D1622488

A True Love of Mine

a&b

A True Love of Mine

Margaret Thornton

First published in Great Britain in 2007 by
Allison & Busby Limited
13 Charlotte Mews
London W1T 4EJ
www.allisonandbusby.com

Copyright © 2007 by MARGARET THORNTON

The moral right of the author has been asserted.

A CIP catalogue record for this book is available from
the British Library.

10 9 8 7 6 5 4 3 2 1

ISBN 978-0-7490-8047-1

Typeset in 11/16 pt Sabon by
Terry Shannon

Printed and bound in Great Britain by
MPG Books Ltd, Bodmin, Cornwall

MARGARET THORNTON was born in Blackpool and has lived there all her life. She is a qualified teacher but has retired in order to concentrate on her writing. She began by writing articles and short stories for magazines and has since gone on to have fifteen novels published, most of which are set in Blackpool. Her family sagas range from the late Victorian period, through to the Twenties, the Second World War, and the Fifties and Sixties. She has two children and five grand-children.

For my husband, John, once again; with
my love and remembering the happy holidays we
have enjoyed in Scarborough.

And for my friend, Gladys Royston,who
also loves Scarborough. Thanks to Gladys for her
information about the work of an undertaker!

Chapter One

'Casey would waltz with a strawberry blonde,
And the band played on...'

Maddy Moon joined in enthusiastically with the song
along with the rest of the audience, although she had
no idea who Casey was, or what was meant by a strawberry
blonde.

She knew that she, too, had blonde hair; a sort of golden
colour which waved a bit and which shone with a reddish
tinge when it was newly washed or when it caught the
rays of the sun. So maybe that was what the words meant;
hair that was golden-red, but not so red as to be called ginger.

Now the girl sitting near her, at the other end of one of the
long forms that were provided for the children to sit on, she
was a ginger-nut all right. Her hair, done up in two little
bunches and tied at the ends with blue ribbon, was bright
orange. Maddy wondered if it earned her the name of Carrots,
like the boy in her class at school. She had noticed the girl
before; she looked nice and friendly, and Maddy guessed she
might be about the same age as herself; ten years old. She had
the pale skin and hundreds of freckles that went with ginger
hair. Suddenly she glanced in Maddy's direction, as though
aware of the other girl's scrutiny, and Maddy saw that she had
bright blue eyes. The girl raised her eyebrows, smiling at her
a little curiously. Maddy smiled back, rather uncertainly, and

then looked away quickly because she knew she had been staring. Her mother had told her it was rude to stare.

'...He'd ne'er leave the girl with the strawberry curls,
And the band played on.'

The song came to an end and everyone clapped, and several of the children cheered as the troupe of Pierrots – the six men and three ladies, all dressed alike in white costumes with black pom-poms on their fronts and on their pointed hats – bowed and bowed, waved to the audience, then disappeared through the curtain at the back of the wooden planks that formed their stage, and into the bathing huts which they used as dressing rooms.

Immediately one of the men started to make his way around the spectators, shaking his wooden box, smiling and winking and chatting cheerfully to the children and to the grown-ups – especially the young ladies – in the crowd, encouraging them to part with another copper or two from their purses.

'Enjoyed the show have you, luv? That's good; we aim to please...

'Aye, I'll be singing for you again after the interval; doing a bit of dancing an' all and cracking a few jokes...

'And may I say that is an extremely fetching hat you are wearing this morning, miss...'

Maddy turned her head and saw the young lady who was wearing a straw hat – trimmed with pink ribbons and a big pink rose at the side – blush a little as she smiled back at the Pierrot.

Maddy knew that he was called Pete and that he was known as the 'bottler'. That was according to her grandfather,

Isaac Moon, who knew a good deal about the Pierrot shows, especially those that performed along the east coast, and most particularly the ones in their own town of Scarborough.

'But he doesn't carry a bottle, Grandad,' Maddy had insisted. 'It's a wooden box that people put the money in. Why d'you call him the bottler?'

'Ah, well now, it's only what I've been told,' Isaac had replied. 'From what I've heard tell, they put all t' money they collect into a big bottle, like, so that it can't easily be got at. And then at the end o' t' week they smash it and share the money out amongst all t' members of the troupe. At least that's what they used to do. Happen they're a bit more businesslike now. I believe they charge a copper or two more for the folk who sit on t' deckchairs. Aye, they say a good bottler's worth his weight in gold – well, copper, I suppose, to be quite honest – to a Pierrot show…'

This particular troupe which performed each day – three times each day, not just once – on Scarborough's North Bay, was known as 'Uncle Percy's Pierrots', and was a source of great delight to Maddy. She came to watch them at least once each day during the long August holiday from school. Her parents knew that she was safe enough there. It was not far for her to walk down to the beach – or to the promenade if the tide was in – from her home on North Marine Road. Her mother and father were both very busy in the family business and were glad she had something to occupy her mind. They insisted, though, that she went straight home after each performance. On no account was she to speak to anyone that she did not know, or go wandering off into the town, or get involved with the other beach entertainers; the fortune tellers and pedlars of dubious products and remedies, who aimed to make a living on the sands. Most of those, however, plied their trade on the South Bay beach, on the other side of the headland. The North Bay was a good deal quieter.

Maddy dropped her penny into the slot and heard the satisfying clonk and the jingle of coins as Pete shook his box and said, 'Thank you kindly, miss. We've seen you here before, haven't we?' She nodded, feeling pleased that he had noticed her.

'Well, that's just what we want – satisfied customers.'

She smiled happily to herself. The show was just as good as ever. They had already heard a lot of singing. The Pierrots had sung songs with which all the audience joined in; a lady with a high voice had sung about a garden of roses; and a man with a deep voice had sung a song about the sea. And there had been the man who made you laugh – a comedian, and another man who was called his 'stooge', so Grandad said; and a lady with two little white performing dogs. And there was still a lot more to come.

She turned her head at the sound of a voice in her ear. 'Hello... You don't mind if I come and sit with you, do you? I'm on my own, and it looks as though you are as well.'

It was the girl with the ginger hair whom Maddy had noticed a few minutes ago, and the day before. 'No, I don't mind,' she said. 'Here – I'll budge up, then you can sit next to me.' There was plenty of room on the form, especially as the two smaller children who had been sitting next to her had disappeared. Her mother had told her not to talk to strangers, but she was sure that did not mean she hadn't to speak to a girl of her own age.

'I've seen you here before,' said the girl. 'Are you on holiday here, same as me?'

'No, I live here,' replied Maddy. 'Not far away, just over there.' She gestured towards the ruined castle on the headland. 'This side of the castle, but lower down; North Marine Road, that's where I live.'

'Gosh, aren't you lucky?' said the girl. 'Living at the seaside all the time. I wish I did.'

Maddy shrugged. 'I dunno,' she said. 'I s'pose it's all right living here. I've never really thought about it. I only come down to the beach during the school holidays, to watch the Pierrots. I love the Pierrots, don't you? The rest of the time I 'spect it's the same as living anywhere else. Where do you live then?'

'York,' said the girl. 'It's the capital city of Yorkshire.'

'Yes, I know that,' said Maddy. 'We learnt that at school, but I've never been there. How did you get here then? On the train?'

'Yes, we came last Saturday; my mother and me and my brother, and the twins. They're four years old, our Tommy and Matilda – Tilly, we call her. But my father is staying in York. He works at a bank in the city, so he'll just be coming to see us at weekends. At least he might... He said he would see.'

'You mean...you're staying here for a long time?' Maddy knew that most of the visitors to the town stayed for only a week or so, at one of the various boarding houses. Unless they were very rich, of course, and stayed at the Grand or the Crown, or one of the other posh hotels on the South Bay.

'Well, we're staying for a few weeks – all of August. We'll go back in time for Samuel and me to start school again. We rent a house for the season; we come every year. We're staying on Blenheim Terrace this time, leading up to the castle. You can just about see it from here.'

'You're only just round the corner from where I live then,' said Maddy excitedly. 'Oh, isn't that great? We'll be able to come down together to see the shows. Oh...' She put her hand to her mouth. 'D'you know, you haven't even told me your name, and I haven't told you mine. Aren't we silly?'

'I'm Jessie,' said the ginger-haired girl. She grinned and held out her hand. 'How do you do?' she said, in a pseudo-refined voice. 'That's what my mother has told me to say when I meet somebody I don't know. I'm called Jessica, really,' she said in a more normal voice, 'Jessica Barraclough, but everybody calls me Jessie.'

Maddy laughed. She knew she would like this girl; she was good fun. She, too held out her hand, and they shook hands, just like two grown-up ladies. 'And I'm Maddy,' she said. 'Madeleine Moon, really, but they just call me Maddy.'

They discovered that they had been born within a few days of one another, in the month of June, 1890, and now, in the first week of August, 1900, they were both ten years old.

There was no time to talk any more because the second half of the show was about to start. The Pierrots were coming out from their bathing huts, one on each side of the stage.

'Here we are again, happy as can be...' they sang as they ran on to the stage. Maddy and Jessie grinned at one another, then settled down to watch the second half of the performance.

The man called Pete, the 'bottler', sang and danced a bit, as he had said he would do; then he told a few jokes assisted by his 'stooge', another of the Pierrots who was pretending to be stupid, although Maddy didn't think he was anything of the sort really.

'Who was that lady I saw you with last night?' asked the stooge, in a daft sort of voice.

'That was no lady – that was my wife!' retorted Pete, followed by a quick rat-tat on the tambourine from a man at the side of the stage. That was to make the audience realise it was a joke and that they were supposed to laugh, thought Maddy. They all laughed obediently, although they had heard the same joke many times before, and Maddy joined in with them. She didn't really understand it; why was his wife not a lady? she wondered. But she was enjoying the show more than ever today because she had somebody with her to join in the fun.

The lady with the high voice who had sung about the garden of roses came on again, this time carrying a huge teddy bear, and she sang a song about how much she loved him. Two men performed a tap dance, all the while grinning broadly at the audience, their feet darting back and forth and in and out, making a loud clattering sound on the wooden boards.

There was a funny sketch with two men who both wanted to win the affection of a young lady. They changed out of their Pierrot costumes for this, the men appearing as quite the dandies in their striped blazers and straw boaters, and the lady, in a bright pink dress with a large hat made of feathers, obviously enjoying the flirtation and having both the men 'dangling on a piece of string', as Maddy had heard her mother say.

All too soon the show came to an end and all the Pierrots, including the lady who had played the piano for them, came to the front of the stage and bowed to the audience.

'That was good, wasn't it?' said Maddy, and Jessie agreed that it had been a 'splendid show'. Maddy had noticed that she used rather grown-up words and that she spoke in quite a posh-sounding sort of voice. She didn't appear swanky though, or at all stuck-up; but she did not sound like she, Maddy, sounded, or like the rest of the boys and girls in her class at school.

They made their way across the sand and up the wooden steps to the lower promenade, chatting together all the while, then up the steep path which led up to the cliff top and the hotels on Queen's Parade. The backs of these hotels opened on to North Marine Road, which was where Maddy lived, but her home was on the other side of the road.

'Will you come again this afternoon?' asked Jessie.

'No, I don't think so,' replied Maddy. 'I 'spect I will have a few errands to do for my mother. She's busy, y'see, working in our shop, or else she's out helping my dad with his job. So I help her during the school holidays. She doesn't let me go into town on my own, not yet, just to the shops along our road. Some of my friends have to work really hard when we finish school, 'cause their parents have boarding houses, so I 'spect I'm lucky, really, just running a few errands, and helping to wash up and keep my room tidy. I'll probably go to the show tomorrow, though. Will you?'

'I would like to,' replied Jessie. 'It all depends on what the rest of the family are doing. My brother likes fishing; that's where he's gone this morning, down to the harbour. It's all he ever thinks about when we're here, when he's not reading his books, that is. I should think the twins might like watching the Pierrots though – they were too little last year – but if they get restless my mother could take them away to play on the beach.'

'Is your brother older than you then?' asked Maddy. 'I s'pose he must be, if he's allowed to go fishing on his own.'

'Yes; Samuel's fourteen, four years older than me.'

'But... I thought you said he was still at school?' said Maddy, a little perplexed. All the boys she knew had left school at thirteen, fourteen at the very oldest, and were working for their living. Many of them went out in the fishing boats, as did their fathers, or were apprenticed to some trade or other. Her own brother, Patrick, who also was fourteen, had left school the previous year and was now an apprentice in the family business.

'Yes, he is still at school,' replied Jessie, in answer to Maddy's query. 'Samuel and I both go to private schools in York. Mine is just for girls, and Sam's is just for boys. We will both be staying there until we're sixteen at least. My father would like Samuel to get a position in the bank, like he has.'

'Oh, I see...' said Maddy. 'My school's over there, near the Market Hall. But there's lads in my class as well as girls.' She waved her arm vaguely to the left. 'My brother went there as well, and my mam and dad, ages ago. But Patrick, that's me brother, left last year – we all leave when we're thirteen or so – and now he's working with me dad, learning to...well, to do what our dad does.'

'You said you have a shop, didn't you?' said Jessie. 'What sort is it? Do you sell sweets and tobacco and newspapers?' She didn't wait for an answer. 'When I was a very little girl I used to say that I wanted to be a sweet shop lady.' She laughed, a merry sort of giggle. 'But I've grown out of that idea now. I think I would like to work in a really elegant dress shop.' Maddy would have said 'posh', not elegant. 'But my mother wants me to go to a college where they teach shorthand and typing, then I could be a private secretary to someone... Go on, you said you would tell me what sort of a shop you have.'

Maddy, in fact, had not said so. She found it difficult to explain to people who did not know just what the family business entailed and what they sold in the shop. 'Well, I suppose it is a sort of dress shop,' she said. 'It's just round this corner.'

They had reached the top of the cliff path, near to the terrace where Jessie and her family were staying. 'I tell you what,' said Maddy, 'you come with me now, and then you can see for yourself. It's not very far for you to walk back, is it? Or will your mam be cross with you if you're late?'

'No, Mother doesn't often get cross,' smiled Jessie. 'So long as I'm home by half past twelve, in time for lunch.'

They turned the corner into North Marine Road and walked northwards for fifty yards or so. 'Here it is, this is where I live. That's...our shop,' said Maddy, stopping in front of a double-fronted shop with two large plate-glass windows.

Jessie gave a gasp of surprise and stared, open-mouthed, for a few seconds. Then, 'Goodness gracious!' she said. 'How very peculiar...'

Chapter Two

Maddy felt a little annoyed at her new friend's remark, which she considered rather rude. But when she looked at the windows herself – the windows which she passed by every day without so much as a second glance – she realised that to someone who was not used to such an establishment as this, it might well appear to be a trifle...peculiar.

'Moon's Mourning Modes', proclaimed the sign, in gold writing above the shop, and if anyone was in any doubt as to the meaning of the words, a glance at the windows would tell them. They were filled with black clothing, the right-hand window containing men's apparel, and the left-hand one clothes for women and children. Suits, waistcoats, overcoats, top hats for the men; silken dresses, cloaks, skirts and jackets, wide-brimmed hats trimmed with feathers for the women, and even a small black dress for a little girl of seven or eight years old and a knickerbocker suit for a boy of a similar age; all in unrelieved black.

But no, not quite. If you looked more closely you could see, here and there, a touch of colour. A mauve ribbon or a purple feather on a hat, a silk blouse with a high stand-up collar in a shade of pearl grey, and a white lace edging on the little girl's dress.

At the front of the windows, on the floor, were boxes of white handkerchiefs with black edges; notepaper and envelopes, also edged in black; black stockings, gloves, muffs, fur stoles, beads and brooches made from jet... Everything, in fact, that you might require when a death occurred in the family, to see you through the funeral and during the – often extensive – period of mourning.

Jessie glanced uncertainly at her companion and gave a sheepish grin. 'I'm sorry,' she said. 'That wasn't a very polite thing to say, was it? But it gave me quite a shock, seeing all that black stuff. They're clothes to wear when somebody dies, aren't they?'

'Yes, that's right,' replied Maddy. 'That's what "mourning" means.' She pointed to the sign. 'My dad told me that it means...well...showing how sorry you are when somebody has died.' She nodded knowingly. 'And you wear black as a sign of respect. I've got used to it, 'cause I've always lived here, and I remember my mam and dad opening the shop when I was...ooh, about five, I think.'

'Oh... I see,' said Jessie. 'And where did you live before that?'

'I've just said; I've always lived here, ever since I was born. But before we had the shop we just had the undertaking business. My dad's an undertaker, you see, and my grandad an' all – he lives here with us. Well, it was his business really, and his "father before him".' She laughed. 'He's always saying that, me grandad.'

Jessie was looking quite startled. 'You mean your father...makes coffins? That's what undertakers do, isn't it? And that he goes round to see...dead people?'

'Sometimes he does, yes, and my mam as well, she goes with him. He has to measure the body, you see, so that he can make the coffin the right size.'

'Oh, stop it! Stop it! You're giving me the creeps,' cried Jessie. 'You don't...you don't have to see dead bodies, do you?

I've never ever seen anybody that was dead...' She was staring anxiously at Maddy, her blue eyes wide with alarm.

'Of course I don't,' said Maddy. 'They don't bring them here. My dad takes the coffin round to the person's home, the day before the funeral. I did see my grandma, though, when she died two years ago. Dad said he thought I was old enough to understand. I didn't think it looked like me grandma though... I told you, didn't I, that my brother, our Patrick, he's learning to be an undertaker as well.'

'You told me he was going into the family business,' replied Jessie, 'but I didn't know then what it was. Doesn't he mind? Wouldn't he rather do something more...more cheerful?'

'I don't think so. He seems quite happy about it all. If he's not, then he doesn't tell me. Patrick's always laughing and joking. That's what he's like, and my dad, too; he's very jolly and friendly. You can come in and meet them if you like. They'll be working round at the back, I expect.'

'Making coffins?'

Maddy nodded. 'Probably.'

'No, I... I don't think so,' said Jessie, a little hesitantly. 'I won't come and meet them right now. Some other time perhaps. I'll have to go now, or else my mother might be wondering where I am. It's been very nice meeting you, Maddy, and I hope we'll be able to see one another again.'

''Course we will,' said Maddy. 'Why shouldn't we? It's not frightened you, has it, all that stuff I've been saying about coffins an' all that? I didn't mean to scare you. And I'd really like us to be friends...wouldn't you?'

'Yes...yes, I would.' Jessie nodded. 'I really would. I was being a bit silly. You can't help what your father does for a living, can you? I mean...it's a very important job, isn't it?'

Maddy nodded. 'Yes, I suppose it is.'

'Shall we meet on the beach then, tomorrow morning, to watch the show again? My mother and my little brother and sister might be with me, but you don't mind, do you? I would like you to meet them.'

''Course I don't mind. If the tide's in, though, they'll have the show up on the promenade. They have to watch the tides, but I think it's all right for the rest of this week, in the mornings anyway... See you tomorrow then, Jessie. And I'm really glad you came to talk to me.'

'So am I,' said her new friend. 'Goodbye then, Maddy, till tomorrow.'

'Ta-ra,' said Maddy, giving a cheery wave as she opened the shop door and went inside.

The bell gave a jingle as she pressed down the latch, not a jolly tinkling sound, though, such as you might hear on entering a sweet shop or a toy shop, but a more sombre tonking tone, as befitted the funereal establishment. Not that the emporium – which was a posh name for a big shop, her mother had told her – was at all gloomy inside. It was well lit with electric light bulbs hanging from the ceiling. William Moon had insisted on having electricity installed when the shop was opened, although their living quarters upstairs were still lit by gaslight.

The length of carpeting on which the clients walked on entering the shop had a deep pile and was patterned in a swirly design of maroon and black. The flooring consisted of highly polished wooden boards and there was a long mahogany counter along the rear of the shop, behind which the assistants stood to complete the purchases.

There was a comfortable plush sofa, also maroon, on which customers could take their ease, and discreet cubicles on either side of the shop behind maroon velvet curtains, one for gentlemen clients and two for ladies. There they could discuss their requirements in private with the sales assistants, and try on their choices from the myriad items of clothing in stock.

There were several racks holding the suits of black and charcoal grey and the ladies' dresses, costumes and blouses, not only black ones but others in shades of grey, purple, violet and mauve, which were suitable to wear when the first period of mourning – usually lasting for several months – had come to an end.

A few of the most elaborate hats – wide-brimmed creations fashioned from velvet or straw and lavishly adorned with sweeping ostrich feathers, or more discreet toques of swathed silk trimmed with ribbons and flowers – were displayed on stands, but most of them, and the top hats for the men, were kept in round hat-boxes on the high shelves.

Maddy's mother, Clara, assisted in the shop when she was not helping her husband with his other duties. Bella Randall, a family friend – or so Maddy's mother said – worked there too, and they had recently acquired a new assistant, a fifteen-year-old girl called Polly who was still undergoing her training. To cater for the gentlemen's needs there was an able young man in his early twenties, Martin Sadler, who had been employed at the shop ever since it opened.

Clara Moon was, virtually, the manageress of the shop, but it often seemed to Maddy – and to others as well – that it was Bella Randall who was really in charge. It was true that she sometimes had to take over and hold the reins in Clara's absence, but at other times, too, she loved to make her presence felt and to strut about as though she owned the place. At least, that was Maddy's opinion, although she had to admit – to herself, if not openly to her mother and father – that she might be somewhat biased because she did not like Bella at all. And she knew that the dislike was mutual.

On entering the shop Maddy realised, too late, that her mother was not there, but the other assistants were. Polly was serving a lady at the end of the counter with a pair of black gloves, and Martin, at the other end, was placing a top hat in a box for a gentleman customer. And Bella was standing in the centre on the carpeted area as though she was the Queen Bee.

'Madeleine,' she began as soon as Maddy stepped over the threshold, her forehead creasing in a frown and her black eyes glowering at the girl, 'how many times have you been told that you must not come in through the shop, especially when you have been down to the beach. Look at you now, treading sand all over the place!'

Maddy looked pointedly down at her feet and at the carpet. There was not a grain of sand to be seen, but she knew better than to argue. 'Sorry,' she said, but not very graciously. 'I forgot.'

It was true that she was supposed to go round the back, by the workshop, and enter the premises through the back door. But it was a ruling that was made to be broken and neither her mother or her father minded too much if she did not always keep to it. It was only Bella who kept harping on about it. Maddy was supposed to call her Aunty Bella, but she usually got away with calling her nothing at all.

'I was looking for my mam,' she said. 'I wanted to tell her something. Where is she?'

Bella sighed. 'Where else would she be at this time of the day but getting your dinner ready?' she snapped. 'Off you go now, quick sharp, out of the shop. We have work to do down here.'

Well, I'm not stopping you! Maddy was tempted to reply. Bella certainly didn't look as though she was exactly run off her feet, standing there like 'cock of the midden'. That was an expression she had heard her grandad, Isaac, use about Bella. He didn't seem to like the woman any more than she did, but that was their secret, hers and her grandad's. She was annoyed now that Bella should have reprimanded her in front of the other shop assistants, and customers as well. Her mam and dad would never do that, and Bella, too, was more careful what she said to the little girl when either of her parents were around.

Maddy went through the door at the back of the shop, into the kitchen-cum-stockroom where the assistants could sit for a few minutes' respite if they were not too busy, or make a cup of tea or eat their lunchtime sandwiches if they wished. Then she went through the door which led to the spacious living quarters of the Moon family.

Her mother was busy in the kitchen and she looked up from the stove as Maddy entered the room. Her face was red from the heat of the oven and she pushed back a lock of hair, almost the same golden shade as Maddy's, as she smiled at her daughter. 'Hello there, love. Have you had a nice morning?'

'Yes, it was lovely, Mam, an' I've got such a lot to tell you. I met a girl down there watching the show. I know you said I shouldn't speak to strangers, but she's a nice respectable girl – quite posh she is, really – and she's called Jessie. She's ten like me, and—'

'It all sounds very exciting,' said Clara, continuing to smile fondly at her. 'You must tell me all about it later. But now…do you think you could lay the table for me? I've just been checking on the hotpot and I think it's nearly done. And then you can go and tell your dad and grandad and Patrick that we're ready.'

'Yes, 'course I will,' said Maddy. She sniffed appreciatively. 'It smells good. Is it lamb chops in it then?'

'Yes, proper Lancashire hotpot,' laughed Clara. 'I know we're Yorkshire folk, all of us, but there's some things they do in Lancashire that aren't so bad, and their hotpot's one of 'em.'

Maddy opened a cupboard drawer and took out a blue-and-white checked cloth and the ordinary cutlery which they used when they dined in the kitchen. They ate at the large pine table which stood in the centre of the room and was used at other times for baking and pastry making and bottling of pickles and preserves. On Saturdays and Sundays and on special occasions they dined in the dining-cum-living room, from the mahogany table, using the best silver cutlery, a white damask cloth and rose-patterned china cups and saucers. But it was blue and white earthenware for every day and the large plates were already warming on the plate rack over the gas stove.

'Wash your hands first,' her mother reminded her, so Maddy swilled them under the kitchen tap at the stone sink and wiped them on a striped towel, instead of going into the bathroom.

'There, that's all done,' she said, a few minutes later, looking at the five places she had laid with the wooden table mats, knives, forks and spoons, blue and white table napkins, and the glass salt and pepper shakers in the middle.

'Just get the pickled onions and beetroot out of the larder,' her mother told her, 'and the red cabbage an' all. Your grandad's partial to a bit of red cabbage. Then I think we're all done and dusted… Thank you, luv; you're a good help to me. Now, off you pop and tell the menfolk as we're ready.'

Chapter Three

There were five of them, all the members of the Moon family, seated round the table. Isaac was at the head where he always sat, as William and Clara still deferred to him as head of the household. William and Patrick sat at one of the long sides and Clara and Maddy at the other.

'We'll just say grace, shall we?' said Isaac, as he did at the start of every formal meal; and they all dutifully bowed their heads.

'For what we are about to receive, may the good Lord make us truly thankful,' said Isaac.

'Amen,' they all said.

'Right then, Clara lass,' said Isaac, in a much more jovial voice. 'Let's make a start of us dinner. Me stomach's beginning to think me throat's cut.'

The saying of grace was a ritual in their household, something that Isaac had been brought up with and with which he felt it was his duty to continue, more out of habit than anything else. He could not say that he was an overly religious sort of fellow, although he still, more often than not, attended the morning service each Sunday at the Methodist chapel on Queen Street.

His father, Joshua, had insisted that all the family – his wife, Abigail, and their five children – should attend chapel. Joshua had been a strict adherent to the principles and practices of Methodism, as preached by John Wesley. Indeed, his own father, Amos – Isaac's grandfather – was said to have heard the great man himself preach on several occasions. John Wesley had been a frequent visitor to Scarborough between 1770 and 1790, preaching at the chapel on Church Street Stairs, leading down to the harbour, which the local Methodists had built as their first meeting place.

Joshua's God, and that of Amos, his father, had been a harsh disciplinarian sort of figure. The young Isaac had felt the weight of his father's hand, and of his broad leather belt, many times whilst he was growing up, for quite minor misdemeanours; none of the five children had dared to step too far out of line. Joshua had mellowed, however, as he grew older, and when he started his own undertaking business in the middle years of Queen Victoria's reign, it had been Isaac, the youngest son, who had learnt the trade along with him. The other brothers and sisters by that time had broken away from their father's harsh regime.

Isaac had been determined, were he to be blessed with a family, that he would be a kind and loving father, strict when it was necessary, but understanding as well. He and his beloved wife, Hannah, however, had been granted only the one son, William. When Hannah had died two years ago Isaac had felt as though the light had gone out of his life. But William was a good son – he couldn't wish for a better one – and he had found consolation in his grandchildren, Patrick and Maddy, and his dear daughter-in-law, Clara. Now she was a grand lass if ever there was one.

He had been pleased to see William adopting the same affectionate tolerance to his own children as he, Isaac, had always tried to show. And William had the same easy acceptance of his faith in God as well.

It was difficult to understand sometimes, though, why God should act in the way He did; allowing little children to die, or cutting off a young man in his prime, when he had a brilliant future ahead of him. They came across many such instances in their day-to-day work, and were unable to offer any explanation to the often shocked and anguished relatives. But that was not really their place; it was their task just to show sympathy and compassion and to take care of the more practical matters regarding the disposal of the loved one's earthly body.

Isaac believed it would be impossible to do the job that was his without a belief in God and in the life hereafter. But one must also try to maintain a certain detachment and, perhaps above all, a sense of humour.

That was something that William was not short of, nor his son, Patrick. Isaac watched them now, laughing at something that Maddy had said.

'Honestly, Maddy,' Patrick was saying, 'that joke's so old it's sprouting whiskers. Haven't they come up with any new ones this year, those Pierrots of yours?'

''Course they have!' retorted Maddy. 'There was one about seagulls. Pete's stooge says, "Have you noticed how clean and spotless everything is in Scarborough this year?" And then Pete says, "Aye, I have that. They've even taught the seagulls to fly upside down." But I don't think I really understand that one. I mean, they don't, do they? Seagulls can't fly upside down...'

Patrick roared with laughter, banging his spoon on the side of his dish, which earned him a disapproving look from his mother. ''Course they can't, you ninny! That's why it's a joke, and not a bad one neither.'

Isaac smiled at Maddy's perplexed frown. 'Seagulls drop their mess everywhere, you see, luv. You've only to take a walk along Royal Albert Drive and see what a mess they've made on t' cliffs.'

'And if they flew upside down, then they wouldn't be able to… Oh yes, I see it now,' said Maddy.

'Well, well, well; the penny's dropped at last!' said Patrick, grinning at his sister. 'Give the girl a round of applause, everyone.'

'And you stop teasing yer sister, young feller-me-lad,' said Isaac, although he knew there was no malice in the lad's remarks. The brother and sister were good friends most of the time. 'She's just as clever as you any day of the week, is our little Maddy. Go on then, luv; tell us what else they did.'

'Tap dancing and singing – they've got quite a few new songs – and the lady with the performing dogs; that was a new act…'

'And you were going to tell us about a girl that you met, weren't you?' said Clara. 'Didn't you say she was called Jessie? Does she go to your school?'

'Oh no, she's from York,' replied Maddy. And whilst they ate their baked apples and custard she told them about how she had met Jessie Barraclough, how well they got along together, and what a nice respectable girl she seemed to be; that, she knew, would mean a great deal to her parents. They were not snobbish by any means, but they were quite fussy about the sort of friends that their children mixed with. 'She walked back home with me, an' I'm seeing her again in the morning. She wouldn't come in with me, though… She seemed a bit – you know – scared, like, when she found out about us being undertakers.'

'What d'you mean, us?' quipped Patrick. 'I didn't know you were one.'

'Don't be silly, Patrick,' his mother chided. 'You know perfectly well what your sister means. Yes, people do sometimes think that what we do is rather...odd, but when you've been brought up in the business, you get used to it.'

'You weren't brought up in it, Mam,' Patrick observed.

'No, that's true,' said Clara. 'But I've been involved in it ever since I married your father, and it suits me fine.' She smiled lovingly at her husband and he smiled back at her.

Isaac, watching them, thought, once again, how glad he was that his son had had the sense to settle for Clara and not that other hussy, the one that served in the shop downstairs. The shop would be closed now, of course – between the hours of one and two – and Bella Randall would be having her lunch in the back room, or on a bench on the seafront, like the other two assistants. Isaac knew that she would dearly love to get her feet under their table, but William and Clara had made it clear, obviously to the woman's displeasure, that she was not to be regarded as a member of the family, but as an employee. Except, of course, on special occasions when she might be included as a family friend.

'I don't want your new friend to think that there's something strange about us,' Clara was saying now. 'Would you like to ask Jessie to come and have tea with us one day, then she can see that we are quite normal? What about Wednesday? That's our half-day closing at the shop, and it will give me time to prepare a specially nice tea and do a bit of baking.'

'Wednesday; that's the day after tomorrow,' said Maddy.

'Well done, Maddy!' Patrick clapped his hands loudly.

'Thank you for that information. We would never have known.'

'Shut up, you!' Maddy stuck her tongue out at him.

'Oh, take no notice of him,' said Clara, laughing. 'Do you think that's a good idea, Maddy?'

'Yes, thanks ever so much, Mam,' said Maddy. 'I'll ask her tomorrow. And she said her mother would probably be with her as well, so she'll be able to tell me straight away if she can come. And don't you go frightening Jessie either, Patrick.' She turned to her brother. 'None of your tales about putting pennies on the corpses' eyes, or trying to get their false teeth in.'

'As if I would...' Patrick's brown eyes opened wide with innocence. 'No, honestly, Maddy, I won't. I shall be on my very best behaviour. Is there any of that apple and custard left, Mam?'

Isaac pondered on Clara's words later that afternoon, as he worked alongside his son and grandson, about how, when you had been brought up in the undertaking business, you became used to it. In the end you thought very little about it, realising that death, in fact, was a part of life; the one inescapable part that everyone, sooner or later, had to face. The making of coffins and the organisation of funerals, for rich and poor alike, was just a job, the same as any other job. Isaac supposed he could understand, however, that some folk might consider it an odd sort of way to earn a living. And he had long become accustomed to quips that he would never be out of work.

At the moment he was keeping a sharp eye on his grandson who had been entrusted with assembling and lining a coffin, for the very first time. And a good job he was making of it too. He had fastened together the various sets – the wooden pieces of differing lengths, already cut to form the shape of the coffin – and now he was engaged in the task of lining the sides with pitch, which would make the box waterproof.

The lad seemed to be taking to his apprenticeship like a duck to water, as the saying went. Just as William, his father, had done, and, before that, Isaac himself. He reflected, though, that he had had little choice in the matter. His father had ruled him with a rod of iron, and so, when Joshua had started up his own business, in the mid-nineteenth century, after working as an undertaker's assistant for many years, he had insisted that his youngest son should join him in the venture. Isaac, at that time, had been apprenticed to a carpenter, but had soon been released from his tenure.

The business had started off in quite a small way, until Joshua Moon and Son had started to make a name for themselves as a reverent and sympathetic partnership. They were frequently called out to the homes of the poorer townsfolk who, in spite of their shortage of money, had, nevertheless, ensured that their loved one would have a good send-off. The most widespread form of insurance had been that of saving for a funeral payment; indeed, at the start of this new century, it still was. A pauper's funeral, in a plywood box in an unmarked grave, was to be avoided at all costs.

Most coffins, in those early days, had been black; black wood covered with a black cloth. It was a tradition which had gone on for a long time. Nowadays coffins were also made from elm or oak wood, waxed or highly polished and with brass handles, according to what the family could afford. For children of five years of age and under, though, it was still usual to have a white coffin. There had been a dreadful number of children's deaths in those early years; stillborn babies, and others who had died from diphtheria, scarlet fever or whooping cough. And, regrettably, there were still too many infant deaths. That was the one thing to which Isaac had never become accustomed and he knew he never would. The sight of a little child laid out in a nest of white satin, no matter how peaceful he or she looked, never failed to bring a tear to his eye.

They had not often been asked to do the laying out of the body in those early days, and even now they were not always requested to do so. There was generally a 'handywoman' in the district whose job it was to do the laying out, before the undertaker was called in. This same woman often acted as midwife at the births as well. Nowadays, though, the undertaker usually dealt with every aspect of the death, sometimes not a task for the squeamish or faint-hearted, but Isaac was relieved to see that young Patrick was coping very well with it all. He was a sensible, well-balanced lad who, Isaac was sure, would be pleased to follow in his father's footsteps. The sign above the workshop now read 'Isaac Moon and Son'. And one day, no doubt, it would say 'William Moon and Son'.

Not that Isaac had any intention of departing this earthly life just yet, not if he had anything to do with it. He was very hale and hearty for his almost seventy years and, if God was good, he hoped to continue to be so for many years. He was forcing himself to slow down, though, to a certain extent, leaving the more arduous jobs to his son and grandson because they would, ultimately, inherit the business.

They were in quite a big way now, of course, and Isaac was proud of the manner in which their business had increased. There had been a rapid growth in the social importance of funerals during the last half on the nineteenth century, due to the death of Queen Victoria's beloved husband, Prince Albert, and the Queen's subsequent mourning of him. Even now, almost forty years after his death, she still dressed entirely in black, although she sometimes condescended to wear a white lace cap.

The Queen's interminable grieving for her husband had captured the imagination of the public. It had become customary, following the death of Prince Albert, for a woman who had lost her husband to wear her widow's weeds for up to two years, and then to replace them with dresses of grey, purple or mauve. Nowadays, however, the strict adherence to periods of mourning had relaxed somewhat, several months being the norm, rather than years. But the shop that William had opened some five years before – his own enterprise – was still doing a good trade.

Isaac well remembered the grand funerals of eminent members of the public in those early years, when he and his father had been only a small and insignificant firm, striving to make their way amidst fierce competition. A town councillor, or a prominent lawyer, for instance, would take his final journey in a glass-sided hearse drawn by four black-plumed horses. At the front of the hearse there was often a man who wore a head-dress of black feathers, walking slowly and stately, flanked by two other men, known as mutes – because of their silence – whose job it was to open the doors. Or sometimes it would be the undertaker walking in front, as it was now with their own firm, wearing a black top hat, frock-tailed black coat, black gloves, and a white handkerchief with a black border in his breast pocket. Young Patrick had taken a turn at leading a funeral procession, but on seeing his sister watching him from the sidelines he had had difficulty in controlling his giggles. But he was gradually learning to behave with the dignity and solemnity due to the occasion.

Now that Isaac Moon and Son were themselves a prestigious partnership, they too were able to conduct funerals in a grand manner, according to the requirements of the family. They now owned their own hearse and two black horses, Jet and Ebony, who were stabled at the rear of the premises; in the early days they had hired the horses. Isaac could see the day when the hearse would be contained in one of those new-fangled horseless carriages, but not, he hoped, in his lifetime.

He had seen many changes, though. He remembered, in his early years as an apprentice undertaker, funerals taking place in the churchyard of St Mary's, the 800-year-old parish church of Scarborough, on the top of the cliff facing the castle. It had been a stiff climb for the horses up the steep incline of Castle Road. As for the less affluent families, a pony or donkey might pull the coffin on a cart, or four pall-bearers would bear the burden on their shoulders all the way from the home of the deceased.

Now, the graveyard of St Mary's was full, and funerals took place at the cemetery on Dean Road on the northern outskirts of the town. The ill-fated Anne Brontë had been one of the last persons to be buried in St Mary's churchyard. She had died whilst on holiday in Scarborough in 1849 and was buried in the annexe to the main graveyard, which had already been full, on the other side of Church Lane.

'Aye, I can see you've made a good job of that, my lad,' Isaac said now, bringing his wandering thoughts back to the present time and casting a keen eye over his grandson's efforts. 'We'll leave that 'un to dry out...

'Now, how about trying your hand at lining this 'ere coffin? You've watched me and your dad often enough, haven't you? Cotton wool padding first, then cover it all over wi' this white satin. It's quite a costly one, is this. It's for one o' t' local bigwigs, a fellow from Merchants Row, so mind you do your best...'

Chapter Four

Maddy skipped along the path which led down to the lower promenade. She couldn't wait to get to the beach this morning to meet Jessie again, and probably her family as well. She stopped by the railings, looking out at the wide expanse of golden sand and the bluey-green sea in the distance, with little white waves lapping at the edges like a frill of white lace.

She could see two men assembling the wooden platform which the Pierrots would use; and there was the 'barrer man' pushing their piano on a handcart, down the broad slope which led to the beach; her grandad had told her that that was what they called him. There were a few bathing huts drawn up at the edge of the water; nearer to the sea wall there was an ice-cream stall and, further along, the gaily striped box of a Punch and Judy show. It was far enough away from the Pierrots' stage, so that there would be no distraction between the competing entertainments, although it was unavoidable sometimes to prevent the sound of laughter and singing being carried on the wind.

It was quite early in the morning, but there were already several holidaymakers on the beach, ladies with parasols and men in white flannels, blazers and straw boaters, strolling along by the edge of the sea, and others taking their ease on deckchairs or on rugs spread out on the sand. One or two brave souls were emerging from the bathing huts into the sea. The men and women alike were clad in knee-length bathing drawers and round-necked bodices, and bathing caps which completely covered their hair.

As Maddy stood and surveyed the scene below her she caught sight of a familiar head of bright ginger hair. She had met her only the day before, but surely there could not be another girl with such flaming orange hair as Jessie. Yes, it was Jessie, and there were three other figures with her who must be her mother and her little brother and sister. They were walking in her direction from the stretch of sand below the castle.

Maddy started to wave, but they had not seen her yet. She opened her mouth to shout, 'Yoo-hoo, Jessie...', and then she realised that perhaps she shouldn't. Her mother had told her that it was rather vulgar to shout in the street, and she supposed that went for the sands as well; and Jessie's mother, Maddy guessed, was a rather posh sort of person who would be sure to disapprove of such uncouth behaviour. She hurried down the nearest set of steps and ran to meet them.

'Hello, Jessie...' she began, a little out of breath. 'I saw you coming from up there.'

'Hello, Maddy.' They smiled at one another, but somewhat shyly now after their easy friendship of the day before. Then Jessie remembered her manners, and in a grown-up voice she said, 'Maddy, this is my mother. Mummy, this is Maddy.'

'How do you do, my dear?' said Mrs Barraclough, smiling very charmingly and holding out a white-gloved hand. 'Jessica has told me all about you.'

'Has she?' said Maddy, rather nonplussed. 'Er...how do you do?'

She was a very pretty lady with ginger hair, but of a darker hue than Jessie's. It was the colour and sheen of a sleek chestnut horse, and she had bright blue eyes. Maddy thought that her own mother was pretty, but she guessed that Jessie's mother might be considered beautiful. Her dress was the blue of the sky on a sunny day, and it made her eyes seem even bluer. It had a high white lace collar and lace cuffs, and her straw hat was trimmed with a posy of bright blue cornflowers.

'This is Tommy, and this is Tilly,' she said. 'Say hello to Maddy, you two. She is Jessie's new friend.'

'Hello,' said Tommy, looking at her curiously and rather boldly, with eyes of the same blue as those of his mother and elder sister.

His twin, clearly less confident than her brother, glanced at Maddy shyly from beneath her eyelids. 'Hello,' she whispered, then quickly looked away again. Her eyes were grey rather than blue, and she appeared to be altogether a paler version of her bright and exuberant brother. Her hair was a lighter shade of ginger and she was shorter and less sturdily built than Tommy.

Both children were dressed in sailor outfits, which were still very popular. This style of dress for children had come into fashion in the middle years of the last century, when Queen Victoria had had a portrait painted of her eldest son, Bertie – now the notorious Prince of Wales – wearing one. Tommy's navy jacket had shiny buttons, a large collar with three white stripes and a lanyard, and his knickerbockers fastened at the knee. Tilly's dress, also navy blue and made from shiny stiff cotton, had white stripes around the wide collar and the hem.

'Hello. You look very smart, you two,' said Maddy. She was not really used to smaller children, having no young brothers and sisters of her own, but the boy, at least, looked as though he wanted to be friendly.

'Mummy bought these special for our holiday,' said Tommy. 'They're for best an' we haven't to get them messed up. Mummy says we can go paddling in the sea, p'r'aps another day. Do you go paddling, Maddy?' he asked, looking at Maddy in her far less elaborate clothing.

Her cotton dress was dark green, a colour which would not show the dirt, with long sleeves and a high neck with a rounded collar. She had noticed that Jessie's dress was a much paler shade than her own; green also, but a pretty leaf green trimmed with white braid. Both girls, however, were wearing long white socks as a concession to the summer weather. For most of the year, and always for school, Maddy wore black stockings and black button boots, rather than the brown lace-ups she had on today.

'Yes, I sometimes go paddling,' she replied in answer to the little boy's question. 'Not often though, because my mam says I have to have someone with me when I go in the sea, and she and my dad are usually too busy to come to the beach.'

'That is very sensible of your mother, dear,' said Jessie's mother. 'The sea can be quite dangerous, even if you are only paddling. It is far safer to keep to the rock pools. But we are not paddling today, are we, Tommy? Don't you remember? We are going to watch the Pierrot show. Jessie was telling us how much she enjoyed it.'

Tommy nodded. 'Can Maddy go paddling with us another day? Can you, Maddy?' He looked at her, his blue eyes alive with curiosity.

'Yes... I think so. That would be very nice,' she replied. 'I'll

have to ask…my mother.' She had been about to say 'me
mam', but just a few minutes in the company of this family
had made her think that she ought to try and speak nicely, as
she knew she could do when she was on her best behaviour.

'And we've got new fishing nets, haven't we, Tilly?' Tommy
turned to his twin, who nodded silently. 'And buckets and
spades, and we're going to make a big sandcastle, aren't we,
Tilly?' The little girl nodded again. 'Can you make
sandcastles, Maddy?'

'Yes… I can,' she answered, realising that it was quite a
long time since she had engaged in such a pastime. Both she
and Patrick had made some wonderful ones when they were
small, but that seemed ages ago. Patrick was grown up now,
a working member of the family, and building sandcastles was
not much fun on your own. 'Perhaps Jessie and me could help
you one day,' she said.

'We don't need any help, thank you,' said the little boy
seriously. 'Do we, Tilly? We made some big ones last year, just
Tilly and me.'

'You're a little fibber, Tommy!' Jessie broke in; for the last
few moments she had been very quiet. 'Don't you remember
me helping you? And Daddy as well.'

Tommy scowled at her. 'Daddy's not here very much. I
'spect you might have helped a bit…' he added doubtfully.

'Come along now,' said their mother, laughing. 'Let's have
no squabbling, especially on such a lovely day. I have told
you, Tommy, you will make it rain if you frown like that.' He
looked up wonderingly into the blue, blue sky. 'All these
exciting things can wait for another day. We are here for a
whole month, aren't we, and Maddy is very welcome to join
us if she would like to, and if her mother is agreeable.'

'Thank you,' said Maddy. 'That would be lovely.' Already she felt as though she was falling under the spell of this nice little family from York.

'Let's go and sit down and watch the show,' said Mrs Barraclough, taking hold of Tommy's and Tilly's hands, one on either side of her, and heading off in the direction of the Pierrots' stage. 'Now, you two, I shall sit here on a deckchair and you can sit at the front with Jessie and Maddy. Behave yourselves now, won't you? And I'll give you some pennies to put in the box when the man comes round.' She opened a dainty little bag on a silver chain which was hanging over her arm and took out a purse. 'Here you are.' She handed the twins and Jessie a couple of copper coins each. 'Put them in your pockets now, until the interval.' She glanced at Maddy. 'And what about you, dear? Do you have…?'

'Oh yes, I've got my own money,' said Maddy. 'My mother always gives me a penny.'

Jessie's mother smiled serenely. 'That's all right then. Off you go now and sit down. I think they are just about to begin.'

The show was very much the mixture as before; singing and tap dancing, the same man and lady singing solos, the performing dogs and the comedian and his stooge with pretty much the same jokes as they had heard the previous day. Maddy remembered that they changed the programme each week, so there might well be different acts to look forward to next week. All the same, it was very enjoyable, and Tommy and Tilly watched intently, captivated by their new experience.

However, when the Pierrots had disappeared from the stage and they had dropped their pennies into the man's wooden box, the twins started to grow restless.

'Where've they gone?' asked Tommy. 'Is that the end?'

'No; they've gone to have a little rest,' said Jessie. 'It's what they call the interval now. They'll be coming back again in a few minutes. Did you like it?'

'Yes, it was good,' said Tommy. 'I liked the funny men.' He had, indeed, done a good deal of laughing, joining in with the rest of the audience, although he could not really have understood the jokes. But laughter was infectious and Tommy was, for most of the time, a happy little boy.

'I liked the doggies best,' said Tilly in a timid voice. She smiled shyly at Maddy, edging nearer to her on the bench. 'Did you like them?'

'Yes, I did.' Maddy nodded enthusiastically, pleased that the little girl, also, was now showing a desire to be friendly. 'They're very clever, aren't they, doing all those tricks? Have you got a dog, Tilly?'

'No,' she replied, looking rather solemn. 'We'd like one, Tommy and me, but Daddy says they make too much mess. Have you got a dog, Maddy?'

'No,' replied Maddy, 'but we've got two horses...'

'Horses? Have you...really?' It was Tommy who spoke now. 'Can you ride them, Maddy?'

'No, we don't actually ride on them,' she replied. 'They're for...well...they pull a carriage.'

'You've got a carriage, too?' Tommy's eyes were like saucers.

'Well, sort of,' she replied, realising she was getting herself into deep water. She wasn't sure whether or not Jessie had explained to her mother about the Moons' family business. At all events, the twins would not understand about it.

'Can we come and see your horses?' Tommy asked. 'Me

and Tilly?' His sister was looking much more animated now.

'Yes, I 'spect you could, one day,' said Maddy, somewhat unsurely. 'You will have to see what your mummy says.'

'I'll go and ask her now,' said Tommy, jumping up from the bench. 'Come on, Tilly; let's go and tell Mummy about Maddy's horses.'

'Don't you want to watch the rest of the show?' asked Jessie. 'If you go running off you might lose your seat.'

'No,' said Tommy. 'I want an ice-cream now. Mummy said we could have one this morning. Come on, Tilly.'

The two little ones ran off and Maddy and Jessie looked at one another and grinned. 'That's what our Tommy's like,' said Jessie. 'Always wanting to do something different. And Tilly just follows him. If I know Tommy he'll be wanting to watch the Punch and Judy show next. I don't really mind not seeing the second half of the Pierrot show, do you, Maddy?'

'No, of course not,' Maddy replied. 'We saw it yesterday, and there'll be lots more days.'

'And we won't always have the twins with us,' said Jessie.

Mrs Barraclough agreed that all the children should have an ice-cream, and they made their way across the sand to the ice-cream cart. She bought them each a cornet, but declined to have one herself. Maddy guessed it would not be ladylike for such an elegant person to be seen eating an ice-cream; besides, she might mess up her lovely dress and her white gloves.

'Thank you very much,' said Maddy. 'That's very kind of you... But I could've paid for my own cornet.'

Mrs Barraclough laughed, such a merry melodious sound, and smiled at her. 'I wouldn't dream of it, my dear. I am so pleased that Jessica had met such a nice polite little girl. I hope you two will be good friends whilst we are in Scarborough.'

'We are already,' said Maddy proudly. 'Oh... I nearly forgot. My...my mother says that Jessie can come for tea at our house on Wednesday, that's tomorrow. If she'd like to, and if you say that it's all right.'

'Oh, Mummy, can I, please?' asked Jessie.

'I don't see any reason why not,' replied her mother. 'Yes, of course you can go.' She turned to Maddy. 'Perhaps, on the way back, I could call and see your parents for a few moments? I would like to make their acquaintance, if it is convenient?'

'Yes, I 'spect it will be,' said Maddy. 'They'll probably both be there, but sometimes they have to...to go out.' She looked at the lady a little anxiously. 'Did Jessie tell you about my dad, what he does and...all that?'

'Yes, my dear. I understand, and you don't need to feel embarrassed about it. Why should you?'

'Maddy says they've got some horses,' Tommy chimed in now, having suddenly remembered about them; he had been distracted momentarily by the ice-cream. 'So we'll be able to see them, won't we, if we go to Maddy's house?'

'Just for a moment or two, maybe,' said his mother. 'We don't want to be a nuisance. People have work to do, but I thought it might be a good idea for us to meet.'

Maddy understood perfectly. She knew that her parents would react in exactly the same way. They always wanted to know about her friends' families; what job the father was in, for instance, and if they were nice respectable people.

'There's Punch and Judy over there,' said Tommy, pointing to a spot further along the beach where a crowd was gathering. He had dealt with the question of the horses and had finished his ice-cream and was now ready for the next exciting event. 'Can we go and watch it, Mummy?'

Mrs Barraclough nodded complacently, then helped the twins to wipe their sticky fingers on the hankies that were in their pockets, and Jessie and Maddy did the same.

The children and the few grown-ups in the crowd stood, rather than sat, to watch the antics of Punch and Judy on the little stage of the red-and-white striped box. The dog Toby, a real live dog, sat patiently at the side whilst the ugly hook-nosed Mister Punch berated his poor wife, Judy, knocking her about with a big stick and shouting, 'That's the way to do it!' in his funny squeaky voice. Poor Judy, thought Maddy, although she knew they were only wooden puppets and that it was all supposed to be in good fun. Tommy laughed uproariously, although Tilly seemed a little unsure about all the brutality. Anyway, the policeman came eventually to take Mister Punch away to prison, so perhaps he would get the punishment he deserved.

'Shall we go and see Samuel?' asked Mrs Barraclough when the Punch and Judy show had finished.

'No... I want to make a sandcastle,' said Tommy. He was jumping up and down excitedly, having found a pile of soft churned-up sand discarded by a couple of children who were engaged in building a castle of their own. 'You said we could, Mummy; didn't she, Tilly?' Tilly nodded a little doubtfully.

'No, I didn't; not today,' replied his mother, quietly but firmly. 'You are not dressed for playing in the sand today. We have already done two – no, three – exciting things, haven't we? We've watched the Pierrot show and the Punch and Judy; and you've had an ice-cream...'

'And we're going to see Maddy's horses...' added Tilly, nodding reprovingly at Tommy.

'Yes, so we are, dear,' said her mother. 'Just be satisfied, Tommy, and don't pull your face. It will stay like that!'

'As well as making it rain?' quipped Tommy.

His mother laughed, knowing he was not really being cheeky. He was as bright as a button, was Tommy, always ready with an apt comment. He wouldn't mind too much about the sandcastle and would soon be looking forward to the thrill of seeing the horses.

'Samuel – that's Jessica's older brother – has gone fishing off the end of the pier,' she told Maddy. 'He doesn't often catch very much, but he enjoys himself and that's the important thing. He's rather a solitary boy, my elder son. Not like his little brother, or Jessica for that matter.'

'Tilly's a quiet little girl though, isn't she?' said Maddy. The two of them, Mrs Barraclough and Maddy, were together now, walking up the steps that led from the beach with the other three children following behind. Maddy had decided that she liked this pretty lady very much. Not just because she was pretty, though; she was friendly, too, and made you feel as though she really wanted to talk to you.

'Yes, so she is,' she replied. 'I'm afraid that Tilly had always been overshadowed by her twin brother. But she is starting to think for herself a little bit more now, I hope. It is surprising how different children in a family can be. On the other hand, maybe not... I suppose two of them take after me and the other two after my husband.' She did not say which two, so Maddy supposed it was Jessie and Tommy, the bright and cheerful ones, who took after their mother.

'Do you have brothers and sisters, Maddy?' she asked. 'Jessie did mention that you had a brother...'

'Yes, our Patrick,' replied Maddy. 'There's just him and me; I haven't got any sisters. Patrick works for me dad, and me grandad lives with us an' all...as well. It was his business, y'see, the...undertaker's. Well, it still is really; Isaac Moon and Son, it's called; that's me grandad – he's Isaac – and me dad's called William. And we have a shop as well. My...mother's in charge of that.'

'Yes, I am looking forward to meeting your parents...and perhaps your grandad and your brother,' said Mrs Barraclough.

They walked along the cliff path leading to the pier entrance.

'Did you ever see such a monstrosity?' said Mrs Barraclough pointing – but in a refined manner – to the tower which had been erected two years ago on the cliff top near to the castle. It dominated, and to many minds, spoilt the view of Scarborough's North Bay.

Maddy was able to answer knowledgeably because her parents, also, had protested against the building of the tower. They, too, had used the word 'monstrosity' about the 'Warwick Revolving Tower', as it was called. 'Yes, my mam and dad think it's ugly too,' she replied. 'They said it should never've been allowed. I suppose you can see for miles, though, from up there. That's what it says at the entrance, doesn't it?'

'Yes, stupendous marine views, so they say. It's a hundred and fifty feet high, I believe.' Mrs Barraclough laughed. 'All I know is that it is ruining the view from our front windows, and I certainly won't be going up there! Never mind; perhaps they will remove it if too many people complain. But we are not going to let it spoil our holiday...

'Come along now, all of you.' She gathered the children around her at the pier entrance. 'Off you go, through the turnstile. One at a time... Tommy, don't push like that.'

They went through the pier turnstile, then walked along the wooden boards which stretched out over the sand, and then over the sea. Tilly came up to Maddy and took hold of her hand. 'It's a bit scary, isn't it?' she said. 'Look – we can see the sea underneath us.'

'D'you know, I used to feel exactly the same when I was a little girl,' said Maddy, with all the wisdom of her ten years. She remembered feeling as though the waves, which sometimes could be quite rough on a windy day, were pulling her down into their depths. 'But there's nothing to be frightened of. Don't look down; just look in front of you and tell me when you can see your brother.'

'He's there!' the little girl cried in a few moments, when they had almost reached the end of the pier.

The boy was leaning against the railings, his eyes looking fixedly ahead to the end of his line where it entered the sea.

'Sam... Hello, Sam,' called Tilly. 'We've come to see you!' She sounded more excited than she had done all morning.

The boy turned round and Maddy thought she had never seen a more good-looking lad. He was dark-haired, unlike his mother and his sisters and brother, and his eyes were dark too, an arresting feature in a face that resembled, so she thought, a picture of a knight of old that she had seen in a history book; sombre and serious-looking, but so very handsome. His stern look disappeared, however, at the sight of his little sister.

'Hello there, Tilly,' he said, smiling broadly at her; then he looked questioningly at Maddy.

'This is Maddy,' said Tilly. 'You know – Jessie told us about her new friend. Well, she's my friend as well now, aren't you, Maddy?' She turned her pointed pixie-like face towards Maddy, smiling at her in a proprietary manner.

'Well then, hello Maddy,' said Samuel. He nodded at her in quite a friendly way, but the bright smile that had lit up his face on seeing his sister had faded a little. 'Nice to meet you… Excuse me not shaking hands. I don't want to let go of my rod.'

'Oh yes, so I see,' said Maddy. 'Your mum said you were a keen fisherman. Have you caught anything this morning?'

'One or two,' he answered casually, 'but I always throw them back again.'

'Yes, so you do,' said his mother, who had now joined the group with Tommy and Jessie. She laughed. 'I am still waiting for a nice juicy herring or two to cook for our tea.'

'He never catches any!' said Tommy. He was jumping up and down enjoying the hollow thud that his shoes made on the wooden planking.

'Yes I do, I catch plenty! And we'll have less of your cheek, young Thomas,' said Samuel. 'Now, Mother, you know that you wouldn't like the job of gutting and boning the fish, would you? Besides, I've told you that the best fish, particularly the herrings, are much further out to sea. And I wouldn't want to deprive the fishermen of their trade, now would I?'

His brown eyes twinkled with just a shade of humour and his mother smiled at him fondly. 'You are right, of course, Samuel. I prefer to buy my fish all cleaned and ready to cook from the stalls near the harbour.

'Well then, we will leave you to your fishing,' she added as

Samuel turned back towards the sea, pulling at his rod as though there might be a catch at the end of the line. 'Your lunch will be ready in about…let me see…' She looked at the dainty fob watch which was pinned to her bodice. 'In about in an hour's time; well, perhaps an hour and a half. We are going to call in to see Maddy's parents on the way back.'

'And her horses,' added Tommy, who was still jumping up and down.

'Yes, and the horses,' said his mother. 'Do try and keep still for a moment, Tommy… You will be coming home for lunch, will you, Samuel? Or did you bring a sandwich with you?'

'No, I'll be there, Mother.' He did not turn round. 'Not for long though. This afternoon I intend to go to the museum, the Rotunda. I've heard they have some interesting archaeological specimens there.' He was still staring out to sea, winding in his line.

'Each to his own, I suppose,' said Mrs Barraclough musingly, as though to herself. 'Come along now; let's leave him in peace. Goodbye for now, Samuel.'

'Bye, everyone,' he answered vaguely.

'My brother's real stuffy,' said Jessie, coming to walk next to Maddy as they strode back along the pier. 'He's not much fun at all sometimes.'

But Maddy thought that Samuel was excitingly different from all the other boys she knew. He was not much like her brother, Patrick, that was for sure.

Chapter Five

William and Clara Moon had been out on an assignment that morning, and they were surprised when they arrived back, almost at midday, to find that they had visitors. Isaac was deep in conversation with a lady whom William decided at once was one of the most beautiful women he had ever seen.

'William, Clara...' called Isaac as soon as they entered the yard. 'Come over here and meet Mrs Barraclough; she's our Maddy's friend's mother.'

The vision of loveliness turned and smiled at them, holding out a lace-gloved hand as they approached. 'How do you do?' she said. 'I am so pleased to make your acquaintance, both of you. Our daughters have already become good friends. I am Faith Barraclough.'

'And I'm William Moon and this is my wife, Clara,' said William, shaking her hand very gently. Such an exquisite creature surely deserved the most careful handling. 'How you do? I'm very pleased to meet you.'

'Yes indeed,' echoed his wife. 'I'm glad you've come to see us. Like you say, our Maddy and your little girl seem to have hit it off at once. Sorry we weren't here to greet you, but I see you have already met my father-in-law.'

'Aye, we've said "how do" to one another,' said Isaac. His grey eyes, still very sharp and perceptive, were gleaming with more than a spark of admiration. Although almost seventy years of age he still had an eye for a pretty face.

'And the youngsters are all getting to know one another.' He pointed towards the stable at the end of the yard where the two black horses, Jet and Ebony, were being fussed over by the group of children. 'The little 'un, Tommy, was all for running into t' workshop, but Patrick caught him just in time. So we avoided any awkward questions, you might say.'

Tommy at that moment was offering a sugar lump to Jet on his outstretched palm. 'Keep your hand real flat, there's a good lad, Tommy,' Patrick was saying, 'and then Jet can get her lips round the sugar and not your fingers... No, she doesn't bite, not as a rule, but it's better to be safe than sorry.'

Ebony had a white star on her forehead and that, to folk who did not know them, was the only way of distinguishing between the horses. Tilly was tentatively stroking her sleek mane, all the while looking anxiously at Maddy.

'It's my turn now,' said Jessie. 'Come on, Tommy; you've had your go. May I give Jet a sugar lump, please, Patrick?'

'They are fine-looking animals,' observed Faith Barraclough. 'Have you had them very long?'

'Getting on for two year now,' replied Isaac. 'We used to hire the horses before that.'

'They're both female,' added William. 'We felt they'd be easier to handle than stallions. And we've our own hearse now; we got it when business started picking up for us.'

'And the shop as well,' said Clara. 'Would you like to come and see round the shop some time, Mrs Barraclough? We have a nice range of dresses and costumes, not just black mourning wear. I've been trying to get away from too sombre an image lately. We stock a lot of black, of course, but by no means is all of it funeral wear. We have dresses in different shades of purple and lavender, and that's a colour that anyone can wear anytime. Maddy didn't bring you through the shop, did she?'

'No; we came round the side, but I would certainly like to see it when I have a little more time to spare.' Faith Barraclough looked at her fob watch. 'We really ought to be going now. I just wanted to meet you and to thank you for inviting Jessica to come to tea. I had to make sure the invitation had come from you; I know what children are like.'

'Yes, indeed it did,' Clara assured her. 'Wednesday afternoon; that's our half-day closing. And perhaps another time you all might like to visit us. Maddy says you are here for the whole month.'

'Yes, that's right. This is our third summer here in Scarborough, but it is the first time we have stayed in the North Bay. Jessie, come along now, dear. And you as well, Tommy and Tilly. It's time we were getting back. We mustn't hold up Mr and Mrs Moon any longer; they are very busy people.'

'She seems a very pleasant woman,' said Clara to her husband when all the goodbyes had been said. Maddy had been bright-eyed with excitement at the visit of her new friend's family and had insisted on accompanying them off the premises and onto the street, where she stood waving to them until they turned the corner.

'Yes, I thought so too,' replied William. 'A very charming woman. You realise why she wanted to meet us, don't you? To find out if we were suitable people for her daughter to mix with.'

'Of course,' smiled Clara. 'But you can't blame her, can you? We might well have done the same thing ourselves. Anyway, I think we met with her approval. A very beautiful

woman, isn't she? I know you must have noticed that, Will...'
She grinned at him. 'But she doesn't appear to have any airs
and graces about her, does she? I thought she seemed a
bit...well...not very sure of herself.'

'Yes, I know what you mean. I thought so too. Aye, I
noticed she's a good-looking woman. Lovely blue eyes; you
couldn't help but notice 'em. But they looked a bit sad to me,
as though there's summat worrying her, deep down. Or maybe
I'm being fanciful.' William shook his head bemusedly.

'But you can rest assured, luv, that there's only one woman
in the world for me, and you know who that is, don't you?'
He put his arms around Clara, giving her a quick kiss on the
lips as they stood together outside the back entrance to their
home. 'I can admire a pretty woman, wouldn't be human if I
didn't, but there's only one lass for me and don't you ever
forget it.'

'I won't, Will; I don't,' replied Clara, looking at him
lovingly. 'When have I ever had cause to doubt you? Never.
Now, I'd best go and get the kettle on and see to our dinner.
It'll be a pot-luck meal today, I'm afraid; soup and sandwiches
or something of the sort. What with going out on that job
unexpectedly and then having visitors I've got a bit behind
with meself. Tell your father and Patrick it'll be about twenty
minutes or so...

'Oh, there you are, Maddy love. Come and help me to lay
the table, there's a good lass. We like your new friend; she
seems a very nice polite girl. A lovely family they are; I'm very
glad you've met them.'

William was thoughtful after his wife had gone into the
kitchen. What he had just told her was perfectly true; there
would never ever be any other woman for him than his

beloved Clara. He had grown to love her more and more deeply over the years of their marriage. She was a completely selfless person who saw the good in everyone and was slow to judge or to find fault. Admittedly, she was particular about the friends their children made, but that was because they meant the whole world to her and she wanted them to choose the right pathway through life.

Clara was not a beautiful woman, not one that you would notice in a crowd or give a second glance; William guessed that Faith Barraclough would cause quite a few heads to turn. Clara's face and features were unremarkable, her nose a little too snub, her chin a little too pointed and her forehead a little too high. Maddy had inherited her mother's delicate looks and dainty figure and her golden hair as well, but both mother and daughter had a wiry strength which belied their seeming fragility. But when Clara smiled – and Maddy, too, for she resembled her mother in so many ways – then you might almost say that she was beautiful. Her smile transformed her face, lighting up her deep brown eyes which shone with a radiance, a goodness of spirit that came from deep within her.

Her smile had been the first thing that William had noticed about her when he had first met her in the dressmaker's shop in Eastborough, where she had worked. He had gone in to collect a skirt which his mother was having made and had been completely won over, not only by her smile, but by the pleasant manners and the gentleness of the young woman who was serving him. It wasn't long before he paid a second visit to the shop to buy a pair of gloves for his mother's birthday.

There was good selection of accessories to be purchased there as well as the bespoke items for which the shop was best known. He had an ulterior motive, however: to become better acquainted with the personable young assistant. To his delight, the attraction that he had felt towards her on their first meeting seemed to be mutual. He learnt that her name was Clara Halliday and that she 'lived in' at the premises on Eastborough, working as assistant to Miss Montague, the middle-aged spinster lady who owned the establishment. She showed a little surprise, but was clearly delighted as well when he asked her if she would like to accompany him to a musical concert at the Spa Pavilion.

Other outings followed, and both young people soon knew that they had found something special in their regard for one another. William at that time – some sixteen years ago – had been twenty-two years of age and Clara two years younger. Both her parents had died four years previously when a virulent form of influenza had swept through the neighbourhood where they lived: the little old streets behind Sandside, near to the harbour. Her father had been a fisherman and when he died, followed by her mother a few weeks later, Clara had been left almost penniless.

It was then that she had been invited to share Miss Montague's home; she was already a valued assistant in the dressmaking business and in the shop. The two of them had lived and worked together very companionably ever since. The advent of William Moon had made a difference, of course, but Louisa Montague had been very happy that such an agreeable and charming young man was courting the girl she had almost come to regard as her own daughter, the daughter she had never had.

Louisa had never married and had never had any wish to do so. She lived for her work as a skilled dressmaker. Women of all levels of society, the rich as well as those who were less well-to-do, had over the years found their way to her little shop. Her leisure time, such as she allowed herself, was occupied largely in good works for her Methodist church, with occasional visits to a play or concert or – more frequently – to the library and lecture hall on St Nicholas Street.

When William and Clara had married the following year Louisa had been as delighted as anyone. Those who did not know her, in fact, might have thought her to be the mother of the bride, seeing her in a large-brimmed hat, trimmed with flowers and sweeping ostrich feathers, which could have put even Alexandra, the Princess of Wales, to shame. She was losing her dear Clara, to be sure, both as assistant and as living companion, but she soon became a welcome visitor to the home they shared with William's parents near to their undertaker's yard. She made sure that she did not visit so often as to be considered a nuisance; but the friendship had continued and several of the gowns which were now sold in Moon's Mourning Modes had been made by Louisa and the two young women who now worked for her.

Patrick had been born the year after their marriage in 1886, and Madeleine – Maddy – four years later in 1890. William knew he was a very lucky man. Clara was not only a wonderful wife and mother but a willing business partner as well. She had never baulked at any of the tasks she had been called upon to do and had worked unstintingly alongside him and his father to help to make Isaac Moon and Son the highly respected business it was today.

William's only regret was that he had not been completely honest with his wife about his former relationship with Bella Randall, the woman who now worked in their shop...

* * *

By the second half of the nineteenth century Scarborough had become known as the 'Queen of Watering Places'. The town had prospered in no small way following the opening of the railway line from York in 1845, followed by further branch lines to Whitby, Bridlington, Pickering and Hull. People were finding it easier to travel to the coast and the fashion for day trips began, as well as the longer holidays which had always been popular.

The building of the Spa Bridge near to the sea and, some thirty years later, the Valley Bridge, further inland, had led to easier access between the North and South Bays of the town. All types of accommodation could be found, both on the North and South Cliffs. They varied in quality and in price, too, ranging from the prestigious hotels such as the Crown, the Pavilion, the Prince of Wales and the Grand Hotel – which, at the time of its opening, was the largest hotel in Europe – to the more humble boarding and lodging houses.

In 1880, when he was eighteen years old, William was enjoying himself, when he was not working, as a young man about town. The business was thriving and his father allowed him a decent wage, and so he was affluent enough to be able to patronise, occasionally, the fashionable shops – the hatters, gent's outfitters, hosiers and shoemakers – which were springing up in Westborough, St Nicholas Street and Aberdeen Walk. But he was often to be found at the lower end of the town in the Remnant Warehouse which had been opened by an enterprising man named William Boyes. The six hundred feet of counters in the store were filled with factory remnants and much else besides. The periodical, the *Remnant Warehouse Messenger*, advertised everything one might need in the home or garden or for personal use. Many a

Scarborough housewife, even from the Esplanade or the Crown Terrace, might be found having a rummage there. Yorkshire women as well as the men, even the most well heeled of them, would not say no to a bargain.

There was a good deal of street selling too, although the opening of the new Market Hall in the middle of the century had replaced much of the outdoor trade. Prior to this and for many years afterwards – for the Scarborough Corporation was not altogether successful in limiting the street stalls – it was possible to buy poultry, butter and eggs in St Nicholas Street, hardware and pots in St Thomas Street, drapery and hats in Queen Street, and all sorts of items from the myriad stalls on Newborough.

Not only was there street selling, but many other attractions as well; itinerant singers and musicians, hurdy-gurdy players and organ grinders, hawkers of towels and household linens, and girls selling apples and oranges. The streets echoed with the familiar cries of 'Cockles alive-o', 'Any fish today?', 'Meat pies, all hot', and on the sands the Italian ice-cream seller shouting 'Hokey pokey penny a lump, that's the stuff that makes you jump!'

In the busy harbour stream trawlers and drifters arrived daily to land their catches, and the Sandside cockle and whelk stalls did a roaring trade. Dripping fish carts, passing through the town from the harbour to the railway station, were often to be seen on the roads, jostling with the cabs and carriages and horse-drawn omnibuses. All told it was a colourful scene adding to – or detracting from, according to your point of view – the atmosphere of fashionable Scarborough.

It was down at the harbour, where he had been choosing a lobster for a teatime treat, that William had first set eyes on

Bella Randall. There were six or eight of these girls all busily working at their task on a large stone slab near to the harbour wall. These 'herring girls', as they were called, were well known in the town and had been for many many years, though there were different girls, of course, each season. Sometimes they were known as 'fisher lasses'; they originated mainly from Scotland and the north-east, and from other parts of the country, too, following the herring fleets as the fishermen gathered in from the North Sea the annual harvest of herrings. They worked long and tedious hours at their job, gutting the fish and preparing them for transport to the local shops and stalls or further afield. Skilled workers could gut a fish in a second, using a sharp-bladed tool called a gipping knife. The fish were then salted and packed head-to-tail in tightly sealed barrels with extra salt sprinkled between the layers. It was a method of preservation that had been used for centuries.

These girls had become something of a novelty in the resort and folk often stopped to watch them, even, sometimes, to take their photograph. The fisher lasses, on the whole, grew quite used to the attention, though some were far more friendly than others towards the gawping spectators.

It was one girl in particular whom William had been watching that afternoon, as she grabbed hold of one silver fish after another, slicing them open with a dexterity born of experience and scooping out the guts into a waste bin at the side. She was a rosy-complexioned lass with strong sunburnt arms. She was dressed in a similar way to the other young women, in a dark-hued blouse and a calico apron, the bib of which strained against her fulsome figure. Some of the girls wore white bonnets to shield their heads from the heat of the sun, but her hair was uncovered, a curly mass the colour and sheen of shining coal. When she glanced up, turning her head in his direction as though suddenly aware of his scrutiny, he saw that her eyes were the same shade as her hair, jet black and gleaming, as she regarded him with a brazen stare. He realised that he must have been guilty of staring, although he had seen the girls many times before.

'Got yer eye full, have yer?' she called. Her mouth was wide with red lips, naturally red and not painted, and when she smiled, as she soon did, he could see that her teeth were white and even. She was a very striking young woman, bold to be sure, but William was not averse to a show of spirit in a girl. He was tempted to stop and talk with her.

—

Chapter Six

'I'm sorry,' said William. 'I didn't mean to stare. I was just admiring your...er...your skill with that sharp-looking knife. You seem very experienced, if you don't mind me saying so.'

'Aye, you're right.' The girl grinned, her black eyes alight with humour and a hint of coquetry. 'And I'll tell you summat else an' all, bonny lad. This 'ere blade not only looks sharp, it is bloomin' sharp! One slip and before you can say "knife" the ends of your fingers could be joining the fish guts in the waste bin.' William felt himself giving a shudder.

'But I know what I'm doing,' said the girl. 'Like you say... I'm pretty experienced.' She gave him a bold look, her eyes glancing from his straw boater down to his casual, but smart, jacket and grey flannel trousers and his highly polished black boots. 'Anyways, what's a toff like you doing round here? Ain't you got nothing better to do than stare at us lasses?'

'I've been choosing a nice lobster for our tea,' he replied, indicating the brown-paper parcel in his hand. 'There's nothing like a freshly caught lobster from the North Sea.'

'And you know what to do with it, do you?'

'Aye...well, my mother does at any rate. We're all of us partial to a bit of lobster, my mother and father and myself.'

'You live here then, do you, in Scarborough? You're not just here on yer holidays?'

'Oh no...no; we're a local family. Quite well known in the town, actually, though I say it myself.'

'Aye, I thought you might be. You have that look about you.'

'What do you mean? What sort of look?' he asked.

'Oh...a canny look. One that says, "I'm somebody round here. I know my way around".' The girl gave him another impudent glance, but then her eyes softened a little as they looked straight into his. 'How's about you showing me the way around – round Scarborough, I mean – seeing as how you're a local lad?'

William was a little taken aback. He was not used to such bold behaviour from members of the opposite sex. The girls that he knew, from his neighbourhood and from his local chapel, would not dream of behaving in such an unseemly manner. He had taken one or two girls out, to concerts or for walks on the promenade or up to Oliver's Mount on the outskirts of the town. He had indulged in a few innocent kisses and cuddles with a couple of them, but nothing more. William, despite his self-confident air, was quite inexperienced with the ladies, probably because he had not, as yet, met a young woman who appealed to him in a certain way.

He had many friends of his own sex and was a popular young man in all the various aspects of his life: at work, at the Methodist chapel he attended with his parents and at the one or two drinking places he visited in the town. William did not adhere to the strict principles of his religion with regard to abstinence; neither – thankfully – did his father Isaac. It had been William's grandfather, Joshua, apparently, who had been a strict follower of all the tenets of his faith, ruling his family with the proverbial rod of iron which had verged at times on harshness and near cruelty. Isaac was a much more tolerant father and William knew he was fortunate, blessed indeed, with such kind and loving parents as Isaac and Hannah Moon. He had never knowingly disobeyed them in any way. But what they would think of this fisher girl he had just met he was not sure...

Well, he did know, deep down, if he was honest with himself. They would consider that she was not at all a suitable companion for him and that he should say a polite goodbye to her now, before he got himself any more deeply involved. But William was becoming mesmerised by the look in her jet black eyes; not a brazen look now but one that seemed to be imploring him to befriend her and spend a little time with her. And there could be no harm in that surely? He sensed that beneath her brash exterior there might be a much softer complaisant person hidden inside. Well, he would never know if he did not try to find out...

'Yes...' he replied. 'I...er... I don't mind showing you round a bit. Is this the first time you've been to Scarborough?'

'Aye, so it is. I've worked at Whitby and Hull, and up north at South Shields and Tynemouth – that's near where I come from.' He had already guessed that. 'But I must say I've taken quite a fancy to this place.'

'Where are you staying then?' he asked.

'Oh, at one o' t' little cottages over yonder.' She pointed in the direction of Sandside. William guessed she might be staying in the area known as The Bolts, a not very salubrious part of the town, but no doubt all that the young women could afford. 'Me and two more o' t' lasses... And I can see that me pal Mona has got her eagle eye on me an' all. She likes to think she's in charge of us all, see...' She waved her hand to another lass, one in a white bonnet, who was standing at the other end of the stone slab, staring at her with her arms akimbo.

'All right, Mona,' she shouted. 'Just 'aving a breather. I'll catch up with you in a mo'.'

'Aye, just think on as you do,' replied the other young woman, picking up her gutting knife again and waving it menacingly at William's companion. It struck him that he did not know the girl's name, and neither did she know his.

'I'm sorry,' he said now. 'I haven't even introduced myself, have I? My name is William – William Moon – but my friends usually call me Will.'

'How d'you do then…Will?' grinned the girl. 'We'd best not shake hands, eh, or you'll get yerself all muckied up. I'm Arabella Randall, but me friends call me Bella. And now I'd best get on with me work if you don't mind. I'm getting some pretty filthy looks and I don't want to end up with a knife between me ribs.'

'You're joking, aren't you?' he asked in some alarm.

'Aye, I suppose I am. But tempers gets frayed, y'know, and one thing soon leads to another. Some o' these lasses are tough customers and we all have to learn how to look after ourselves.'

William guessed his new acquaintance might be well able to do that, and he knew it was time he took his leave. 'May I…may I see you tonight then?' he asked. 'Bella…' he added, rather liking the sound of her name.

'Aye, I reckon so…Will,' she grinned. 'Where d'you fancy taking me then?'

'Do you know the Three Mariners' Inn?' he asked her.

'Aye, of course I do. It's not far from where I'm lodging.'

'Well, shall I meet you there then? Say about eight o'clock?

We can have a stroll around and then pop inside for a drink, if that's all right with you?'

'It's fine by me, bonny lad. And I promise I'll have scrubbed meself up a bit by then.' She threw back her head and gave a merry laugh and William found himself becoming more and more fascinated by her. 'Cheerio then, Will. It's been nice meeting you. See you later.'

'I shall look forward to it,' he replied, touching the brim of his boater. As he turned and walked away he heard peals of laughter following him. He told himself not to be surprised if she did not turn up, recalling the outburst of – had it been mocking? – laughter that he had heard as he walked away from the quayside. Maybe she had only been amusing herself with him. But that evening as he approached the point where Sandside joined Quay Street he could see her, standing at the corner near the Three Mariners' Inn. As she had said she would, she had scrubbed up more than a little since their encounter earlier that day. Her black skirt might have been the same one – he could not tell – but she was now wearing a blouse, long-sleeved and low-necked, made from a shiny material in a bright shade of green; he remembered his fashion-conscious mother referring to such a colour as emerald green. Perched on top of her mass of curly black hair, which flowed loosely almost to her shoulders, she wore a straw hat trimmed with a ribbon the same shade as her blouse.

His heart gave a leap as he set eyes on her; she really was a most attractive and alluring young lady. Or, rather, young woman he supposed, reflecting briefly that his mother would certainly not consider this person to be a lady! Neither of his parents were snobbish – indeed there could be few men more down-to-earth than his father – but they both had certain standards which they had tried to instil upon their only son.

He quickened his footsteps as he drew nearer to her. 'Bella,' he greeted her warmly. 'I'm so pleased you decided to come. I thought you might…well…change your mind.'

She smiled at him, her red lips parting to show her rather large and even white teeth. Obviously she took good care of them; there was no sign of decay or discolouring such as he had noticed in some young women's teeth and which he always found repellent. William, despite the unpleasant sights he saw from time to time in his daily work, was fastidious about his personal appearance and that of others.

'Now whyever would I want to do that?' she said. 'Turn down the best offer I've had in a month of Sundays? Not bloomin' likely!' She laughed out loud, opening her mouth wide and throwing back her head. 'Hello again, Will. Glad you decided to come an' all. I thought you might've been the one to change yer mind.'

'Never let it be said that I should let a lady down.' He inclined his head towards her gravely. 'You will find that William Moon is a man of his word.'

'I'm pleased to hear it,' she replied. 'I've found that they're few and far between. Righty-ho then; where are you taking me?'

'Oh, let's just stroll along by the sea, shall we?' said William. 'Happen as far as the Spa Bridge, then we could come back here and have a drink or two. How would that suit you?'

'That would suit me just fine, bonny lad,' said Bella, tucking her arm companionably through his and smiling at him.

They were much of a height. William, at five-foot six or thereabouts, was not very tall, whilst Bella was quite a reasonable height for a woman. She was a well-built lass; not what you would call fat or even buxom, but Will could not help but notice how her ample breasts strained against the shiny green fabric of her blouse, the low-cut neckline revealing a tantalising glimpse of her cleavage. He looked away quickly, smiling into her dark eyes; eyes that were already full of mystery and promise.

'Hmm...' He cleared his throat. 'Come along then; let's make the most of the fresh sea breezes,' he said as they set off walking southwards along Sandside.

Bella gave a deep sniff and laughed. 'Not all that fresh,' she remarked, wrinkling her nose. The stalls which did a busy trade during the day selling fresh fish and shellfish of many kinds had now closed, but the aroma still lingered on the air, as did the smell of herrings from the spot where Bella did her daily work. 'Let's keep to this side o' t' road, shall us?'

William nodded. 'You get used to it, though; the smell, I mean. It's part of Scarborough; I don't mind it. In fact, I quite like it.' It was, indeed, preferable to some of the rather less pleasant odours that he came across in his occupation, but he did not say so. Time enough, later, to acquaint his new friend with the details of his work, although he did not imagine that anything much would disturb her.

'You're not working in it though, are you?' said Bella. She was eyeing him appraisingly and he was aware that she was taking in his smart appearance. He was casually dressed in what was known as a Norfolk jacket, with a soft cap, such as that favoured by Bertie, the Prince of Wales. William always dressed fashionably, according to the company and the situation in which he found himself. He knew that Bella had already sized him up as a bit of a toff.

'What is it that you do?' she asked now. 'No…don't tell me, let me guess… I think you work in a bank…' He shook his head, smiling a little. 'Well, an office of some sort anyroad. I don't reckon you get yer hands dirty.' He burst out laughing at that, but still did not let on.

She frowned a little. 'Or you might work in one o' them big posh shops. Floor walkers, don't they call 'em? I can just see you in a black coat and pin-striped trousers.'

'You're not so far off the mark there, with the dress at any rate,' he replied. 'Well, some of the time I have to dress up… No, I'm not going to tell you, not yet, but I promise that I will, later. I work in my father's business, and that's all I'm going to say for now.'

'I suppose it don't matter much anyways,' said Bella, briefly squeezing his arm. 'I like you, William Moon. I've decided I like you a lot, whatever it is you do.'

'I'm glad to hear it,' he replied. 'And I've decided that I like you too… Now, how about a stroll over the Spa Bridge. You'll soon get the smell of fish out of your nostrils over yonder.' They had passed the harbour where the fishing vessels and leisure craft were moored for the night and, reaching the end of Foreshore Road, they started to climb the steps which led up, through a laid out garden area, to St Nicholas Cliff. Above them loomed the magnificent edifice of the Grand Hotel.

'What d'you reckon to that then?' he asked as they reached the top. 'The Grand Hotel. It's supposed to be the finest in all Europe.' They stood and admired it whilst getting their breath back from the climb.

'Aye, very lah-di-dah,' said Bella. 'Not for the likes of you and me though, bonny lad. Well, not for me anyways. Dunno so much about you, but I don't reckon I'll ever have the brass to stay in a place like that. I wouldn't mind though...' she added wistfully.

It occupied a commanding position on the headland overlooking the South Bay, but it was considered by some to be overpowering in its enormity. You could not fail to be aware of it, looming over the town and dominating the skyline.

'I've heard it has three hundred and sixty-five bedrooms,' said William, 'One for each day o' t' year. And twelve floors...'

'One for each month, I suppose,' said Bella.

'Aye, that's right. And four domes, one at each corner, one for each season.'

'How long has it been there?'

'Oh, I'm not quite sure. They were building it for years, it seemed, and then the company ran out o' money. Anyway, a businessman from Leeds came to the rescue, and it opened in 1867, about thirteen year ago. And doing very well an' all, so they say. Now, let's have a walk on t' bridge, shall we?'

William paid their pennies at the toll gate and they stepped on to the broad walkway which spanned the valley. Halfway across they leant on the railings, gazing out to sea across the stretch of golden sand. There were still a few people strolling on the beach in the balmy air of the June evening, but soon they would be forced to leave as the tide was advancing. The view was quite breathtaking in its beauty, although William had seen it many times before. To the left the harbour and the sweep of the South Bay, with the ruined castle on the cliff top and, below it, the parish church of St Mary and the hotels facing on to the North Bay; and to the right, in their wooded setting, the Spa buildings after which the bridge was named.

'D'you like listening to music?' asked William, gesturing towards the newly renovated building of the Spa below them. 'They have concerts there. I thought perhaps, sometime, we might...?'

'What sort o' concert?' asked Bella. 'I've never had much chance, y'see, to listen to what you might call proper music, and I don't know as it'd be my cup of tea.'

'Oh, they put on all sorts of shows at the Spa,' said William, 'especially since it's been rebuilt. There was a terrible fire a few years ago and it only opened up again last year. There's a theatre there now and they put on summer shows and a pantomime at Christmas.'

'I shan't be here at Christmas, shall I?' said Bella, turning to give him a quizzical glance.

'No... I don't suppose you will.' He looked into her dark eyes which were fixed steadily on him, reflecting that it was most likely she would be here today and gone tomorrow; well, not tomorrow, of course, but certainly at the end of the herring season. It was up to him to make the most of their time together, that was if she wanted to go on seeing him. 'They have brass band concerts, though, on a Sunday afternoon.'

'Brass bands?' said Bella. 'Now you're talking! I'm all for a bit of tiddly-om-pom-pom.' She moved her arms back and forth as though playing a trombone, her voice tootling a popular air from HMS *Pinafore*. 'I've heard 'em on the prom at South Shields. An' I like the music hall...' Her voice rose on a cadence with enthusiasm. 'Aye, I'm quite partial to – what do they call it? – that there vaudeville? My pal Nancy and me, we've had many a good night out at the music hall in Newcastle.'

'Oh, we've any amount of theatres here,' said William. 'Highbrow and lowbrow, whatever you fancy. And shows on the beach an' all. Minstrel shows, they're all the rage at the moment.'

'Y' mean the ones wi' black faces?'

'Aye, that's right. They're not really black, of course; they're white men that paint their faces. Negro minstrels, they call themselves. My father, now, he's become a right keen follower of 'em. Morgan's Merry Minstrels; they're his favourites. They've got a pitch over on the North Bay and he's there every chance he gets.' He chuckled. 'He's got me quite addicted to 'em an' all.' Both Isaac and William had found that watching the jolly antics and listening to the music – the oftentimes haunting and nostalgic songs – afforded a welcome respite from the more unpleasant aspects of their daily work.

'I've never seen any of 'em,' said Bella. 'But it sounds as though it might be right up my street. Nowt too educated like; I'm only an ordinary sort o' lass.'

'You seem all right to me,' said William as, by mutual agreement it seemed, they started to walk back the way they had come, along the bridge then down the steps to the promenade.

Bella told him, as they walked, that her home was in Morpeth, or, rather, that was the place where she had been born; a 'canny place', she said, a market town surrounded by the rolling Northumberland hills. But she had left home when she was thirteen to go into service at one of the big houses in the area. He gathered that she had not been happy at home. As the eldest of six, she had been nothing more than a skivvy for her ailing mother; a pitiful woman, so it seemed, worn down by continual child-bearing. By the time the last child had been stillborn and her mother had also died, due to inadequate care, Bella had already been in service for nearly two years, working herself up from scullery maid to kitchen maid, and then to housemaid. She had ignored her father's pleas for her to return home and, within a year, he had married again to the twenty-year-old daughter of a neighbour who had agreed to be a mother to his five remaining children.

William had heard similar stories many times before. Frequently their clients were the husbands of women who had died in childbirth, and it was the task of Isaac Moon and Son to do their job with as much sympathy as they could muster, and not to criticise or condemn. William, now aged eighteen, had had his eyes opened to the grim realities of life. He had already decided that when he found a wife he would treat her with the respect due to her sex and status; he had been given a perfect example with his own parents.

He was aware now that Bella was telling him only as much of her story as she wanted him to know. She told him, somewhat hesitantly, how she had left the house where she was working when she was sixteen years old. There had been a disagreement – that was as much as she would say – and the lady of the house had not quibbled when she had said she wanted to leave. She and her friend, Nancy, had then decided to follow the herring fleet down the east coast during the summer months. They lived together in 'digs' during the winter, finding whatever work they could, cleaning or working in bars. But now Nancy was married and Bella, in her third summer as a herring girl, would be on her own during the coming winter.

'But that's a long time off, ain't it?' she said cheerfully. 'Tomorrow can take care of itself. I believe in making the most of today.'

'A good philosophy, I suppose,' said William thoughtfully.

The Three Mariners' Inn was crowded around the bar area, but they managed to find a secluded corner away from the crowds. William ordered his usual pint of bitter whilst Bella asked for a port and lemon. One soon disappeared and he bought her another, but his pint would last him all evening. He had seen too many fellows – even some of his own friends – the worse for drink and did not want ever to be in that state himself.

'Now, bonny lad,' she said, putting down her glass and licking her lips appreciatively. 'Hows about telling me about this mysterious job of yours? I reckon you've got time to do a fair bit of gadding about, watching minstrel shows and going shopping for fresh lobsters, eh?'

He grinned at her, putting his elbows on the scarred and pitted wooden table and leaning towards her. 'I'm an undertaker,' he said.

'What!' She threw back her head and laughed. 'You're not! You can't be! Tell me you're joking…'

'Of course I'm not joking. Why should I be?' he replied, feeling somewhat indignant. 'It's a respectable trade and one I'm not ashamed of. Somebody has to do it, the same as somebody has to sweep chimneys, or gut herrings…' He nodded at her meaningfully. '…Or go down the mine or…anything.'

'Aye, I s'pose so.' She nodded. 'That's what my old man does; he works down the pit. I'm sorry I laughed.' She was looking a little more serious now. 'I shouldn't've, but it was such a shock, like. I never dreamt…'

'No, I don't suppose you did. You're not squeamish, are you, about what I do? It's just a job, same as any other.'

'Squeamish? No; why should I be? I've seen a few dead bodies if that's what you mean, an' it doesn't worry me that you have to touch 'em.'

'Talking about me having time to gad about,' he went on, 'well, it's not strictly true. I'm as busy as the next man. But our work comes in fits and starts, you might say. Sometimes there's a lull, and then suddenly there might be a rush of jobs that we're called out to attend to.'

'In the winter, I suppose?'

'Aye, or if there's an outbreak of summat or another. Believe me, I sometimes feel it's wrong to be making money out of folks' tragedies, but it's got to be done.'

'You're a sensitive sort o' lad, aren't you?' She smiled at him, not at all teasingly now. 'I like fellers that show a caring side, but I ain't met many of 'em. I reckon you're different, William Moon.'

'Thank you,' he replied, a little nonplussed. He had always tried to be thoughtful towards others and to respect womenfolk especially, as his father had instilled in him that he should. Some of the lads he knew boasted about their conquests with girls – the girls who hung around the bars in the less salubrious areas of the town – although he was never quite sure how much to believe. There were a few such young women there tonight in the Three Mariners'. He had seen Bella wave to one of them and guessed it was another of the herring girls. He knew they were considered by some to be not quite respectable. But Bella was there at his invitation. She had not tried to entice him and he was sure that, given a chance, she would turn out to be a decent sort of girl.

So he told himself all through that summer. He walked her home that first evening, kissing her discreetly on the cheek as he said goodnight to her at the end of her street. She would not let him take her any further, assuring him it was only a stone's throw from where she was lodging.

He asked her to accompany him to a brass band concert at the Spa on the following Sunday afternoon. They both enjoyed the rousing music, singing along or lah-lahing to the marches and the inevitable selection of Gilbert and Sullivan tunes. William was glad they shared this interest and he was sure they would find other things they agreed upon as time went on.

He knew, deep down, that Sunday afternoon, that had she been a different sort of girl – one from the chapel maybe – he would have invited her home to have tea with him and his parents. His mother always put on quite a spread for Sunday tea, with boiled ham and salad and thinly cut bread and butter, followed by tinned peaches and cream. But he did not do so. Neither did he invite her to his home at any time throughout the whole of that summer, and Bella did not seem to expect that he would.

'Shall I see you tonight?' he asked tentatively that first Sunday, after the concert had ended. 'My parents...er...they've got visitors for tea today...' He felt awful lying to her. '...So I'll have to go home and pay my respects. But I could see you later...?'

'No, not tonight; I'm busy,' she replied, a little abruptly. He wondered if she was aware that he was not being entirely straightforward with her. She seemed to relent, though, almost immediately, smiling at him ruefully – as though she understood he was fibbing? – and saying, 'Hows about tomorrow night then, or Tuesday? I could manage to see you then.'

They met on the Tuesday evening, taking a stroll around the North Bay area of the town, a quieter, more select part which Bella had not visited before. They returned to the harbour area for a drink and this time, with Bella's encouragement, William was tempted to kiss her on the lips, and much more ardently.

He became a different person during the three months he spent with her, giving little heed to what the future might hold for both of them. It was inevitable that their increasingly passionate kisses and embraces should ultimately lead them to the room in the fisherman's cottage, and to the double bed that Bella shared with another young woman. Her friend was out for the evening, she said, and would not be back until much later, and William had little doubt that Bella had planned it that way. His eyes took in briefly the shabbiness of the room where she and her colleague slept, lived, ate and did what little cooking they required; but, fortunately, he did not find the place dirty or too repellent. Besides, he had eyes only for Bella as she lay, eventually, naked in his arms.

It was the first time for him, but he was not surprised to discover that Bella was far from inexperienced; nor sorry either as she led him along every step of the way. 'Aye, I guessed you might be wet behind the ears, bonny lad,' she told him teasingly. 'But you weren't half bad for a beginner. An' it'll be better next time...'

And so it had proved to be, although William told himself it was not just 'that' that was important in their relationship. He enjoyed her company and the things they did together;

visits to the theatre, brass band concerts and minstrel shows and long walks along the beach, or along the promenade when the tide was in. His parents did not question his whereabouts, but then they had never done so, trusting him to abide by their standards.

One night, however, when they were enjoying a drink in a bar on Castle Road, William caught sight of his father. He had tried to avoid the pubs that he thought Isaac frequented, but obviously he was not fully conversant with all his father's haunts. He gave a start, spilling some of his ale on to the table and causing Bella to ask him, 'What's up?'

'My father,' he replied truthfully. 'He's over there. I didn't realise he came here.'

'So what? What does it matter?' she asked. 'You're a big boy now, Will. You don't have to ask your father's permission to go in a pub, do you?'

'No, of course not,' he replied. 'It's just that…well…we're supposed to be strict Methodists and…' But that, he knew, did not explain the fact that his father was there as well, partaking of strong liquor. He did not need to explain further, however, because at that moment his father noticed them and, after a startled glance, raised his hand in greeting.

'Aren't you going to introduce me?' said Bella, already jumping from her stool and making her way across the saloon.

To give her her due she behaved impeccably as William introduced her as a friend he had met earlier that summer. She had been dressed fairly decorously that evening in a blouse with a higher neckline that the ones she usually favoured. But its bright scarlet colour and the matching ribbon on her hat were eye-catching enough; and Isaac was not fooled into thinking she was a girl from the chapel or the sister of one of his friends.

All he said to William the next morning was, 'Watch your step, lad. That young woman's not our sort. Happen she's a pleasant enough lass to take around a bit, but...just think on. Watch what you're doing. That's all as I'm saying.'

'She's just a friend, Father,' William replied, shrugging a little. 'I didn't introduce her to you and Mother because she won't be staying in Scarborough very long. She's only here for the season.'

'Aye; it's happen just as well...' remarked Isaac.

It was halfway through September that Bella told him she was pregnant with his child.

Chapter Seven

William felt himself blanch visibly and he put down his tankard of beer with trembling hands. 'But...you can't be!' he gasped. 'I've been so careful...' At least as careful as he knew how.

'Not careful enough, bonny lad...'

'How can you be sure though? And how do you know it's mine?'

Bella was indignant then. 'What sort of a girl do you take me for? Of course it's yours. Who else's would it be? Aye, I know I'd been around a bit afore I met you; I told you so, didn't I? But since I've been seeing you there's been nobody else, nobody at all.'

'But how can you be so sure...so soon? I mean...' He counted on his fingers. 'It's only just over three months since we met. Perhaps you're just... I mean, perhaps you'll find out soon that you're not expecting a baby.' Despite the intimacy that they had shared William knew it would not be proper to make any reference to a woman's monthly cycle.

'You mean I might come on?' Bella said, without any such reticence. 'Not a hope I'm afraid. I'm as regular as clockwork. Anyways, I know; I just know I'm pregnant.' She grinned. 'I've got a bun in the oven, as some of my mates might say.'

'They don't know, do they?' he asked.

'No, why should they? It's got nowt to do wi' them, only you and me. So...what are you going to do about it, eh lad?'

He stared at her in astonishment. He felt ashamed, looking back on it afterwards, at how little effort he had made to support her, how quick he had been to shift the responsibility on to her. 'What do you mean?' he said. 'What am I going to do about it? Surely it's up to you, isn't it, to do...something?' He had heard of such situations. Unwanted babies could be got rid of. Bella would know girls, he was sure, who had been in a similar predicament. There was sometimes a risk involved, but she was a big strong lass...

His thoughts had barely formed before she yelled at him, her black eyes flashing with anger and a deep red colour suffusing her already sunburnt cheeks. They had, until then, been speaking quietly, but now her voice could have been heard at the other end of the room, were it not for the sudden outburst of laughter breaking forth simultaneously from a crowd of fishermen at a nearby table. 'You're telling me I should get rid of my bairn – your bairn – are you, Will Moon? How could you even suggest I might do such a thing?'

'I'm sorry...' he mumbled, reaching out and putting his hand on her arm. 'I didn't mean it to sound like that...' He scarcely knew himself what he had meant. He had said the first thing that had come into his head.

'Well, what did you mean then?' she retorted, speaking rather more quietly now but spitting the words out with a venom that disturbed him.

He rose to his feet. 'Come along, Bella; let's get out of here.'

She quickly drained her second shandy of the evening and William left the dregs of his ale in the tankard and made towards the door. She followed him out into the gathering dusk of the September night. They crossed the road and leant on the railings gazing out across the dark sea.

'I'm sorry,' he said again. 'But you've taken the wind out of my sails...'

'Aye, I can see that, lad,' she replied.

'I didn't really mean... Of course you mustn't get rid of...the baby. But...what are you going to do?'

'What am I going to do?' she repeated, using the selfsame words that he had uttered a few minutes earlier. 'You mean what are *we* going to do, don't you, Will? The way I see it there's a simple solution. It's your child...and you're a single chap, aren't you?'

'You mean...' He stared at her, aghast. 'You don't mean...you can't mean that we should get married, do you?'

'Why not? You've got me into this pickle. It takes two, y'know, an' I can't recall you ever being unwilling.'

'But we can't... I mean, it's out of the question. I'm only eighteen.'

'Lots of lads are married at eighteen, and lasses an' all. And you're not short of a bob or two neither, are you?'

'No, I suppose not. But it's such a big step and...'

William, to his consternation, found he was near to tears now. He was disgusted at himself for his reaction, but it was something, in his naivety, that he had never envisaged happening. What a stupid bloody fool he had been! He couldn't marry Bella. He was fond of her, he supposed, and they had had some good times together. And he had taken willingly of all that she had to offer... He knew that, and it didn't make him any easier in his conscience remembering how, in the beginning, she had led the way in their lovemaking. But he had been a keen follower... She had made a man of him; that was what he had thought, but now he felt like a callow inexperienced lad again. His father was right, though;

she was not their sort of girl, not the sort you married; just the kind of girl you might amuse yourself with for a while. Feeling heart sore and remorseful beyond words he turned to look straight at her. 'Bella, I'm sorry, but—' he began.

'But you can't – won't – marry me,' she interrupted. Her eyes were burning with what looked like dislike, hatred almost, and an undisguised contempt which he had no doubt he deserved. 'Huh.' She gave a bitter laugh. 'So much for your fine words, eh, Will Moon? You'll find I'm a man of my word... Remember saying that, eh? Never let it be said that I should let a lady down,' she mocked him. 'All right then, I know where I stand now, don't I? An' I suppose it's only what I might've expected. Yer father didn't reckon much to me neither, did he?' He opened his mouth to answer but no words would come.

'Oh, don't bother to try and explain yerself. Get back to yer dead bodies. I might just as well be one of 'em for all you care.'

'Bella, that's not true...' he protested.

'I've got me answer, an' as far as I'm concerned that's that. So why don't you just bugger off now to where you belong?' It was the first time he had heard her use such language and he was rather shocked. She had moderated her colourful speech when she was in his company, but he knew she had just cause to be angry now.

'Go on, clear off! Don't worry – you won't be seeing me again, not yet awhile, p'r'aps not ever. But I shan't forget what you've done, William Moon.' She gave him one more baleful glance before turning away and heading off back in the direction of the harbour.

'Bella...' He took a step towards her, but she held up her hand.

'No, Will. I've said all as I'm saying and that's an end to it. Don't come after me. Goodbye, Will Moon.'

He stood and stared as she walked briskly away from him. He saw her turn up an alleyway near to where she was lodging. He was not to see her again for more than five years. He did not go down to the harbour the following day to see if she was there. After all, what could he say to her? He had tossed and turned all through the night but he knew that nothing could make him change his mind. Two days later, though, feeling reluctant and fearful but unable to help himself, his steps took him towards the harbour. He stood a little way away, watching the familiar scene of the herring girls at their work. Bella was not amongst them. He despised himself more than ever for the sigh of relief that escaped him. Stepping forward he asked the girl called Mona if she knew where Bella was.

'Oh, it's you, is it?' she said, looking him up and down in a provocative manner. 'No, I don't know where she is. She's skedaddled. She took off yesterday morning wi'out so much as a cheerio or anything. She might've gone up to Scotland or down to Grimsby. Who knows? Sorry an' all that, but I can't help yer.' She grinned at him. 'Not unless you're wanting a bit o' company, like?'

'No...thank you,' he muttered. He turned away finding himself trembling a little.

He still had not recovered from the shock that Bella's news had given him and for a few days afterwards he found himself looking over his shoulder, half expecting that she might suddenly reappear. His work, as always, was an antidote to his preoccupation. Not that it was work that was likely to cheer him up, at least not some aspects of it, but there was great fulfilment to be found in working with timber, in the satisfying sweep of the plane in his hand and the satiny smooth feel of the elm or oak beneath his fingers.

'Is there summat wrong, lad?' his father asked him, after he had been more than usually quiet for a few days. It was inevitable that Isaac would enquire. He was always quick to notice when one of his family was worried about something. 'You've not been yerself just lately.'

'Oh, it's nowt much, Father,' he replied. 'Happen it's because the summer's coming to an end…' Then he decided he would be honest; well, as honest as he could be under the circumstances. 'Actually… I'm feeling a bit lonely. You remember that lass you saw me with? Well, she's gone back home now. And I liked her quite a lot, I must admit.'

His father gave him a searching look but one, William felt, that held a touch of sympathy as well. 'Aye well, maybe you did, but you'll get over it, son. She weren't our sort…' He shook his head. 'But there's nowt wrong wi' sowing a few wild oats afore you settle down.' Isaac sniffed, then gave a chuckle. 'Not that I ever had much chance to do that, not wi' my old man around. Just think on how lucky you are, my lad.'

'Oh, I do, Father,' replied William, beginning to feel a little better already.

His culpability, the wrong that he felt, deep down, that he had done to Bella, was to remain with him for a while. But gradually the memories of her began to recede to the back of his mind, and he started to pick up the threads of his former friendships and social life again. By the time he married Clara in the summer of 1885 he was looking back on the brief time he had spent with Bella – if he ever thought of it at all – as a hazy recollection of something that had happened, long ago, to a young and immature lad. He had become a far different person in the intervening years. He knew exactly what he wanted from life; a satisfying job – he already had that – and a blissful marriage to his beloved Clara. His main desire was to make her happy; to be a faithful and loving husband to her and never, never to let her down. He still could not believe his great fortune in having found such a lovely young woman who was all in all to him.

They were both thrilled when they discovered that Clara was expecting a child. The baby was due in the July of 1886, almost exactly a year after their marriage. William was on top of the world. Not only was he married to the most wonderful woman in the world, she was soon to give birth to his child. He was hoping for a boy, although he had not admitted it to Clara. But all men wanted a son, didn't they?

His head was full of plans and dreams for the future as he walked down Eastborough one afternoon in early May. He had just passed the Market Hall when his wandering thoughts were brought to a halt by the sound of a – once – familiar voice.

'Hello there...William Moon. What a surprise, eh?'

He blinked, staring around him in bewilderment, then he stopped dead in his tracks at the sight of the young woman on the other side of the road. She was already crossing over towards him, hurrying her footsteps a little in front of an approaching hansom cab. It was Bella, Bella...Randall; he had almost forgotten her surname. He had, in fact, tried, and almost succeeded, in forgetting her existence. After all it had been five – no, nearly six, he reckoned up quickly – six years since she had disappeared so abruptly.

'Bella...' he gasped. 'Yes; it is a surprise. I didn't know...

How long...?' He had no idea what sort of expression was showing on his face. Surprise, shock...horror? He hoped not. The least she deserved was for him to acknowledge her and to show some sort of pleasure at seeing her. But she was taking her time in answering his incomplete question. He tried to move his lips in a smile although his face felt frozen.

'You look...well,' he said, because it was no less than the truth. She did look well. A little slimmer than she had used to be, he thought, and there was something else different about her too. She was smarter, much more well groomed than the rather blowsy young woman he remembered. She was wearing a trim-fitting jacket and skirt in a shade of mid-green, with a high-necked white blouse and a neat little straw hat.

'Very well indeed,' he went on. 'So...what brings you here then?' He was fearful as to what sort of tirade she might let fly at him. The old Bella would not have hesitated to do so, but she was looking at him quizzically, half smiling, and the glint in her eyes was a humorous, not a malevolent one.

'What brings me here?' she repeated. 'Oh, this and that. As a matter of fact, I'm working here.'

He felt a stab of fear, although he tried not to let it show on his face. Then she was not here just for a visit, as a holidaymaker, as her attire might have suggested. 'You mean...? You're not working...at the harbour, are you?'

'No, of course not.' She laughed. 'That's a thing of the past I'm glad to say.' There was something different about her speech too. She sounded...not exactly refined, but she had certainly lost much of the broadness of her native accent. And she had not called him 'bonny lad' once. 'No, I'm working over there.' She pointed along the street. 'At Boyce's store, but it's my half day. I'm after something better, but it'll do for now. I've only been here a couple of weeks, so it was any port in a storm, you might say. As a matter of fact, Will, I was going to look you up. I've been asking around and I know you're still on North Marine Road, still in the same line of business.'

His heart gave a jolt then. What else had she heard, he wondered? Did she know he was now married and very happily so? If not, he must make sure that she did know and without delay. What a mercy he had met her before she had come to look him up. 'Yes, we're still there,' he replied. 'But... I'm married now,' he added hurriedly. 'My wife's called Clara. We got married last year.'

'Oh...oh, I see.' Bella looked at him steadily, her glance more serious and more calculating now, he thought. 'Well, that puts a different complexion on things, doesn't it? Well, it does and it doesn't...' she deliberated. 'Actually, there's something I want you to do for me, Will.'

He stared at her stolidly, not answering. Then, 'What?' he managed to ask, at last.

'I'm after a different job. A more...select sort of job, you might say, and one that pays a bit more. There's a job going at the top of Westborough where all the posh shops are. It's at a high-class ladies' gown shop. I've been there now to enquire about it, and I think Madame – Madame Grenville, she calls herself – I think she was impressed with me; I can put on the style when I want to, you know. But she wants a reference, somebody to say I'm trustworthy and honest an' all that.' She raised her eyebrows. 'I think you could do that for me, couldn't you, Will? Write and say that I've been a friend of the family for – how many years is it? – six years by my reckoning.'

He fingered around his collar which was beginning to feel rather tight, and he could feel beads of sweat breaking out on his forehead. 'Look, Bella... I'll have to think about it,' he said, although he knew he owed her something for their shared past; and she still had not made any reference to what had gone on between them, or about the baby.

'I shouldn't hesitate too long if I were you, lad,' she said, with just a shade of menace and a slight reversal to the rougher tones she had once used. 'You don't want to lose your good reputation in this town, do you? And that nice little wife of yours... I really wouldn't enjoy spoiling things for you, Will.'

'All right then,' he said at once, glancing around anxiously. Somebody he knew might have seen him already, talking to a strange woman in what was the busiest part of the town. 'I'll meet you...tonight if you like. I can't talk to you anymore now but I'll meet you later. I promise I'll be there... Where are you staying, by the way?'

'I've a couple of rooms on Queen Street. Quite clean and comfortable; they'll do for now. Will...' She was looking at him less threateningly now. 'I don't want to cause trouble for you, but I do need a leg-up, a chance to get meself started again.'

He sighed. 'Very well; I'll see what I can do. I'll put in a good word for you, if you're sure that's all it needs.'

They arranged to meet later that same evening at a secluded part of the lower promenade, just south of the Spa buildings. William felt he was unlikely to see anyone he knew in that area. He hated deceiving his beloved Clara – he told her he was meeting some of his pals for a drink, something he did from time to time – but he could not see that there was any point in telling her, now, of his past indiscretions. Neither should there be any need to tell her anything in the future, if Bella could be persuaded to keep her silence in exchange for his promise to help her.

They leant on the sea wall, looking out across the North Sea, as they had done many times before but in a different spot, listening to the crash of the waves as the incoming tide pounded against the rocks below them.

'I've written this for you,' said William, handing her an envelope. 'I've not sealed it, so you are at liberty to read it. I've said that you are an honest and God-fearing woman and that my family has been acquainted with yours for several years. I do, in fact, know Mrs Green – Madame Grenville, as she calls herself. We buried her father a couple of years ago. But may I ask you, please, not to contact me again, Bella? I am sorry about what happened between us…but it seems as though you have not done too badly for yourself since then.'

'I've done all right,' she replied briefly. 'I'm ready for a change, though, an' I've got a soft spot for Scarborough, in spite of everything.' William knew he must find out something of what had happened to her in the meantime, particularly about the child she had been expecting, but he was unsure how to broach the subject.

She looked directly into his eyes, and as though she could read his thoughts she said, without preamble, 'I had the baby adopted. It was a girl. I called her Henrietta, after my mother.'

'Oh…oh, I see. That must have been a wrench for you, giving her up.' He looked at her, feeling sorrow – as well as a good deal of relief – but she was staring out to sea, unaware of his sympathetic glance.

'It was for the best.' She gave a shrug. 'I had no choice at the time, the way things were. It was a case of needs must.'

'And do you know where...? I mean, are you in touch with...?'

'With the child? I'm not supposed to be. She's five years old now, five last month... I try not to think about it.'

'I'm sorry,' said William, feeling a tug at his heartstrings. He was, after all, partly to blame for this whole sorry situation. 'But you are still a young woman, and a very attractive one...'

'An' you think that makes up for losing my first-born, do you? Aye, maybe I'll get wed one o' these fine days, but that can't alter the past, can it?'

He shook his head. 'I'm sorry,' he said again, although he knew it was a futile thing to say.

'Then don't be, lad.' Bella gave a wry half-smile. 'I was hard on you at the time, I know that, and I was just as much to blame as you were. You were only a bit of a lad, weren't you, hardly into long trousers? An' I should have known that if I played wi' fire I'd get burnt. Anyroad, I made out...without your help. I soon found out who my friends were.'

'You weren't on your own then? Did you go back to your father and your family?'

'Not on your life! But I've told you, I managed. And you're asking too many questions. I've said as much as I'm saying.' They looked at one another in silence for several seconds. Then, 'Thanks for this, Will,' she said, putting the envelope into her handbag. 'That wipes the slate clean, doesn't it? I promise I won't be bothering you again...not unless I have to,' she added, giving an eloquent nod. 'Now, you'd best trot off back home, hadn't you? Back to that little wife of yours. Just leave me here. It wouldn't do for us to be seen together. I'll stay and look at the waves for a while; it's very soothing, watching the sea... Cheerio, Will. I'm glad we've met up again.'

'Goodbye, Bella,' he replied, raising his hand in farewell as he walked away from her.

He did not say, as she had done, that he was glad they had met. He would be glad – more than that, he would be thankful from the bottom of his heart, and full of praise for the God he hoped was looking after him – if he knew that this unfortunate little episode in his life was now at an end. He would be a good deal happier, certainly, if Bella were not in Scarborough. It was not a large town – not compared with York or Leeds, for instance – and it was not unlikely that his and Bella's paths would cross from time to time, quite unintentionally. Her words about not bothering him again, 'unless I have to', had given him a moment's disquiet. He thought about them as he made his way back, walking briskly over the Spa Bridge then up past the Grand Hotel and through the town to his home; home to his adoring wife who would be waiting for him.

He would have to trust Bella to keep her word, and hope that she would keep to her part of the town as well. 'Madam Grenville', the exclusive gown shop owned by Maud Green was a good distance from their own premises. William had passed by it several times, but only half noticing the stylish garments on display in the windows. This part of the town was becoming the fashionable area in which to shop. Several of the small shops – jewellers, hosiers and milliners, as well as cabinetmakers, upholsterers and furniture salesmen – had expanded to larger sites in Westborough, as the centre of trade moved further west towards the railway station. William Rowntree's great department store and house furnishers dominated the scene, its plate-glass windows glowing with hundreds of the new electric incandescent lamps.

As far as William knew, his wife still bought her clothing from the small shop on Eastborough at the other end of the town; the dressmaker's shop owned by Louisa Montague where Clara had worked until her marriage. No doubt she wandered up to the other end of the long High Street now and again, as all ladies did. He recalled how he and Clara had window-shopped there from time to time, admiring the deep-piled carpets, the rich damask and velvet curtain materials, mahogany tables, cabriole-legged chairs and button-backed Chesterfield sofas. And then they had gone back home, more than contented with the comfortable, if a little shabby, premises that they shared with his parents.

Clara greeted him with a warm kiss, after rising rather laboriously from her chair at the fireside. Seven months into her pregnancy, she was much less active than she would wish to be, but she insisted on going into the kitchen and making tea for them all: his mother and father as well as the two of them. How lucky he was, he thought again, seeing the contentment on the faces of all his dear family, and the deep affection in the eyes of his lovely wife. He felt more determined than ever that nothing was going to spoil this perfect marriage.

Chapter Eight

Bella was disappointed that William Moon had married, but wasn't it only what she might have expected? she asked herself. A personable young man such as he would be sure to be snapped up by the first girl to take his fancy; the first suitable girl, of course. The way he had rejected her so abruptly on discovering she was pregnant had rankled with her for a long time. She had been growing very fond of him; she had even thought she might be falling in love with him. Then, to be dropped like a hot potato at hearing what, if he had any sense at all he might have realised could be a possible result of their intimacy…well, it had shaken her faith in him. She had believed he was different from the fellows she had known before.

Had she really imagined, though, that he would marry her? And had she, in fact, led him on in the hope that she would fall for a child and thus force the issue? Bella herself was not sure of the answer to that. All she had known at the time was that she was enjoying his company and the developing ardour between the two of them, and what had seemed like his admiration, touching almost on adoration at times. Her hurt had been so great that she had known she could not stay in the same town as him. She had known she could cause trouble for him if she wished to do so, but despite her anger her better nature had prevailed. He was only a lad, whereas she, Bella, although only the same age as him in years, was far older in experience and understanding of the ways of the world.

Now, though, he had become a man; she had noticed the difference in him straight away. And the glimmer of hope that had always remained with her was kindled anew as she spoke with him on Eastborough. Maybe, now that she too was changed, now she had taught herself to dress more respectably and to speak and behave in a more dignified manner, maybe he might be persuaded to resume his friendship with her.

But her hopes had been dashed almost at once by the news that he was married. She had been determined, though, not to let him see that she was fazed by this. She had pressed on with her request that he would help her to procure the job she was seeking – that had been her intention anyway – but she had been unable to resist throwing out a faintly malicious hint that she might need his help again...sometime.

What sort of a girl had he married? she wondered. A sweet and biddable miss who would do as she was told? Not that she could imagine William would be a domineering sort of husband, the archetype of the Victorian male, ruling the roost in the home and having his wife and children obey him in all things. Maybe, she pondered, when all was said and done Will Moon would not have been her, Bella's, type of man at all... It could be that she needed someone more forceful who would give her a run for her money, someone she could stand up to and give as good as she got. At all events there was no point in hankering over what she couldn't have; but she would keep her eyes and ears open and try to find out what she could about William's wife; Clara, he had called her. Clara Moon... She must be careful, though, not to appear too inquisitive.

As she had hoped, Madame Grenville agreed that she would take her on for a trial period as sales assistant, then, if she proved suitable she would be given the position on a permanent basis. Bella was determined that she would make good. The reference from William Moon had impressed Madame. She clearly regarded the Moon family as being of some importance in the town, but Bella was relieved that she didn't enquire too closely into how well or how long she had known them. She had worked as a sales assistant, though never in quite such a prestigious salon, during the years she had spent in Northumberland after her hasty retreat from Scarborough. But Madame Grenville seemed satisfied with the one reference regarding Bella's character and reliability and did not ask for further credentials from previous employers. Bella was glad about that too. She had returned to the town to make a fresh start; and although things had not turned out entirely as she might have wished, she was determined to put the last six years behind her and to begin again.

She soon discovered that her employer had more of the 'Maud Green' about her than the 'Madame Grenville'. Obviously she was not short of 'a bit of brass', as Yorkshire folk termed it, but her pretensions regarding her position in society were only skin deep. She was, in fact, quite ordinary and came from a humble background. Her father had been a fisherman and the family had lived in one of the little cottages near to where Bella had lodged during her time as a herring girl. Her airs and graces and pseudo-refined accent had been acquired and improved upon since she took a step up in the world, as Bella, being of the same ilk, was quick to realise; it took one to know one. As the women came to know one another more closely they realised they were two of a kind. They both had their eye, ultimately, on the main chance.

Maud had married a local businessman, Archibald Green,

who owned a string of small shops and stalls in the resort, catering for the holidaymakers. They sold buckets and spades, fishing nets, sun hats, paddling shoes, sweets, bottled 'pop', picture postcards, cheap toys and a selection of gifts – ashtrays, vases, cups and saucers and ornamental plates, often emblazoned with the Scarborough crest – suitable to take back as a memento or as a present for those left at home. It was mainly seasonal trade, but Archie Green had made enough over the years to set his wife up in a nice little business and buy a house on Esplanade Road, just off the promenade in the South Bay area. It was far too large for the two of them, without children and now in their early forties. Maud did not seem to be worried about her childless state. Her thriving business had become her main interest in life and hob-nobbing with the elite, although only in a position of servitude, was all she had ever wanted.

Bella grew to like her although she could not help but be envious of the other woman's wealthy husband and her splendid home. She hoped that some day Fate would deal her, Bella, such a hand. It was surely no more than she deserved. She suffered pangs of regret and remorse now and again – what mother would not do so? – about the baby girl she had given up for adoption. But it had seemed to be the best solution at the time, and the child had gone to a loving couple who would do their very best for her. How could she make her way in the world and achieve what she desired with a child – an illegitimate child – on her hands? She still had not attained her desire, but she would, one of these days. It was only a matter of time...

'Oh look, isn't that William Moon's wife?' said Maud one afternoon in early December. The two of them, Maud and

Bella, had just finished re-dressing the window ready for the Christmas season.

There were two models in the window, which was quite a small one. One model was wearing an afternoon dress of deep red silk in the fashionable close-fitting princess line. The bodice, boned to create the hour-glass shape that women desired, was covered in black lace, a band of which also surrounded the bustled skirt, near to the hemline. The other model was dressed in an outdoor coat in a shade of dark olive green, trimmed around the neck and down the front with Russian fur. Both garments, and many more that hung on the racks inside the shop, would be suitable for the forthcoming Christmas season. They had already sold a satisfying number of gowns and mantles.

Bella gave a start at her employer's words. She did not know Clara Moon, not even by sight, but it would not do to let Maud know that. 'See, over there, looking in the book shop window.'

Bella looked through the glass panel of the door, making sure to keep out of sight. Across the road a smallish woman was studying the selection of books which Charles Bamforth had arranged in the window of the shop he had recently opened. She was neatly, but fashionably, dressed in a brown coat with a small bustle at the back and a small close-fitting hat trimmed with fur. Hair of a reddish-golden colour curled around her ears and over her forehead. A pretty woman, mused Bella.

'Yes, I do believe it is,' she said. 'I don't really know her very well, though. I've only met her a couple of times. It was William Moon's parents, really, who knew my parents. They had business dealings with them, you see. We had some relations in Scarborough and they – the Moons – dealt with the funerals,' she went on, improvising rapidly. 'But they're both dead now, of course – my parents, I mean.' She had never had need to explain, before, what her connection was with the Moon family, and she hoped that the hastily concocted story would satisfy Maud. But her employer did not appear to be listening too closely. She nodded.

'Yes, it is Clara; not that I know her all that well either, to be honest. She doesn't shop here, of course. I wouldn't expect her to.'

'Oh, why not?' asked Bella, relieved all the same that the said woman did not patronise the salon. That could prove difficult.

'She's quite a skilled dressmaker herself,' Maud replied, 'although I don't suppose she has time now, since she's been involved with the undertaking business. I believe she's helping out there with young Will just as though she was born to it. Summat I couldn't do, I can tell yer.' She gave a shudder. Madame Grenville's cultured tones slipped a little at times when there were no customers around. 'And then, of course, she's got the bairn. A little boy, they had, a few months back. But you knew about that, didn't you?'

'Yes, I read it in the newspaper,' said Bella, who had, indeed, done so, not without a pang of regret and envy. 'And you mentioned it, too, didn't you?'

'Oh yes, happen I did. Patrick, they called him. I wonder who's looking after him today. I 'spect it'll be his gran. Grandmas are useful like that and I dare say Clara needs a break. They'll be getting busy soon, I reckon. Folks start popping off after Christmas with bronchitis and influenza. She'll find it a big change from working in a shop. Like I was saying, Clara was a dressmaker. She worked for Louisa Montague at t' other end of Eastborough. But she left when she got wed... Anyroad, we'd best get on. Standing here nattering all day isn't going to keep the wheels turning.'

There was a jingle from the bell as the door opened and a middle-aged woman entered. Maud stepped forward with a beaming smile. 'Good afternoon, madam. How can we help you?' she asked in a cut-glass accent.

Maud and Archie Green invited her to spend Christmas with them at their home on Esplanade Road and Bella was pleased to accept. Archie was a benevolent host. He was a corpulent red-faced man in his early fifties, well known for his cheerfulness and conviviality. He plied her with more food, wine and spirits than she had been accustomed to of late. For Bella was now quite a different person from the one she had been during her days as a herring girl. She had tried to better herself in several ways.

Gone were the days when she would enter such places as the Three Mariners' on her own. She doubted that Will Moon went there either, now that he had a wife and family. Well, the beginnings of a family; she did not doubt that there would be more children as time went on. Bella had joined a lending library since returning to Scarborough and she occasionally attended lectures on such subjects as the history of the resort, or the works of Charles Dickens, with readings from some of the novels. She had not made any real friends, apart from Maud – who was becoming as much of a friend as an employer – although she and another woman she had met at the library occasionally went to concerts at the Spa, and once to the music hall which was held at St George's Hall in Aberdeen Walk. She feared, however, that this type of more raucous entertainment was not entirely to the liking of her new acquaintance; Florence Bland was a 'maiden lady', some years older than Bella.

She was happy to relax in Maud and Archie's comfortable home. As she had realised almost at once, Maud was a very down-to-earth woman when away from her 'Madame Grenville' persona, and she and Archie, who was several years her senior, were ideally suited to one another. Although Archie was known in the town as a 'hale fellow well met' sort of man, he and Maud appeared to seek little company apart from that of one another when they had finished their daily work. Their evenings were usually spent alone in the home they had created with their combined – quite considerable – wealth.

The parlour was furnished and carpeted with the best that money could buy. How the home was furnished was an indication of one's social standing, and Maud, clearly, was determined not to be found lacking. The room was filled to overflowing, as was the custom, with plush armchairs, occasional tables and glass-fronted cabinets, and on every surface there was a plethora of Staffordshire figures, vases, potted plants, candlesticks, lamps, and a huge floral arrangement beneath a glass dome stood on a whatnot in the corner.

Bella was flattered that they had invited her to share their cosy intimacy. She gathered that, contrary to what she might have thought, they did not do a great deal of entertaining. She spent a pleasant two days in their company, eating, drinking, chatting and playing card games. They even invited her to stay overnight on Christmas Day in one of the sumptuously furnished – though seldom used – spare bedrooms.

When she returned home in the evening of Boxing Day she felt somewhat deflated and more than a little depressed, a state of mind which she always tried to shake off whenever she felt the black cloud descending. The worst of the winter was yet to come. She could not afford the coal for the blazing fires which burnt almost continually in the Green residence – in the bedrooms, too – and her two-roomed living place seemed even more paltry now by comparison.

She had only her own company to look forward to in the evenings, that of Florence having already started to pall. The shop was due to open the following day, but trade was sure to be slow after the Christmas rush. There might be a few women choosing gowns for the New Year festivities, but on the whole Bella could foresee nothing but a succession of long tedious days ahead.

Her rooms had grown chilly during her absence, but it was not worth lighting a fire until the next day. She took off her outdoor things, staring around gloomily and sighing. Then she went over to the sideboard and took out the whisky bottle – now almost empty – that she kept there. She poured an inch of the golden liquid into a tumbler, boiled up the water in the kettle on her not-too-clean gas stove and added the same amount of water. A hot toddy would warm her up and liven her spirits as well.

'Cheers, Bella,' she said, raising her glass to her reflection in the fireplace mirror. A woman who was still young stared back at her; a woman who, at twenty-five, still had the copious black hair, though now worn more decorously in a chignon, and the flashing black eyes that she had had at eighteen. Her face had settled now into lines of maturity; she had lost the girlish chubbiness of her cheeks and much of the healthy redness that had betrayed that she was an outdoor worker, a herring girl…

She smiled, revealing her still-perfect teeth, and her reflection smiled back. She was not displeased with what she saw. And one of these days, she was convinced, there would be someone who would notice her as she deserved to be noticed, admire her, desire her... There must be someone, she told herself, as she had done many times before, as she tried desperately to rid herself of thoughts of William Moon; those niggling intrusive thoughts that still plagued her from time to time, bringing feelings of discontent and jealousy in their wake. She must, must try to forget him.

'Here's to the future, Bella!' she said, raising her glass again. What the hell? she thought as she drained the whisky bottle into her glass and, this time, drank it neat. She went straight to her bed, shivering as her body touched the icy sheets. But the liquor warmed her inside and, gradually, outside as well. Tomorrow would take care of itself, she thought as, after a few moments, she felt her eyelids closing. It was some six weeks later, in the mid-February of 1887, that Bella first met Ralph Cunningham...

Trade had been slack in the period between winter and spring. The inclement weather had kept many people indoors, and those who ventured out had other things on their minds rather than thinking of choosing new spring clothes. On this particular morning, however, there was a break in the clouds and, though it was still cold, there was a small patch of blue in the sky.

'Nearly enough blue there to make a sailor a pair o' trousers,' said Maud. 'That means it's going to be a fine day. At least that's what my old gran used to say.'

Bella nodded. 'Well, it's not before time. Happen we'll have a few more customers if the sun keeps on shining. Are we going to change the window display, or is it too soon?'

'No, it's not too soon to be thinking about spring, new Easter bonnets an' all that,' said Maud. 'We'll tackle it this afternoon, eh? How about that? Shades of green, I think, and happen a touch of yellow.'

'What about those new parasols you've just bought?' said Bella. 'And the bonnets and gloves and the Brussels lace collars? If we put a few at the bottom of the window – tastefully arranged, I mean, not too many of them – they should be eye-catching.'

'Yes, you're good at that sort o' thing, Bella. I'll leave that to you.'

Madame Grenville had recently been persuaded, by a zealous commercial traveller, to purchase a line of accessories to complement the gowns and mantles of well-dressed ladies. These had been unpacked but not yet displayed to the clientele. But by three o'clock that afternoon the small window was a symphony in shades of green and yellow.

The two models stood in front of a dark green velvet curtain, which was now surplus to requirements in Maud's newly furnished home. One wore an apple-green gown made of stiff silken taffeta, trimmed with golden binding, and the other a light woollen travelling costume of jade green with a fitted jacket and flared skirt. Gay parasols in green and yellow, some trimmed with lace, lay half opened on the floor of the window, with several pairs of gloves, stockings of the finest silk, and three straw hats, one trimmed with emerald green ribbon, another with a cluster of silken primroses, and the third with a positive cornucopia of dainty spring flowers around the brim.

'Well, if that doesn't bring in a few customers I don't know what will,' Maud declared, as both women stood on the pavement, viewing their handiwork from outside. 'It's making me feel quite spring-like already. Come on, lass, let's go and make a cup of tea before the rush starts.'

Maud gave a laugh at her own words. She knew only too well that there was not likely to be a sudden influx of clients. Yorkshire women liked to weigh up the pros and cons before parting with their money, especially if they were dependent upon their husband's generosity, and would sometimes peek into the window a few times before venturing inside the shop.

There were, however, a few of what you might call impulse buys that afternoon. One elderly lady purchased a pair of leather gloves, another a much daintier lace pair, and a pretty young girl, attracted by the pale green parasol in the window, came in with her mother who duly agreed to buy it for her. She went out highly pleased with herself, swinging it jauntily on her arm.

At a quarter past five they thought they had finished with customers for the day. Maud was starting to reckon up the day's takings and Bella was tidying the counter – the woman who had bought the lace gloves had viewed practically the whole stock before making a decision – when the door was opened quite forcefully. The bell gave a loud jingle as a man entered, quite clearly in a hurry. He took off his trilby hat as he spoke to them, revealing sleek dark hair beginning to grey slightly at the temples.

'Good afternoon, ladies,' he began. 'Please excuse me bursting in on you in such a rush. I feared you might be about to close.'

'Not for a few moments yet, sir,' said Maud with a welcoming smile. She glanced at her fob watch, pinned to the bodice of her black dress. 'In fact we won't be closing for a quarter of an hour or so, or longer if necessary. How may we help you?'

'The parasol in the window,' the man replied. 'The pale lemon one with the lace edging – may I see it, please? It will be my daughter's sixteenth birthday on Sunday...'

'And it would make a perfect gift for a young lady, if you don't mind me saying so,' said Maud, with just a touch of obsequiousness. 'Bella, would you take it out of the window for the gentleman, please?'

'Of course, Madame Grenville,' replied Bella, with the same hint of servility; it was an act they sometimes played out, depending on the customer.

'Yes...' said the man. 'That is the one I would like. I don't need to look any further. Would you mind opening it out for me, my dear? Or...you don't think it is bad luck, do you, to open an umbrella inside?'

Bella laughed. 'I'm not superstitious. And this is a parasol, not an umbrella, isn't it, if that makes any difference?' She opened it and twirled it around. 'Lovely, isn't it, sir? It's a new line; we've only had them delivered recently.'

'Yes, it is indeed...lovely,' replied the man, his eyes resting for a moment on Bella's face and figure rather than on the parasol. Or so she thought... 'I like the lace round the edge, it's very becoming.'

'That's broderie anglaise, sir,' she replied. 'It's very fashionable just now. You will take this one then? Shall I wrap it up for you?'

'Yes, if you would, please.' As he smiled at her Bella noticed that his eyes were grey, deep-set, with eyebrows that almost met in the centre. He sported a moustache, as dark as his hair. She took him, at a glance, to be in his mid-forties. At all events he had a daughter of sixteen, which meant that he was married, or a widower, maybe…

Stop it, Bella! she chided herself. She really must stop weighing up every man she met – every personable man, that was – with a view to…what? Friendship, courtship, marriage…? And she must stop imagining, too, that such men were the slightest bit interested in her.

Maud intervened at that moment. 'I will take care of the bill,' she said to Bella, 'whilst you are wrapping the parcel. Will you be paying for it now, sir? And may we deliver it for you, perhaps? It is rather an awkward shape to carry.' They did deliver items occasionally to important customers, the delivery 'girl' being Bella on 'Shanks's pony'.

'I'll settle up with you straight away,' he said, taking a leather coin case from an inside pocket, 'and I will take it with me, of course. I am going back to York very soon. There is a train in half an hour or so; that is another reason I was in rather a hurry.'

'Oh, you live in York, do you?' said Maud, showing more than a little curiosity. 'I thought we hadn't seen you around here before.'

'Ah, but you will be doing quite soon,' said the man, with a satisfied glint in his eye. 'As a matter of fact, we are going to be neighbours. Well, pretty close, at any rate. I had better introduce myself, hadn't I? I am Ralph Cunningham…and you, of course, must be Madame Grenville.' He held out his hand to Maud who took hold of it with an embarrassed little laugh.

'Oh…oh yes; I'm…Madame Grenville. And this is my assistant – my valued assistant – Bella.'

When the 'how-do-you-dos' had been uttered Ralph Cunningham, bowing a little over each hand, went on to tell them that he would, very shortly, be opening a shop in the vicinity.

'Just round the corner, on Huntriss Row,' he told them. 'A perfumery. I already have such a shop in York, on Low Petergate, and I thought it was time I branched out and came to Scarborough.'

Maud was agog with interest. 'Perfumes, is that what you'll sell? Like…Yardley and Rimmel…?'

He smiled and nodded. 'Yes, but not just perfumes. Beauty products of all kinds; soaps, powders, lotions… I hope we will be open and running in about two months' time.'

'So you will be living here?' enquired Maud.

He pursed his lips. 'Part of the time, maybe. I am not sure yet. My home is in York; I have a house there as well as the shop. But I am hoping, soon, to be able to leave my daughter in charge of the York shop; my daughter, Rosalind, for whom I have bought the parasol. So I shall divide my time between the two places, all being well. All I want now is a reliable assistant for Huntriss Row, possibly two…

'Well now, ladies, I mustn't take up any more of your valuable time. I have kept you long past closing time, haven't I? My apologies.' He smiled a little ruefully, but humorously, at Maud and then at Bella. A rather more lingering glance, or had she only imagined that? 'Good afternoon to you then, ladies.' He bowed as he placed his trilby hat on his head.

'Good afternoon, sir,' they chorused.

'Well, what d'you make o' that?' said Maud as the door closed behind him. 'He's a right bobby-dazzler and no mistake, isn't he?'

'He certainly is,' replied Bella, feeling quite weak at the knees.

Chapter Nine

William had made discreet enquiries from one and another of his business associates in the town, and he learnt that Bella Randall had settled down nicely to her position as assistant to Madame Grenville, otherwise Maud Green. Her employer, it was said, was very pleased with her. William had strolled up to the shop once or twice; then, quite nonchalantly and taking good care not to be observed, he had peeked through the window and had seen for himself how Bella smiled pleasantly at the customers and appeared to be the ideal sales assistant. He guessed that the two women, Maud and Bella, would get along well together, especially if the pretences and the barriers were broken down.

He doubted that Bella would tell her employer the truth about her former relationship with him; in fact he hoped and prayed fervently that she would not do so no matter how friendly she and Maud became. But he was aware of Maud Green's aspirations to be a 'somebody' in the town, and he knew as well that Bella was seeking to take a step up the social ladder. Yes, Maud and Bella could well be an ideal partnership. The shop, however, was not one that was patronised by his wife, so he had no fear that Bella and Clara might meet.

He hoped, for Bella's sake as well as his own, that she would find happiness, in her job and in her personal life too, and that she would be able to look forward instead of back.

He had found deep contentment and fulfilment in his marriage to Clara. The birth of their first child, Patrick, in the June of 1886 had been a great joy to them and to his parents as well. They had all settled down comfortably together in the place that had long been the Moon family home. Will and Clara, although they hoped to have more children as time went on, saw no need to move to a place of their own. It was convenient to live at their workplace and it was what Isaac and Hannah wanted as well.

However when, in the spring of the following year the shop next door – a run-down second-hand clothes shop owned by an elderly couple – became vacant, Isaac and William decided it would be a good idea to purchase the property and extend their own premises. The business was thriving and they could do with more space in their living accommodation as well.

It was around the same time, towards the end of April, when William, walking along Newborough one afternoon on his way to visit a client, came face to face with Bella. She was arm in arm with a well-dressed man, tall and distinguished-looking, who wore an overcoat of fine woollen tweed and a trilby hat. Bella was smartly turned out too, he noticed, in the brief glimpse he caught of her, in a sky blue costume and a neat felt hat with a matching long blue feather; purchased from Madame Grenville, no doubt. He did not stop to speak, as Bella, after a brief smile, seemed anxious to walk on. William tipped his hat, murmuring 'Good afternoon', as he went on his way.

The man looked vaguely familiar, although William could not put a name to him and he was sure he had not met him through business or socially. Mid-forties, he surmised, well set up, reasonably handsome... It seemed that Bella might have done quite well for herself if the fact that they were arm in arm meant anything. He had not heard much about her recently and had not enquired, nor could he do so now without alerting suspicions as to why he should be interested in her.

The following day, however, as he walked along Huntriss Row, he caught sight of the same man entering the shop that was due to open the following week. William remembered then why his face had seemed familiar. There had been a photograph of him in the local evening paper a few days previously; and an article – William guessed it was more of an advertisement paid for by the man himself – stating that 'Cunninghams' would be open for business very shortly, stocking perfumes and beauty products of many kinds to suit women of taste and discernment. There would be items to suit all pockets, too, the article went on to say; but William, stopping now to look in the window, pondered that the ladies who shopped there would need to be quite well heeled.

He could see the man inside the shop lifting a cardboard box on to the mahogany counter, and there were other boxes of all sizes on the floor. There was a notice on the door which stated that the shop would be open for business on Monday, 2nd May; that was the following Monday. So that must be Ralph Cunningham, preparing for his grand opening.

The window was only partially dressed but William could see that the display, when completed, would be tasteful and eye-catching, but in a discreet way. A curtain of dark blue velvet hung in swathes at the back and covered the floor of the window in rippling folds. There were glass shelves on which were arranged just a few products but with room for many more. The few that were on show were of the highest quality.

There was a large bottle of the famous 4711 eau de cologne with its distinctive label of blue and gold, and a smaller bottle of fluted glass with a spray attachment holding the same perfume; fancy boxes of soaps – rose, heliotrope and violet – by Vinolia; honey and flower brilliantine for shining hair; and gaily decorated tins of tooth powder.

William walked away lest he should be thought to be taking too much interest, although he did not think the man had noticed him. He hoped he would do well with his innovative plan. There was no other such shop in the town, at least William did not know of one, although chemists' shops often sold perfumes and beauty products. A 'perfumery', he supposed would be the correct name for such a shop, like the ones that were found in London and the larger cities. The article had said that this Ralph Cunningham already had a similar shop in York, so it must he a thriving business for him to think of opening one in Scarborough.

He went further along the row to the gents' outfitters where he had two white Irish linen shirts on order, one for himself and one for his father for funeral wear. Maybe he would pay a visit to Cunningham's when they opened on Monday, he mused. It would be nice to buy Clara a little present. It wasn't her birthday, but he felt sure she would appreciate a bottle of perfume; she didn't often treat herself to such luxuries and his lovely wife deserved the best that money could buy. They had a funeral on Monday, he remembered, in the morning, but he should be able to manage a visit to the shop in the afternoon.

When he arrived there again on the said day the window display was complete; a colourful array of bottles and boxes, fancy cartons and jars, all pleasing to the eye, but in a refined and tasteful manner. An advertisement for Pear's soap in the bottom corner of the window stated that it had been recommended by Mrs Lillie Langtry for improving and preserving the complexion.

William smiled, his hand reaching out to press the latch on the door. Then he stopped, staring in surprise at the woman – the sales assistant – standing behind the counter. It was Bella. She was wrapping a small parcel in gold-coloured paper, at the same time talking and smiling with her customer. He did not think she had noticed him. He took a step back. Perhaps it might be not such a good idea after all to buy his wife a bottle of perfume. He would buy her a box of chocolates instead...

He wondered afterwards why he had not entered the shop. Why be afraid of encountering Bella again? It appeared, from what he had seen, that she was doing quite well for herself. She was an assistant in a shop of some quality and, although he could not be certain, it seemed as though she was on friendly terms – rather more than friendly, maybe? – with the owner of the establishment. William had decided, though, when they met up again the previous year, that the less dealings he had with Bella the better it would be. It might well be that their paths would cross again sometime. Possibly, at some future date, he might make a purchase at the shop; it would be a perfectly reasonable thing to do, to buy a gift for his wife's birthday in September.

In the meantime, though, he had to admit that he was curious about Bella and her change in circumstances. She had been working for Madame Grenville for less than a year. Had they parted amicably, he wondered? Or had Maud Green been annoyed that her assistant had left so hastily? He kept his ear to the ground and learnt from the gossip of his business associates that Maud, in fact, was not too pleased at all. Men, it seemed, were just as keen to hear and to pass on titbits of scandal, whether they were true or not, as were their wives.

She had been left in the lurch, Maud declared, and after all that she had done for that 'jumped-up madam' who was 'no better than she ought to be'. William had never understood that expression – to him it did not make any sense – but he knew it was meant to imply that the said person was a 'trollop', a woman of easy virtue. He was pretty sure that Maud Green had not learnt anything of Bella's past history, certainly not about that which concerned himself. What she was referring to in her scathing comments about the woman who had let her down was the fact that Ralph Cunningham was a married man. He had a wife and family back home in York; and yet there he was setting up this Bella Randall in a love nest above the shop, and visiting her there as bold as brass!

The attraction between Bella and Ralph had been instantaneous. She could not stop herself from thinking about him after their first encounter in the shop. But he was a married man – hadn't he just admitted to having a grown-up daughter? – so she determined to put all thoughts of him out of her mind at once. But that was easier said than done, especially as he came into the shop again a few days later. This time Bella was on her own, Maud having gone out on an errand.

'Good afternoon…Bella,' he greeted her. 'I am sorry to be so presumptuous, but I do not know your other name, and I heard Madame Grenville address you as Bella. It means beautiful, as I am sure you know; a very suitable name for a lovely lady.'

'Miss Randall,' she replied, without smiling. She was not going to be influenced by such smooth talk. 'My name is Arabella Randall. So, how may I help you...Mr Cunningham?'

He smiled at her. 'I have been thinking about the conversation we had the other day. I was telling you about the shop I will be opening round the corner, and you showed such an interest...' Bella recalled that it had been Maud who was agog with curiosity and asking all the questions. She, Bella, had been interested too, of course, but she had been busy wrapping up the parasol and had not said a word. 'So I was wondering,' he went on, 'if you would like to come round and see for yourselves something of what I am planning to do. I am sure our two businesses could be beneficial to one another. We are both seeking to beautify women, in one way or another, are we not?'

She nodded gravely. 'That is true. I will tell Madame Grenville. I am sure she would be most interested in your plans.'

'Where is Madame?' he enquired. 'I...er...noticed you were on your own this afternoon.'

'She has gone out on an errand of some importance,' replied Bella. She knew that Maud was meeting her husband at the nearby Rowntree's furniture store, where they were to choose some chandeliers for the hall and landings of their already impressive home. 'She has asked me to lock up if she is not back before closing time.' She glanced at the wall clock. 'And it looks to me as though she will not be back.'

'Well then, in that case...' He was looking at her expectantly, 'would you like to come round now, Miss Randall, on your own? I will wait whilst you lock up and see to things here. That is, if you would like to come? And then, perhaps Madame could come some other time?'

'I am sure that would be perfectly in order,' Bella replied, keeping up what she knew was just a pretence of formality. She guessed that he had known all too well that she was on her own and had been for the last half-hour or so. 'But there are ten minutes to go yet before closing time, and Madame insists on keeping open till the very last minute. You go on ahead, Mr Cunningham, back to your shop, and I will follow when I have finished what I have to do here.'

'Yes, of course,' he agreed. 'I understand.' As a shop owner himself he would be aware of the safety precautions that one had to take. There was no safe in the shop, as there were in some of the larger premises, but the day's takings were placed in a strong tin cash box which was locked with a key. Maud took it home with her every evening – a cab came to collect her at the end of each day – but today Bella would leave it in a secret place in the stockroom and Archie would call and collect it later. That was the arrangement whenever Bella was left in charge. She was gratified that her employer trusted her and she had never been tempted to steal so much as a farthing. Whatever sins she might be guilty of, stealing was not one of them.

She crossed her fingers, hoping that Maud would not return before half past five, and her luck held. She tidied up, hid the cash box, pulled down the window blind and, after locking the door behind her, hurried round the corner to Huntriss Row.

'Do you live over the shop, Bella?' Ralph asked her as he welcomed her into his premises; he had been waiting at the door for her. 'By the way, you don't really mind if I call you

Bella, do you? And you must call me Ralph... I am sorry if I seemed rather forward, but that is how I have been thinking of you as Bella ever since we met.' His smile was sincere now, with no hint of boldness, and she smiled back.

'No, I don't mind...Ralph,' she replied. 'Not at all... Do I live over the shop, you asked. No, I don't. I have rooms in Queen Street. I'm quite comfortable there; well...it's adequate, I suppose; it will do for now. I agree that it would be handy to live over the shop, but Maud – that's Madame Grenville,' she corrected herself, 'already had tenants living there. A middle-aged couple, and she can't move them; well, it wouldn't be fair to try. She says she feels easier in her mind with somebody living over the shop. They would hear if there were any intruders, and Mr Evans – that's the lodger – he's a great big fellow; he works down at the harbour an' he'd be a good match for anybody who was up to no good...

'Mmm... It all looks very nice, Ralph.' She looked around admiringly at the glossy mahogany counter with glass shelves beneath it, the blue carpeting on the floor, the wallpaper of Regency stripes in pale blue and gold, and at the boxes lined up on the floor and on the shelves behind the counter. 'Have you got anybody to help you to unpack this lot?'

'No...not yet,' he replied. 'I will be advertising for staff, of course. For a suitable lady to be in charge, and possibly a younger girl to help out. There's a lot to be done yet; I would like the window dressing in blue velvet...' He waved his hands expressively, 'to match the carpet, and the goods on display in the window will be of the best that we can offer, and not too many of them. I think it is better to show a little rather than a lot. A cluttered window only confuses the eye.'

'That is just what Madame says,' agreed Bella.

'So I have noticed,' he replied. 'Your window is a perfect model of elegance. And I am sure you must have had a lot to do with that?' He glanced at her questioningly.

'Yes, I help to dress the window,' she answered. 'Of course Madame has taught me a lot.'

'Have you worked in similar shops before?' he asked. 'Forgive me if I'm wrong, but I have a feeling you were not from these parts originally. Am I right?'

'Aye, I'm from Northumberland,' she smiled, exaggerating for a moment the accent that she hoped she had almost lost. She was not too pleased that her manner of speech had betrayed her. 'I worked in shops up there, a few different sorts of shops.' There was no need to go into that part of her life that she had put behind her. 'But I'm quite settled in Scarborough now. It's a good place to live.'

'And you are happy with...Madame Grenville?'

'Yes, perfectly happy; for the moment, that is.'

'But you wouldn't say no to a change...?'

'What are you suggesting?' she asked, raising her eyebrows. The thought had already entered her head, in fact it had been lingering at the back of her mind even before Ralph came back to the shop. And she had no doubt that the same thought was in his mind now. But she was loath to be disloyal to Maud who had been so good to her.

'I think you know,' he replied. His deep-set eyes looked into hers with an intensity that disturbed her, even though she knew she was attracted to him; and he to her. 'How would you feel about coming to work here, as manageress of the shop, I mean?'

'But...you don't know me. You don't know anything about me.'

'I know enough to feel that you would be ideal for the position,' he replied, now in a much more matter-of-fact manner. 'And the upstairs rooms are vacant. I have leased the whole property, and I will be looking for someone who could live here as well as manage the shop.'

That, indeed, was most appealing, and she felt like saying yes there and then. Instead, 'It's too soon, Ralph,' she said with a show of reticence. 'We hardly know one another. Besides, what would Madame Grenville say? It wouldn't be very loyal of me.'

'All's fair in love and war...and in business too, I believe,' he replied. 'But I do see what you mean.' He nodded seriously. 'You and I do not know one another very well. But I hope to remedy that very soon. Would you come out with me, shall we say...tomorrow evening, Bella? I thought we could dine at the small hotel where I am staying; it is on St Nicholas Cliff. Then we could go to a concert at the Spa. What do you say?'

She answered the question that was not only on his lips but in his ardent grey eyes as well. 'Yes, I would like that very much,' she replied. 'Thank you for inviting me.'

When she had been out with him a couple of times, to a concert as he had suggested, and then another evening to the Theatre Royal on St Thomas Street, Bella knew it was time she found out more about his marital status. He had behaved most circumspectly, taking her arm as they walked along the street and escorting her back to her lodgings at the end of the evening, his farewell to her just a light kiss on her cheek. But his admiration was there in his eyes, with an ardour not very far below the surface.

She broached the subject at their next meeting, which was on a Sunday afternoon in the middle of March. Ralph had arrived soon after midday on the train from York and now, after listening to a brass band concert at the Spa Pavilion they were strolling back towards the hotel on St Nicholas Cliff. They would partake of 'high tea', the meal which was always served on a Sunday at the quite modest establishment where Ralph stayed on his frequent visits to Scarborough. He had already mentioned his daughter, whom he intended to leave, quite soon, in complete charge of his shop in York, so that provided her with a suitable opening.

'Your daughter...' she began. 'She sounds to be a very capable young woman. Does she look after your home as well, Ralph, while you are away?' At the moment he was spending at least two nights each week in the seaside resort, and this time he had come early, he said, in order to get to grips early in the week with some of the jobs that were in progress in Huntriss Row, and to keep the workmen on their toes. He was silent for a moment, then he stepped aside, leaning on the railings of the Spa Bridge. Bella joined him there, looking out across the sea.

'Yes, as you say, Bella...' He put his hand on top of her gloved one as it lay on the railing. 'Rosalind is a very capable girl. She has needed to be for the last...' He shook his head. '...goodness knows how many years. My wife...' She felt the pressure of his hand increase, as his eyes met hers in a look full of apology and sadness. 'Yes, I have a wife... I am sorry, my dear. I know I may have given the impression that I was a widower. Maybe that was what I intended you to think; I don't know...' He shook his head again in a bewildered manner.

'But believe me, I might just as well be a widower,' he continued, his voice betraying more than a touch of bitterness.

'My wife has been an invalid ever since Rosalind was born. She took to her bed then and has scarcely left it since.'

'Oh, I see...' Bella was at a loss as to how she should react. Should she be angry that he had misled her? But no, he had not actually said that his wife was dead, and she had heard of women, of the upper and middle classes, who took delight in being ill and confined to bed, sometimes when there was, in fact, very little the matter with them. Maybe Ralph's wife was one of these; a malingerer, or she might, of course, be really ill.

'What...what's the matter with her?' she asked. 'What does the doctor say? The doctor visits her, I suppose?'

'Oh yes, once a week at least.' He gave a wry chuckle. 'He dances attendance on her, just like Rosalind does. Rosalind loves her mother, though. There is a bond between them and I suppose I can understand that. They were very close when Rosie was little, she and Prudence...that's my wife. Maybe I shouldn't judge her too harshly. I knew when we married that she hadn't much stamina. She was a delicate little creature; maybe that was part of the attraction. But we...well, I believed that we loved one another.' He glanced at her apologetically. 'But I've watched her change over the years She's selfish now, selfish and demanding, and she delights in her frailty. She believes it is part of a well-brought-up woman's nature to be frail and in need of care. As you can imagine, we haven't enjoyed a real marriage for more than twelve years...not that we ever really enjoyed it,' he added, thoughtfully. 'Twelve years ago; that was when our son was born...stillborn, I should say.'

'Oh, I see...' said Bella again. 'I'm sorry...'

'It was a difficult birth when Rosalind was born, long and

drawn-out. The doctor helped all he could – she had far more help, I am sure, than some poor women get – but Prudence regarded it as an experience never to be repeated. She was unwell for ages afterwards, and all the love she had was centred on Rosalind, never on me... And she began to suffer from every complaint you can imagine, or convinced herself that she did.

'But I badly wanted a son; I feel ashamed sometimes when I think about it. It was a difficult pregnancy and the birth was even worse than it had been with our first child; and in the end the poor little mite was stillborn. Edward, we called him, after the prince... But she has never forgiven me and nothing has been right since then between Prudence and myself. I do what I can to take care of her, financially and materially. She doesn't go short of anything. Actually, she had a considerable dowry from her father when we married, and so...' He shrugged. 'As I've said, I do what I can.'

'I'm glad you have told me,' said Bella. 'It can't have been easy for you.' She was somewhat discomfited, though, by Ralph's story. What had he been saying? That his wife had been unwilling, but that he had forced himself upon her and claimed his rights as a husband? Such an act would, indeed, be abhorrent to a woman of Prudence's temperament. She found herself feeling almost sorry for the woman. But from what she knew of Ralph, personally, he seemed to be a kind and considerate man, and a wife such as he had must have driven him to distraction at times. She knew that his situation was not unique. There must be many men, and women too, trapped in unhappy marriages such as theirs from which there was no escape.

'I can't pretend that I have lived like a monk,' he said now.

'I have been – what shall I say? – friendly with one or two ladies. But please believe me, Bella, I am not a philanderer. As soon as I met you I knew there could be something special between us, and I think you felt the same…didn't you?'

She nodded silently.

'And…dare I hope that you still feel the same?'

She nodded again. 'Yes, I do. But neither am I a…philanderer, or I suppose it would be a trollop in my case. But I'm not! I might have been rather indiscreet once or twice when I was younger. But it's all in the past now.'

'And I will never enquire into the past unless you want to tell me about it,' said Ralph. 'But as far as I'm concerned I felt I had to put all my cards on the table. And I will be very happy to go on enjoying your friendship, Bella, and, maybe…a little more than that?'

Chapter Ten

It was inevitable that the friendship between Ralph Cunningham and Bella Randall should continue, and it lasted for almost eight years.

They came to be regarded in the town as a 'couple', although it was known that they were not married, at least not to one another. She had always been something of a mystery woman, appearing suddenly, as she had done, as if from nowhere, then climbing the social ladder, via Madame Grenville, into the comfortable love nest with Ralph Cunningham. Tales of his unhappy marriage to a woman in York – it was said that she was an invalid – gathered momentum in the town. Some tongues were malicious. Maud Green, for instance, was unwilling to forget how she had been slighted, which was how she saw it.

But most folk thought of Ralph as a good sort, well respected in business circles, and a man who was ready to help associates who might find themselves in a spot of financial trouble. He and his lady friend were soon accepted into the social scene. After all, the Prince of Wales had a string of lady friends and nobody thought any the worse of him. 'Good old Teddy' was regarded as a grand sort of chap, with his six-inch cigars, bellowing laugh and genial bewhiskered countenance. Bella was contented; more than contented; she felt that she had found what she was seeking – security, happiness and love. She was sure that Ralph loved her and she believed that she loved him. They were almost like a married couple. Almost...because she knew he could never marry her whilst his wife was still living, and Prudence was what was often referred to as a 'creaking gate'. This situation could continue for years and years.

Ralph had never taken up residence in the rooms above the shop, although he stayed there quite openly on his frequent visits to Scarborough. This was Bella's domain, to furnish as she wished, and Ralph had insisted that she should choose whatsoever she wanted with regard to the furniture, carpets and curtains. She was proud of her 'little palace', which was how she thought of it. It was as posh as Maud Green's any day of the week, and, she believed, rather more tasteful. Ralph had assured her she would always be financially secure and that he would make provision for her. But she paid little heed to the future; the present was turning out to be just what she had dreamt about.

It was unavoidable that they should encounter Maud and Archie Green sometimes at social gatherings, and gradually a truce was arrived at between the two women. Their two businesses were, as Ralph had predicted, proving to be mutually beneficial. And Ralph and Archie had never had any problem in rubbing along together. Different personalities, but both of them shrewd businessmen.

She had wondered if they might also meet William Moon and his wife socially, but this did not happen. Obviously they moved in different circles. Will had been into the shop, though, during the late summer of the year they had opened. They had greeted one another without embarrassment and, with Bella's help, he had chosen some perfume for his wife; Rimmel's 'Bouquet', advertised as being 'as sweet as a May morning'. Bella's assistant, Sally, who had not long left school, wrapped up the little parcel in floral paper whilst Bella dealt with the money transaction.

It was later in the year that Clara, his wife, had come into the shop for the first time. The window was dressed ready for the Christmas season and Bella was pleased with the colourful and arresting display. She had, with Ralph's permission, ordered several new lines which needed to be on show in the window, and so the rule of simplicity first and foremost had been overlooked temporarily. There were tortoiseshell and ivory combs from Spain, exquisitely hand carved, some to use for combing the hair and others as fashionable hair ornaments; natural sponges for use in the bath; toothbrushes with bone and ivory handles; exotic perfumes – 'Phul-nana', 'Sweet Pea Blossom', 'Scent of Araby' and 'Parma Violet', in glass-stoppered bottles with pretty flowered labels and ribbon around the neck.

Bella thought she recognised her as soon as she came through the door, but she could not be certain; she had only caught a glimpse of her, once, from across the road. She smiled welcomingly as she always did.

'Good afternoon, madam. And how may we help you?'

Clara – for Bella very soon realised that it was, indeed, Clara Moon – smiled back. 'What a lovely smell,' she exclaimed, taking a deep breath of the air, heavy with the scents of perfume, powder and pomades. Then she gave a little laugh. 'I suppose I should say perfume, shouldn't I, not smell, in such beautiful surroundings? But it really is quite breathtaking.'

Bella had remembered her from her coat and hat, the same ones, brown and fur-trimmed, that she had been wearing before. Clearly she did not waste money on too many changes of clothes. She was a pretty woman, Bella thought again; of medium height, slim build and with dainty finely drawn features. Her wisps of reddish-golden hair and her warm brown eyes, shining out from beneath her fur hat, reminded Bella of a bright little squirrel.

'Yes, I suppose we get used to the...odour,' Bella laughed, 'working in it all day. Don't we, Sally?'

'Yes, Miss Randall,' replied the young assistant dutifully.

'I'm glad you find it pleasant,' Bella continued. 'Some people think it is overpowering. Now, madam – what would you like to see?'

'Those lovely combs you have in the window, please.'

'Certainly, madam. Sally, would you find a selection for the lady?'

Clara bought two fancy combs, one to enhance a lady's dressing table and the other as a hair ornament. 'Not for myself, of course,' she explained. 'My hair is too fine for me to wear anything like that; it's a Christmas present for a friend.' She glanced admiringly at Bella's glossy black locks and the carved and jewelled comb which secured the chignon at the back. 'That comb looks lovely in your hair, Miss Randall,' she said, 'if you don't mind me mentioning it.'

'Of course I don't,' laughed Bella. 'I believe in advertising our goods any way we can. But I shall treat myself to it. I shall have to, won't I, now that I've worn it?'

Clara also chose three boxes of floral soaps for presents and a tin of cherry-flavoured tooth powder. Then she said, tentatively, 'I was wondering whether to go really mad and treat myself...' She looked, Bella thought, like an excited little girl in a sweet shop. 'My husband bought me some perfume for my birthday; "Bouquet" it was called, by Rimmel, and I liked it so much. In fact, the bottle is nearly empty.'

'Ah yes... I think I remember the gentleman,' said Bella, who had taken over serving this customer, leaving Sally to deal with an elderly lady who had just come into the shop. 'A very popular perfume, madam. We have recently ordered some more; it's sure to be in demand at Christmastime. Are you sure that is the one you want, or would you prefer to try something different? Forget-me-not, perhaps, or this essence of Lily of the Valley?'

'No...no, thank you. I'll take the "Bouquet". I had never used perfume very much before, but this one seems to suit me.'

Bella smiled at her, not in an obsequious manner but more as woman to woman. 'And you are doing the right thing,' she said, leaning towards her and speaking confidingly. 'It is every woman's privilege to treat herself now and again.'

And Clara, without any coaxing, purchased, in addition, a jar of face cream, also by Rimmel, which promised to beautify and preserve the complexion. Bella was surprised at how much she had liked the woman, William Moon's wife. She realised, too, that she no longer felt any jealousy or antagonism towards her. But then why should she? Bella, also, now had someone who cared for her.

They did not become friends, but Clara Moon visited the shop now and again and was always ready to chat and pass the time of day. During one visit she mentioned, confidentially, that her husband was an undertaker and that she, too, helped out with the work. A dab of perfume on her handkerchief was necessary at times, she said, to mask other less pleasant odours.

'Ah yes, I see...' Bella had nodded, not admitting that she

already knew of the profession of Clara's husband. Neither did she ever let on to William Moon, who also paid infrequent visits to the shop, that she had made the acquaintance of his wife.

She was aware when Clara was pregnant again in the spring of 1890. She did not see her again for several months, but she had read in the evening paper that William and Clara Moon were pleased to announce the arrival of a daughter, Madeleine, on the twenty-first of June.

A daughter... Although several years had gone by Bella could not help but think, with a stab of pain, of her own little daughter; Henrietta, the daughter she had been forced to give up for adoption. She would be nine years old now, the little girl who was – she realised with a jolt – half-sister to the child to whom Clara Moon had just given birth.

Bella told Ralph, little by little, about most of the incidents of her past life. She even admitted that she had worked as a herring girl during her last sojourn in the town. He had shown little surprise at her revelations, not even when she told him her reason for leaving the resort and going back up north; that she had found herself pregnant and that the young man – no more than a lad, really, she had explained – had been unable to stand by her. His name was not mentioned. Probably Ralph assumed that he was no longer on the scene and Bella did not refute his belief.

When William Moon had let her down she had gone back to Northumberland with a vague plan in her mind. There was someone whom she believed she could rely on to help her in her predicament...

Tobias Lonsdale was the son of the local squire, Sir Horace Lonsdale, one of the largest landowners in the area around

Morpeth, and it was this young man, Toby, who had been responsible for Bella's dismissal from Lonsdale Hall at the age of sixteen. He had been a few years older and engaged to the daughter of another of the gentry families. Although he had an eye for a pretty girl Toby was not a lascivious sort of young man who thought only of his own lust and gratification, as did some of his peers. He was genuinely fond of Bella although their friendship had never progressed beyond a few kisses and covert meetings away from the house. But when their trysts had been discovered by Toby's irate mother, Bella had been sent packing.

'I'm sorry... I'm so very sorry,' Toby had told her, disobeying his mother to snatch a few moments with her before she departed. 'Honestly, Bella, I feel dreadful about this. If there's ever anything I can do for you – when all this has blown over, I mean – then you must let me know, please, Bella...'

She had tossed her head, too hurt and bewildered to talk to him, but his words had stayed in her mind because she believed they were sincere.

When she returned to Morpeth after a couple of years away, and following her summer in Scarborough, Toby Lonsdale was married, quite happily, it was said. He had given up his mild philandering and had become a responsible young man. It had not been difficult to arrange a meeting with him.

She had found temporary lodgings in Ashington and a job as a barmaid, but Toby, on learning of her plight, found accommodation for her at a farmhouse a few miles from Lonsdale Hall; not one of his father's tenant farms, but one of the few that was privately owned. Bill and Madge Stockton were a middle-aged couple willing to offer Bella bed and board in exchange for her labours. She was a strong lass and was able to work almost to the end of her pregnancy. So it was there that she had stayed for the next few months, and when it was time for her confinement she was competently cared for by Madge Stockton.

As she held the baby girl in her arms – not a red and wrinkled brat, as she had anticipated, but a pink and white round-cheeked infant with black curly hair and a tiny puckered mouth like a rosebud – her maternal instincts had surged, but only for a moment. Bella knew she must not allow her feelings to influence her. She had been persuaded over the past months that there was only one course open to her, to let her child be adopted. Especially as Madge and Bill knew a couple who were desperate for a child but were unable to have any of their own.

They were an honest and decent couple, she was told, steady and reliable, and the child would have a good home with loving parents. They were both in their mid-thirties. The man worked at the pit in Ashington, but in the office; he did not go down the mine. And that, Bella, believed, was all to the good. She knew of many poor little mites who had lost their fathers in pit disasters.

Anyway, how could she, Bella, find employment, which she knew she must do, with a baby to look after? Madge and Bill had been kind to her, but she could not go on living there. It had been Toby, of course, who had persuaded them to take her in and had rewarded them, too, for their pains. And it was Toby who took care of the details when the week-old child was handed over to its adoptive parents.

Bella was not supposed to know the whereabouts of the child, but she pleaded with Toby to tell her the address. She promised she would not make any trouble and she was true to her word. Only occasionally did she go up to Ashington to snatch a glimpse of the child, watching her grow into a sturdy, stocky little girl with Bella's dark eyes and hair and bold features. She was satisfied that the child was happy and well cared for. As for Bella, she had moved down to Newcastle where she found lodgings and employment, first in a haberdashery shop and then in the gown department of a large store.

But when, early in 1886, Toby fell from his horse and broke his neck in a riding accident, Bella felt that it was time for her to move on. She could not have said what made her return to Scarborough, apart from, of course, a vague idea that she might meet up again with William Moon, but as the years passed by she came to believe that it was Fate.

She had never met Rosalind, Ralph's daughter, although she had spoken with her once or twice on the newly installed telephone, regarding business matters. She did not enquire about his wife, whether she was still ailing or whether there had been any improvement in her health or temperament. She was content to leave things as they were, not to muddy the waters, so to speak, by any undue poking and prying. She and Ralph were happy and that was all that mattered to her for the moment. The future could be left to take care of itself. She realised afterwards that she had been living in a fool's paradise. Ralph still spent half of his time in York. He stayed in Scarborough every other weekend, and these were times that Bella looked forward to; the times when they were able to be together as a couple, enjoying the company not only of one another but of the several friends they had made. These were married couples who invited them to their homes or accompanied them on an outing to a concert or to the theatre. It was known that Ralph was leading a double life, but their friends were broad-minded enough to accept this. The consensus of opinion was that his wife, also, must know about his lady friend in Scarborough and be quite resigned to the situation.

The first weekend in February Ralph had stayed in York and Bella was looking forward to his return on the Monday; he usually arrived back at the shop by mid-morning. This time, however, he was late. The shop closed between the hours of twelve-thirty and two, but when two o'clock arrived he had still not appeared. Bella had drawn up the blind and was turning the notice on the door to read 'Open' when the telephone rang, its discordant tone sounding loud and shrill in the small shop.

She recognised the voice who spoke, addressing her as Miss Randall, as that of Ralph's daughter, Rosalind. The line was crackly and it was difficult to hear clearly; but what she could make out between the buzzing and the interference made her gasp in shock and horror. She grabbed hold of the counter behind her, leaning against it for support. Rosalind was telling her about an accident; she seemed to be saying that Ralph had been...killed!

'No, no...' Bella cried out, shaking her head and refusing to believe what she was hearing. 'I'm sorry – I can't hear you very well. I thought you said that your father was...dead. But he can't be...'

'Yes, that is what I said.' The young woman's voice sounded flat and emotionless, but Bella had no doubt that she, too, was still in a state of shock. 'He was involved in an accident on Lendal Bridge on Sunday night,' she went on, the line sounding rather clearer now. 'He was crossing the road and there was a runaway horse... He was trapped under the wheels of a cab... They took him to the hospital, but he was already dead.' Her voice broke and Bella could hear a strangled sort of sob.

'Oh, that's dreadful,' she said, her voice, escaping on a drawn-out breath, was scarcely audible. 'I am so sorry. So completely...stunned. I can't believe it.'

'No, neither could we. We would like you to close the shop for today at least, as a sign of respect, Miss Randall.' Rosalind sounded more in control now, quite brusque, in fact.

'Yes, of course,' said Bella. 'That goes without saying.'

'And I will come over to Scarborough to talk with you later this week. There will be several matters to discuss... I will let you know, of course, when I am coming.'

'Yes...yes, that would be helpful...'

'So that is all for now, Miss Randall. I know the news will have been a considerable shock to you, but there is no more to be said for the moment.' Bella heard the telephone receiver being replaced with a sharp click.

Sally had entered the shop and was staring at Bella, her eyes wide with anxiety, although she had heard only a little of the conversation. 'Whatever's up, Miss Randall?' she asked.

'Oh, Sally...' Bella cried, reaching out her arms to the young girl, something she would, normally, never have dreamt of doing. 'It's Ralph; Mr Cunningham... He's been killed. Oh, Sally...he's dead. I shall never see him again.'

'Eeh, deary me,' said Sally, putting her arms round the older woman. 'That's a bad do. Such a nice man he was an' all. And you and him, you were so fond of one another, weren't you? Oh dear! Happen I shouldn't't've said that,

Miss Randall. I'm sorry, but I noticed, see...'

'That's all right, Sally,' said Bella, holding the girl's hands and trying to smile at her. 'I dare say a lot of people noticed. We weren't ashamed of it... Now, would you go and make a pot of strong tea for us, please, dear, while I see to closing the shop again. I'll make a notice for the door. Closed owing to bereavement. That's what I'll have to say...'

She shut up the shop and sent Sally home for the rest of the day and for the whole of Tuesday. She planned to reopen on Wednesday, just for a few hours, as Wednesday was half-day closing. She was still not able to believe, fully, what she had heard, but if there was any vestige of hope remaining in her mind it was soon wiped out by the stark headline in the evening paper. There it was in black and white, LOCAL BUSINESSMAN KILLED IN ACCIDENT WITH RUNAWAY HORSE... followed by three inches of print extolling Ralph Cunningham as a prominent shopkeeper in the town, respected and well liked by everyone. He owned thriving businesses in York and in Scarborough, and was succeeded by his wife and his only daughter, Rosalind.

When the shop reopened there were only a few customers, but quite a number of callers expressing their sympathy and – in some cases – commiserating with Bella on her sad loss. She told them to watch the evening paper for details of the funeral, which was sure to be held in York. She was as much in the dark as anyone.

She was not looking forward to the meeting with Rosalind. The young woman had sent her a brief note saying that she would arrive at the shop at eleven o'clock or thereabouts on the Friday morning. She arrived almost on the dot of eleven and Bella turned the notice round to 'Closed'. Sally had already had her instructions to make herself scarce for at least twenty minutes and then reappear with coffee and biscuits.

Bella thought that the young woman, who must be in her mid-twenties now, had a definite look of Ralph, in her deep-set grey eyes and dark hair, but her face lacked the spark of animation that had transformed his features. But the poor lass had nothing much to smile about, Bella reminded herself, and the unrelieved black of her coat and large feathered hat did nothing to enhance her sallow complexion.

'How do you do, Miss Randall?' Rosalind extended a black-gloved hand, allowing Bella to barely touch the finger tips. She did not smile, but was regarding appraisingly the shop manageress whom she was meeting for the first time. Bella had no doubt as to what was going through her mind. So this is the woman who was my father's mistress...Bella had long assumed that both Rosalind and her mother were fully aware of what had been going on for the last...almost eight years it had been.

'How do you do, Miss Cunningham?' said Bella. 'Do sit down.' She indicated a small spoon-backed chair upholstered in blue velvet, often used for important customers. She herself perched on a stool which was kept behind the counter.

Rosalind slowly drew off her gloves and placed them tidily in her lap before looking fixedly and still unsmilingly at Bella. 'I do not intend to beat about the bush, Miss Randall,' she began. 'There is no point in either of us pretending. I know, and so does my mother, that you have been my father's mistress for several years. He has never admitted it, but neither has he denied it.'

Bella returned her look just as unflinchingly. 'And I will not deny it either,' she said. 'I loved your father and I believe he loved me. And I was given to understand that the marriage – that of your mother and father – had come to an end long ago.'

Rosalind shook her head a little impatiently. 'In many ways, yes, I admit it had. But my mother was still his wife, and now she is his widow. From what she has told me it didn't take long for him to start looking elsewhere, even in the early days of their marriage. If you believe you were the first, then I am afraid I must disillusion you. There had been several others.'

What she was hearing came as a shock to Bella, although Ralph had admitted that he had not been a saint. She did not react in any way, though, except to say, 'No, I may not have been the first... But I was most definitely the last!' She was quite certain of that.

Rosalind inclined her head. 'Yes... I think that is probably true. But the fact remains that you have no rights in law. You are not even what they call a common-law wife.'

'I believe your father will have made provision for me,' Bella answered. 'He said that he would do so.' That, indeed, was what he had said at the start of their relationship, but he had not mentioned it since that time. She was beginning to have grave doubts. 'There is a will, isn't there?' she enquired, trying to imbue her words with more confidence than she was feeling.

'There is a will...but you are not mentioned,' replied Rosalind. She gave a tight little smile, but Bella noticed that her eyes were no longer hostile, not so cold and unfeeling as they had appeared at first. There was a certain softness in them, a glimpse of understanding there as she murmured, 'I'm sorry...'

'But I was led to understand...' Bella began, then she stopped, shrugging her shoulders. 'I was wrong, wasn't I?' Was there any man, anywhere, who could be trusted, she wondered? Even Ralph had let her down.

'There is a copy of the will with our solicitors, if you are in any doubt,' said Rosalind, before the thought of duplicity could take root in Bella's mind. 'I am afraid my father was inclined to put things off until another day. He may have intended to do something. I am sure he didn't think he would die at fifty-two. Oh yes, he had a good head for business in some ways, but as far as money was concerned, my mother was the one who was in control.'

'Oh...?' Bella raised her eyebrows in surprise, although she did recall, now, Ralph telling her that Prudence had come to the marriage with quite a substantial dowry.

'This property, for instance – the Scarborough shop and living accommodation – it was bought in my mother's name. She had money in her own right. When the law was changed she made it her business to claim what was rightly hers. She is no fool, my mother. She has had poor health for many years, but her mind is still very astute.'

Bella vaguely remembered hearing of a law being passed, several years ago, allowing women to keep their own property after marriage. Until that time all a woman's possessions, by law, belonged to her husband to do with as he pleased. She was taken aback now by these revelations but she had no intention of going to pieces. She must stick up for her rights. It was a shock to hear that the shop and property had belonged to Prudence Cunningham all along; even if it had been in Ralph's name, though, it would have passed to his wife now. But she, Bella, had worked long and hard to make it the successful business it had become. She said as much now.

'I have been a faithful employee. I have managed the shop, virtually on my own, for the last eight years and I believe I have been responsible for its success. You father was very pleased with the annual turnover...and I'm sure your mother, too, will agree that it is most satisfactory.'

'Yes, that is true,' Rosalind conceded. 'There is no cause for complaint. However, we have decided that it is no longer possible to keep both shops going. So we will be closing the Scarborough shop and concentrating on the one in York.' Bella was unable to suppress a gasp of surprise.

'Yes, I realise this may come as a shock,' said Rosalind. 'We appreciate all your hard work and we do not intend to let it go unrewarded. Nor do we intend to turn you out immediately.'

'I'm very pleased to hear it,' said Bella, a mite sarcastically.

'No...you may stay in the flat until the end of the month. And in the meantime the property will be put up for sale. The shop will close down at the end of next week, and I will make arrangements for the remaining stock to be transferred to York, if you could pack it up, please, Miss Randall. With the help of your young assistant, of course.' She smiled, quite charmingly, at Sally who had entered with a laden tray. 'Ah, coffee. Thank you, my dear. That smells lovely.'

Bella was glad of the diversion to gather herself together. Silently she handed the cup of coffee and the plate of biscuits to her unwelcome guest. So that was that, was it? After eight years of loyal service she was back on the scrapheap again. She took a sip of her coffee, then another, savouring the full-bodied flavour and warmth, despite the feelings of hurt and insecurity which were beginning to steal up on her.

'So that's it, is it?' she asked.

'No, just one more thing, Miss Randall. Well, two more things, really. Firstly, the funeral will be held in York on Monday.' Bella already knew because there had been a notice in the paper the previous evening. 'My mother and I do not wish you to attend.' Rosalind looked at her uncompromisingly.

'And secondly...as I have mentioned, we do not want your efforts to go unrewarded, and so we have decided to grant you a supernumerary payment of one hundred guineas.'

Bella nodded briefly. She had no intention of saying thank you. But she almost smiled, even in the midst of her despair, as an amusing thought crossed her mind. She was remembering a favourite quip of one of the fisher lasses. 'Ah well, ne'er mind,' she thought to herself. 'It's better than a slap in the gob with a wet herring.'

Chapter Eleven

In the spring of 1895 building work was going ahead as planned, and William Moon hoped that the shop – 'Moon's Mourning Modes', as they intended to call it – would be completed and ready for customers in a few weeks' time. His father had been all in favour of this innovative plan; another string to their bow, Isaac said, in a business which went from strength to strength with each passing year.

Two small run-down shops – a greengrocer's and a bakery – becoming vacant at the same time had proved fortuitous for the Moon family, especially as these shops adjoined their existing property. The landlord had been persuaded to sell them for a reasonable sum, in view of their dilapidated condition, and Isaac and William had lost no time in employing builders to make the two small shops into one and to convert the upstairs rooms into a large stockroom, and living accommodation which could be let to a suitable person.

A tenant was very soon found when it was known that there was a flat to let. This was a bachelor friend of William – a friend from childhood days – who worked as a porter at the railway station. Fred Archer was a big burly chap who would be handy to have on the premises if there were any intruders. And with regard to what happened later, William was to thank his lucky stars time and again that the rooms were already occupied.

Clara was excited about the new venture. 'You will be the

manageress, of course,' William told her. 'My father is leaving the running of the shop entirely in our hands, yours and mine.'

'Does that mean I won't be going out with you on your assignments, in future?' asked Clara.

William smiled. 'I thought you might have wanted a change from all that side of things,' he replied. 'Looking after a shop would be a much more congenial occupation, surely?'

'Yes, that's true, and I shall love it. I know I will. I always enjoyed serving in the shop when I worked at Louisa's. But I shall miss being with you and helping you, Will,' she said pensively. 'You father doesn't often get involved with the laying out any more, does he? He's spending more and more time in the workshop and...well, I don't think you can manage on your own, can you?'

'I dare say I could,' replied William, 'but I must admit that I've got used to having you with me, and there's nobody who would be able to work along with me as well as you do.'

'Anyway, I won't be able to manage the shop single-handedly, will I?' Clara pointed out. 'I will need an assistant, maybe more than one in time. How would it be if we appoint someone as under-manageress, a sort of second-in-command, who could take over whenever I need to go out on a job?'

'Yes, a good idea; why not?' said William. 'What shall we do? Put an advertisement in the local paper? The stock will be arriving in a few weeks' time, all being well, and you will need someone to help you to sort it out.'

They had already made excursions to warehouses in York and Leeds to choose garments and accessories, which would be delivered when the finishing touches – the carpentry and decorating, the installation of electricity and the carpet fitting

– had been completed in the new premises. Their two children, Maddy, who was almost five, and eight-year-old Patrick had been left, as they often were, in the care of their grandmother whilst their parents were absent on shopping expeditions. Both of them were at school now, so they were very little trouble.

'I don't really think we will need to need to advertise,' said Clara thoughtfully. 'Leave it to me, William. I think I know somebody who would just fit the bill.'

William was relieved that his wife had forewarned him regarding the woman she had invited to come round to their premises, to see if she would like to work in their soon-to-be-opened shop.

'Bella Randall?' he had said, unable to keep the surprise out of his voice, and also the hint of censure that he realised must have been obvious in his tone. 'The...er...woman from the perfume shop?'

'Yes, that's right,' replied Clara, looking at him keenly. 'Why, what's the matter? You sound rather disapproving. Don't you think she would be suitable? I didn't realise you knew her, anyway.'

'I don't,' answered William quickly, too quickly. 'I mean... I know who she is, of course, from going into the shop to buy perfume for you. Yes, she's always been very helpful. Her position has come to an end there, hasn't it, with the death of Ralph Cunningham?'

He had heard about the tragedy on the local grapevine as well as seeing the account in the local paper. Some said that Bella had been left penniless and homeless; others thought that she had been left a small legacy. At all events, the news had given William quite a jolt. He had not given much thought to the woman for years, believing she had found the comfortable little niche that she had been seeking. He could not help but wonder, with a stab of trepidation, whether she might seek his help again as she had half threatened to do. And now here was his wife preparing to offer her a job.

'Yes,' said Clara. 'I feel so sorry for her losing her job so suddenly and her security, to say nothing of...er...the man she loved.'

'He was a married man,' said William. 'He had a wife and a daughter in York.' He stopped, aware of the note of reproach in his voice which would, indeed, be most hypocritical. 'Still, from all accounts they were happy together, he and...Bella. But you must be careful, Clara. We don't really know all that much about her – her background, I mean – do we?'

Clara frowned at him. 'That doesn't sound like you, William. Why are you being so disapproving all of a sudden? I agree that we don't know everything about her, but it would be the same with whoever we employed, wouldn't it? And what I do know about Bella Randall I like very much. She is a very good sales assistant – most helpful and obliging – and she seems to be a nice friendly person as well. I believe she worked at Madame Grenville's before she was at Cunningham's, so she has some experience of the gown trade as well. I think she would be ideal for us.'

'Obviously you've already mentioned it to her,' said William. 'And what did she have to say about it? I expect she jumped at the chance, didn't she; a good position dropping straight into her lap?'

'No...no, she didn't,' said Clara. 'As a matter of fact she

seemed rather unsure at first. Probably the thought of working in a shop that's part of an undertaking business. I suppose the idea might be rather off-putting. That's why I invited her to come round and see us, then we could put her at her ease if she has any problems.'

It is more likely to be us who will have the problems, thought William, but he was not able to give voice to his doubts. 'Very well, my dear,' he said to his wife. 'You are the one who will have to work along with the lady, and if you like her and you feel that you can trust her then...well...maybe that's a good start.'

'You still sound rather unsure, Will.'

'No...no, I'm not. Anyway, it must be your decision.' He knew that any misgivings he might have must be set aside or else Clara would become suspicious. 'Where is she at the moment, by the way? The shop on Huntriss Row has closed, hasn't it? And what about the rooms above? Is she still living there?'

'No, she had to be out by the end of February.' It was now almost the end of March. 'She's gone back to the place where she had rooms before, when she first came to Scarborough, on Queen Street. And she's got a temporary job at Boyce's store.'

'Mmm; I see. Rather a come-down for her.'

'Yes, so it is. I saw her there when I went in to buy some odds and ends. So when we started talking about engaging an assistant, that's when I thought about Bella. It's rather a pity the rooms over our shop are already spoken for,' she added wistfully. 'It would have been ideal for her to live on the premises, as she did at the perfumery.'

William found himself breathing an inward sigh of relief. 'But we've already promised Fred, haven't we?' he said.

'Anyway, we don't know that she's going to take up our offer, do we?' But he had a very strong feeling that she would.

He shook hands formally with her when they met a few days later. Bella also made the acquaintance of Hannah Moon, William's mother, over a cup of tea. Hannah said afterwards that she thought the young woman would be most suitable. She was polite and respectful and decorously dressed.

Isaac had been busy working at his carpentry and had seen no reason to come out and meet the woman who would be employed in the shop. It was inevitable, though, that they should meet eventually. When that happened Bella smiled and shook hands with him, her eyes showing no glimmer of recognition, but something stirred at the back of Isaac's mind.

'That lass,' he said to William later, 'the one that's just started working in t' shop, I've seen her before, haven't I?'

William nodded. 'Yes, Father; so you have. But I didn't think you would have recognised her.' He might have known, though. Isaac had a memory like an elephant and there was no point in trying to pull the wool over his eyes now.

'Aye, I recognised her all right,' Isaac nodded. 'It's the lass you were with in t' pub all those years ago. Not quite so flashy now I've got to say, but you'd best watch yer step, lad... There's nowt going on between you and her, is there?'

'Of course not,' said William, feeling hurt and indignant. 'She's been back in Scarborough for ages, but I've had no contact with her. As if I would! Actually... I had my doubts about employing her, but Clara knows her and likes her, so I don't see that there can be any harm in it.'

'You've got a grand little wife there,' said Isaac, as he had said many times before. 'One o' t' best.'

'And don't you think I know that very well?' retorted William. 'You must know, Father, that I would never do anything to hurt Clara or the children.'

'Aye, well; make sure as you don't,' said his father. 'And – if you'll take a tip from me – don't let yon Bella get too familiar, not with any of you. Don't let her get her feet under t' table. She's an employee, that's all, now just think on.'

William knew that he could have told Clara there and then about his former friendship with Bella. But how much or how little could he have admitted to? That was the problem. In the end he decided not to tell her anything at all.

Five years later Bella was still employed at Moon's Mourning Modes. She now had comfortable rooms in Trafalgar Square, only five minutes' walk away. It would have suited her better to have had the rooms over the shop, but Clara had explained at the beginning that they were already spoken for. And the tenant, Fred, was still there. Moreover he was married now and there seemed to be no possibility of them ever moving.

Bella had liked Clara Moon the first time she met her in the perfumery. Indeed, there was nothing to dislike about the friendly and kind-hearted woman. By the time they had worked together for a few months they were quite good friends, on Christian name terms with one another.

She had felt right from the start, however, and she still felt that she was being held at arm's length, not to be admitted into the close intimacy of the Moon family circle. She blamed William for this, and his father. If the decision had been left to Clara or to Hannah Moon she thought she might have been treated much more as a family friend and less as an employee.

She had liked Hannah, a sweet-natured grandmother figure who had stayed very much in the background of the family business, and when that lady had died of a bout of pneumonia two years ago, Bella had felt sad. She had, of course, been invited to the funeral and to the meal that followed. Similarly, she was sometimes asked along to happier events; the children's birthday teas and for a meal at Christmas. That was usually on Boxing Day, Christmas Day itself being reserved solely for family members.

She knew that Isaac had recognised her at their first meeting. What a memory he must have, to be sure. She realised that nothing much escaped old Isaac, and she felt that it was his say-so which had prevented her from being accepted whole-heartedly as a friend. There was a constraint between them, herself and Isaac, just as there was between her and William.

Why had she stayed, she often asked herself, on the outer fringes of the Moon family but never quite one of them? She had a secure and well-paid job; an interesting one, too. That was one reason for staying, she supposed. And her rooms in Trafalgar Square were spacious and comfortable and convenient for the shop. Her social life had dwindled in the years since Ralph's death. Couples with whom they had been friendly no longer sought her company. It might have been different were she a widow, but the bereaved mistress – or 'other woman' – was now treated with a certain amount of pity, but not a good deal of friendliness.

Strangely enough, the couple who still regarded her as a friend were the Greens, Maud and Archie, Maud having long since recovered from her show of pique on losing her valued assistant. It had become customary for Bella to spend

Christmas Day with them and she was sometimes invited round for Sunday tea.

There were times, though, when she was lonely, and it was then that the acrimonious thoughts that were always lingering on the periphery of her mind began to intensify. And she knew, deep down, the reason that she stayed was because she could not break away. It was a bitter-sweet agony watching this family who were so happy together.

She had seen the children, Patrick and Madeleine, grow and mature as children should. Patrick, now aged fourteen, was working with his father and grandfather, learning the various aspects of the undertaking business. He was a cheerful even-tempered lad with a look of his father – dark-haired and brown-eyed, with a ruddy healthy-looking complexion – but possessed of a much more outgoing disposition than Will had ever had. Bella liked Patrick and the lad treated her with the same easy friendliness that he showed to everyone.

Madeleine – Maddy – who was now ten years old, was the image of her mother. Bella had to admit that she was a nice friendly little girl, well brought up, of course, and usually polite. But Bella had never been able to take to the child. Her feelings for her bordered on dislike, which she always tried to hide when other members of the family were around. She guessed, though, that Maddy was aware of these feelings of animosity – she was a perceptive child – and, what was more, Bella had come to realise that the antipathy was mutual.

The reason, as far as Bella was concerned, was a simple one. She, too, had a daughter with whom she had lost touch many years ago. Indeed, she was not supposed to have had any contact at all since the adoption, although she had stolen a glimpse of the child very occasionally, until she was five years old. Henrietta would be nineteen now; a young woman. She might even be married, but Bella had no idea of her whereabouts. None of this was Maddy's fault, and Bella knew that it was unreasonable of her to feel the way she did about the child, but she could not help herself.

There had been times when she was with Ralph that she had almost forgotten about her daughter. She had loved Ralph and there had been other things to fill her life and occupy her mind. In the same way, thoughts of William Moon had receded to the back of her mind. But since Ralph's death, the memories and the remorse she had felt regarding the adoption, had returned a hundredfold. And along with them came bitter feelings about the man whom she believed had loved her. She had blindly gone on believing that, one day, they would be married; or if that were not possible, that she would be comfortably provided for in her advancing years.

In spite of all this she was fond of Clara, so much so that she was almost able to forget at times about the unspoken secrets that lay between them. At other times her envy of Will Moon's wife – a woman who had everything she wanted in life – would surface to the forefront of her mind. She, Bella, was now thirty-eight years of age – fast approaching forty – and sometimes her embittered thoughts convinced her that life had handed her a very raw deal.

Chapter Twelve

1900

'Patrick, you won't start teasing my friend because she's got red hair, will you? And I've told you before, you don't even mention corpses!'

'Of course I won't!' Patrick answered his sister with a look of wide-eyed innocence. 'Fancy you thinking I would! Surely you know me better than that, Maddy.'

'Yes, I do know you,' retorted Maddy, 'and that's why I'm telling you. We've got to make her feel welcome. Mam says so, and I know what an awful tease you can be.'

'What, me?' Patrick gave a good-natured laugh. 'No, honestly, Maddy, I won't call her Carrots or Gingernut if that's what you're afraid of. I'll be a model of good behaviour. I saw her yesterday – have you forgotten? – and I was extremely polite to her then. She's called Jessie, isn't she?'

'Yes, short for Jessica. And I think she's going to be my very best friend while she's staying here. I wish she could stay here for ever; go to my school and everything.'

'You've only known her a few days,' replied Patrick. 'If I know you girls you'll have fallen out by next week.'

'Oh no we won't!' retorted Maddy. 'Jessie's really nice and I shall never fall out with her.'

'Well, make the most of it while she's here then,' said her brother. 'Summer holidays don't last all that long.'

'Theirs do,' said Maddy. 'They're here for a whole month.'

'Well, lucky old them,' said Patrick. 'We have to be satisfied with a day in Whitby or Bridlington, don't we?'

'You don't do too badly, neither of you,' said their mother, coming in from the kitchen and catching the tail end of the conversation. 'You don't go short of much. We're always too busy to have proper holidays anyway, if that's what you were saying. Your dad and I have been promising ourselves a weekend away for ages; happen to Llandudno or Colwyn Bay,' she added wistfully, 'but we never seem to be able to get round to it... Maddy, come along now, there's a good girl. Put that book down and come and give me a hand in the kitchen. You said you would and I don't usually have to remind you. It's your friend who's coming to tea, remember.'

'Sorry, Mam,' said Maddy. 'I'd just got to a good bit, you see, and then Patrick came in and started talking to me.'

'I like that!' replied Patrick. 'It was her, Mam, going on about me behaving myself while Jessie's here. Honestly, she's so worked up, anybody'd think it was a bloomin' princess coming for her tea.'

'Well, just think on that you treat our guest as though she is a princess,' said Clara. 'Are you ready now, Maddy?'

Reluctantly Maddy put down the book she had been reading and followed her mother into the kitchen. *Treasure Island* had been a birthday present from her brother; a boy's book really, she supposed, but she was enjoying it immensely.

It was true that she was in quite a lather of excitement about Jessie coming for tea. She and her mother had discussed at length what they should have to eat. They had decided on three sorts of sandwiches; salmon paste, egg and cress, and a special potted meat from the butcher's on the next block.

Maddy had insisted they should be cut 'fancy', in triangles instead of straight across, but Clara had refused to cut off the crusts. She believed that children should be encouraged to eat the crusts; her two had always done so. Then there were Clara's specialities; sausage rolls, home-baked gingerbread, curd tarts, and iced buns with cherries on top. She had been busy baking all morning. And as a party was not a proper party without a jelly, as far as Maddy was concerned, there was a quivering red jelly in a fancy shape – which, fortunately, had turned out perfectly from the jelly mould – to be served with tinned pears and evaporated milk.

Maddy set to her tasks with a will now, to make up for her former dilatoriness, helping her mother to arrange the sandwiches onto large plates and then to set the table in readiness for their guest; the best rose-patterned china cups and saucers today and the damask cloth because it was a special occasion.

Patrick had finished his work a little early – they were not very busy at the moment – and had had a wash and brush-up, as he called it. He was now sitting reading the daily newspaper, something he had done since he started work, showing himself to be a man of the world. And, like the other men, Isaac and William, he would sit and wait until the meal appeared on the table.

Jessie arrived promptly at half past four. Maddy had gone out to wait for her on the pavement and to bring her in. The shop was closed on Wednesday afternoon, so they could not enter that way, and Maddy thought her friend might be nervous of coming through the undertaker's yard on her own. Maddy noticed that Jessie had her pretty leaf-green dress on again underneath her short coat. Maddy was glad she had decided to wear her pale blue dress with the large white collar, one she usually wore only for very best. She wanted to look just as nice as Jessie and she felt that perhaps she did.

'Hello, Jessie.'

'Hello, Maddy.'

They greeted one another a little timorously at first; after all they were only quite new friends. But Maddy soon overcame her shyness.

'Come along,' she said, linking her friend's arm. 'I've been dying for you to come, and we're going to have a lovely tea. I've helped my mum to get it ready.'

Clara decided that they would start their meal almost straight away, after everyone had said hello to their guest. There was only the tea to be brewed, everything else was ready, and it would help to dispel any awkwardness that there might be if they were left to sit and smile at one another. Once the meal started Clara knew she could rely on Isaac and Patrick to keep the conversation going if Jessie proved to be a little shy. Her father-in-law and her son were alike in a number of ways, one being their ability to put people at their ease.

Jessie looked a little surprised when Isaac said, as he did at the start of every formal meal, 'Shall we say grace?' Probably it was something they did not do in their household, but she bowed her head dutifully with all the others.

'Nah then, let's tuck in, shall we?' said Isaac when they had all said 'Amen'. 'Help yerself to a few sandwiches, Jessie love, and a sausage roll. If you're not quick our Patrick'll have scoffed them all.'

'No...no, Grandad, that's not true,' replied Patrick. 'I'm on my best behaviour today.' He picked up a plate of sandwiches and one of sausage rolls, offering them to Jessie who was sitting opposite him. 'Jessie, do have one of these lovely salmon sandwiches,' he said politely. 'They are really extra special because Maddy has helped to make them with her own fair hands.'

They all laughed and the ice was broken as everyone helped themselves to sandwiches, and hot sausage rolls, straight from the oven.

'Well then, have you two lasses got any new jokes to share with us?' asked Isaac. 'You've been to see the Pierrots again this morning, haven't you?'

'Only for a little while,' replied Maddy. 'We didn't stay for it all, did we, Jessie? It started raining and everybody ran to shelter under the pier.'

'Aye, if wet, under the pier,' laughed Isaac. 'That's what they advertise. You can never tell what the weather's going to be like, but they carry on in th' open air as long as they can.'

'We decided to go home,' said Maddy. 'I thought I'd better come back and help Mum, and Jessie went to find her brother, didn't you, Jessie?'

'Yes, he was fishing on the pier, but he wouldn't go home. Samuel says a bit of rain never hurts anybody.'

'So how about those jokes?' said Patrick. 'I hope they're good ones.' He smiled encouragingly at Jessie, but she suddenly turned shy.

'I... I don't think I can remember any,' she said, 'but I expect Maddy can.'

'Yes, I've got a good one,' said Maddy. She thought for a moment, frowning slightly. 'Just let me think... Yes, I can remember. I saw two little boys paddling in the sea this morning... That's what the comedian said,' she explained. 'I don't mean that I actually saw them.'

'Come on, get on with it,' said Patrick. 'We know what you mean.'

She pulled a face at him. 'Well...one little boy said to the other one, "Haven't you got dirty feet?" And the other one said, "Well, we never had a holiday last year."'

'Very good,' said Clara, leading the round of applause.

'I didn't have a holiday last year, but my feet are lovely and clean,' said Patrick with a show of innocence.

'But you wash them, don't you?' said Jessie seriously. 'That little boy never washed his feet, you see, except when he went paddling. That's what's supposed to be funny...' She sounded rather puzzled.

'Yes, I understand, Jessie.' Patrick grinned at her and gave a slight wink, and Maddy, sitting opposite him, noticed that his eyes were kind and warm with not a hint of the impishness they held when he was teasing her. And she noticed that Jessie blushed bright pink beneath her freckles.

'I must go and see one of the shows myself,' said Patrick, 'when I have time. I've not been since I left school; I've been too busy working. But I used to love them when I was a little boy. Grandad used to take us, me and Maddy, didn't you, Grandad?'

'Aye, so I did,' said Isaac, 'and your dad as well, before you.'

'But there weren't any Pierrots when I was a lad, were there, Father?' said William. 'If you remember, those were the days of the minstrel shows. The Pierrot troupes have only been going for the last ten years or so, haven't they?'

'Yes, of course you're right,' agreed Isaac. 'I was forgetting. Minstrel shows were still all the rage when you were a lad,

William. And then Henry Morgan came along and started his troupe, Morgan's Merry Minstrels… They were a good troupe an' all,' he said, addressing his remarks to Maddy and Jessie. 'Negro minstrels, they called themselves – a minstrel's a sort of travelling singer – and they had black faces and they played banjos and tambourines.'

'You mean… they were black men, from Africa?' asked Jessie.

'No, they weren't really black,' laughed Isaac. 'I expect the very first ones were; they started off in America. But the ones we're talking about, they used to black their faces with burnt cork soaked in water; quite a messy business it must have been. Henry Morgan, he was the leader of the troupe. The leading man was always called the "Uncle", and he did all the organising. Aye, I got to know Henry Morgan quite well. We did a funeral for them when one of the men died sudden like, but that's just by the way. He's still going strong is Henry. He's about the same age as me and he's still active in the business.'

'But they're called "Uncle Percy's Pierrots" now,' said William. 'That's the troupe you've been watching, Jessie and Maddy, and Percy Morgan – the main man – he's Henry Morgan's son; he took over from his father.'

'Yes, that's right,' said Isaac. 'In the olden days – the black face days – there were only men in the troupe, but now they have women as well. All to the good, I reckon; it adds a bit of variety. And it's Percy's wife who plays the piano for them; Letty, she's called.'

'She acts as well, doesn't she, Maddy?' said Jessie. 'Do you remember? She was the dressed-up lady in that little play they did.'

'Aye, a sketch they call it,' said Isaac.

'Oh...a sketch then,' said Jessie. 'She was the lady that had two gentlemen friends.'

'Lucky lady,' said William and they all laughed.

'I like the costumes they wear,' said Jessie, who was becoming much more talkative now. 'Those white suits and pointed hats with pom-poms. The men and the ladies dress the same, don't they? Well, nearly the same. The ladies have dresses and the men have baggy trousers.'

'That's right,' agreed Isaac. 'Actually, Percy Morgan's a bit of an innovator in that respect – I mean he was the first to think of it,' he added, as the girls looked puzzled at his unusual word. 'Dressing the men and the women in the same garb, I mean. Come to that, it's quite a new idea to have any women in the troupe. Now if you were to go along to South Bay, near to t' Spa, and watch Will Catlin's troupe, he doesn't have women in his company at all.'

'His was the first Pierrot troupe to appear in Scarborough, wasn't it, Father?' asked William. 'Will Catlin's?'

'No...no, lad. He was nearly the first, mind. But it was actually a fellow called Tom Carrick,' replied Isaac. 'He was the first. His Pierrots had red pom-poms on their suits, and Will Catlin's have black ones.'

'Ours have black ones too,' said Jessie, with a knowledgeable air. 'I mean...the ones that we watch,' she added.

'Ours – I mean Uncle Percy's – isn't it the only one then?' asked Maddy. 'You mean there's lots of other Pierrot shows as well?'

'Aye, two others at least in Scarborough,' said her grandfather. 'Not just here, though; they're all over t' country now. They're in Bridlington and Filey and Whitby. And

Blackpool of course, and some o' t' resorts down south; Eastbourne and Margate and all them places. There's never been any ill feeling though, here in Scarborough, at least not as far as I know; happen just a bit of friendly rivalry between the troupes.

'Shall I tell you how it all started?' Isaac went on, pleased to have a captive audience in Maddy's new little friend Jessie. 'About why they wear them fancy costumes?'

'Yes, please,' said Jessie.

'Yes, go on, Grandad,' said Maddy. She had heard it all before, many times, but she did so love her grandad and never tired of hearing him talking about one of his favourite subjects.

Patrick affected a yawn behind his hand, which his grandad noticed, as he was probably intended to do.

'Less of yer cheek, young feller-me-lad,' Isaac reproved him, but with a laugh in his voice. 'You might not want to hear about it but these young ladies do. Just get on with yer tea and close yer ears up if you don't want to listen.'

'All right; sorry, Grandad,' grinned Patrick. 'Mam, isn't it time for the jelly and fruit now?'

So while Clara served the dessert Isaac told, once again, the tale of how the Pierrot troupes, which were now becoming part of the British seaside tradition, had begun. They were descendants of the group of travelling players, the 'commedia dell'arte' of Italy.

'You see there were these characters called Harlequin and Columbine, and Punchinello. As a matter of fact Mister Punch that you see on the sands – you know, Punch and Judy – well, he's a descendant of the Italian Punchinello; an ugly fellow with a hooked nose and a bad temper. And Harlequin and

Columbine, well, they were the two lovers; boyfriend and girlfriend, you see...

'And then France got hold of the story, and the French folk called them Pierrot and Pierette; and then they ended up here in Britain as our Pierrot shows, with the same white costumes as the French people dressed 'em in. And we hope they'll be here for many years to come.' Isaac gave a satisfied nod when he had come to the end of his tale, beaming at the two girls.

'Thank you,' said Jessie. 'That was all really interesting.'

After tea was finished Maddy helped her mother to clear the table, and Jessie, although of course she had not been asked, offered to help as well. Clara piled all the plates and dishes to one side, saying that she would tackle the washing-up later. The dining table was cleared and covered with a brown chenille cloth, which it always wore when it was not being used for dining, and they all sat round it to play card games; snap, beggar my neighbour, and happy families.

'I've had a lovely time,' said Jessie, glancing at the clock on the mantelshelf. 'Thank you very much for inviting me, Mrs Moon. I have really enjoyed it. My mother said she would come for me at seven o'clock.'

'We are very pleased you could come,' replied Clara. 'Perhaps you would like to come again sometime? You still have three weeks of your holiday left, haven't you?'

'Yes, thank you; I would like that.' Jessie turned to Maddy. 'Are you going down to the sands again tomorrow morning, Maddy? Shall I see you there?'

'I think Maddy will be busy here in the morning,' replied Clara. 'There are a few jobs that need doing.' Enough is enough, she was thinking. Jessie was a lovely little girl and an ideal friend for Maddy, but she did not want them living in one another's pockets. And Maddy needed to calm down a little and remember that life did not consist wholly of holidays and Pierrot shows.

'There's a sandcastle competition on Friday,' said Maddy. 'D'you think I could go to that, please? Uncle Percy is arranging it after the afternoon performance. If it doesn't rain, of course.'

'I hope he has checked that the tide is out then,' observed Clara. 'Yes, Maddy; of course you can go, provided you tidy your bedroom in the morning. That's her Friday job, Jessie,' she explained.

'Thanks, Mam,' said Maddy. 'I'm sure he'll have checked and made sure the tide'll be out... Oh, that'll be your mam...your mother,' she added, hearing a knock at the back door, the entrance from the yard. 'Shall we go and let her in, Jessie?'

'No, you stay here and find Jessie's coat for her,' said William. 'I'll go and open the door for Mrs Barraclough.'

When William opened the door he was surprised to see a strange young man standing there. About Patrick's age, he guessed; tall and dark with thoughtful brown eyes. He had expected to see Faith Barraclough and he could not have explained his slight disappointment.

'How do you do?' said the lad, for that was all he was really, despite his air of maturity. 'I am Samuel Barraclough. I have come to collect my sister.'

'Of course, of course,' said William heartily, shaking the boy's outstretched hand. 'How do you do? I'm William Moon, Maddy's father. Do come in; Jessie is just about ready.'

'What are you doing here?' asked Jessie at the sight of her

brother. 'I thought Mother was coming for me.'

'Well, that's a fine greeting,' said Samuel, with just a hint of a grin. 'Mother is busy with the twins. They were acting up a bit, at least Tommy was, so she's decided to put them to bed early.' He looked round at the rest of the company. 'How do you do, everyone? I am Samuel, Jessica's brother.'

Isaac and Clara shook hands with him as that was what he seemed to expect. 'I have met Maddy before, of course, on the pier,' he said, smiling at her. 'Hello again, Maddy.' She was pleased to see that this time his serious brown eyes lit up with a touch of friendliness.

'Hello,' she replied, hoping that nobody could see that she was blushing. He was such a good-looking lad.

'And I'm Patrick,' said Patrick, not to be outdone. 'How do, Samuel?'

'How do you do?' replied the other boy, shaking his hand. They managed a brief grin at one another, two fourteen-year-old boys, but poles apart in lifestyle and experience.

'By heck, he's a sober-sides, isn't he?' remarked Patrick, when the brother and sister had gone. 'He'd make a good undertaker,' he grinned. 'Wouldn't he, Grandad?'

'Aye, well, I suppose he looks more like one than you do,' laughed Isaac. 'But I dare say the lad was a bit overcome, meeting all these strange folk.'

'Oh, I don't think so,' said Clara. 'He seems a very self-possessed young man to me.'

Maddy was quiet, thinking that, indeed, Samuel Barraclough was very different from her cheeky irrepressible brother. But there was something about his earnestness that appealed to her.

And Jessie, walking home with Samuel and answering his

probing questions about all that had gone on in the Moon household, was thinking how very different from her own brother was Maddy's brother, Patrick. He was so lively and funny and good-natured, and she had decided that she liked him a lot.

Chapter Thirteen

It was on the Saturday of that same week that Percy Morgan and his troupe of Pierrots met together in Percy's lodgings to talk about the success – or otherwise – of their recent shows and to discuss future plans and tactics.

Percy and his wife, Letitia, his father, Henry, and three other members of the troupe were staying in Castle Road with Mrs Ada Armstrong, a warm-hearted woman whom Henry Morgan and his son had known for many years. The rest of the company had lodgings in Tollergate, not very far away. Several lodging-house keepers in that vicinity took only 'pros' as paying guests; those folk who were connected with the theatrical profession, either performing at one of the theatres in the town or on the sands in one of the Pierrot shows.

Saturday was known in the resort of Scarborough, and in other seaside resorts as well, as 'change-over day'. It was the day on which one lot of visitors left and another lot took their place; the day when the landladies changed the bedding and did not serve a midday meal (as most of them did on the other six days of the week) to enable them to get the house shipshape again for the incoming visitors. This rule, however, did not apply to Ada Armstrong or to her friend Mrs Ethel Bradbury, round the corner in Tollergate. Their lodgers would be staying put for several more weeks and both ladies, therefore, had served their guests a hearty meal of locally caught fish and crispy golden chips. And now, at two o'clock in the afternoon, the nine members of the troupe, plus Henry Morgan – who no longer performed but was still very active in the party – were gathered in Ada's comfortably cluttered parlour. It was rather a tight squeeze, but they appreciated her generosity in vacating her private little sanctum and, moreover, providing them with a cup of tea so strong that the spoons would almost stand upright.

Uncle Percy's Pierrots had given their usual morning performance and would be back again on the sands that evening, but they did not perform on Saturday afternoons as the beach would be pretty well deserted.

'Of course, you know what Will Catlin and his gang will be doing this afternoon, don't you?' said Percy to his fellow members whilst they were sipping their tea.

'Aye, he'll be driving around Scarborough in one o' them wagonettes,' replied his father. 'Him and all t' rest of his troupe, all dressed up in their costumes. And you can be sure they'll stop at t' railway station and chat to t' folk who are getting off the trains. There's nowt like getting yer oar in first, like; letting 'em know about his show and telling 'em it'll be summat they'll be sure to enjoy.'

'Well, jolly good luck to him, that's what I say,' replied Percy. 'He thought of it first, and it wouldn't be right to steal his thunder, but we will have to try and think of ways of promoting our own shows; we don't want to get left behind. Catlin's a great entertainer, that's for sure. And it isn't only today, Saturday, that they show themselves in the town. He insists on his troupe getting dressed up in their lodgings – full make-up an' all – and parading through the streets down to their pitch on the sands.'

'I don't think I would fancy the idea of doing that,' replied

Letitia, his wife. 'It's better that we should stick to our bathing huts to get changed in. When I've finished my act or my piano playing I prefer to be incognito. Of course there are some people who recognise you. I was in Boyce's store the other day and a lady came up to me and asked me if I was the one who played the piano for the Pierrots. So I said that I was and we had a nice little chat. But, like I said, I prefer to keep myself to myself when I'm not on the stage.'

Percy smiled at her. His wife was a reserved, self-contained sort of person, unlike many theatrical ladies – and men, too – who behaved in an extrovert manner both on and off the stage. Letty could play the coquette as well as anyone, as she did in some of their sketches, but only when she was acting. Normally she had eyes for no one else but him, and he felt the same way too. After more than eight years of marriage they were still devoted to one another and were the envy of many of their show business colleagues.

Letty had been playing the piano at a charity concert in a church hall in Bradford when he had first met her. He had been asked to sing, as he often was during the winter months, the time when he was not performing in Scarborough as part of his father's minstrel troupe. Letty had accompanied him as he sang 'Where e'er you walk', and they had fallen in love almost at first sight.

Letty – Letitia Rigby – aged twenty-two at the time of their meeting – had been working as an assistant in a milliner's shop, and Percy, some three years older, was a builder by trade. Both he and his father, Henry, had served their apprenticeship as builders, but neither of them had intended this to be their only profession. The reason was that they were 'stage-struck'...

And so, when his wife had died of a sudden attack of bronchitis, eight years previously, Henry, despite his sorrow, had decided to take the bull by the horns, so to speak, and do something which had always lingered at the back of his mind. He would never have taken this momentous step if his dear wife, Bertha, had lived. She had regarded it as a lot of nonsense and he had respected her opinion, knowing that it was up to him, as the breadwinner, to support her. But when there remained just himself and his only son Percy, aged seventeen, to consider, he knew that the time had come to pursue his dream.

After a suitable time of grieving – for both Henry and Percy were shocked and saddened by the loss of their wife and mother – Henry mooted the idea that they should form their own minstrel show. Percy had not needed any persuading. He had inherited his love of performing from his father and had a good baritone voice which he used to its best advantage in the chapel choir and at concerts. Henry sang, too, and was well known as something of a comic and could strum quite expertly on the banjo.

Consequently, Morgan's Merry Minstrels had been formed with the cooperation of a small group of like-minded friends and acquaintances – all men, no women at that time – from their home town of Bradford. Scarborough had been the resort of their choice and they had soon made their name there, setting up their pitch on the North Bay sands and performing three times daily – tides and weather permitting – throughout the summer months. During the winter they returned home and took whatever part-time work they could – as builders, joiners, barmen, shop assistants, road sweepers, delivery men – knowing that when the next summer came round they would return to the occupation that was nearest to their hearts.

At the time when Percy and Letty first met, during the winter of 1891, Percy and his father had been discussing various changes that they intended to bring about with regard to their troupe. No longer would it be 'Morgan's Merry Minstrels', a troupe of black-faced entertainers, but 'Uncle Percy's Pierrots'. Pierrots were white-faced performers – sometimes their faces were artificially whitened with zinc oxide – the very antithesis of the Negro minstrels, and they were, in fact, beginning to supersede them. Their ruffled white suits and pointed hats with black pom-poms were adding a touch of romance and novelty to the seaside resorts, and Percy and Henry had resolved not to be left behind. Moreover, Henry had decided, magnanimously, that it was time that he handed the reins over to his son, although he would continue to take part in a smaller way and to give advice when it was needed.

All thoughts of Pierrots and minstrels, though, fled out of Percy's mind for a while when he met Letty, the girl of his dreams. They enjoyed an idyllic courtship throughout the winter and were married a few months later in the spring of 1892. What was equally wonderful to Percy was that Letty shared his passion for the world of the theatre. She was a very competent pianist and she was delighted when Percy suggested that she should play for the newly formed group of Pierrots, which, in reality, consisted mainly of the original minstrels, but in a different guise. It was Letty's idea that they should include a few women in the troupe, although that was quite a novel concept. She had not wanted to be the sole woman amongst a totally male caste, and Percy agreed that the addition of a couple more ladies could only be advantageous. It was at Letty's advice, also, that he decided not to have his troupe members whitening their faces with substances which might well prove to be dangerous.

All in all Letty had been a great asset to Uncle Percy's Pierrots, as well as being a loving and loyal wife. Their only regret was that they had not been blessed with a family. Letty had had a miscarriage in the second year of their marriage, and after that they had waited and waited to no avail, and had finally resigned themselves to their childless state. But as they were all in all to one another it didn't matter as much as it might otherwise have done.

Now, in the summer of 1900, Percy was realising that there would need to be some changes if his troupe was to maintain its popularity; and, also, some incentives to ensure that the troupe members – seven of them, excluding himself, Letty and Henry – remained loyal to him. He had heard one or two murmurs, not exactly grumbles, but comparisons with other troupes which, in some ways, were more enterprising than their own.

That was why he had mentioned Will Catlin. The man was becoming a force to be reckoned with, that was for sure, although Percy did not wish to cause any ill feeling by pinching his ideas or setting up in direct opposition to him. Percy's troupe had its own band of loyal followers. His pitch on the North Bay, near to the pier, was far enough away from that of his rival. Catlin's was on a site on the other side of the headland, near to the Spa Theatre, one he had always favoured, and he, too, had his faithful supporters.

Will Catlin's name was becoming quite a byword in

Scarborough. And not only there; he also had a company which appeared at Bridlington, further down the coast, for a four- or five-week period between Easter and Whitsuntide. But Scarborough remained his chief centre of interest.

Percy had heard quite a lot about the man, although he had never been a friend of his or even an acquaintance; they were on nodding terms and that was all. Percy knew, though, that the young man – Catlin was a few years younger than himself – had been interested in the stage from an early age and had entertained as an amateur on concert platforms around Leicester, just as he, Percy, had done in Bradford. Having formed his first Pierrot troupe at an early age he had, thereafter, insisted that all his performers must be men. He was said to have very strict rules for his company and he was keen to present his boys, as he called them, as desirable bachelors. They did, indeed, cause several female hearts to flutter, and this ensured a keen following at the shows. Never must his Pierrots be seen walking arm in arm with a lady through the streets of Scarborough, even though some of the 'boys' had wives.

'No, I'm not suggesting that we should parade through the streets in our costumes,' Percy said, in answer to his wife's objections, although he knew that, were he to insist on it, she would gradually conform to the idea. 'That would be too blatant, but happen there are a few of Catlin's ideas that we might be able to use for ourselves.

'For instance, how about us having some photographs taken, as a group, and in ones and twos, and selling 'em before and after each performance? We could have one of you with your dogs, Nancy; and Barney and Benjy doing their tap dancing...'

'We would have to strike a pose though,' said Barney. He was the sleek dark-haired, pale-faced member of the duo who was, in fact, well known for striking poses. 'What I mean is, one has to keep very still to get a good clear photograph, so we wouldn't have to be jigging about.'

'Jigging about!' exclaimed his dancing partner, Benjy, with a touch of exasperation. 'Our dancing consists of a great deal more than jigging about, as you well know, Barnaby.'

Benjy was the other member of the duo, rosy-cheeked and with curly blonde hair, the very opposite, with regard to looks, of his partner. In spite of their different appearances many people assumed them to be brothers, which they were not. Barnaby Dewhurst and Benjamin Carstairs were just very good friends. They were both in their late twenties – unmarried – and had been with Percy's troupe for the last five years.

'Just a figure of speech, my dear,' replied Barney with a casual wave of his hand. 'You know what I mean so don't try to cause an altercation.'

'I am sure we will be able to arrange the two of you in a suitable pose,' said Percy with a wry grin. 'And of course we won't forget you, Susannah,' he added smiling at the young woman who was known as the 'soubrette' of the group.

Susannah Brown sang light-hearted songs in a somewhat shrill soprano voice; she was also a comedienne and the audiences appreciated the pert and rather impudent way she put over her act. Nobody was quite sure how old she was. In her mid-twenties, maybe; but she still acted and dressed as though she were seventeen or so, the age many people believed her to be until they came closer to her. At that moment she was leaning forward in her chair, gazing at Percy with wide blue eyes and a slightly open mouth as though hanging on his every word.

'You could pose charmingly with your teddy bear,' he said, 'or perhaps with a large basket of flowers. In fact I hope we will be able to have photographs taken of all of you. There's a firm in Holmfirth, Huddersfield way, that specialises in that sort of thing; picture postcards to send home from holiday. Bamforth, they're called. Of course I've left it too late for this year; I don't know why I didn't think of it before, but I've had a lot on me mind. Anyroad, I'll make enquiries as soon as we get back to Bradford. That is if everyone is agreeable...'

'Yes, of course we are...'

'Good idea...'

'It's worth a try...' There were mutterings of agreement from the rest of the troupe. Only Charlie Wagstaff, the character man, shook his head a little dolefully.

'I don't know as you'd want my ugly mug on a postcard,' he said, 'although I dare say it'd be all right for the rest of you.' He was the eldest member of the group, turned sixty years of age, but still very popular with audiences for his portrayal of different characters. A Chelsea pensioner, a policeman, or an old tramp; these were just some of his acts for which he dressed accordingly and always succeeded in bringing out the essence of the various characters. He did monologues too, specialising in such poems as 'Gunga Din', 'The Wreck of the Hesperus' and 'The Green Eye of the Little Yellow God'.

'Of course we want you, Charlie,' said Henry Morgan. Charlie had been with him for ages, ever since the days of the Negro minstrels. 'Don't talk so daft! You know what they say;

There's no show without Punch. And you're one of our mainstays, as you well know.'

'Hear, hear,' agreed Percy, and all the other members murmured in assent.

'Your impression of that pompous policeman, I've heard folks say they've never laughed so much in their lives,' Henry went on. 'And you look real grand dressed up as a Chelsea pensioner. It's a pity the postcards wouldn't be in colour though.'

'It's good of you to say so,' said Charlie, looking a mite embarrassed. 'But the fact of the matter is...I don't think I shall be with you, come next year.' They all appeared startled and looked at him questioningly. 'Aye, I'm thinking it's about time I retired, hung up me shoes, as they say. It's the missus, y'see, my Ada. She's been harping on a bit more than usual lately about me being away during t' summer. She's not getting any younger neither, and I reckon she's feeling a bit lonesome like. She's got the shop, of course, and that keeps her busy, but I'm thinking of packing in me job with the brewery an' all and helping her full-time in the greengrocer's shop.' Charlie worked as a barman during the autumn and winter when he was back home in Leeds and the family also owned a thriving little greengrocery. 'It's hard work for a woman, although I know she's got our Clive to help her and he sees to the buying an' all that. In a few years' time we'll be handing it all over to him and Mavis, then the missus and I can retire and enjoy our last years together.'

'Your last years?' echoed Henry. 'Good grief, Charlie! You're nobbut a spring chicken yet. I can give you a few years an' I'm not thinking of packing it in yet awhile. I don't do as much as I used to, though, and if that's the way you feel... But we shall miss you.'

'And it means we shall have to look out for another character actor, or summat o' t' sort,' said Percy. 'That's bad news, Charlie, but you must do whatever you think is best. As a matter of fact, I have summat else in mind that I want to tell you about. I'm working on it at the moment.' He looked round at them all. 'How would you feel about us carrying on as a troupe all through the winter? That is, if we can get the bookings, and that's what I'm trying to do just now. I've got a few contacts in Leeds, and Bradford, of course – with it being my home town – Halifax, Huddersfield, Sheffield... I've been concentrating on Yorkshire at the moment. Just small theatres, y'know, or even church halls and assembly rooms. They're glad of some entertainment during the winter months. They have repertory groups and amateur operatics an' all that, so I thought, why not us? Anyroad, I've put out a few feelers an' I've already had a few replies. So...what do you reckon to it?'

It seemed as though they were all in agreement apart from Charlie, who laughed. 'Seems as though I'm packing it in at the right time, don't it? The missus certainly wouldn't stand for that! But jolly good luck to you, Percy lad. I think it's a grand idea. That's how Catlin manages to keep his troupe together, isn't it, by getting bookings all through t' winter?'

'Yes, I admit that's where I got the idea,' said Percy. 'And I don't want to lose any of you... I know some of you have been casting your eyes elsewhere and I can't say I blame you. But let's give it a try and see how we go on.'

He saw Barney and Benjy, and Susannah exchange surreptitious glances and realised he had been right in his suspicions. They had been looking around at other troupes, but he hoped that this would provide sufficient encouragement for them to stay. All three of them could be temperamental at times, but they had acts which went down well with the audiences.

'It suits us fine, wouldn't you say so, Benjy?' Barney asked his partner.

'Ra-ther,' Benjy replied, 'especially as we've a few new routines to try out, haven't we, Barney?'

The duo were the only members of the troupe who were not from Yorkshire. They came from not far over the border, from Rochdale, but no one was quite sure what jobs they did when they returned to Lancashire at the end of each season. It was believed that both men still lived at home with their parents.

'And I think it's a wonderful idea,' enthused Susannah, fixing her blue-eyed gaze on Percy. 'Thank you, thank you, Percy my love. It's just what I've been hoping for.'

Susannah's home was in Halifax. She was a shop assistant and usually managed to find casual work when she was not on the stage, and she shared the home of her sister and brother-in-law. No one knew why she was still unmarried; like the tap-dancing duo she played her cards very close to her chest. But Letty, who had probably come to know her better than anyone else, had gathered that she had suffered an unhappy love affair and had been badly let down. Consequently she was mistrustful of men and her friendships with them, though not infrequent, were of short duration.

'Good, good,' said Percy. 'How about you, Pete and Nancy?' Percy, in fact, had already mentioned his plans to Pete, who might be called his second-in-command, and he already knew that he and his wife were in full agreement. 'You think we would be making the right move, do you? It's a big step, but I'm hoping it's the right one for us.'

'Yes, we're both of us right behind you, Percy,' said Nancy.

Peter and Nancy Pritchard were a childless couple, both in their early forties. Their home was in Bradford and they had been with Percy almost since the Pierrot show had begun. They were both good all-rounders, the sort of performers who were an asset to a group, being able to dance, sing and act, in addition to which Pete was the comedian and Nancy had her act with the performing dogs. Pete was also the 'bottler', collecting the money at each performance and exchanging wisecracks with the crowd in his inimitable manner. It was well know that they had private means, or were 'not wi' out a bit o' brass', as Yorkshire folk might say. They owned a detached house in Baildon. Pete did not seek employment during the winter, but used his leisure time to help out with amateur dramatic performances, and to write humorous articles, some of which were published by newspapers and magazines.

The only other member of the troupe was Frank Morrison, who was also a man of several talents, the chief of which was as a musician. He played both the banjo and the concertina and could sing quite passably.

'And how do you feel about this idea, Frank?' Percy asked him now. 'Or perhaps I should say, how will your wife feel about it?'

'Oh, she'll get used to it no doubt,' said Frank, grinning. 'She hasn't much choice, has she, if I say it's what I intend to do? And I'm right behind you an' all, Percy. The wife's got her own little business anyroad, so there'll be no need for her to complain about what I'm doing.'

Hilda Morrison ran a second-hand clothes shop – a rather exclusive one, though, Frank always said – on the outskirts of York. The rest of the troupe had seen her only occasionally when she paid a rare weekend visit to Scarborough to see her husband. He was not noted for his faithfulness to his wife and was often to be seen about the town with a lady on his arm, a different one each week or fortnight. But Hilda was by no means the downtrodden little wife. She was a striking-looking woman in her mid-forties, Frank being a few years older, and it seemed more than likely that they each went their own way, keeping up their marital status mainly for appearance's sake.

'Very good. We all seem to be agreed then that this is the way ahead,' said Percy. 'I shall keep you all informed about our plans, and I'm hoping we will be able to get enough bookings to keep us busy for the best part of the winter.'

'It'll involve a lot of travelling, won't it?' said Nancy. 'To-ing and fro-ing across Yorkshire. You're not thinking of going any further afield, are you, to Lancashire...or to the Midlands or the south of the country?' Anywhere south of Sheffield, say, which was on the very fringe of the West Riding, was foreign territory to most of them.

'No, not yet at any rate,' smiled Percy. 'But who knows what might happen if we find we make a success of it. Aye, it'll mean a good bit of travelling, but we'll be on the move on Sunday, won't we, like the rest of the theatrical folk?' It was a well-known fact that the trains and railway stations, especially the junctions like Crewe or York were crowded on Sundays with travelling companies moving from one booking to the next.

'Ooh, it all sounds terribly exciting!' said Susannah, clapping her hands together like a little girl. 'I can hardly wait!'

'Do you intend us to perform as Pierrots?' asked Pete. 'You know, in our Pierrot costumes? Would that be appropriate, do you think, when we're not at the seaside?'

Percy scratched his head. 'Aye, I know what you mean, Pete, and it's summat I've been puzzling about. Happen we could do an opening number dressed in our costumes – and a closing one an' all, maybe – but wear different clothes for the rest of the acts. And if anyone can think of a suitable name for us in the winter months rather than "Uncle Percy's Pierrots" I'll be glad to hear of it. I've been wracking me brains but I've not come up with anything yet.'

'Very good, boss,' said Frank, giving a mock salute. 'We'll put our thinking caps on.'

'Talking about costumes,' said Letty, 'I can't help thinking that ours are not quite as fresh-looking and crisp as they used to be. Of course, I know we've had them a good few years, but they need a lot of keeping up to, washing and ironing and starching them.'

'And every time they are washed some of the life goes out of them, doesn't it?' said Nancy. 'Yes, Letty, I agree with you. Maybe it's time we were thinking of replacing them. Is that what you have in mind?'

'Hey, steady on! Hold yer horses!' Percy broke in. 'We're not made of money. I think the ones we've got will see us through to the end o' t' season. And in the meantime happen we can be thinking about new ones. Had you got anywhere in mind, Letty, love? We sent away for the last lot and I know some of 'em don't fit as well as they might.'

'As a matter of fact I do know of someone,' said Letty. 'There's a little shop near the bottom of Eastborough, quite near to the Market Hall, and I know that the lady who owns it is a really skilled dressmaker. She altered a skirt and jacket for me soon after we arrived. I'm afraid they both wanted letting out a little…' She laughed, patting at her hips, slightly more rounded now than when Percy had first met her. 'Miss Montague, she's called, Louisa Montague. She's quite an elderly lady now but she's still making fashionable garments; they're in show in the window. She has some younger assistants, of course. So I thought perhaps we could give her a try. She'll be more reasonable, I'm sure, than the big firms.'

'Sounds like a good idea,' said Percy. 'And I trust your judgement as always, my dear.' He noticed that Charlie Wagstaff, who had earlier announced his intention of retiring, had gone rather quiet and pensive-looking. Was he having second thoughts already? wondered Percy. He had always loved being involved in everything the Pierrots did or planned to do.

'Everything all right, Charlie?' he asked in an aside, as the older man was sitting quite near to him.

'Aye… I'm all right,' Charlie replied. 'I'm just sitting here and listening, quietly like. It'll be strange not to be a part of it all no more, but don't you worry; I'm doing the right thing. I don't think I could cope with all that dashing about, Bradford one week, Barnsley the next and all that carry-on. And I know Ada'd tell me it was too much for me. We'll come and watch you though, me and the missus, when you're performing in Leeds. We shall insist on t' best seats, mind.'

'You'll be the guests of honour, Charlie,' Percy told him. 'And we will be holding a benefit performance for you, of course, towards the end of your time here, you can be sure of that.'

It was the custom amongst seaside entertainers to hold benefit concerts at the end of the holiday season, the proceeds going to the performer who had been named for that particular evening. He – or she – often received gifts from patrons and from delighted members of the audience in addition to the benefit money. It was not something that Percy often did, believing that his artistes received sufficient reward for their efforts, although he sometimes held a benefit performance and gave the proceeds to a worthwhile charity. However, he felt that Charlie was worthy of receiving such an honour. And there were 'Hear, hears' from the rest of the caste.

'Well, I never expected that,' said Charlie, and Percy could see that his kindly brown eyes, a little faded now with age, were starting to fill up with tears. 'But I'll not say no to it. Thank you... Thanks very much indeed. I'll invite the missus to come for it an' all. She'll be tickled pink, will my Ada.'

'And how about a real slap-up farewell concert during our last week?' suggested Henry Morgan. 'For the local folks, I mean, rather than the visitors, although we can't keep 'em away if they want to come. I know the landladies would appreciate it, an' if it were Friday night, the guests'd be getting ready to go home the next day.'

'Good idea, Father,' said Percy. 'Best bibs and tuckers for that an' all, of course. By that I mean evening dress, and happen a slightly different programme from our usual Pierrot routine. A foretaste of what we'll be doing when we start our concert party. Now – does anyone have any other matter they'd like to bring up? Any more ideas?'

'Song sheets,' said Frank. 'That's something else that Catlin's troupe has. Song sheets with the words of all the songs. They sell 'em for a penny or a penny ha'penny. Perhaps we could do that, come next year?'

'Mmm... I don't see why not,' said Percy. 'But if we sold the music as well as the words, that'd be even better,' he pondered. 'Anyway, thank you, Frank. Something else for me to look into.'

'I must say that the sandcastle competition was a great success,' said Susannah. 'The children all enjoyed it, and we enjoyed watching them as well. Do you intend to have another one, Percy?'

'Yes, in a couple of weeks' time,' he replied. 'I must admit it was very popular and it was grand to see the kiddies' happy faces, bless 'em.'

He smiled fondly, remembering particularly the golden-haired little girl and her friend with the fiery red hair who had won the second prize. Those two were on the front row of the audience at many of the performances. Percy found himself looking out for them and missing them if they were not there.

Chapter Fourteen

'We'll win next time. You just see if we don't,' said Maddy to Jessie after the prizes had been awarded for the best sandcastle in the competition.

'Aren't you pleased that we've come second?' asked Jessie. 'I think we've done really well.'

'And we helped as well, didn't we, Tilly?' said Tommy. 'You couldn't 've done it without us, could they, Tilly?'

Tilly shook her head, clinging tightly to her bar of Fry's chocolate with the picture of five boys on the wrapper, which was her prize. The prizes that had been handed out were really only tokens, the main object of the competition being the enjoyment in taking part and the honour of winning. The first-prize winners had each been given a slightly larger bar of chocolate, that was the only difference, and all the children who entered were given a lollipop.

'It's a splendid castle,' said Faith Barraclough, who had stayed with the children to await the results at the end of the afternoon. 'You mustn't be disappointed because you didn't win first prize, Maddy. And, as you say, there is always another time. You can try again. But it's been great fun, hasn't it?'

'Yes, it has,' agreed Maddy. 'I'm not really all that disappointed. I'd just like us to have come first, that's all. 'Specially as it was those boys who won. They can dig faster than us and get deeper.'

The winners were two brothers who had been building

quite near to Maddy and Jessie, and the twins, of course, who had insisted on helping. During the snippets of conversation they had had with them they had learnt that the boys were on holiday from Darlington and would be going home the following day.

'Perhaps we could ask your Patrick to come and help us next time,' suggested Jessie, and Maddy noticed that her friend turned a little pink as she mentioned his name.

'Oh no, I don't think that's a good idea at all,' retorted Maddy. 'We can manage perfectly well without him. You don't know what he's like. If we won he would say it was because of him. I'd never hear the last of it. Anyway, he might be working. He can't just take time off whenever he feels like it, you know... What about your Samuel, though?' she added casually, as though she didn't really care either way. 'D'you think he might be interested?' She liked Jessie's brother and hoped she would see him again before very long.

'He wasn't interested this time, was he?' said Jessie. 'All he thinks about is his fishing and his bloomin' old fossils. No; I don't think we want my brother there either, not if we can't have yours.' She sounded a trifle peeved and Maddy knew that it was because, secretly, Jessie liked Patrick.

'Why don't you ask both of them?' said Mrs Barraclough with a knowing smile. 'You never know; Patrick might be able to spare the time. I'm sure your grandfather would let him have an hour or two off, wouldn't he, Maddy? And I feel sure Samuel won't want to be left out of things. Maybe you would be able to have two teams then?'

'You mean...our family and yours?' asked Maddy. 'But that would be four against two...' And she certainly didn't want to work just with Patrick.

'Not necessarily,' said Mrs Barraclough. 'It was only an idea. You could have two teams of three... Provided the boys are allowed to enter,' she added as an afterthought. 'They might be considered too old.'

'Let's go and ask Uncle Percy,' said Maddy. 'Quick, there he is; I think he's ready to go home.' She set off running across the beach, with Jessie following her, to where Percy and his wife, Letty, had just emerged from the bathing hut where they changed back into their ordinary clothes.

They looked quite different when they were not in their Pierrot costumes. When Percy took off his pointed hat you could see that he was going bald on top and the rest of his fairish hair was turning grey. He had quite an ordinary face, but one that was able to change in an instant from serious to jovial. When he sang his songs about the sea and fishermen, or love songs to a lady he could look suitably sombre or romantic, but that expression could be replaced, very quickly, by one of jollity and friendliness.

When he saw the two little girls running towards him and Maddy shouting, 'Uncle Percy' – that was what he liked to be called – he smiled broadly at them and his pale blue eyes shone in a friendly welcoming manner.

'Yes, that's me,' he grinned. 'And what can I do for you two young ladies? Maddy, isn't it? And Jessie?' He prided himself on learning the names of the children who made up their audience whenever it was possible. 'You made a lovely sandcastle, the pair of you. A pity you were just pipped at the post, but better luck next time, eh? Although it's not the winning that's important, is it? It's the taking part.'

'That's what my mother says,' said Jessie, feeling more bold about speaking to him when she had her confident friend,

Maddy, with her. 'And we're staying for a few more weeks, so we can have another try next time, can't we? Maddy lives here though, in Scarborough, don't you, Maddy?'

Percy already knew that. He had made enquiries and discovered that the little golden-haired girl was the granddaughter of Isaac Moon, the undertaker. He recalled that many years ago when one of their troupe had died suddenly – it was in the days of the minstrels, of course – Isaac Moon had organised the funeral for them. It was Percy's father, Henry, though, who had had most contact with them; but Percy remembered meeting William, the son, and his wife, Clara, when they had not been married very long. A nice family.

'Yes, I know your grandfather, Maddy,' said Percy, 'and your father and mother. I met them a long time ago before you were born. Now...what was it you wanted to ask me?'

'When you have the next sandcastle competition...' Maddy began. Then she hesitated a moment. 'You are going to have another one, aren't you?'

'Oh yes, most certainly we are. In a couple of weeks' time, I hope.'

'Oh, that's all right then. Well, we were wondering, me and Jessie, if our brothers could take part in it as well. Or are they too old?'

'How old are they?' smiled Percy.

'Fourteen.' It was Jessie who replied. 'Both of them. My brother and Maddy's, they're both fourteen. My brother, Samuel, still goes to school. We could manage without them,' she added, 'couldn't we, Maddy? But we thought it might be nice if they could be in it as well. We enjoyed it so much...'

Percy looked at his wife and they both smiled.

'I don't see any reason why not,' said Letty. She was a pretty lady with dark curls and kind brown eyes. 'They could give you a hand, why shouldn't they? It is supposed to be for children, of course...' But both she and Percy had seen grown-ups helping in a surreptitious way, doing the more strenuous digging or adding a few final embellishments, although this was taken into consideration in the final judging. But what did it matter? It was meant to be fun for all the family.

'And you two would be the ones in charge, wouldn't you?' said Percy, with a twinkle in his blue eyes.

'Yes, of course we would,' said Maddy, although she was wondering what her brother would have to say about that. 'So long as they can help us if they want to. Actually, we thought we might have two teams. It's something we have to sort out,' she added seriously.

'Yes, I can see that's a matter of vital importance,' agreed Percy, nodding in a thoughtful way. Then he grinned. 'Well, off you go then, the pair of you. We'll see you soon. And you tell your brothers, the more the merrier.'

Both Patrick and Samuel showed an initial reluctance to the idea of taking part in a sandcastle competition.

'Kids' stuff!' Patrick had remarked scathingly to Maddy; and Jessie reported that Samuel's reaction had been pretty much the same.

'I am far too busy,' he had said, 'to take part in such trivial pursuits.'

Nevertheless, by the time the day of the contest arrived, two and a half weeks later, both boys had agreed to come along and lend a hand. Isaac had said that of course Patrick could have a few hours off. They were not very busy at that time, summer being the time when folk stayed reasonably healthy.

And Samuel decided he was not too busy after all. There had been arguments, albeit friendly ones, about the fair division of the two teams, it being agreed that one team of six would be too many.

'Boys against girls,' Patrick suggested, but that was soon overruled.

'Because you knew we'd win,' scoffed Patrick to his sister. 'We're bigger and stronger than you.'

'No, that's not the reason at all,' she argued. 'Anyway, Uncle Percy would take that into consideration at the judging.'

One family against the other would have meant four against two, which was unbalanced. Eventually it was decided to have two teams of three; Patrick, Jessie and Tommy in one, and Samuel, Maddy and Tilly in the other.

Maddy was quite excited at the thought of spending more time with Samuel, although she was a little in awe of him. He seemed so clever and grown up and she wondered if she would be able to think of things to say to him. But when they were involved in the task of castle building there was not much opportunity to have long conversations.

Samuel had been working on a grand design, even though he had at first scorned the idea. But he had come to the conclusion that if a job was worth doing, it was worth doing well. If he was to take part at all then he must make sure that his team was the winning one. Maddy, when she was told about it, was quite happy to go along with his suggestion of a castle with not just one, but several turrets, and a surrounding moat, resembling the Tower of London. She had, of course, not seen that building, only heard of it, but Samuel had seen it on a visit to London. He had also asked his father, when he had come on a fleeting visit to Scarborough the previous weekend, to bring his toy cannons with him – long discarded as playthings, but still kept as mementoes of his childhood – and he had even constructed a Traitor's Gate out of wooden spills.

The castle of the other team, that of Patrick, Jessie and Tommy, was nowhere near as elaborate. Patrick, who had heard from Jessie that her brother was working on something special – she had sneaked a look at his supposedly secret plans when he was not there – had tried to think of something comparable. Then, Why not Scarborough Castle? he thought, seeing that it was right there on top of the cliffs for them to copy. The facsimile which they built was, indeed, a good representation and they were awarded second prize for being topical and showing originality. But Samuel, Maddy and Tilly were the undoubted winners. Everyone agreed it was a magnificent sandcastle and Samuel was not unstinting with his praise of his two helpers.

'You have worked like a Trojan, Maddy,' he told her. 'I couldn't possibly have done it without you, and you, of course, Tilly.' Maddy didn't need to ask him what he meant. They had been learning about the hard-working Trojans and the wooden horse at school, so she was pleased at the compliment. She was, indeed, very tired and red-faced with all the exertion. Her arms ached with the effort of digging and her hair had lost its ribbon and was all over the place.

'See, here's your pretty green ribbon, Maddy,' said Mrs Barraclough, picking it up from the sand. 'Let me tie your hair up again. Goodness me, child! You've tired yourself out, haven't you? Never mind; you'll feel better when you've had a nice drink and something to eat.'

They were all going back to the Barracloughs' lodgings to have tea, which Maddy thought was a wonderful ending to a happy afternoon. Regrettably they said goodbye to their works of art. All the sandcastles had been built near to the sea wall, to keep them out of danger from the encroaching sea for as long as possible. They were still standing upright, but they all knew that if they were to return in an hour or two the sea would have done its worst. It was far better to remember them as they were, and fortunately Faith had had the presence of mind to bring along their Kodak camera and take a few photographs. That was just one memorable event amongst many that the two families enjoyed during that summer of 1900. It seemed, especially to the children, looking back on it, that there had been days and days of endless sunshine. They knew, of course, that there had been wind and rain, and occasionally, as August drew to a close, the mists that Scarborough was accustomed to. A 'sea fret', the locals called it. But Maddy chose to remember only the sunshine and the friendships she had enjoyed during those few weeks in the summer, before things started to go wrong.

Faith Barraclough, also, looked back on those few weeks as an idyll, a most welcome respite from the humdrum reality of her life back in York. For a short while she had been able to leave her problems behind her and to enjoy herself in the company of her children and her new friends, the Moon family. She had been happy, she had laughed a lot, and Jessica, the most sensitive of all her brood, had remarked to her mother how nice it was to see her smiling so much.

Edward had been to visit them for only one weekend, and that, Faith knew, was a duty visit; the children might well have asked questions if he had not come at all. As it was, she was aware that they were not overjoyed to see their father and showed little enthusiasm for his presence; apart from the exuberant Tommy who was full of stories of all the exciting things they had done and were going to do. Samuel had made use of his father's visit by asking him to bring some necessary embellishments for his castle; and he did deign to show his father the master plan, a secret he had not divulged to his mother.

She wondered if Samuel would always regard the female sex as the one of lesser importance, in the way his father had always done. The tendency was there in her elder son, but she had noticed a certain softening of his attitude over the last few weeks, especially in his dealings with little Maddy. What a delightful child she was, to be sure. Even Samuel had taken notice of her; more than that, he had really seemed to like her. He had previously treated girls of any age with indifference, apart from the soft spot he had always had for his little sister, Tilly. If there was a chink in his armour it was his fondness for Tilly; and Faith thought she had seen the chink widen a little more when he met and came to know Maddy. She feared her husband's influence on the boy, but Samuel surely could not fail to notice the deepening rift between his parents, and she trusted him to be able to evaluate the situation without prejudice.

It was a morning in mid-September and Faith was alone in their home in a leafy suburb, just outside the walls of the city of York. It was a large greystone house in a pleasant avenue near to the road which led on to Knaresborough. From the upper front windows you could see the towers of the Minster – Faith was looking towards them now from her bedroom window –

and from the back ones the view was across the rolling plains that was the Vale of York. They had lived in the house for sixteen years, ever since she and Edward had married.

She had believed she would be happy with Edward. She had known him for many years. He was the son of family friends of her parents and she had grown up admiring the handsome young man who was four years older than herself. The age difference was too great at first, and so he had taken little notice of her until she was seventeen years of age and developing into a beautiful young woman. That was not her own estimation of herself. She remained modest and self-effacing although she could not be unaware that she had many admirers. It was Edward Barraclough, though, for whom she had long had a fondness, who won her hand and her heart. Both sets of parents were delighted, believing it to be an ideal match. They were married when she was twenty-one and he was twenty-five.

She had realised before less than a year had passed that what Edward wanted was a presentable wife – one who was docile and knew her place – to accompany him to functions and to dinner parties in the houses of his influential friends, and to act as hostess for the reciprocal gatherings in their own home. With the help of servants of course, because Edward was already climbing fast in the banking world and commanding quite a substantial salary. The bonus for Edward was that his wife was not merely presentable, she was beautiful; and he did not stint on the amount he let her spend – indeed, encouraged her to spend – on clothing and items of luxury for their home. She wanted for nothing in the material sense, but she soon learnt that Edward was self-centred, arrogant, and not at all loving or affectionate.

He had been attentive at first during their period of courtship, but after he had wooed and won her his interest in her had gradually waned. They had slept in the same bed at first and she had become accustomed to his unemotional way of making love. It seemed always as though his mind was elsewhere. Consequently, this was something she had come to tolerate rather than enjoy, and when he suggested that they should have separate beds and then, later, separate rooms she had agreed without question. He needed more privacy, he said, and he was sure that she did too. As the house was plenty large enough she had been more than happy to concur.

She knew, of course, that he was not faithful to her. His frequent absences from home confirmed this in her mind, but she had not bothered to find anything out about what he did or his whereabouts when he was not at home. She had become as indifferent to him as he was to her. Both sets of parents, hers and Edward's, living on the other side of York, knew nothing of the state of their marriage, or if they did they had chosen not to become involved. Faith could not say that she was happy with the situation; how could she be? But she had built around herself a wall of complacency and detachment so that nothing Edward did could touch her. In truth, she knew she had little to complain about in her husband, apart from his total indifference to her. He did not bully or beat her as she knew some husbands did, nor did he lose his temper or criticise her unduly. Many women, she knew, might envy her comfortable lifestyle and her elegant clothes. Only she knew how empty her life would be were it were not for her children.

It was only when she got away from her home that she became fully aware of what she was missing. Her outer shell of aloofness and self-restraint started to crumble as she began to really enjoy herself. As it had done during those few glorious weeks in the summer when she and the children had met the Moon family…

She sat down on her bedroom chair, looking once again at the photographs she had taken during the happy times they had spent together on the beach. Tilly and Tommy paddling at the edge of the sea; Jessica and Maddy, who had become bosom pals, with their arms around each other's shoulders; and the ones of the sandcastle competition which they had all enjoyed, even Samuel. Most particularly Samuel, she smiled to herself, as his team had won, and her elder son always strived to be a winner.

There they were, Samuel, Maddy and Tilly, looking pleased and proud, with Percy Morgan – Uncle Percy – standing behind them. He had asked if he could be on the photograph. What a charming and friendly man he was and popular with the children and grown-ups alike. Then he had posed with Patrick, Jessie and Tommy, the team which had come second, realising that Tommy, particularly, might be disappointed if they were left out.

There were very few photos of Faith herself; only one that Maddy had insisted on taking – after being given strict instructions to hold the camera still – of Faith, Jessie and the twins; and another, taken by Jessie, which included Maddy. She was sorry that there were even fewer of William and Clara. They had always been hard at work whilst she had been taking her ease with the children on the sands.

There were two group photographs, though, taken at the rear of the Moons' house. They had all gone back to enjoy a tea party there after attending the benefit concert which had been held for Charlie Wagstaff, the character man, who was retiring from the company of Pierrots. Grandfather Isaac had taken one of the photographs of the families, standing in two rows with the children at the front. They were all smiling broadly at the camera; William, Clara and Patrick, Faith and Samuel, and Bella Randall at the back; with Jessie, Maddy, Tommy and Tilly on the front row. Then William had changed places and acted as the photographer so that his father could be included. Faith had wondered at the time why Bella, who was the only one who was not 'family' had not volunteered; but she guessed that the woman could not resist taking her share of the limelight when the occasion arose.

Faith had found herself developing a mild antipathy to Bella the first time she met her, which was when Clara had invited her to visit the shop and view the merchandise. She had tried to conquer her instinctive dislike – she always sought to see the best in people whenever she could – telling herself that there was no reason for her to feel that way; she did not even know the woman. But when she was in her company again, at the tea party, Faith knew that her feelings had not changed; indeed, they were intensified. For one thing, she was aware of the animosity between Bella and Isaac Moon and, likewise, between the woman and little Maddy; although the unfriendly vibrations seemed to be coming mainly from Bella. She was sure there must be a reason for this; some secret hidden in the past, maybe. Both Isaac and Maddy were, to her mind, most friendly and likeable, and she could not understand why Bella should be hostile towards them.

She had also noticed that Bella harboured a fondness – possibly a good deal more than a fondness – for William Moon. There were times, Faith had noticed – as she observed the woman surreptitiously – when her dark eyes smouldered with passion and desire as she looked at him. But William had seemed to be unaware of her regard; so did his wife. Clara had told her that Bella was a family friend and she had worked at the shop ever since it had opened five years ago. She had become much more than a shop assistant, and so Clara liked to include her now and again at family gatherings to show how much she was appreciated. And it was clear that the two women, Clara and Bella, did appear to get along very well together; there was no sign of animosity in their relationship.

But Faith had a suspicion that all was not as it seemed. Could it be that William and Bella Randall had known one another rather well at one time, unbeknown to Clara? She was a striking-looking woman, with jet black hair swept back in a chignon, lustrous dark eyes and a well-rounded figure. She almost had the look of a gipsy, and Faith could not help but wonder about her background and her past.

But whatever had taken place, maybe long years ago, there was one thing of which Faith was sure; William Moon now had eyes for no one but his beloved wife. They were a loving and well-matched couple, perfectly attuned to each other's ideas and feelings. Faith had felt a pang of envy as she watched them together, but at the same time she wished for them continued happiness in their marriage. Would, though, that she could experience the same affinity with Edward as her new-found friends had found with one another.

Faith was not immune to the appeal of the opposite sex, although she knew she would never be tempted to behave in the same way as her husband was doing. William Moon was a most attractive and amiable man. Reasonably handsome – although she supposed Edward was the more striking as far as looks were

concerned – but it was William's personality that she had found
so pleasing. He was kind and modest, not as outspoken as
either his father or his son, but not without a wry sense of
humour. In short, she had liked him a lot and, moreover, in the
time she had spent with him she had felt that he liked her too.
But she knew only too well that Clara was the love of his life.

Charlie Wagstaff's benefit performance had been held on a
Wednesday afternoon during the last week of August.

'Wouldn't it be grand if we could all go?' Clara had said to
her husband. She enjoyed the Pierrot shows although not with
the same intensity as did her father-in-law and her daughter;
but she had been only once this year, to an evening
performance way back at the beginning of the season. 'Maddy
has kept on and on about it. Jessie and all her family are
going, so I thought I could ask them to come back here for tea
afterwards. What do you think, Will?'

William pondered. 'I'll see what my father has to say. At the
moment I can see no reason why we shouldn't go, Dad an' all
if he can manage it. Aye; unless somebody kicks the bucket
unexpectedly we should be able to spare the time. We've been
fairly quiet these last few weeks as you know.'

'I thought about asking Bella along as well,' said Clara,
'seeing as it's on a Wednesday afternoon and the shop will be
closed.' William looked at her keenly, raising his eyebrows in
an unspoken query. 'Yes, I know what you mean,' she went
on. 'I know you said I hadn't to get too intimate, like, with
her, but she's been a good friend to me. And it's ages since she
was included in one of our get-togethers. Of course I know
your father's not too keen on her, though I've never really
understood why.'

'Oh…just a clash of personalities, I dare say,' replied William with a shrug. 'I think he regarded her as something of an upstart at first when she started working for us. Yes…that's all right with me, love. Invite Bella by all means. You'll go to the show though, won't you? I mean, with you suggesting they all came back for tea?'

'Yes, of course I will. I shall prepare everything well in advance, then I'll only have the tea to brew and odds and ends to finish off when we get back. It'll be a nice farewell for the Barraclough family, won't it? They'll be going back the following weekend. It's amazing, isn't it, how time flies?'

'It is indeed,' said William with a sigh.

'The boy I love is up in the gallery,
The boy I love is looking down at me…'

Several heads looked sideways and people smiled at the little golden-haired girl who was joining in so exuberantly with the singing. Susannah, the soubrette, dressed in a red satin gown full of frills and flounces, in emulation of the great music hall star Marie Lloyd had invited the audience to join in with the second chorus.

'…There he is, can't you see, waving of his handkerchief,
Merry as a robin that sits on a tree.'

'That was good; I enjoyed that,' said Maddy as Susannah curtsied and waved her hand, then blew kisses to the audience and disappeared behind the curtain at the back of the stage. It was the end of the first half of the show.

'Yes, I could see you did,' said Jessie. 'You have a really nice voice, haven't you, Maddy? I've noticed you singing before. Do you have singing lessons, or are you in a choir or something?'

''Course I'm not,' Maddy laughed. 'I just enjoy singing, that's all.'

'You're just as good as that Susannah,' said Jessie, nodding in a decided manner. 'I say, Maddy, perhaps when you're old enough you could join the Pierrot troupe. You could be one of Uncle Percy's Pierrots.'

Maddy smiled. She wasn't sure whether her friend was joking or not. It was an interesting idea – she rather liked the sound of it – but she didn't think her parents would agree. 'Mmm...perhaps,' she said, 'but somehow I don't think so. My mam and dad'll want me to do...something else.'

'Have you thought though, really, what you want to do when you leave school?' asked Jessie. 'You said that Patrick had to go and work for your father and grandfather. You don't think you will have to do – you know – what they do, will you?'

'Go into the undertaking business,' said Maddy, grinning. 'I know you still think it's weird, Jessie, but I've got used to it, y'see. Patrick didn't mind; in fact it was what he wanted to do. But my mam has already said that she doesn't want me to do it, and neither do I. They would never make me do something I didn't like.'

'What would you like then?'

'Oh...to work in a shop, I think. I could work in our shop. P'r'aps Mam thinks I'll do that, but the trouble is I don't like Bella very much.' She glanced briefly behind her to where Bella, a couple of rows further back, was chatting to her mother and Jessie's mother.

'No, I didn't think you did,' replied Jessie. 'I've noticed.'

'She doesn't like me much either,' said Maddy. 'I don't know why… Anyway,' she shrugged, 'I don't really bother about it any more. I might learn to be a dressmaker. That's what my mam did before she was married, and she still makes nice dresses and things when she has time. What about you? Are you still thinking of going to that college where you'll learn to type an' all that?'

'I expect so. It's six more years though for me, before I leave school.' Jessie sighed. 'It's too far off to think about really…' She broke off as Samuel and Patrick appeared at the side of them.

'Come on and we'll treat you to an ice-cream,' said Patrick. 'Won't we, Samuel?'

'I think that would be a jolly good idea for all of us,' agreed Samuel in his usual precise tones. He was smiling though, and Maddy felt that his smile was for her rather than for his sister.

'And us as well,' Tommy chimed in. 'Me and Tilly. We'd like an ice-cream, wouldn't we, Tilly?'

The twins jumped up, leaving the sand pies they had been making. They had brought their buckets and spades to keep them occupied during the interval.

'Of course we won't forget you two,' laughed Patrick. 'How could we?'

'The trouble is we don't want to lose our places,' said Jessie. 'If we get up somebody might pinch them. Could you fetch the ice-creams for us, please?'

'Oh…all right then,' said Patrick. 'Anything to oblige a lovely young lady.' He winked at Jessie and Maddy noticed that she turned a pretty shade of pink.

Jessie's pale freckled skin had not changed colour very much during the weeks they had spent in Scarborough. Unlike

Maddy's, whose arms, bare from the elbows down, were brown and her cheeks ruddy, like rosy apples. Both the girls kept their sun hats on, though, for most of the time, and Maddy noticed that Jessie's summer frocks, like those of her mother, had long sleeves. She knew that proper ladies – like Mrs Barraclough – tried to preserve their pale complexions by wearing large-brimmed hats and holding a parasol. Her mother had told her so, although Mam didn't fuss about it too much herself, and she, Maddy, liked to feel the warmth of the sun on her face and arms.

'I think we should swap brothers, don't you?' said Maddy, as the two lads went off to the ice-cream cart with the twins dancing along behind them. 'Patrick's a lot nicer to you than he is to me. And you said your brother was real stuffy. But I think he's...quite nice.'

'No, I don't want to swap,' replied Jessie decidedly. 'I think it's more fun when they're not brothers...if you see what I mean.' She turned rather pink again. 'Anyway, brothers are often horrid to their sisters, aren't they?'

'Yes, you're right,' said Maddy. She hadn't really meant that she would like to swap. As Jessie said, it was more fun having Samuel as a friend. But it would not be for very much longer. By the time they returned with the ice creams it was almost time for the second half of the show to begin.

'Be careful you don't spill your ice cream,' said Jessie to the twins. 'And wipe your hands when you've finished. You've got your hankies, haven't you?' Tommy and Tilly nodded and perched on the end of the form to watch the rest of the performance.

It was more interesting to them than the first half had been. Nancy came on with her performing dogs, then the tap-dancing men, Barney and Benjy, and the funny man who always made Tommy laugh so much. They fidgeted a little when the man called Charlie came on although the rest of the audience clapped and cheered like mad. He had already entertained them with his monologues, 'Drake's Drum' and 'The Charge of the Light Brigade'. But this time he was dressed in the bright red uniform of a Chelsea pensioner.

'We're the soldiers of the Queen, mi lads,
Who've been, mi lads, who've seen, mi lads...'

he sang in his loud, but not very tuneful, voice. Then followed a recital telling of his days as a soldier, fighting for his Queen and Country. Several of the grown-ups were wiping their eyes as he came to the end of his last song, with the audience joining in.

'...Steady and strong, marching along,
With the boys of the old brigade.'

All the Pierrots came in and joined in the singing as a fitting end to the performance, and then Percy Morgan spoke glowingly about Charlie, wishing him well in the future and saying how much he would be missed. He was presented with a large bouquet of flowers which he handed to his wife, who was seated on the front row of chairs, as well as several parcels from members of the audience. It was known, of course, that the proceeds of the show would be given to Charlie, and it was believed that folks would be generous. He was a popular member of the troupe.

'That was a most delicious meal,' said Faith, when they had all eaten their fill of the magnificent spread put on by Clara. Sausage rolls, meat pies, all kinds of sandwiches and mixed pickles; fruit cake, almond tarts, and iced buns (specially for Tommy and Tilly), and a large trifle in a cut-glass bowl, decorated with cherries and tiny silver balls. 'It was very kind of you to invite us, and we all want to say thank you, don't we, to Mrs Moon?'

She glanced at each of her children who all smiled and said their thank yous.

'We have been pleased to get to know you all,' said Clara. 'It's a pity you'll be going back soon, but all good things have to come to an end, as they say. And we do hope we will see you again next year.'

Maddy and Jessie, in particular, were looking rather downcast as they glanced at one another. Faith looked at them and smiled. 'Don't look so glum, you two,' she said. 'Actually... I have a surprise for you. I have decided we can stay another week!'

'Can we really, Mummy?' said Jessie. She looked at Maddy and they both grinned with delight. 'Why have you changed your mind?'

'You and Samuel don't go back to school until the week after next, do you?' said Faith. 'And I decided...well...there's nothing much to rush back for. Your father is out on business most of the time...' Her voice petered out and she looked pensive for a moment.

'So we'll have another week together, Maddy,' said Jessie.

'Ye-es...only part of the time though,' replied Maddy. 'I go back to school next Monday, earlier than you do. I 'spect it's because you go to – you know – a sort of posh school, don't you, you and Samuel?'

Faith laughed and Samuel, too, gave a wry smile. 'I expect school is school, whatever sort of an academy it is. Anyway, thanks very much, Mother. Lots more time for fishing.'

'You and your fishing!' said Jessie. 'Never mind; we've got the rest of this week, haven't we, Maddy? And perhaps one day next week you could come round for tea at our place, when you finish school, couldn't she, Mummy?'

'Most certainly,' said Faith. 'I'm pleased you two have become such very good friends.'

'And a week next Friday,' said William, 'it will be the final performance of the Pierrots for this year. It's usually quite a grand occasion. They wear evening dress instead of their usual costumes. Clara and I are thinking of going, aren't we, love? We went last year and it was real grand. Perhaps you would like to come with us, Faith? It'd be a nice ending to your holiday.'

'That's very kind of you, William,' said Faith, 'and you, too, Clara. Yes, I would love to come.' She did not dare to glance at Bella Randall, but she was aware that the woman had suddenly gone very quiet. She hoped fervently that Bella would not be included in this proposed outing, and somehow she felt that she would not be invited.

'And us,' chimed in Maddy. 'What about me and Jessie?'

'Oh...it's rather too late for you, I'm afraid,' smiled Clara. 'It doesn't start until half past ten at night. It's just for grown-ups, you see, and it gives the local landladies a chance to see the show, as well as the holidaymakers.'

'I reckon I shall be holding the fort here,' said Isaac. 'Many's the time I would have been there meself, on t' front row an' all, but I'll give it a miss this time. I'll take care of Maddy and Patrick.'

'I don't need taking care of, Grandad, thanks all the same,' said Patrick. 'But I'll stay behind and look after my dear little sister.' He laughed out loud as Maddy stuck her tongue out at him.

'And I will take charge of Jessica and the twins, Mother,' said Samuel. 'You go and enjoy yourself. But I was wondering, Patrick…would you like to come fishing with me, perhaps on Sunday afternoon?'

'Yes, why not?' said Patrick with his usual cheerful grin. 'Ta very much. I'm ready to try anything once.'

Chalk and cheese, thought Maddy. Wasn't that what grown-ups said about people who were absolutely different in every way? But who could tell? Perhaps the two young men would come to be good friends, just as she and Jessie were. The two girls had already promised to write to one another and vowed they would be best friends for ever.

William, Clara and Faith also promised that they would keep in touch, although the two women guessed that it would be up to them to do the letter writing. Faith had invited them back to her lodgings after the evening Pierrot show which ended soon after half past eleven. William held out both his arms to assist Clara and Faith up the steep cliffside path. Faith showed no embarrassment; they had been so attentive towards her all evening, making her feel that they were pleased to have her company. But she could not help but feel a pang of…not exactly jealousy, but certainly sorrow that her marriage was so different from their own.

The performance had been a happy occasion, but nostalgic too, as the Pierrots said their goodbyes in comedy, dance and song. They had chosen some specially plaintive songs; 'The Last Rose of Summer, and 'Will ye no come back again?'. But the last chorus of,

'Goodbye-ee, don't cry-ee,
Wipe the tear, baby dear, from your eye-ee...'

had everyone laughing again. Fortunately it was a still, fine night. The moon shone brightly and the stage was lit by oil lamps which cast a radiant yellowish light on the men in evening suits and the ladies in dresses of shimmering satin.

Back at Faith's lodgings all was silent as the children, including Samuel, surprisingly, had all retired to bed. Faith poured pale golden sherry into glasses of crystal and handed them to her friends. 'Thank you both,' she said, 'for helping to make our stay here so enjoyable.'

'And here's to our friendship,' said William raising his glass. 'Long may it continue. We are very pleased to have met you all. And – God willing – may we all meet again next year. Here's to the future...'

'To the future...' echoed Clara and Faith as they lifted their glasses, all smiling happily at one another.

Chapter Fifteen

Queen Victoria died on the evening of 22nd January, 1901, at her beloved holiday home, Osborne, on the Isle of Wight. She was eighty-one years of age.

She had been a distant, shadowy figure to most of her subjects. After the death of her beloved husband, Prince Albert, in 1861, she had become a recluse for many years, shutting herself away in her Highland retreat at Balmoral. People's sympathy at her bereavement had soon turned to impatience and resentment that, even now, she would not allow her son, the Prince of Wales – Prince Teddy – to take over some of the responsibilities of monarchy. Instead, she remained hidden away, swathed in the deepest black, which she wore for the rest of her life, gazing sorrowfully, it was said, at the bust of her dear Albert.

However, by the time of her Golden Jubilee in 1887 she had emerged from her retreat. Ten years later, at the celebration of her Diamond Jubilee, she had been gratified by the cheers of the vast crowds as she was driven through the streets of London to St Paul's Cathedral.

Now the grand old lady was dead, and she was mourned by her loyal subjects throughout the land. Clara Moon, like thousands of others, read in the newspapers of her death and then of her elaborate funeral. It was said that she 'died peacefully' with the members of her family at her bedside. 'In the arms of her grandson, the German Kaiser...' said some reports; and another said that her last word was 'Bertie...' uttered to her eldest son who was, at long last, to become king.

'Poor old lady,' said Clara, one evening in early February, as she read of the prolonged ceremonials which followed the death of the queen. 'It's strange we should feel so saddened by her passing. I mean to say, it isn't as if we knew her, but she's always been there, hasn't she, for as long as we can remember?' Most of her subjects, however, knew her only as a corpulent, frumpish and somewhat grumpy old lady, judging from the photographs which appeared from time to time in the newspapers.

'Aye, that goes for me an' all,' said Isaac. 'It's the end of an era, all right. Victorians, we called ourselves, didn't we? Now we'll have to get used to summat else. Edwardians; I reckon that's what we'll be called. It was King William the Fourth – Silly Billy, they used to call him – when I was born. Not that I remember owt about him. I'd be about five years old when Victoria came to t' throne. Aye, she'll be missed, will the old girl.'

'When you come to think of it, she's done a lot for our business,' said William. He gave a wry grin. 'I don't want to sound disrespectful, like, but I'm thinking of our shop, Moon's Mourning Modes. It was the queen who started the mourning cult, wasn't it, after Prince Albert died? And you could say that we've cashed in on it. Folks wanted to follow her example with black clothing and all the paraphernalia. Aye, she's certainly not done us any harm, God bless her.'

'Perhaps King Edward will have a different outlook,' said Clara. 'But I've tried to steer away from too much black in the shop, as you know. Actually, I'm wondering if it's time we had a change of name. 'Mourning Modes' sounds so terribly depressing.'

'Happen so,' replied William, 'though I don't know what else you'd call it.'

He glanced anxiously at Clara before returning his eyes to the book he was reading, one of the latest of the adventures of Sherlock Holmes. His wife continued with the perusal of the morning newspaper. William was concerned about her. Apart from the fact that she had been singularly moved by the death of the queen, she was not herself at all. She had had a succession of colds during the winter months and now she seemed to be developing a nasty cough. Clara was not one for consulting the doctor with every little ache and pain, but William decided that very soon he would have to insist that she did so.

Clara felt her eyes watering, and she blew again into her handkerchief. If she were truthful she felt quite unwell, but they had been busy recently – it was always the same in January and February – and she had wanted to help William as much as she could. Not only was her head aching and her throat a little sore, but she felt low in spirits as well. The death of the queen, of course, had not helped. It had cast a dark pall over the nation, but maybe now that she had finally been laid to rest they could all get back to normal. And maybe she, Clara, would begin to feel a little brighter.

It was only now, two full weeks after her death, that the queen's body had at last been laid alongside that of Prince Albert in the mausoleum at Frogmore; whilst, it was reported, 'the snow fell softly outside'. The newspaper that Clara was reading gave a detailed account of the funeral. After the lying-in-state at Osborne House the coffin had been moved to the royal yacht, Alberta, for its journey to the mainland, and then by train to Victoria Station. Black drapes over the coffin had been replaced by white and gold ones as Queen Victoria's last public journey was made through packed, silent streets, escorted by troops from around her vast empire. All along the route people stood bare-headed, many of them in tears. A gun carriage took the coffin to Paddington Station for its second train journey to Windsor. A salute of eighty-one guns was fired from the park, one for each year of the queen's life. After a brief service in St George's Chapel at Windsor there was a second lying-in-state in the Albert Memorial Chapel. And then, at last, on the 4th of February, the queen was laid to rest beside Prince Albert.

'God bless her,' Clara said quietly to herself. 'And God bless King Edward too.' He could not know what lay in store for him at the start of his reign any more than she, Clara Moon, did.

'You're not at all well, are you, dear?' said Clara's old friend, Louisa Montague, when she came to visit her the following morning. 'If you don't mind me saying so you look very peaky; and tired, too. I think you need a jolly good rest.'

'You're right, of course,' replied Clara, giving a weak smile, 'and that's what I'm trying to do. Will has insisted that I do nothing at all today. He's gone out on a job, but he's taken Patrick with him instead of me. And Bella can manage very well without me in the shop.' She gave a little chuckle, in spite of feeling so wretched. 'In fact, I know she likes to feel that she's in charge.'

'Hmm... I had noticed,' said Louisa with a meaningful sniff. 'She was acting like the Queen of Sheba when I came through the shop just now, giving that young Polly the run-around. She'd put a box of gloves back in the wrong place, from what I could make out. But I didn't stop to chat; I just said I was coming to see you. That Martin seems to have got her weighed up, though. He gave me a sly wink as I passed him. There's no flies on him, that's for sure.'

'Yes, Martin Sadler's a very capable assistant,' said Clara. 'And young Polly is shaping up very nicely. She does need to be told though, now and again.' She was well aware that there was no love lost between Bella and Louisa. Many people seemed to find her chief assistant high-handed and 'full of herself' – that was often said of Bella – but Clara felt that she should try to defend her. She was, of course, an invaluable help in the shop as well as being a good friend. A loyal friend, Clara had always believed, despite knowing that her father-in-law and her daughter, also, were not too keen on the woman.

'I realise Bella may seem rather...uppity,' she said now, 'but I really couldn't manage without her. And she and I do get on very well. I'm afraid she will have to be in complete control until I'm feeling better. It's not like me to give in, but Will is insisting that we should get the doctor. I've persuaded him to wait till tomorrow and see how I feel then, but it does seem to be more than just a cold... Don't come too near me, Louisa. I don't want to pass my germs on to you. It's very good of you to come and see me.'

'Oh, don't worry about me,' said Louisa. 'I'm as strong as an old war horse. I had a bad cold after Christmas so I don't think I'm likely to catch another one. I met William on Eastborough, and he said you were very much under the weather. But to tell the truth, I was coming anyway... I don't know whether you feel like discussing business matters now, do you, dear?'

'Yes, why not? I mustn't give up entirely. You want to

know about the blouses you made, I dare say?'

'Yes, that's right, dear. Would you like a few more? Say another half-dozen, or is that too many?'

'No, not at all. We've only one left now. They sold like hot cakes over Christmas. Daft expression, that, isn't it, but we always say it. Goodness knows why hot cakes should sell any better than cold ones... Yes, Louisa; we'd like six more blouses, please, if you can manage them. We have found that a lot of our garments are selling not just for mourning wear now. In fact, I was saying to William that it might be a good idea to change our name. We've got a new king on the throne now, haven't we, so maybe it's time for a change. What shall we say then? Two white ones, two lilac, and maybe two pale blue. I know it's not a mourning colour, but like I say, maybe it's time we bucked up our ideas a bit.'

The blouses that Louisa made were exquisite, of fine cotton or silk, trimmed with lace or finely pleated and with a high stand-up collar, like the ones worn by the new Queen Alexandra. Clara realised she was starting to feel a little brighter as she talked with her friend, her mind being momentarily distracted from her aching head and streaming eyes and nose.

'Certainly,' said Louisa. 'I shall be pleased to oblige. I'll get on with them as soon as I can. I'll probably make them all myself and let the girls get on with some of the more ordinary garments. You did know, didn't you, that I had a big order from the Pierrot troupe, Percy Morgan's lot?'

'Yes, you did mention it a while back,' said Clara. 'You're going to be kept busy, aren't you?'

'Yes, it seems so. They all came in to be fitted before they left last September. Same thing as usual, more or less, that's what they want. You know; baggy trousers, frills round the neck, pom-poms and all that. I thought I might add a few nice little touches; an extra frill for the ladies or maybe a touch of lace. We'd best be getting started on them soon.' Louisa counted on her fingers. 'February, March, April, May... They'll be back again in four months' time or just over. And it's surprising how time flies.'

'Doesn't it just?' said Clara. 'And this morning's flying past, as well. Maddy will be back from school soon, ready for her dinner, and the menfolk of course. It's really kind of you to bring the soup and everything, Louisa. You'll stay and have some with us, won't you?'

Louisa had arrived armed with a basket full of goodies, like Red Riding Hood visiting her grandmother, Clara had said; a huge flask of home-made chicken soup, baked custard tarts, a dozen bread rolls and a pack of butter.

'Yes, I will stay, dear,' Louisa replied, 'then I can see to things and wash up afterwards. I guessed from what William said that you could do with a bit of cheering up. Now, you stay just where you are and I'll lay the table and warm the soup up. There'll be six of us altogether, won't there? There's plenty to go round.'

'You're an angel of mercy,' smiled Clara. Maddy would have helped her to put a meal of sorts together when she came home, but this was an unexpected treat. She felt tears of gratitude and affection for Louisa welling up in her eyes, but they were a sign of her weakness, too, she realised. She sniffed, trying to keep a sob out of her voice. 'I really don't know how to thank you... The plates and bowls are in the top cupboard and the knives and spoons in the drawer...'

'Don't you worry yourself,' said Louisa, 'and don't start getting upset. I should know where everything is by now, and that's what friends are for, to lend a helping hand when it's needed.'

Clara smiled fondly at the woman who was bustling around so cheerfully and energetically. Louisa had been a good friend to her for many years. She, Clara, had started out as an assistant in the dressmaker's shop, and then, after her parents had died she had been invited to share Louisa's home. She had stayed there until her marriage to William. Louisa had been like a second mother to her and their friendship had continued until the present day. The older woman appeared pretty much the same to Clara as she had done twenty years before. She was small and sprightly, her movements were quick and nimble, like a little sparrow, and her dark brown eyes did not miss a trick. Her once dark hair was now entirely grey, but that seemed to be the only difference.

The rest of the family members were pleased to see Louisa and were relieved that Clara appeared to have bucked up a bit, as her husband put it.

'This soup's delicious,' he told Louisa. 'Just what the doctor ordered, you might say.' He smiled at his wife. 'I'm sure it'll do you a power of good, Clara love. But speaking of the doctor, I still think we should let him have a look at you, just to be on the safe side.'

'Let's see how I feel in the morning, shall we, Will?' said Clara quietly. She was not too happy at being the focus of attention, especially with regard to her health. She turned to Maddy. 'Aunty Louisa has been telling me about the costumes she will be making for Uncle Percy and the rest of the Pierrots. That's exciting, isn't it? And it won't be all that long before they're back again. Our Maddy's a great admirer of the Pierrots, you know, Louisa.'

'Aunty Louisa...' said Maddy – both children had always called her 'Aunty' – '...I've been thinking. When I leave school, d'you think I could come and work for you in your shop? And learn how to be a dressmaker, like my mam did?'

Louisa laughed. 'Good gracious me! You're looking a long way ahead, aren't you, Maddy? I don't even know if I shall still be there in...how many years is it?'

'Not all that many,' retorted Maddy. 'I shall be eleven in June, and it'll only be two years after that, won't it?'

'Yes, of course you're right,' said Louisa, nodding thoughtfully. 'And there was I thinking it was ages away. Your mother and I were saying earlier, Maddy, how time flies. I dare say I might still be there in two or three years' time, but I'm nearer seventy than sixty, you know, now.'

'But nobody would think so,' said Clara. 'You mustn't think of giving up, Louisa, so long as you've got your health and strength. Anyway, Maddy...' She turned to her daughter. 'What has brought this on? You haven't mentioned to me that you would like to work for Aunty Louisa. Not that I don't think it's a good idea, mind.'

'Oh, it's something that me and Jessie were talking about in the summer,' replied Maddy, 'and it just reminded me when you said about the Pierrots' costumes. I told Jessie that I might like to work in a shop... Not our shop,' she added, 'and then I remembered Aunty Louisa and that you used to work there, Mam.'

'And if you are anything like your mother, Maddy – and I'm sure you are – then you would be a grand little worker. Clara was always such a godsend in the shop as well.' Louisa smiled reminiscently. 'So friendly and patient with the customers. A lot of them remarked about how pleasant she was.'

'One of them in particular,' said William with a chuckle. 'That's where I first met your mam, Maddy, but I think I've told you before, haven't I?'

'Many times,' interrupted Patrick with a grimace.

'Well, never mind,' said William. 'It's a tale well worth the telling. Aye, there she was, standing behind the counter, so pretty and cheerful. "How can I help you, sir?" she said, and I was completely bowled over.'

'Give over, Will,' said Clara laughing. 'Yes, Maddy; it's something we shall bear in mind when the time comes.'

'And what about your friend...Jessie, isn't it?' enquired Louisa. 'What does she want to do when she leaves school?'

'Oh, she'll be staying at school till she's sixteen,' said Maddy. 'She's at a posh school, y'see, and then she thinks she'll be going to a college to learn how to type and do something they call shorthand.'

'Oh, I see. She's got a lot of years at school still ahead of her, hasn't she?' said Louisa. 'But I don't suppose she'll turn out to be any brighter than you, for all her book learning.'

'She's a lovely little girl,' observed Clara, in Jessie's defence. 'Well, I shouldn't really say "little" any more, should I? Maddy often reminds me that she's not a little girl now... Yes, Jessie was a very good friend for Maddy during the summer. You had a Christmas card from her, didn't you, love? And Will and I had one from "Edward, Faith and the children". That's what it said, although we didn't meet her husband.'

'Mmm...' William nodded soberly. 'We had to draw our own conclusions about him. Still, enough said... They were a very nice family and we enjoyed their company.'

'And Jessie says they'll be coming again this summer,' said Maddy. 'Her mother's talking about it already. She sent me a letter as well as the card; Jessie, I mean, not her mam.'

'So that's something to look forward to,' said Clara. She realised that her spirits had lifted a little and she was not coughing or blowing her nose quite as much.

Louisa's visit had been a pleasant diversion. Clara went to bed early that evening, convinced that she would waken the next morning feeling much better.

But her optimism proved to be unfounded. When she woke, suddenly, in the early hours she was sweating and feverish. She lay quietly in the darkness, realising she felt wretched, but not wanting to disturb her husband, sleeping peacefully at her side. But when the pearly grey light of dawn at last stole through the curtains she was hardly able to lift her head from the pillow.

William phoned for the doctor without delay and he was with them in less than an hour. Dr Metcalfe looked concerned when he came out of the bedroom after examining Clara. William was hovering on the threshold and the doctor beckoned to him to move out of earshot.

'I am afraid your wife has contracted a rather virulent form of influenza,' he said, as they stood together in the living room.

'Oh dear, that sounds bad,' said William. 'She kept insisting that it was just a cold. In fact, she was so much brighter yesterday that I really felt she was over the worst. But as you can see...' He looked keenly at the doctor. 'Is she...seriously ill?' he asked in a low voice.

The doctor paused. 'At this stage...no, I don't think so. I am sure we can get her right again. She has had a severe cold, of course, and that hasn't helped, but influenza is something else. It's an infection, picked up from contact with another person.

And, unfortunately, it doesn't need to be close contact. There is a lot of it about at this time of the year, as I'm sure you will know, Mr Moon, in your profession.'

'Yes, indeed. We've had a lot of…clients,' William replied grimly. 'And we can't avoid meeting people who have coughs and colds or goodness knows what else.'

'Your wife has all the usual symptoms of influenza,' the doctor continued. 'A sore throat and a cough and aching limbs, and her temperature is rather high. The danger is that this condition can sometimes lead to pneumonia, but that is more likely in elderly people. Your wife is generally pretty strong, isn't she? I know you don't often require my services.'

'Yes, she's usually in good health,' replied William. 'So, what can you do for her, Dr Metcalfe? Obviously she must stay in bed and keep warm…'

'That is the most important thing, warmth, and bed rest – in fact she will probably sleep a lot – and plenty of hot drinks. I doubt if she will feel much like eating for a while.'

'And what about medicine? Can you prescribe something to ease her cough and bring her temperature down? It worried me sick when I felt her forehead; she's so hot she feels as though she's on fire.'

The doctor nodded. 'Most certainly. As a matter of fact, I have been able to get my hands on a new drug. It's not readily available in our country yet, but I have a contact in Germany, a fellow I was at medical school with in Edinburgh. He's working over there now, in Munich, and we've always kept in touch. He keeps me up to date with any new developments, and apparently this is being hailed as a wonder drug. Acetylsalicylic acid – I think I've got that right, but don't ask me to say it again! They're calling it aspirin, for short.'

'And...you can let me have some for Clara?' asked William. 'We're not worried about the cost, you know. All I'm concerned about is getting her right again.'

'Yes; it's available in powder form at the moment. I've put some in a jar for you, with the instructions on the label. I guessed when you called me that your good lady might be suffering from influenza, so I came prepared.' The doctor opened his black bag and took out a small jar, half filled with a white powder. 'I've used it for a couple of patients with very good results. It brings the temperature down and eases the fever and the aches and pains. We're hoping it will be in general use before long.'

'It sounds wonderful,' said William, feeling a good deal relieved already. 'Thank you for suggesting it, and thank you for coming so promptly.'

The doctor nodded. 'I'm hoping there will be a big improvement in your wife's condition before long. I'll call again in a couple of days. In the meantime, though, if you are worried about her, please let me know.'

'Thank you, I will indeed,' replied William as he saw the doctor off the premises. 'We'll look after her and make sure she takes the medicine.'

They were busy, though; extremely busy, as the airborne germ which had attacked Clara had also attacked many more other people in the town. Some of them, older and weaker than Clara, had not recovered. Isaac and Patrick were out on a job at that very moment, there was a great deal to be done in the workshop, and there were two funerals booked for later in the week.

William hurried back to his wife's bedside. Her face was flushed and she was sweating profusely, but her eyes were open and she smiled when she saw him. 'We'll have you as right as rain in no time,' he said, sitting on the edge of the bed and taking hold of her hand. 'Dr Metcalfe has give me a new wonder drug and I shall make sure you take it regularly.' Clara frowned a little. 'No... I know you're not keen on taking medicine, but it will do you good. Now, I'm going to make you a drink of hot lemon juice and give you your first dose, and then perhaps you will sleep for a while.' He laid his hand on her forehead which was hot and damp to his touch.

She nodded and smiled weakly, but she had uttered hardly more than a dozen words or so since she woke that morning. He knew that her throat was painful from the way she grimaced when she swallowed, and to be so listless was not like Clara at all. He knew he would be unable to be with her as much as he would like. There was a coffin to be finished even now, and when his father and son returned there would, doubtless, be more work to be done.

And what about their meals? They could make a scratch meal for themselves at lunchtime, although none of them – neither he nor Isaac nor Patrick – were used to helping in the kitchen, doing what they called 'women's work'. Maddy, though, was getting to be a very capable girl.

When Clara had sipped at her lemon juice and taken her first dose of the new medicine he could see that she was already very drowsy. He tucked the bedclothes around her, wondering whether or not he ought to leave her on her own. He was beginning to realise how indispensable was his wife; she had always been there to see to their every need. What about their evening meals, for instance? He couldn't expect Maddy to cope with all that. And Clara, too, would need to be attended to regularly; when she started eating again she would need nourishing food. In spite of the doctor's reassurances and his own words to his wife that they would have her right in no time at all, William was very worried about her.

There was someone, though, whom he knew he could turn to for help. At one time he would have dismissed the idea out of hand. How many times had he warned Clara that it was not advisable to get too friendly with Bella Randall? But in spite of his advice the two women did seem to be very good friends. He was starting to feel now that he might have been too harsh in his judgement of Bella, too anxious about what she might let slip if she felt inclined. After all, what had gone on between himself and Bella was history. It had all happened ages ago and neither of them ever referred to it.

He pondered for a few moments, and then, still feeling a certain reluctance, he made his way to their shop, Moon's Mourning Modes, where Bella, dressed in the customary black, was standing behind the counter.

Bella guessed from the concerned look on William's face that he was worried about his wife's state of health. She knew that Clara had been suffering from a cold and a cough, but when she had come into the shop towards closing time on the previous day she had said that she was feeling much better. She had just popped in, she said, to make sure that everything had gone smoothly during her absence. As if I wasn't used to coping without her, Bella had though, a trifle irritably. Clara was often out on a job with William leaving her in charge of the shop and the two assistants.

'Louisa called to see me,' Clara had told her, 'and her visit seems to have bucked me up no end. I should be back with you in a day or two, but it's best if I keep my distance now.

The customers don't want to be served by someone with a streaming cold. Although a lot of them were coughing and blowing their noses, I noticed.'

'I'm glad you're feeling so much better,' Bella had told her. 'You've certainly got more colour in your cheeks now.' Although she had noticed that Clara's face was flushed, and not, she thought, with the rosiness of good health, but with the symptom of an incipient fever. And about half an hour ago she had seen the doctor arrive…

She had not commented on Louisa's visit. Louisa Montague, to Bella's mind, was a meddlesome little woman who pushed her nose in where it was not wanted. It could be, of course, just that the two of them did not hit it off. Bella always suspected that Louisa knew more about her than she let on.

She had been sincere when she told Clara that she was pleased she was feeling better. She had grown fond of Will's wife over the years, despite her former antagonism. She had felt at the start that she would dislike, even hate, anyone who was the recipient of William's affections. But she had found that there was nothing she could possibly dislike about Clara. She was the kindest, sweetest and most amiable of women, and Bella had been pleased when she knew that Clara regarded her as a friend. There had always been a certain amount of restraint, though, on William's part. There had been times, Bella suspected, when she might well have been invited to some gathering or outing; but William had advised against it and Clara, ever the dutiful wife, had gone along with his wishes. Now, though, she could tell from the way he was approaching her, with an uncertain smile on his face, that he wanted her help.

'Good morning, William,' she said, with only a hint of a

smile. 'I couldn't help noticing that the doctor has called. Is it Clara? She's not...too poorly, I hope?'

'Yes, you're right,' nodded William. 'I had to call the doctor. I'm sorry to say that Clara is not well at all. She's got influenza; it wasn't just a cough and cold after all. I could kick myself now for not calling the doctor sooner, but she kept insisting it was just a cold.'

'You weren't to know, Will,' said Bella. 'It seems as though everyone you talk to has got a cold. So, you've come to tell me that Clara won't be in the shop for a while? Well, I can manage as I'm sure you know. Martin doesn't need any supervision. And Polly...you're managing very nicely now, aren't you, dear?' She smiled at the young assistant in a much more friendly manner than usual.

'Yes, Miss Randall,' replied the girl, nodding her head in a deferential way as she looked up from her task of writing labels for a new assignment of scarves and gloves.

'But could Polly manage if you left her in charge for part of the time?' asked William in a low voice. 'She and Martin, I mean; I can see that he is very capable. The thing is, Bella, we really do need some help in the house, with Clara being ill and the meals and everything.'

'And you are asking me?' Bella could not help her wry smile.

'Yes,' said William without preamble. 'You are a good friend to my wife and I know she thinks well of you.' He did not go on to say he regretted being distant with her, not did he refer to their past history, but Bella knew that the unspoken thoughts were there in both their minds.

She listened in some amazement as he asked her if she would be willing to help out with tending to Clara's needs.

He feared she might be in bed for several more days, if not longer, and would need constant care. Also – he asked this rather hesitantly – could she possibly help out with their evening meals? Maddy was very capable and she would do what she could, but he couldn't leave it all to a ten-year-old girl.

And – this was the deciding factor in Bella's mind – would she consider moving into the vacant premises over the shop? Fred Archer and his wife, who had been the tenants for several years, had moved out just after Christmas to a flat with an extra bedroom as Mrs Archer was now expecting a baby. Would she consider it? thought Bella. She would jump at the chance of living there, so near to her work; and so near to William... But she did not let that treacherous thought take hold in her mind. She would have suggested it herself when Fred moved out but she had been afraid that the answer would be no, and she could not face the idea of rejection. Now it was being handed to her on a plate.

She did not show her delight, however, but answered thoughtfully that that might be a very good idea. She could sleep there that very same night, in fact, and move the rest of her belongings at a later date. She would be required, she guessed, to give at least a week's notice at her present accommodation.

'Thank you ever so much, Bella,' said William. 'That is a great load off my mind and I know that Clara will be very grateful to you.' He smiled more warmly at her than he had done for years. 'I'll leave you to explain the situation to the assistants and then...perhaps you could go up and see how Clara is? She's sleeping at the moment, but I want someone to be near in case she needs anything.'

'Don't worry, William,' said Bella. 'You can be sure I'll take very great care of her. I'm very pleased that you asked me. Now, you get off back to your work. She'll be in safe hands with me.' She smiled encouragingly at him, but he did not realise that it was also a smile of triumph and self-satisfaction.

Chapter Sixteen

Bella had always known that one day William would need her. That was why she had stayed close to the Moon family all those years. Close enough, that was, to be considered an indispensable assistant in the shop, but not close enough to be admitted into their intimate circle. Well, now all that was to change. She could hardly cook their meals and dance attendance upon Clara without sitting down with them at their family table, could she? She made up her mind that she would make it clear to William that she was not to be regarded as a servant. What she was doing was because of her affection for Clara, and she did not require payment other than the normal wage she received as a sales assistant. That, of course, would be ongoing.

She knew, however, that she would need to be more gracious in her dealings with old man Isaac and with Maddy. Over the years a mutual antipathy had developed between herself and Isaac Moon, and likewise with young Madeleine. Bella had the good sense to realise that this was largely her own fault. She had sensed from the start that William's father did not like her; that he mistrusted her and had probably guessed that there had been something more than friendship between her and William. And so she had behaved off-handedly towards him, only speaking to him when it was absolutely necessary.

As far as Maddy was concerned, Bella certainly knew she

was at fault there. There was really nothing to dislike about the little girl any more than there was about her mother. Maddy was inclined to be outspoken, a little precocious maybe, but Bella could not help but admire the child's spirit and her self-confidence, although she would never admit it. But this was William's daughter, the only one that he could acknowledge, and that was the rub. He had another daughter; Henrietta was a young woman now, almost twenty years old. But she might just as well be dead for all that Bella knew of her, and it hurt when she saw how loved and cherished was his little daughter, Madeleine. Bella decided that she must make an effort to be kinder to her; ask her for help with the evening meal and with suggesting treats that her mother might enjoy when she was feeling better. Maddy might well be a little suspicious at first – and who could blame her? – but Bella was sure she could win her confidence if she tried.

She explained the situation to Martin and Polly, telling Polly, especially, that she was trusting her to look after the ladies department and to be responsible for the sales and the care of the customers; women who were bereaved often needed a sympathetic ear. Should there be any problems, however, she, Bella, would not be far away and Polly must not hesitate to come and find her. And she would, of course, pop in sometime each day to ensure that all was running smoothly.

Young Polly seemed to grow several inches and to swell out with pride at the news that she was to be left in change. 'Oh, thank you, Miss Randall,' she babbled. 'I won't let you down, honest I won't. You know you can trust me, don't you? Just imagine me being t' boss! Me mam'll be that pleased. Just wait till I tell her!'

It was the longest speech Bella had ever heard her make; usually the girl was cowed by Bella's dictatorial manner. Even now she could not resist issuing a word of warning. 'Don't get carried away, Polly. It's only temporary. Just see that you don't let me down, and Mr and Mrs Moon as well. I shall be reporting back to them about how you are managing, so think on!'

'Oh, I will, Miss Randall. I'm real sorry Mrs Moon is poorly. I think she's a lovely lady. Er…will you tell her, please, that I hope she'll soon be better?'

'Yes, I shall tell her,' replied Bella curtly. 'Now stop your prattling and finish off those labels you're writing. I thought they would have been done by now. And make sure your hair is tidy before a customer comes in. You look as though you've been dragged through a hedge backwards.'

'Yes, Miss Randall,' said Polly, her hands reaching up to straighten her mop of tangled curls. No matter how many times she combed her hair it always looked untidy. But Bella had to admit that she was a very clean girl. Her shiny red cheeks had a well-scrubbed look and her black dress was always neatly ironed.

Bella went through the stockroom at the back of the shop and then through the door which led to the Moons' living quarters. She would normally have knocked, but as she had been given carte blanche she walked straight in. William, she knew, had gone into the workshop to carry on with his coffin making.

She went upstairs to find that Clara was still asleep in the double bed that she and William shared. Bella stood and watched her, a welter of thoughts and feelings running through her mind. Affection for the woman who had been a good friend to her over the years, and pity for her now because she looked so ill. Her face was flushed, more so than it had been on the previous day, and her breathing was laboured and rasping, as though there was a tiger growling inside her chest. Beads of perspiration stood out on her forehead and there was a damp patch on her pillow where her head was lying.

It was then that thoughts of a different nature began to steal into her mind. From what Bella could see Clara was quite poorly, maybe even dangerously so. William had mentioned the doctor's fear that this severe form of influenza might turn to pneumonia if she were not nursed diligently over the next few days. And if that happened, then there was the possibility that Clara would not get better at all...

I knew William Moon before she did... Bella thought now. And the bitterness that she had felt all those years ago, and which still surfaced from time to time, crept insidiously into her mind. She, Bella, had been his first love, the first girl to whom he had made love in the fullest sense; she knew that without a doubt. She was sure, too, that he had loved her. He had told her so, and if he had not been so naive, so wet behind the ears and so scared of what his father might think, then she might well have been married to him now instead of Clara. She would have loved him so much, she told herself. Theirs would have been a love which endured, and as well as Henrietta, the daughter whom William could not acknowledge, there might have been others. She, Bella, could have experienced the joys of a happy family life, such as Clara had enjoyed for all those years.

Bella did not think, then, of Ralph Cunningham whom she had loved deeply and who, she believed, had loved her in return...until he had betrayed her by dying so unexpectedly. She forgot the truly happy times that she and Ralph had had together. Her disordered mind was taking her further back to her first encounters with William Moon – Will had always been the only one for her, so she told herself now – and the injustice which she imagined had been done to her. But injustices could be put right. Will Moon owed her a lot, although he would never admit to it. She had sensed a certain softening, however, in his attitude towards her today. And as he became more and more indebted to her, so would his feelings towards her become warmer. She knew that their love for one another could, in time, be rekindled...

Clara, in a few days' time, might be fighting for her life, she pondered. She gazed at the woman dispassionately now, her previous feelings of sadness and friendship gradually dwindling away. William had said something about the medicine, a new drug that she would need to take regularly. There it was on the bedside table, a small brown-coloured glass bottle containing a whitish powder. Bella's eyes narrowed and her mouth set in a determined line as she looked at it. But Clara was sleeping at the moment and she knew she must not disturb her, not yet. It was time for her to go and have a chat with William.

Isaac and Patrick had returned from what she assumed to be a 'laying-out' job, and all three men were busy in the workshop when she went out to the yard. She stood at the door and beckoned to William who came over to her.

'Clara is still asleep,' she told him, 'and I didn't like to disturb her. But I think it might be advisable for her to start her medicine as soon as possible. Her breathing is very laboured, isn't it?' she said in an anxious tone of voice.

'Yes...but I have every confidence in Dr Metcalfe,' said William. 'I'll pop in to see her myself in a little while and see that she takes her medicine. In fact she's already had her first dose.' He smiled, still a little uncertainly, at Bella. 'Thank you...for everything. I know you're concerned about Clara.'

She nodded. 'Yes, I am. Now, what would you like me to do next? Shall I prepare some lunch for you, and your father and Patrick? And Maddy will be in from school before long, won't she?'

'Oh...goodness me!' said William, scratching his head in some perplexity. 'It just shows how much we rely on Clara, doesn't it? She always sees to the lunch. Yes, Bella, if you don't mind. There are some tins of soup in the cupboard, and there's bread...at least I hope there is, in the bread bin. Just a scratch meal will do, and then we could have something rather more substantial, maybe, tonight?' He looked at her expectantly.

'Of course,' she smiled. 'Don't worry; I'll see to everything. I'll go and see what I can find, and when Maddy comes in from school she will help me.'

'What was all that about?' asked Isaac when William went back into the workshop. 'What did she want?' William had already told his father and Patrick about the doctor's diagnosis, but had not got round to telling them who he had turned to for help.

'Oh...Bella's going to help us out for the next few days,' he replied casually. 'Just while Clara's in bed. I hope it won't be for long, but we need somebody to see to our meals and all that, don't we? We're rushed off our feet at the moment.'

'Have you taken leave of yer senses, lad?' said Isaac. He shook his head unbelievingly. 'You've asked Bella Randall – of all people! – to help us? Whatever were you thinking of?'

William frowned at his father, at the same time giving a cautionary nod in the direction of his son. Patrick laughed.

'It's all right, Dad. You don't need to watch what you're saying in front of me. I know "little pigs have big ears", an' all that, but I'm not a kid. I know that Bella isn't exactly Grandad's favourite person.'

'You can say that again, lad.' Isaac tutted loudly. 'Couldn't you think of somebody else as could help us out? One of the women at chapel...or Louisa? Aye, Louisa; she brought us a champion meal yesterday.'

'Louisa is too busy to be running around after us,' said William. 'Besides, she's getting on a bit and it wouldn't be fair to presume on her good nature. And you know that Clara has never got too involved with the other women at the chapel; she always has too much to do. And they all have their own families to see to. No... I'm sure Bella will do very well for us and she's already on the premises. You know as well as I do that she's very fond of Clara...whatever else you may think about her. Anyway, maybe it's time we buried the past...' He stopped, aware that Patrick was looking at him oddly. 'I mean to say, we may have had our differences, but happen it's time to put 'em behind us. And you'll want an evening meal, won't you, Father? You won't want to make it yourself?'

'Aye, that's true enough,' sighed Isaac. 'Well, what's done is done, I suppose. Let's hope it won't be long before Clara's back on her feet again.' He paused, realising how selfish that might sound. 'I mean...for Clara's sake, poor lass. She isn't used to being ill. Anyroad, a few days in bed with nowt to do should do her a power of good. But she does look after us all so nicely, doesn't she? I've told you afore, William, you've got a wife in a million there.'

Maddy stopped in her tracks when she came in through the back door and saw Bella busy at work in the kitchen. 'Where's Mam?' she asked, eyeing the woman suspiciously.

Bella smiled in an unusually friendly manner. 'Oh, hello there, Maddy. Your mother's in bed. You knew she was poorly, didn't you?' Maddy nodded, still mistrustfully. 'Well, the doctor had been to see her this morning and she really is...quite poorly. That nasty thing called influenza, that's what she's got. Now you mustn't worry. The doctor has given her some medicine to take, and if she keeps nice and warm and has plenty of hot drinks she should be as right as rain in a few days. So your dad has asked me to help with the meals and to take care of your mother.'

'Yes... I see,' said Maddy guardedly. 'Can I go and see her now?'

'Yes, of course,' replied Bella. 'Don't get too near her though, dear. You don't want to catch any nasty germs, do you? She's awake now but she's still feeling pretty rotten, I guess. She's had a nice hot drink of lemon juice and a dose of her medicine. The doctor seems to think it's a magic sort of powder, so we hope it will make her better very soon, don't we? Off you go then; run along and see her. And then I'd like you to help me to set the table. Could you do that, please? You know where everything is, don't you, better than I do. And perhaps you could think of something you would like tonight for your evening meal. Something you would all enjoy.'

Maddy pursed her lips. 'I'll think about it,' she replied.

She was puzzled; unable to understand why Bella should suddenly start being so nice to her instead of criticising her and being downright nasty like she was sometimes, when the two of them were on their own. Perhaps Bella really was feeling very sorry for her because her mother was poorly; maybe she was very ill indeed?

Clara smiled weakly at Maddy and said, 'Hello, love,' in a very shaky voice. Then she said, just as Bella had done, 'Don't come too near me, love. You don't want to catch this awful thing.'

She really did look dreadfully ill, thought Maddy. Her eyes were bright, but not a nice normal sort of brightness; they looked glassy, and confused as well. Her face was damp with sweat and her hair was wet and clinging to her forehead. As Maddy stood and looked at her she closed her eyes as though she was too weary to even speak.

Maddy tiptoed out of the bedroom and into the kitchen where Bella was cutting slices of bread off the loaf. 'Aunty Bella...' she began, knowing it might be best to address her in that way. 'Me mam's real poorly, isn't she? She's not... She won't...die, will she?' Her words whispered the dreadful words.

Bella seemed to give a start and she paused before she answered. Then, 'No, of course not,' she said brightly. 'Whatever gave you that idea?'

'Because she looks so ill, that's why,' said Maddy. 'I've never ever seen her look like that. She doesn't like staying in bed, so she must be feeling real bad.'

'I'm sure she is at the moment. But you mustn't worry, Maddy dear. We'll do all we can to make her better... You're so used to having your mother around to look after you all, aren't you?' She sounded rather critical for a moment, more like the old Bella that Maddy was accustomed to. 'Well, it's time now for you to help her, for a change. Would you like to butter this bread for me and put it on a big plate? Then you can set out the mats and the knives and soup spoons. I've already put the cloth on the table.'

It was strange having Bella sitting with them as they ate their meal, instead of Mam, especially as she was sitting in what was Mam's chair. But maybe she didn't know that. Maddy didn't like it though, and she decided she would sit there herself next time. When it was time for their evening meal Maddy sat down first, and it did not go unnoticed by her father that she was sitting in what was normally her mother's chair. He did not say anything, but he gave her a sort of knowing smile.

'For what we are about to receive, may the Lord make us truly thankful,' said Isaac, as he always did, and Bella bent her head like the rest of them.

Maddy noticed that her attitude towards the family, particularly towards Grandad, was now rather different. She had always known that Bella and her grandad did not like one another very much and only spoke when they were forced to do so. But Bella was talking to him now; not exactly chattering, but addressing a few of her remarks in his direction.

'Maddy helped me to make this cottage pie, didn't you, dear?' she said. She turned to Isaac. 'She said it was one of her grandad's favourite meals.'

'Aye, so it is,' replied Isaac. 'And very tasty it is an' all. You've made a good job of it...both of yer.' He looked down at his plate, though, not catching her eye.

'I'm sorry I didn't have time to bake,' Bella went on. 'I'm afraid the apple pie is shop-bought, but I'll try and make time to do a spot of baking before long.'

She had spent the afternoon at the local shops, buying what

she thought they needed, including the minced beef for the pie. Then she had moved some of her belongings from her flat, which was about five minutes' walk away, into her new rooms.

William, meanwhile, had kept a careful watch on his wife, supplying her with drinks and the medicine – every four hours – and changing her damp pillow slip. She was still very feverish and was spending a good deal of the time sleeping. He had decided it would not be advisable for him to occupy the same bed at night. Much as he loved Clara it would not be helpful to anyone if he were to catch the illness as well, although it was possible that the germs had already been passed on. Only time would tell. He would sleep on the couch in the small room, next to the bedroom, which he used as a study. He would be near enough to hear if Clara called out, and he would check on her regularly throughout the night.

Bella, it was decided, would see to Clara's needs during the daytime. It was the busiest time of the year for undertakers. There was a funeral on the following day which it was necessary for all the menfolk to attend, the younger two, William and Patrick, acting as pall-bearers. And the rest of the day they would be occupied with the carpentry part of the business.

'Yes...thanks for all you're doing, Bella,' said William, sounding a trifle preoccupied. 'The cottage pie's champion. It's one of Clara's favourites, an' all. Perhaps we could have it again in a few days' time. Happen by then she'll be able to enjoy it herself. I know she won't be happy about staying in bed for too long.'

'Oh, I'm sure she'll be sitting up and taking notice in a day or two,' replied Bella. 'I think I can see a slight improvement already. Her breathing's a little easier, don't you think so, William?'

'Happen so,' replied William. 'I hope so...please God,' he added under his breath.

The next morning Clara seemed a little better. Her chest did not sound quite so congested, although she was still sweating profusely and her pillow was continually damp and in need of changing. She appeared confused, too; unsure as to what time of the day it was, morning, afternoon or evening. William gave her another dose of medicine and made sure she was comfortable before setting off, with his father and son, for the funeral which had been arranged for the mid-morning. He told Bella that he hoped they would be back by lunchtime. Clara was still not interested in eating and had shaken her head when he suggested that she might try just a mouthful or two of porridge.

'Rest, that's what she needs,' he told Bella. 'Complete rest, and sleep if she feels inclined, and she's certainly sleeping a lot at the moment. It's nature's remedy, I suppose; she must have been exhausted, poor lass. But I've every confidence that she's getting better. Just see that she keeps warm. She'd thrown the bedclothes off when I went in just now and that won't do her any good at all.'

'No, of course not,' Bella agreed. 'She'll feel hot and sticky, though, won't she, with perspiring so much?'

'I've sponged her down and...er...made her clean and comfy,' said William, sounding a little embarrassed. 'So you don't need to do anything of that sort, Bella. She's due for another dose of medicine, happen about eleven o'clock?'

Bella nodded. 'I'll see to it,' she said.

'Well, thanks again,' said William. 'I'll leave her in your capable hands.'

Clara had fallen asleep again. Bella went down to the shop to make sure that all was running smoothly, then returned to the Moon family home. It was the first time she had had a chance to have a good look around; to have a 'good old nosey' in other words.

She noted the homely touches in the living room. Clara's half-finished knitting in a patchwork bag, still where she had left it, shoved down the side of an armchair; Isaac's pipe and tobacco tin on the mantelshelf; William's library book, *The Woman in White* – at least she guessed it was William's – again left on the seat of a chair; they were not the tidiest of families. On the top of the sideboard there was a collection of framed family photographs, some of which she knew had been there for ages. William and Clara's wedding photograph, for instance, and one of old Isaac and his wife, Hannah; casual snapshots of Patrick and Maddy as tiny children, as well as a more formal studio photograph, posed with a huge rocking horse.

There were two that Bella had not seen before, although it was the first time, of course, that she had had the chance to examine any of them closely. There was Maddy with her arm around Jessie, the girl she had got so friendly with during the summer; and there they all were in a second photograph – taken by Isaac, she recalled – standing in the yard after they had returned from that Pierrot show, Faith Barraclough looking elegant and dressed in the height of fashion, with a faraway smile on her – admittedly – beautiful face. Bella had not taken to that woman at all, and she knew that that was because she had noticed the way that William had glanced at her once or twice. Not that William would ever dream of being unfaithful to his beloved Clara, not he! He looked proud and pleased, standing between his wife and his son, and with one of his hands resting gently on the head of his daughter, Maddy, who was seated in front of him. And there was she, Bella, standing at the end of the row...like an afterthought. It had probably been an afterthought to invite her to that family outing anyway.

She felt a spasm of resentment run through her as she recalled, again, her loyalty and years of service to this family. She put the photograph down and went upstairs and into the bedroom. She had seldom entered this room before, except to leave her coat on the bed, maybe, when she had paid one of her infrequent visits to a Moon family get-together. Looking around the room now reawakened her feelings of bitterness and envy, much more than had her forays into the other rooms of the house. There was something so intimate about a brass bedstead, she thought. It was a design loved by the Victorians, to be found in the homes of the rich and poor alike. This one gleamed with constant polishing, and hanging on one of the brass balls at the foot of the bed was William's striped pyjama jacket. She knew he had slept in the small study-room last night – at least, that had been his intention – but the blue and white jacket and the trousers, which were folded and laid on a chair, evoked images in her mind of the two of them in the marital bed.

On top of the dressing table – a dainty piece of furniture with a swing-mirror and a chintz frill – were three mats with crocheted edges. Two silver-backed brushes and a hand mirror, all inscribed with the initials CM lay upon them, a gift, no doubt, for birthday or Christmas from a loving husband;

and a glass hair tidy with a silver top out of which protruded wisps of Clara's red-gold hair. A tall chest of drawers of dark mahogany – a much more manly piece – held William's wooden-backed brushes and a photograph of Clara, a much younger Clara, in a silver frame.

Bella's eyes rested in turn on the chintz curtains with a design of large pink roses, partially drawn to keep the light out of Clara's eyes, although it was a miserable greyish sort of day anyway, with no hint of sunshine. The satin eiderdown and the silken counterpane beneath it were pink as well, as was the fluffy rug on Clara's side of the bed.

The eiderdown, really only for show except when the weather was extra cold, had slipped sideways and the rest of the bedclothes – the sheets, blankets and counterpane – were tangled and only partly covering Clara's body. Automatically, Bella straightened them and pulled them more closely around her. William had said she must be kept warm.

Clara stirred at that moment and opened her eyes. She blinked confusedly then stared at Bella as though trying to remember who she was. Then, 'Oh...it's you,' she said. 'Bella... I was dreaming. What time is it? Where's William?'

Bella glanced at the clock on the bedside table. 'It's nearly eleven o'clock,' she said. 'You've had a nice long sleep. William is out on a job, so I'm looking after you. Are you feeling any better, Clara?'

She closed her eyes again. 'I'm not sure. I think I might be. But I'm so terribly hot... Eleven o'clock did you say? In the morning?'

'Yes, of course,' said Bella, smiling. 'You're a bit mixed up, aren't you? Eleven o'clock in the morning, and that means it's time for your next dose of medicine.' She looked at the bottle, standing next to the clock. There was a small drinking glass there too, a jug of water covered with a bead-edged doily, and a bottle containing orange squash.

'How do you take your medicine?' asked Bella. 'Let me see...' She picked up the bottle and read the label. 'Oh yes; it dissolves in water. Does William mix it with the orange juice?'

'I think so,' said Clara. 'Yes...in a glass, with the orange juice. Or hot lemon juice.'

There was a teaspoon there as well. Bella carried the bottle of white powder and the glass over to the window so that she could see more clearly. Half a teaspoonful... What would be the effect, she pondered, if she were to administer a full spoonful, or two...or the whole bottleful? You would be found out, you stupid woman, she answered herself. William would ask where the powder had gone. He would know how much of it was left, even now. But what if...? A niggling little thought which she had not, as yet, allowed to take control in her mind, was becoming more persistent. This medicine was meant to be Clara's lifeline, her aid to recovery. Supposing, instead of increasing the dose, which would be sure to be noticed, she were to withhold it? It was supposed to be taken regularly in order to bring the temperature down and reduce the feverishness. But supposing Clara was to be deprived of the next two doses, and the same again tomorrow? She, Bella, would have no control over what happened when William was caring for her, but now...now she was in charge.

'I won't be a minute,' she whispered to Clara, even pausing for a moment to touch the hand that was lying on the bed cover. 'I'm just seeing to your medicine.'

Driven by an impulse that seemed, almost, outside of herself, she hurried into the bathroom. She scooped out half a spoonful of the white powder and emptied into the washbasin, turning on the taps and making sure it was swilled away down the drain. Returning to the bedroom she mixed together the orange juice and water and took it over to Clara.

'Here you are,' she said. 'Do you think you can manage to sit up a bit? That's right… Now then, drink it all down in one go, then you won't taste it.' Clara smiled weakly and did as she was told.

'That's good,' said Bella. 'Now, can I get you anything else? A cup of tea? A drink of lemon juice?'

Clara shook her head. 'Nothing, thanks. But if you could change my pillow case, please, Bella? It's wet through again. I'm sorry to be such a nuisance.'

'Don't mention it. Of course you're not a nuisance.' Bella stripped off the pillow case which was soaked with perspiration, exchanging it for a clean one which she found in the airing cupboard on the landing.

Clara smiled her thanks. 'That feels better. I don't want to go to sleep again. I feel as though I'm sleeping my senses away. I'll just lie here quietly… Send Maddy in to see me, please, will you, when she comes home from school?'

She was sounding a little more coherent now, thought Bella. All the same, there was still a long way to go.

At lunchtime, at William's insistence, Clara managed to drink a small amount of the chicken soup which Bella had heated up. Only a few spoonfuls but William seemed well pleased with her progress.

'That's good,' said Bella with a forced brightness. 'She had her eleven o'clock dose of medicine. And I could see to the afternoon one too, if you like?'

'Yes, if you would, please, Bella,' he replied. 'We shall be busy in the workshop all afternoon. We've another rush job on, I'm afraid.'

'Don't worry; I'll see to everything,' she said.

Clara had perked up a little when she had drunk the chicken soup. Bella asked if she would like anything else; a cup of tea, perhaps? To her surprise Clara agreed that she did rather fancy a cup of tea. Bella sat with her whilst she drank it, watching her carefully all the while. She did not seem to want to talk but appeared glad of the company. Soon her eyelids began to close and her head fell forward. Bella put a hand on her shoulder.

'Clara...' she said. 'It's nearly time for your next dose of medicine. I think it would be best for you to have it now, then I can leave you to sleep in peace. I can see that you're feeling tired again.'

'Yes, so I am,' smiled Clara. 'I'm a real old lazybones, aren't I?'

Once again Clara partook of the imaginary dose of medicine and handed the empty glass back to Bella. 'I can almost feel it doing me good already,' she said. Such was the power of self-delusion... In a few moments she was asleep again.

Bella closed the curtains fully, then went down to the shop for her daily visit to make sure that all was running smoothly. Martin assured her that they were managing just fine. They had had several customers during the morning, but it was not likely there would be any more now as darkness was falling early. Bella gave them permission to close an hour earlier than usual. A thick mist was rolling in from the sea and although it was only just turned three o'clock the daylight had almost vanished.

When she returned to the sickroom she found that Clara's bedcovers were once again in a tangled heap, barely covering her, and her pillow was wet again. Her head, in fact, was hardly touching the pillow at all. She straightened the bedclothes and then, instead of covering her up again, she turned them right back to the foot of the bed. She saw Clara give an involuntary shudder, but she did not wake up. Her nightdress was a pretty summery one, not at all suitable for the winter, but Bella guessed that the more serviceable ones might be all in the wash.

Keep her warm and covered up at all times, had been William's instructions. The constant sweating was nature's way of bringing the temperature down. But Bella left her uncovered. Moreover, she went across to the window and drew back the curtains, then pushed up the central sash window until there was a gap of about a foot above the sill. The mist was thickening now; she could scarcely see across to the other side of the road. A chilly blast of air swept across the room and over the bed where Clara was lying. Bella stood for several seconds looking at her. The violent and dangerous thoughts which had lingered at the back of her mind for so long and had recently come to the forefront, now, in that moment, took complete control of her. She eased the sodden pillow away from Clara's head, gently though, so as not to waken her, and stripped off the pillow case. There was a clean dry one lying over the back of a chair where William must have left it in readiness. Quickly she slipped it over the feather pillow.

But she did not replace it beneath Clara's head. She stood at the side of the bed, the pillow grasped firmly in her hands. She held it motionless about a foot or so away from the patient's face. Her mind was a blank, empty of coherent thought, as she stood there – she did not know for how long – probably no more than twenty seconds... Then she heard a voice behind her.

'What are you doing? Why is the window open? And why has me mam got no covers over her? Aunty Bella...what are you doing?'

Chapter Seventeen

Bella felt herself freeze... Yes, indeed; what was she doing? What on earth had possessed her? She turned round to see Maddy staring at her in horror.

'Aunty Bella...' she said again. 'What are you doing?'

Bella's face felt stiff, as though the muscles would not respond, but she managed a sort of a smile. She hoped that the frenzy and the hatred she had been feeling only a few moments ago did not show in her eyes. But she feared that the feeling of guilt which was rapidly taking hold of her now would be all too obvious.

'Oh...hello, Maddy,' she said. 'I wasn't expecting you back so soon...' She stopped, realising too late that that was a foolish thing to say. 'I mean...has school finished early?'

'Yes,' replied Maddy in a flat voice. 'They said we could come home 'cause it was foggy and it's going to get worse... Don't you think you'd better cover me mam up? And why have you opened the window?'

'To let some air in,' said Bella, walking briskly to the window and closing it. 'There we are...that's enough, I think, but it was so very stuffy in here. A room where somebody is poorly has to be well ventilated, you see, or else the germs might spread even more.' She went over to the bed and pulled the covers around Clara's still sleeping form, tucking them in around her shoulders.

'There we are,' she said again. 'She'll feel rather more

comfortable now.' She rested her hand on Clara's head, to give emphasis to her words. 'Your poor mother was so hot and sweaty; that's why I was letting her cool down a bit. See, her hair's all damp. Could you pass me that towel, please, dear? Yes, it's hanging on the end of the bed...and I'll wipe her forehead.'

Bella was still holding the pillow, which she very gently eased beneath Clara's head. 'I was just putting a nice dry pillowslip on when you came in,' she said. She took the towel from Maddy and realised, to her dismay, that her hands were trembling. She grasped the towel more firmly, but her movements as she wiped the invalid's face and forehead were soft and soothing. She was talking all the while, although it was a one-sided conversation.

'All this sleeping will do your mam good. I expect by tomorrow she'll be feeling much more like herself. I wonder if she will feel like eating something tonight. What do you think she might like, Maddy? Is there anything that we might tempt her with?'

Maddy was still staring at Bella with a puzzled expression on her face. 'I don't know...' she said. 'Haven't you already decided what we're going to have? I thought you were seeing to the meals while me mam's poorly.'

'Yes...yes, of course I am. We're having lamb's liver and onions with mashed potatoes and carrots. And an egg custard afterwards.'

'I don't like liver,' said Maddy in an expressionless tone. 'I thought you knew that.'

Normally Bella would have retorted that little girls should eat what they were given and not be so fussy, or words to that effect, but she found herself answering in a very different vein. 'Oh dear, don't you, Maddy? Well...perhaps you could have some bacon instead. I was thinking of cooking some bacon as well to make it more tasty.'

To her relief Maddy seemed to relax a little. She shrugged. 'I can eat it if I have to; liver, I mean. Mam always gives me just a tiny bit. She doesn't like it much either, but we have it because she says it's good for us.'

Bella laughed. Even to her own ears the laughter sounded false and hollow. 'Oh, deary me, yes! Grown-ups are always telling you what's good for you, aren't they?' Maddy did not smile back. Clearly she was not ready yet to be all friends together. She was still eyeing Bella suspiciously.

At that moment there was a slight movement from the bed and the sound of Clara's voice. 'What time is it? Oh dear, I've been asleep again, haven't I? Is it night-time? It's so dark in here...'

Bella felt a great sigh of relief escape from her. 'You've had a good long sleep,' she said cheerfully, 'and I'm sure you'll feel much better for it.'

'I'm thirsty,' said Clara. 'My mouth and throat...they're so dry. And there's a nasty taste in my mouth. But perhaps it's the taste of the medicine. Do you think so?'

'I expect so,' replied Bella soothingly, although she knew it could be no such thing. 'What about a nice drink of blackcurrant juice? And I'll stir a spoonful of honey into it. That's good for a sore throat.'

'Where's William?' asked Clara, raising her head a little and looking round the room. 'Oh...hello, Maddy love. I hadn't seen you there. But it's so dark. Oh dear, I'm in such a muddle I don't know whether it's night or day. Where's William?' she asked again.

It was Maddy who answered. 'He's busy working with

Grandad and Patrick. But I 'spect they'll be finishing soon because it's going dark already. It's real foggy outside, Mam; that's why we finished school early. It's not four o'clock yet. You can't see anything outside, the fog's that thick.'

Clara glanced towards the window. 'So it is. Could you close the curtains, love, and shut it out? And, Bella, perhaps you could light the little lamp at the side of the bed, please? You're ever so good, looking after me like this.'

'Not at all; I'm only too pleased to help,' said Bella as she applied a match to the gas mantle on the bedside lamp. 'There, that's more cosy. It's certainly not a night for being out and about, is it?' Even as she spoke they heard the sound of the foghorn booming out from the lighthouse at the end of the harbour pier. 'Pity the poor sailors on a night like this. Maddy, would you like to come with me and we'll see to your mother's drink, then you can bring it back to her. I'd best be making a start with the meal soon. I dare say the menfolk'll want it a bit earlier tonight.'

Stop prattling, woman! she chided herself. She knew she must act normally and get on with the task that had been entrusted to her, that of looking after the household...and Clara. The enormity of what she had so very nearly done was coming home to her now. If she had not heard Maddy's voice at that moment, if the girl had returned from school only a few minutes later...would she really have pressed the pillow down on to Clara's face and smothered the life out of her? Surely she would not have gone through with it? It must have been a moment's madness, a temporary derangement of her mind that had caused her to act in such a way. Was it also a temporary madness that had made her withhold Clara's medicine and open the window to let the cold air blow over her uncovered body? Had she really intended to bring an end to the life of the woman who had befriended her for so long? But this was also the woman who had been married to the man that she, Bella, had loved for nearly all her life...

Once again the wicked thoughts that had caused the unbalance in her mind were threatening to control her. But she was not going to let them rule her any longer. And the more she thought about it the more she convinced herself that she could not have gone through with her plan to kill Clara. Something would have stopped her. If it had not been Maddy's appearance, then she would have come to her senses at the last moment.

But what had Maddy seen? A pillow being held over her mother's head; had she realised the significance of that? The open window and the drawn-back bedclothes...all of which Bella had tried to explain away. But was there a doubt lingering in the child's mind, and if so, would she tell anyone? Her father, her brother, or might she even tell her mother that her friend had been trying to kill her? If she did, then surely they would dismiss it as nonsense and tell her she was imagining things. It was well known that she and Maddy had never really been the best of friends.

She had to make sure, though, that she behaved in an exemplary manner now. She would do her damndest to make amends for her fleeting loss of sanity. She set to with determination, scrubbing the potatoes clean and then peeling them.

The family were well satisfied with the meal of liver and bacon. Clara did not have any of it – Maddy had said that liver was not her mother's favourite meal – but she managed to eat a small amount of egg custard.

Tomorrow would be Saturday and Bella knew that William would be seeing to Clara's needs himself throughout the weekend. So there would have been no opportunity anyway to inflict any further harm on the patient. That was what the more rational part of her mind was telling her. And with the resumption of the medicine and the loving care that surrounded her Clara would get well again. Bella convinced herself that this would be so, and that it was what she was now hoping and praying for. She turned cold with fright at the thought that she might well have been accused of...murder! But Clara was going to recover... By the next morning, however, Clara's condition had worsened. She had had a restless night and William, still sleeping on the sofa in the upstairs lounge, had been back and forth all night attending to her needs. As soon as daylight dawned he sent again for the doctor.

Dr Metcalfe looked grave as he examined the barely conscious patient. He shook his head. 'It is as I feared might happen. She has developed pneumonia. There are some particularly virulent germs flying around at the moment, but I hoped with the constant care she has been getting that she might have avoided this complication.'

'Do you mean...? She will recover though, won't she?' asked William. But the doctor did not give him the reassurance he was seeking.

'All I can say is that the next twenty-four hours will be critical,' he replied. 'By that time the fever might have broken, or...' he paused ominously, 'there is the possibility that it...might not do so. I do want you to be prepared, Mr Moon, but in your job, of course, you do know something of these matters, don't you?'

William looked at him in desperation. 'You mean...her

chances are not good? But I thought she was getting better. She seemed to be, last night.'

'And with constant care she might pull through,' said the doctor. 'The medicine every four hours, that is essential. I'll call again tomorrow unless you need me sooner. Don't hesitate to call me if you do.' His face was grim as he went out of the door.

'My darling Clara…' William whispered, leaning over his wife and taking hold of her hand. 'Please don't leave me. I couldn't live without you…'

Bella, hovering outside the door, heard him speaking in a low voice to his wife. She could not catch his words, but she could tell from the doctor's expression that the news was not good. She hurried away, not wanting to encounter William face to face, or Maddy either, who was curled up in an armchair with a book. Bella knew that she would be best employed in the shop that morning, until it was time for her to prepare the lunch. Keeping busy would help to occupy her mind and, hopefully, steer it away from the terrible frightening thoughts that were plaguing her.

It was a gloomy sort of day both outside and inside the house. The fog of the previous day was still lingering and the members of the Moon family were dispirited. A pall of anxiety hung over the household. They half-heartedly ate the meals that Bella prepared for them, and when she had seen to their requirements she made herself scarce, returning to her own rooms above the shop. Whatever had she done? Would she ever be able to forgive herself?

William kept a constant vigil by his wife's bedside, sponging her flushed face and clammy limbs from time to time, as the doctor had directed, before covering her up warmly again.

Her parched lips could only sip at the drinks he gave her and the medicine which, alas, seemed to be having little effect.

In the early hours of Sunday morning William fancied that her breathing was easier. He had not tried to sleep, but had sat in the chair near the bed all night, attuned to every slight movement. As he took hold of her hand she opened her eyes.

'William...' she murmured. 'You're so good to me...' Then her eyelids flickered and her lovely brown eyes closed again...for the last time.

As he knelt there holding her hand her body gave a convulsive shudder and a harsh rasping sound came from her throat. As it stopped her head lolled sideways and her hand slipped away from his gentle grasp.

'Oh no...my darling, don't leave me!' he cried. He laid his head against her breast, although he knew that her heartbeat was stilled, and that his own heart was breaking.

William could not have said how long he stayed there, kneeling by the side of his wife's body. Fifteen minutes, half an hour... The passage of time had no meaning for him now. In those first dreadful moments after the stark reality dawned on him that his beloved Clara was dead, he felt that life would never again have any meaning for him. Clara had been his love, his best friend, his very life.

Eventually, when his sobs and weeping had subsided a little, he rose to his feet, looking down on his wife's lovely face and her golden hair curling over her forehead and around her ears. He knew that there was one last service that he must perform for her. He would trust no one else with the task of laying out her body and preparing her for her last resting place.

He stooped and kissed her forehead, then crept through the silent house and down the stairs, not wanting to awaken the rest of the family. It would be time enough in an hour or two, when he had completed this last act for Clara, for his father and his children to be told the devastating news.

The workshop was a creepy frightening sort of place in the darkness of night and early morning; at least it might seem so to those unused to the trappings of death. But William, accustomed to the sight of partially made coffins standing on end and the piles of shrouds and coffin linings, scarcely noticed his surroundings. He collected the items he needed: a laying-out board and trestles on which to stand it, and a temporary shroud to cover his wife's body before she was laid in her coffin. And that coffin would be the very best he had ever made.

Back in the bedroom he lifted her body off the bed and on to the board. He filled a bowl with warm water then, tenderly and lovingly, he washed her face and body. It was fitting that, in death as he had been in life, he should be the one to share such intimacy with her. He covered her with her temporary shroud then crossed her arms over her breast. It was here, in her own bedroom, where she would lie until they finally laid her to rest.

Her limbs were still flexible, but William knew that in a few hours' time the stiffening of the body, the rigor mortis, would take place. His father, a long time ago, had told him of the belief that if the body did not stiffen in an hour or two, then it was a sign that someone else in the family would soon die. But William had long ago dismissed this as an old wives' tale. There had been cases, of course, of broken-hearted spouses very quickly following their husbands or wives to their graves. They had dealt with such a few themselves, but William's practical nature had, hitherto, made him scorn such fanciful ideas.

How different it was, though, when the deceased person

was his own wife. He laid his hand on her forehead; the coldness of death had still not taken hold of her. Her eyes were closed; that had been the first thing he had done, to close her warm brown eyes that he had seen so many times glowing with love for him. He would never be able to look into their loving depths again.

He realised, though, as he gazed down on her, that this was not Clara at all. This was just an empty shell that until only a short while ago had held the vital warm-hearted spirit that was the real Clara. Now, that spirit had departed from her and – if what he had always tried to believe was true – she had gone on to a better place. His despair was so great at that moment that he wished he might soon join her there. Perhaps the old tale held some truth and her still-pliant limbs were a sign that she was waiting for him to be with her in the unknown realms beyond this earthly life.

But his innate common sense prevailed. He had a son and daughter. They would be as distressed as he was at this dreadful turn of events. Only a few days ago his wife and their devoted mother had been alive and well, seeing to all their needs in her cheerful and unassuming way. She was – or had been, he reminded himself – the very linchpin of their life. And it was for Patrick and Madeleine that he had to go on living. And for his father's sake, too. Isaac would be broken-hearted at the untimely death of his daughter-in-law who was as dear to him as any daughter might have been. Daylight was creeping through the chinks in the curtains, but they must remain closed as must all the other curtains at the front of the premises, as a mark of respect. William breathed a heart-rending sigh. It was time to go and break the news to the rest of the family.

Patrick was already awake and stirring when William

entered his bedroom. 'I've something dreadful to tell you, son,' he began. 'The worst possible news...'

'Mam!' cried Patrick, sitting bolt upright in bed. 'She's not...? No, she can't be...?' William nodded slowly.

'I'm afraid so. Aye, lad; she's gone. And I've done all that's necessary...you know. I saw to that during the night. She's at peace now... We'd best go and tell your sister.'

'And Grandad,' said Patrick, with tears welling from his eyes.

'Aye, my father as well. Do you know...' William shook his head in a bewildered way. 'I can't believe it meself yet. It's as though I'm caught up in a bad dream. But I know I'm not. She's gone, son. Your mother's been taken from us, although God knows why.'

Maddy knew from the look on their faces when they had knocked and entered her bedroom that something was badly amiss. She sat up, her golden hair tousled from sleep and her brown eyes, so like her mother's, staring at them in alarm.

'It's Mam, isn't it?' she asked, then noticing Patrick's tears which he was unable to check, she began to sob loudly. 'Oh no, not Mam. Please tell me she's not...?' William sat at the side of the bed and put his arms around her.

'I'm afraid so, love. Your mother died a few hours ago, quite peacefully. She must have been more poorly than we thought. But you know, don't you, that we all looked after her and we did all we could to make her better. It was pneumonia, you see. A lot of people have...have died from it recently. That's why we've been so busy at the yard.' Then, once again, he was overcome by tears.

Isaac was awake. He usually woke early, no longer needing his full eight hours' sleep as he had when he was younger. The

sounds of weeping coming from Maddy's room told him
something was wrong and he immediately guessed what must
have happened. Quickly he pushed his feet into his carpet
slippers, donned his plaid dressing gown and hurried across
the upstairs landing.

'She's gone then?' he asked, embracing his son in a manner
unlike his usual undemonstrative way. Isaac was not give to
great shows of affection, but that was not to say that he did
not care. And William, too, knew of the depth of his father's
feelings for all of them. 'Aye, it's a real bad do, lad, it is that.
She were a grand lass and you'll miss her. Well, we all will.'

He held tightly to his granddaughter's hand as William
removed the muslin square covering his wife's face, and they
looked down on Clara's serene and untroubled features for
the last time. Maddy was the first one to speak, echoing the
very thought that had occurred to William.

'She doesn't look like Mam,' she said. 'I know it is,
but...she's gone, hasn't she? Like they told us in Sunday
school. She's gone to heaven, hasn't she? The real Mam, I
mean; she's not here.'

'Aye, that just about sums it up, love,' said Isaac. 'That's
what we've been taught all us lives and it's what we've got to
hang on to now. But it's hard to understand the ways of the
Lord at times and that's a fact.' He turned to his son. 'Haven't
you sent for the doctor, Will? You didn't get him during the
night then?'

'No...it was too sudden at the end.' William spoke quietly,
his eyes on his sad-faced daughter. 'Run along now, Maddy
love, and get dressed, and you an' all, Patrick.'

He covered his wife's face again and closed the bedroom
door. 'Perhaps I should have called him out as soon as I knew

she'd...gone, but it was the middle of the night and it didn't seem right to disturb him. To tell the truth I never even thought of it. I just wanted to see to Clara myself. I'll phone Dr Metcalfe now. He'll have to come to issue a...death certificate.' He faltered at the words that he had been so accustomed to saying at other bereavements. He turned and looked perplexedly at Isaac. 'Why, Father? Why has she been taken from us? It's so unfair.'

'Aye, I know, son,' said his father. 'Like I was saying just now, I doubt if we'll ever understand.'

Maddy tugged at her brother's arm. 'Come in here a minute,' she said, going into her bedroom. 'I want to tell you something.'

Patrick followed her. Her eyes were red and she had cried a lot, but now she was bravely trying to stem her tears. 'What is it?' he asked. 'Is it something to do with...Mam?'

She nodded. She stared at him for a few seconds and then she said, in a quiet voice. 'It's about Bella...' She lowered her voice even more. 'I think she killed our mam...'

Patrick almost laughed, not that there was anything at all amusing about what she had said, but because it was so...ridiculous, so outrageous.

'Killed her?' he repeated. 'Don't be silly, Maddy. She couldn't have done. Look, I know you're upset, and so am I. And I know you don't like Bella very much, but you can't go saying things like that. Anyway, Mam died last night, didn't she? There was only Dad with her. Bella wasn't anywhere near. And she's not here now.'

Maddy shook her head in exasperation. 'No...what I meant was, I think she tried to kill her. I saw something. Yesterday...no, not yesterday; I'm all muddled up. It was Friday, the day we came home from school early 'cause it was foggy.' She told her brother what she had seen: Bella standing with a pillow only inches from her mother's face, the turned-back bedclothes and the open window with the cold air blowing in. 'She said she was letting some fresh air in because Mam was so hot. And that she was changing her pillowslip. But I didn't believe her.'

'Did you tell her...what you've just told me? That you thought she was trying to...?'

'No, of course I didn't. And she was real nice to me afterwards. I think she must've been feeling guilty.'

Patrick was thoughtful. 'I've no doubt you thought you saw something, Maddy,' he told her. 'And I must admit I don't like the sound of the open window. But Bella's been very good these last few days, making the meals and everything. Don't say anything to our dad, will you? It'd only upset him even more. Or Grandad...he doesn't like Bella very much and we don't want to cause any more trouble. Anyway, even if what you saw was...suspicious – and I don't think it was, really – there is nothing we can do about it.'

'But I saw her!' persisted Maddy.

Patrick smiled sadly. 'I'm sorry, but I think you might have been mistaken. Bella was very worried about Mam, you know; I don't think she'd do anything to harm her; they were good friends.' He turned his sad eyes towards his sister, then, in an unusual gesture, he put an arm around her. 'We're all going to miss her very much, aren't we? Now, promise me you won't say anything.'

'All right,' replied Maddy. 'I won't.' But she knew what she had seen and what she still believed.

Chapter Eighteen

Bella's arrival, to see to the family's breakfast on Sunday morning, coincided with the visit of Dr Metcalfe. It was a solemn-faced William who opened the door to both of them.

'Oh dear,' said Bella. 'Has Clara taken a turn for the worse? I did hope she might be getting better.'

'No,' said William briefly. 'I'm afraid she's gone... Clara died during the night.'

'Oh no!' Bella cried out with shock and dismay which were not pretence. She had been hoping against hope that that would not happen. It must have been very sudden. She thought she had never seen so much anguish on a man's face as there was on William's as he turned to look at her. For a moment he stared at her blankly, seeming not to know who she was or why she was there.

Then, recovering himself a little he said, 'Bella...yes, of course. The breakfast...and dinner, too, I suppose, although I don't think we will feel like eating very much.'

'No, possibly not; I understand,' she said. 'I really am very, very sorry, William.' Tentatively she placed a hand on his arm but he made no response.

His features did not soften into even the slightest semblance of a smile as he said, curtly, 'Thank you. Now, if you will excuse me I must attend to Dr Metcalfe.'

She followed the two men through the doorway and entered the kitchen, whilst they went upstairs to the bedroom.

Isaac and Patrick were seated at the table looking down at the empty plates in front of them. They lifted their heads, staring at her with a vacant look in their eyes. Maddy, busy at the stove, did not even turn round.

'I've...just heard,' Bella faltered, 'about Clara. I saw William...and the doctor. It's dreadful news, Mr Moon,' she said, addressing her remarks to Isaac. 'I'm so sorry...for all of you.'

'Aye, well...so are we,' replied Isaac gruffly. 'If you've come to see to us breakfasts then there's no need. Our Maddy's making a bit of toast, aren't you, love?'

'Yes, Grandad,' replied Maddy. She turned round then, narrowing her eyes and staring across at Bella. The look she levelled at her was, Bella thought, full of hatred. It was a secretive and meaningful sort of look too...or was she only imagining it? Isaac and Patrick were unaware of the malice in the girl's stare, but they did not seem to welcome Bella's presence any more that Maddy did. 'I can manage, thank you...Aunty Bella,' she said evenly.

Her eyes were red and it was clear that she had shed a good many tears. Bella could not have said there was insolence in her tone, but the meaning was clear; we do not want you.

'I understand,' said Bella. 'It's a family time. You will want to be on your own. But if you should need me later...' She hesitated before going on to say, 'There's a shoulder of lamb I bought yesterday. It's in the pantry, and there are the vegetables to see to...'

'Aye, well... I suppose we'll have to try and eat to keep our strength up,' said Isaac. He paused for a moment and Bella guessed at the thoughts running through his mind. However would they manage without Clara to look after them?

'So if you don't mind,' he continued, 'happen you could see to it for us...please, Miss Randall?'

'I can do it, Grandad,' said Maddy quickly and a trifle truculently. But her grandfather shook his head.

'Nay, love. We'd best let...er...Bella come and give us a hand today, and then, well, we'll have to see...'

Bella left them to it for the moment, returning to her own rooms to make herself a cup of tea and a slice of toast. She could not stem the resentful thoughts that sprung to her mind. When all was said and done the Moon family could not manage without her. They needed a capable woman to run their household for them. Isaac knew that very well and so did William. They had been only too willing to make use of her over these last few days. And what would they do now? she wondered...

As she sat by the fire she had laid earlier that morning she felt her hands and then her limbs beginning to tremble. She gripped tightly at the chair arms, trying to get a grip on herself as well. Her sorrow at Clara's death was genuine, but so was her fear. Her wicked thoughts and the action she had so very nearly brought about, had they contributed in any way to Clara's death? It must have been very sudden at the end. Was it because she had been deprived for a time of her vital medicine? Had Clara, in those few moments when the cold air blew in on her, suffered a relapse from which her body could not recover? And there was something else, which might be even more pertinent to the question; what thoughts were going through Maddy's mind right now? Had she told anyone of what she had seen, or who was she likely to tell? The child disliked her, she knew that, and she was grieving over the death of her mother. She, Bella, might be accused of murder!

Her hands flew automatically to her throat. The penalty for murder was hanging; to be hanged by the neck until you are dead...

It would be futile to argue that she hadn't meant it, that she would never have gone through with it. Bella did not know herself what she might or might not have done if the girl had not returned at that moment. But the fact remained that the evil vicious thought had been there in her mind, and now Clara was dead.

But she would – she must – make amends. She must behave with Maddy as though the incident had never happened. And maybe, in a little while, the girl would come to the conclusion that she had only imagined what she had seen. She, Bella, would prove to them all what a devoted friend she had been to Clara.

Clara's coffin was the finest that William had ever made, and he had insisted on completing every last detail of it himself. It was made of oak wood of the very best quality, French polished to a high gloss and with six ornamental handles of silver gilt. It was lined with pitch, as were all coffins to make them waterproof, which was then covered with cotton wool padding. Coffin linings varied in quality; cotton, silk or satin according to what the family could afford. William chose ivory satin with a frill all around the circumference of the coffin. The outer edge hung down over the sides, to be tucked in when the coffin lid was finally screwed down. Clara's head lay on a satin pillow, and her golden hair against the whiteness of the coffin lining and shroud shone just as brightly in death as it had in life. William combed it gently and reverently in soft waves over her forehead and ears.

Her hands were crossed over her breast, the plain gold wedding band visible on her left hand. It was usual, although not always the case, for relatives to request that wedding rings should not be removed. William recalled that family members sometimes asked that cherished items might be buried with the deceased; a brooch or locket maybe, a family photograph or a Bible or prayer book. He had formerly regarded such requests as sentimentality, but at the last moment when he looked down at the body of his beloved wife he realised that perhaps they were no such thing. He reached for the pocket-sized Bible bound in white leather which Clara had carried on their wedding day, and placed it beneath her folded hands.

There... She was as lovely as ever; and although he might wish that it could be otherwise, he knew that friends and neighbours would want to come, as was the custom, to pay their last respects to the woman they had all admired so much. Strangely enough, Clara had never had many close friends – her family had always been all in all to her – but she had been well loved in the community. No one had ever had a wrong word to say about her. Clara had been a truly good woman.

A verse from the Bible came into William's mind as he stood at the side of the coffin, loath to go away and leave her all alone. 'Who can find a virtuous woman, for her price is far above rubies...' It was from the Book of Proverbs, he thought, although he was not an ardent reader of the Bible. He would ask the minister of the chapel if they could have those verses read out at the service. They were to have a service at the chapel on Queen Street before Clara was taken for burial at the cemetery on Dean Road. The arrangements had been made for Friday morning, which was in four days' time.

His father, and Patrick and Maddy came first to look upon

Clara in her coffin. William had decided that she must remain there in the bedroom where she had always slept, given birth to her children, and where she had died, rather than in the family living room. Some households had a separate room, referred to as the 'front room' or the 'best room' where deceased persons could be laid out, but the Moon family had just the one large room, apart from the kitchen, where they ate and spent their leisure time. Both the children were dry-eyed now that a day and a half had passed since their mother's death, but William knew that the funeral would be an ordeal for them. He had told both of them that he would like them to be there. It had been the custom at one time for only the men to attend a funeral, leaving the womenfolk at home, but customs were gradually changing. Patrick, of course, was well used to attending such events; and even Maddy, brought up as she had been in close proximity to the practices and traditions associated with death, knew more about it than did most children of her age. William considered that she was old enough, at nearly eleven years of age, to attend her own mother's funeral.

From Tuesday onwards there was a steady stream of visitors to the Moon family home bringing small posies or larger bunches and sprays of flowers. Wreaths to place upon the closed coffin would arrive on the morning of the funeral. Most touching were the posies of snowdrops or primroses carried by the children; school friends of Maddy or girls from her Sunday school class whose mothers had brought them along to say how sorry they were. Maddy, like her mother had been, was a very popular person. The sprays contained mainly lilies, the conventional funeral flower, or chrysanthemums in shades of gold, bronze and russet-red. Very few flowers were available at that time of the year, although there were some expensive ones grown in hothouses.

William had seen little of Bella since Clara's death. She had appeared shaken and extremely grief-stricken. He had never seen her so subdued. He wondered, again, if he had been wrong in keeping her at arm's length for so long. After all, there was nothing between the two of them now. It seemed that she had been very fond of Clara and was as saddened by her death as the rest of them. She had prepared their meals and then disappeared back to her own rooms which were now over their shop. He appreciated the tact she was showing by not dining with them. It was a time for just the family members to be alone together, although sensitivity was not a trait that he had noticed in Bella in the past.

The shop, Moon's Mourning Modes, had remained closed on Monday and Tuesday, and would close all day Friday, of course, the day of the funeral. William decided to speak to Bella, however, on the Tuesday evening, to suggest that the store should open as usual on the Wednesday and Thursday. It was something to which he had given serious thought. He did not want to appear callous or grasping, especially at such a sad time; on the other hand the shop provided a service for the folk in the area and there was no other shop in the town to compare with it. There might well be people wanting to purchase items of mourning to wear at Clara's funeral. The undertaking side of the business, which was a separate concern, would remain closed all week.

Nor would Clara be the only person to be laid to rest on that day. Influenza and pneumonia as well as the usual winter ailments of bronchitis and asthma had been rife in the town. There had been several funerals planned, but Isaac Moon and

Son had passed their bookings for that week on to another firm.

Bella gave an involuntary start when she answered the knock on her door and found William standing on the threshold. She invited him in and listened to his plans regarding the shop.

'Very well then, William,' she said, with a compassionate nod and the hint of a smile. 'I will contact Martin and Polly and tell them that we will be reopening tomorrow. What about your other arrangements, though? I don't want to appear pushy but...what about your meals? I assume you want me to take over my duties in the shop again, and I don't think...'

'No, of course you can't do that and look after us as well,' replied William. 'I want you to know how much we appreciate all you have done for us. We – that is to say my father and I – we would like you to resume your duties in the shop, though. And now that Clara is...no longer with us, would you consider, perhaps, taking over as manageress? With a suitable rise in your wages, of course.'

Bella inclined her head. 'That would be very acceptable,' she said. 'Thank you.'

'As for our family arrangements,' he continued, 'Louisa has offered to look after us for the next few days. She is heartbroken, as you can imagine, over Clara's death. She regarded her almost as a daughter. We can't put on her good nature, though, for too long. She's an elderly lady and she has her own business to see to as well. When...when all this is over...' He paused, overcome for a moment by an upsurge of grief, '...we will have to see about employing a housekeeper. We intend to ask around in the chapel congregation. There are

one or two ladies who might be willing.' He looked straight at
Bella then, not smiling, but as though he were inviting her, it
seemed, to share with him in his grief. 'We are all going to
miss her so very much,' he said, a sob catching at his throat.
'And I know you were such a good friend to her, Bella. You
will come to the funeral, of course, won't you? I know she
would have wanted you to be there.'

Bella felt so ashamed at that moment, so overcome with
guilt, that she was unable to answer for several seconds. She
felt the colour rising to her cheeks as she looked down at the
floor. She hoped that William had not noticed her
discomfiture. But he could not help but do so.

'Is there something the matter?' he asked gently.

She raised her head, looking him in the eyes and trying to
control her emotions. 'No...no; of course I will be there.' She
knew how odd it would appear if she were to stay away,
which, deep down, she felt she ought to do. What right did she
have to attend the funeral of the woman she had considered
killing? The thought still plagued her that what she had done
might, indeed, have played a part in Clara's death. 'I was just
thinking how very sad it is,' she went on. 'Just a short while
ago Clara was well, and now...' She shook her head. 'It's so
hard to understand... Anyway...thank you for inviting me.'

She had regained her composure now, so she asked, 'Would
you like a hand with the arrangements for the meal? I take it
you will be having something to eat...afterwards. If there is
anything I can do...'

'That's all taken care of,' said William. 'But thank you all the
same. The women at chapel have rallied round and asked if
they can help. A few of them will be coming here on Friday
morning to prepare sandwiches, meat pies...whatever they

decide on; I have left it all to them. And they will draw back the curtains and let the daylight in again, ready for our return.' That was always the custom after a funeral, to attempt to dispel the gloom and help the household to return to normal.

William stood up, and Bella realised that their conversation was at an end. 'Goodnight, Bella, and thank you again,' he said briefly as he took his leave of her.

They had spoken of nothing else but the funeral arrangements and business matters, but it was the longest talk they had had for many years. Certainly the longest since she had come to work for the Moon family. A time would come, she felt sure, when William would realise how much he relied on her. And, maybe, when his time of grieving had passed, he would remember how it had once been between the two of them...

It was something of an anomaly organising the funeral of his beloved wife. William had wanted to tend to her himself; he could not possibly have allowed anyone else to perform such intimate tasks. But as far as the funeral was concerned, he had at first considered handing over the arrangements to a rival firm; a friendly rival, that was, as they all worked amicably together. Then he came to the conclusion that it would be more fitting to use their own hearse, with their own two horses, Jet and Ebony, to pull it. But neither Patrick nor his father nor, indeed, he himself, wanted to lead the procession as they normally did, in their turns, in their professional capacity. Eventually they decided to ask another firm in the town, with whom they had cooperated in the past, to provide them with pall-bearers, an extra carriage in which the family members would ride, and someone to lead the procession in front of the hearse.

It was a sombre little group who gathered together in the

Moon family living room on the Friday morning. The service in the Queen Street Methodist chapel had been arranged for eleven o'clock, to be followed by burial at the cemetery on Dean Road. Louisa Montague joined the family members – William, Isaac, Patrick and Maddy – just before half past ten. She had seemed to age considerably over the last few days since the death of her beloved Clara. She was dry-eyed now, but her pale face still showed signs of weeping and her slight figure looked shrunken into itself in the deep black mourning clothes. They were waiting now for Bella, whom William had asked to accompany them in the family carriage. So when there was a knock at the door at ten-thirty he went to answer it, assuming he would find her there on the doorstep.

He gave an involuntary start of surprise at seeing Faith Barraclough standing there. He had written to tell her of Clara's death and had, indeed, invited her to come to the funeral if she should wish to do so. But it had been out of courtesy more than anything else, and he had not really expected her to attend.

'William…' She stretched out a black-gloved hand and he saw her blue eyes mist over with tears. 'I am so very, very sorry. I hope you don't mind me coming, that you don't think I am intruding, but I felt I had to be here.'

'Mind? Of course I don't mind,' he replied, taking her hand and holding it for several seconds. 'I invited you, didn't I? But I didn't press you too much to come because it's a fair way to travel from York at this time of the year; I didn't want you to feel obligated.'

It was a raw cold sort of morning. The recent fall of snow had all disappeared, but the thawing wind seemed even colder than the frost and ice had been.

'I'm in good time, am I?' she asked. 'I caught an early train because I was worried in case it might be delayed. One never knows…'

'Yes; it's a quarter of an hour or so before we set off for the chapel,' said William. 'We're just waiting for…for the undertaker,' he faltered slightly at the word. 'We decided to ask for some help, although we're using our own hearse, and Jet and Ebony. Clara was so fond of them… Anyway, come along in.' He looked at her cheeks which were pink with the cold wind, as was the tip of her nose. 'You didn't walk from the station, did you?'

'No, I took a cab,' she answered, following him along the passage and into the living room. They all turned to look at her. Maddy, who until then had seemed to be in control of herself, jumped up from her chair and ran across the room.

'Mrs Barraclough!' she cried. She flung herself at the woman, putting her arms around her waist and burying her head in the folds of her black coat. 'Oh…oh, I'm so glad you've come. Oh dear! I didn't mean to start crying again, but I miss my mam so much.' Her shoulders shook with sobs as the tears began to flow again. 'I just don't know what I'm going to do without my mam…'

'I know, dear, I know,' said Faith, stroking the child's golden hair and holding her close. 'I'm so very, very sorry.' She looked around at the menfolk and Louisa, whom she had met only briefly before. 'For all of you…' she added. 'I was just saying to William that I hope I'm not intruding on your grief, but I wanted to be here. In the short time I knew her Clara was a good friend to me and to my children. Come along, dear,' she said to Maddy. 'Let's go and sit down, and we'll try and compose ourselves, shall we?'

'You're very welcome, lass,' said Isaac. 'I only wish it were in happier circumstances. Aye, it's been a real blow to us. You might think as how we'd be used to it, but when it's one of yer own...' He shook his head sadly. 'It were t' same when my wife died, my Hannah. It was as though the bottom had dropped out of me world.'

Faith and Maddy sat close together in an armchair that was large enough to hold them both. And that little scene was what Bella noticed, first of all, when she arrived some five minutes later. She had not wanted to get there too soon. It would be an ordeal for her to spend time alone with the Moon family, especially with Maddy. The girl had scarcely spoken to her since Clara's death except when she was forced to do so, and the looks she levelled at her were mistrustful to say the least.

Bella acknowledged them all with a nod and a mumbled 'Good morning...' although she knew it could not, in any truth, be called a good morning. Then, as she could not ignore that the woman was there, she spoke to Faith Barraclough. 'Hello, Mrs Barraclough.' She had not been invited, last summer, to use her Christian name. 'I didn't realise you were coming. It's a sad day, isn't it?'

'Indeed it is, Miss Randall,' said Faith, inclining her head. 'I knew I had to come...to show my respect for Clara. She was a lovely lady.'

They sat in almost complete silence for the next few minutes. Bella could see that Maddy had been crying again. She could not help but feel a surge of compassion for the girl. It was her mother's funeral when all was said and done and the poor child must be feeling wretched. No doubt Faith Barraclough's arrival had set her off weeping again. The woman's arm was around her now, comforting her as though she was a close relation. And she was nothing of the sort. She was just the mother of that girl, Jessica, who Maddy had been so friendly with last summer.

Bella recalled now how William had glanced admiringly once or twice at the woman, when he had been in her company last August. Faith was, undeniably, a beautiful woman, and she was obviously rich enough to be able to dress in the very height of fashion. Her elegant black coat was edged with silver fox fur and her large-brimmed hat, trimmed with ostrich feathers, sat stylishly on her exquisitely coiffured auburn hair.

Bella experienced a tremor of dislike, such as she had done in the summer, although she was not sure herself what there was to dislike about the woman. The truth was that there was nothing at all. Faith Barraclough was charming and kind-hearted; not over-friendly, to be sure, but that was probably because she was of a shy disposition. Bella knew only too well that her antipathy for the woman stemmed from jealousy, as had her feelings for Clara; those feelings of which, so recently, she had lost all control.

She knew that William was not likely to cast admiring glances at Faith today; he was too steeped in his sorrow and despair, she guessed, to be too much aware of her. But what of the future? There might come a time, sooner or later, when William might want a companion to share his life, maybe even a wife. By keeping her ear to the ground Bella had discovered that Faith Barraclough's marriage was not too happy... She made up her mind, there and then, that if, or when, that time arrived it would be she, Bella, who would be there in William's sights, and no one else.

She watched as William invited Faith to go upstairs to look at Clara, before the arrival of the funeral director. The undertaker arrived very soon afterwards; then the lid was screwed down and the pall-bearers carried the coffin down the stairs and into the street.

William placed a large wreath of white lilies, a loving tribute from himself, Isaac, Patrick and Maddy, on top of the coffin. It was then surrounded by a host of wreaths and sprays, their multicoloured hues of bright yellow, gold, bronze, crimson and orange, as well as dazzling white, making a vivid splash of colour through the glass sides of the hearse, on a gloomy grey and sunless morning. They were tokens of affection to a well-loved friend, neighbour and member of the community.

The procession made its short journey from North Marine Road to Queen Street, with the top-hatted leader walking in front of the horse-drawn hearse. The family carriage, in the end, held only Maddy, Faith, Louisa and Bella. William, Isaac and Patrick had decided to walk, leading the other mourners; several more would be joining them in the chapel.

'How sweet the name of Jesus sounds
In a believer's ear;
It soothes his sorrows, heals his wounds,
And drives away his fear...'

The hymn was one that Maddy knew as they had sung it quite often in Sunday school. She felt Mrs Barraclough's arm go gently round her as she tried to sing the words; but they kept catching in her throat and the sound she was making was coming out all funny and squeaky. She knew she could sing nicely most of the time; people were always telling her what a good little singer she was.

But it was different today. Singing was a happy sort of thing to do and she usually enjoyed it, but this was a very sad day. Lots of people had come to the chapel to show how sorry they were that her mam had died. It was a large building and the downstairs part was nearly half full.

They sat down when they had sung the hymn. The minister said some prayers and read from the Bible, all about a woman who looked after her family, just like her mam had always done. He gave a little talk and said what a lovely person – good and helpful and kind – her mam had been and how they would all miss her. Maddy bit her lip and tried hard not to start crying, and she thought that Patrick, sitting in front of her with their dad, was doing the same. She saw her father put his arm around him and Patrick lowered his head. It was hard not to keep looking at the coffin which was standing at the front on something she had heard Patrick call a bier. The wreath of white flowers from the family – Dad, Grandad, Patrick and herself – covered the full length of the coffin. Her dad had asked her if she would like to write on the card, and she had written 'For Clara; a dearly loved wife, daughter and mother. God bless you and keep you in His care.'

After they had sung another hymn they followed the men carrying the coffin – she knew they were called pall-bearers – out into the street and into the carriage again for the journey to the cemetery. It was not very far and Maddy, sitting next to Mrs Barraclough, could see people on the pavement, pausing for a moment from their shopping or whatever they were doing, watching solemnly as the procession went past. The men took off their hats and the ladies bowed their heads.

She made sure as they stood at the graveside that Jessica's mother was next to her. She clung tightly to her hand as she watched the coffin being lowered into the deep deep hole in the ground. Dad threw some clods of earth on the top and so did Patrick and her grandad, and it was then that Maddy felt the tears starting again. She couldn't help it. It was the very worst thing that had ever happened to her. Whatever would she do? How awful it was going to be without her mam at home...

Eventually, after yet another journey in the carriage, they were back home again. A cheerful-looking fire burnt in the grate, the curtains had been drawn back and the ladies from the chapel had been busy preparing sandwiches, meat pies and all sorts of cakes and things. They handed round cups of tea, just as though it was some sort of party. But how could it be? Mam was not there to share in it.

There was quite a crowd there; friends and members of the chapel as well as the family. She saw some of the people smiling and chatting together and there was even some laughter. She wondered how anyone could laugh. Her father and grandfather and Patrick looked quite solemn, though, and she, Maddy, felt as though she would never laugh again. Bella, too, seemed subdued and rather sad as she sat quietly in a corner talking to Martin and Polly from the shop. Maddy hardly glanced at her. She didn't even want to think about Bella and the awful thing she thought she had seen her doing.

She edged close to Mrs Barraclough on the settee and smiled up at her. A sad sort of smile; but she was very glad to have Jessica's mother there with her. It was not like having her own mam, of course, but she was a lovely kind lady and Maddy had always enjoyed being with her last summer.

'You've been a very brave girl, Maddy,' she said, patting her hand. 'I know how hard it must have been for you.'

'Thank you, Mrs Barraclough,' replied Maddy. 'I couldn't help crying a bit. I still want to cry, but I 'spect my dad and Patrick do as well, and Grandad.'

'You may want to cry for quite a while, dear. That's only to be expected. But you must try to smile as well and think of all the happy times you had with your mother. It will get a little bit easier before long. And you have a dad and grandad, and a brother, who all love you very much.'

'I know...' said Maddy quietly.

'Now, are you going to eat one of these nice sandwiches? I don't suppose you had very much breakfast, did you?' Maddy shook her head. 'Well then; you'll feel better if you get some food into your tummy.'

Maddy nodded and nibbled at her ham sandwich. 'Mrs Barraclough...' she began.

The lady smiled. 'Oh dear! Do you think you could call me Faith? Mrs Barraclough is such a mouthful, isn't it?'

'Oh no! I don't think so,' said Maddy. 'You're Jessie's mam... It would be rather rude, wouldn't it?'

'Not if I gave you permission. But I do know what you mean. How about...Aunty Faith, then? Ladies who are friends of your parents are sometimes called Aunty, aren't they? Isn't that what you call...Bella?'

Maddy frowned. 'I s'pose so,' she muttered. 'Mam said I had to...to call her Aunty Bella. But I don't really...' She stopped, realising she had said quite enough and it would not be very nice to say that she didn't like Bella. 'Yes...thank you,' she said, with a little more of a smile now. 'I'd like to call you Aunty Faith.'

'Well then, that's lovely,' replied her new aunt... What was it you were going to ask me, Maddy?'

'Oh yes... I wondered if you were coming to Scarborough again in the summer. Jessie said you might, in her letter at Christmas, but she wasn't sure.'

'Yes, indeed,' replied Faith. 'All being well we will all be here again. That is to say...myself and the children.' Maddy thought she looked rather troubled for a moment. Then she smiled again. 'It will be something for us all to look forward to, won't it?'

Maddy nodded. 'Yes...' she said, frowning a little. 'Aunty Faith... It's not wrong to look forward to things, is it? Mam would've wanted us to be happy again, wouldn't she?'

'Of course she would,' said Faith.

Chapter Nineteen

Bella had been watching the touching little scene of Faith Barraclough comforting Maddy, firstly in the chapel and at the graveside, and later in the family living room. She felt a spasm of resentment, but she also had the good sense to know that it was her own fault that she could not be the one to offer sympathy and support to the little girl. Firstly, there was the antipathy that had developed between the two of them over the years. And now...well, it was not surprising that Maddy would not turn to her, Bella, for comfort after what she had seen in the bedroom...or imagined she had seen. Bella was still determined to win her round by acting as though nothing out of the ordinary had taken place. And if by any chance Maddy should tell anyone about the incident in the sickroom...well then, it would be Bella's word against hers. That woman, Faith, would be gone by tomorrow; in fact it was likely that she would be departing quite soon. And then Maddy would need a different sympathetic ear.

Bella had noticed, too, that William had not spoken very much to Faith since they had returned from the cemetery. He was standing talking to a couple of men from the chapel; at least, they were doing most of the talking and he was listening, nodding now and again or shaking his head. She had seen him wince slightly at one point at the sound of laughter coming from a corner of the room. As well he might, she thought; although the laughter was fairly subdued it was certainly not a time for hilarity. Some folk had no sense of decorum or feeling for the bereaved.

William's face was grey and drawn, as was only to be expected; but she thought that not only did he look sad and perplexed, but ill as well. He put his hand to his forehead once or twice, then she saw him reach for his handkerchief and mop his brow. William was ill. She was sure of it. It took all her self-control for her not to jump up and go over to him, but she stayed where she was.

'I'm sorry... What did you say, Polly?' she asked. 'I was only half listening. I was watching Mr Moon – Mr William, I mean – and thinking he doesn't look at all well... Were you asking if we would be open again tomorrow?'

'Aye, that's what I wanted to know, Miss Randall... Oh deary me, yes! He does look poorly doesn't he, poor man? He'll be missing her summat awful though, won't he? They were a lovely couple. Happen that's what's wrong with him, eh? Just that he's sad, like. You don't think he's caught that 'fluenza thing, do you, like Mrs Moon had?'

'We must hope not, Polly,' said Bella with a sigh. That girl didn't half chatter lately. She had come out of her shell since being given more responsibility in the shop, but she would have to learn her place again. She, Bella, was manageress now. 'In answer to your question; yes, we will be reopening in the morning and then for a couple of hours in the afternoon. Just to show that we're in business again. And then on Monday it will be back to normal; business as usual. You will be paid, of course, for today, and for the days when we were closed earlier this week. Mr Moon insisted on that.'

'Aye, he's a good boss, isn't he?' remarked Martin, who was sitting with them.

'He is indeed,' replied Bella, graciously inclining her head. 'Although it was Mrs Moon, of course, who was in charge of the shop. And now...' She could not help a slight smile of self-satisfaction, '...I will be taking her place as manageress. We will need to advertise for an under-manageress, although there is no immediate hurry. We will have to be sure we appoint somebody who is suitable.'

'Aye; somebody as we can get on with an' all,' added Martin. 'Mrs Moon now; she was a real lovely lady to work for. If there was owt wrong she always told you nicely and didn't go off the deep end.'

Bella bristled a little, sensing a note of criticism of herself and her exacting standards in his remark. 'Mrs Moon didn't always know what went on in her absence though, did she? She wasn't there all the time. She was quite often out, helping Mr Moon with the other side of the business. But you can be sure I will be keeping a watchful eye on everything. And so will anyone else that I...that we...appoint.'

'So you will be taking over Mrs Moon's job then?' asked Polly.

'Of course I will, you silly girl!' replied Bella. 'I've just said so, haven't I? I will be in charge of the shop.'

'Yes, I know about that. But what I mean is...t' other part of it. You know; going out and helping Mr Moon with...with laying out bodies an' all that? That's what Mrs Moon did, didn't she?'

Bella gave a start. 'No...no, of course not. That won't be part of my duties. At least... I don't think so. Mr Moon will appoint someone else, I'm sure, to help him with that side of things.'

It really had not occurred to her at all that she might be

asked to help William in his undertaking duties. No, of course she wouldn't... There were already Isaac and Patrick, and if they should need another pair of hands then it would be someone more accustomed to the task. But as she thought about it, it came to her, in that split second, that there could be no better way, surely, of gaining William's gratitude and friendship than by offering to assist him in that side of his work. She guessed he might need a woman's help, sometimes, if the deceased person was a female. And who better than herself? She, Bella, was not a squeamish sort of person. Admittedly, she had not had a great deal of experience of death, certainly not of laying out bodies, but she could learn...

She realised that she hadn't spoken for several moments. Martin and Polly were looking at her with puzzled expressions. 'Mr Moon will see to everything in time, I suppose,' she said. 'Now, if you will excuse me; I'll just have a word with Mrs Barraclough before she goes.'

Faith had stood up and was gathering together her gloves, scarf and bag; Maddy, it seemed, had gone to fetch her coat from the hallway. 'You are on your way then, are you, Mrs Barraclough?' Bella asked, smiling at the woman in a friendly manner. 'Are you going back to York this afternoon?'

'Yes, there is a train mid-afternoon,' replied Faith. 'I want to get back before it goes dark. These winter evenings are so dismal... It has been a very sad occasion, hasn't it, Miss Randall? I hadn't known Clara very long, and I could scarcely believe it when William wrote to tell me she had died. I felt I had to be here.'

'Yes, indeed,' Bella nodded understandingly. 'And I was pleased to see you befriending little Maddy. Poor child! She will need someone to confide in for the next few weeks or so.

I will do what I can, of course…Clara and I had been friends for a long time, you know.'

'So I believe…' Faith's blue eyes looked directly into Bella's black ones and, to her annoyance, Bella felt herself looking away from the woman's searching glance. There was no chance to speak any more as Maddy came back with Faith's coat, and then William appeared.

'You're going, Faith?' he enquired. 'Of course…you will want to catch a train to get you home before dark, won't you? Come along then; I'll see you out into the street and we'll call a hansom cab.'

Faith kissed Maddy gently on the cheek. 'Goodbye, my dear,' Bella heard her say. 'Jessie will be writing to you soon…and it won't be all that long before we see you all again. God bless you, darling.'

When Bella looked round Maddy had gone over to the other side of the room to talk to her brother. Her back was turned towards Bella, but whether it was by accident or design she did not know. She didn't feel like talking to anyone else; many of the guests, indeed, were people she knew only by sight. She set about keeping busy by collecting empty cups and plates and placing them on the table.

In a few minutes William returned, and it was even more obvious now that he was most unwell. He had had the sense to put on his coat and hat and muffler before going out into the cold air with Faith, and now he almost staggered into the living room, flopping down into the nearest easy chair without even taking off his hat.

'William… Hey, what's up, lad?' His father hurried across to him. 'You've gone a funny colour… Tek yer hat off and loosen yer coat.' Isaac popped the trilby hat on the nearby sideboard and felt at his son's forehead. He nodded solemnly. 'Aye, you're boiling up, aren't you, lad? Why didn't you say you were feeling poorly, like? I knew meself as you weren't too grand, but I thought it was happen…well, you know…because it's a sad day, for you more than for any of us.'

'I thought I'd be all right,' said William. 'I knew I had to keep going for our Patrick and Maddy's sake. But now, I'd best face up to the fact that I've got what Clara had.'

'Well, we don't know that, do we, but we must get t' doctor right away,' said Isaac. He turned round to see his grandchildren standing there staring at their father, both of them looking worried and frightened. 'Go and phone for t' doctor, Patrick, lad,' he said. 'Quick sharp now. Dr Metcalfe; his number's in t' little book on t' hallstand.'

But Bella was there too, standing behind them. 'It's all right, Mr Moon,' she said. 'I'll do it.' She put a hand on Patrick's arm, who looked too petrified to move. 'I'll phone the doctor, Patrick. I can see you've had a shock. But your father will be all right, I'm sure. You stay and look after your sister.'

'Thank you, Bella,' said Isaac Moon. He did not smile, but he gave her a look which, she thought, was one of gratitude. 'Tell him it's urgent, won't you? We'd best get him into t' bedroom. Here, Jack…' He called to one of the men from the chapel. 'Come and give us a hand, will yer? We'll get our Will upstairs and sorted out a bit afore t' doctor arrives.'

William gave a wry sort of smile as he got to his feet again. 'I can manage to walk a few steps, Father. And get meself undressed an' all. I'm not helpless. I'm not going to argue though.' He gave a deep sigh. 'It seems as though it's my turn now.'

'What does he mean, Patrick?' asked Maddy, clutching hold

of her brother's arm. She had heard her father's last few words as he went out of the door, leaning on his friend for support. 'He said it was his turn now. You don't think he means that he's going to…to die, do you, like Mam did?'

'No, of course not,' said Patrick, although he, too, looked pretty pale and scared. 'He meant it was time that he went to bed, like Mam had to do. But just because Mam died it doesn't mean our dad's going to die an' all. He's strong, isn't he? He'll be all right. Everybody knows that men are stronger than women.'

Maddy didn't comment, as she might have done, at the slur on her sex, except to say, 'Mam was strong too, but she didn't get better. And we know why, don't we, Patrick? I told you what I saw.'

'And I told you to forget about it!' said her brother in a harsh whisper. 'You could cause a lot of trouble if you start going on about something you imagined you saw.'

'I didn't imagine it! I told you…Bella had a pillow…'

'Shhh!' Patrick looked round anxiously, but no one seemed to be taking any notice of the two of them. 'You've got to promise you won't say another word, not to anybody. It's too late now anyway. And you can see, can't you, that Bella's trying to be helpful.' The woman had just re-entered the room after phoning the doctor. She came across to the brother and sister. It was Patrick to whom she spoke.

'Don't worry, Patrick. Dr Metcalfe will be here just as soon as he can. He has no doubt but that it's influenza, and he'll bring some of the same medicine that your mother was taking.'

'But it didn't do her any good, did it?' said Maddy sullenly, looking down and kicking at the hearthrug instead of looking straight at Bella.

'No, dear,' said Bella, shaking her head sadly. 'I'm afraid it didn't, and that's all I can say. But your father will get better; I feel sure of it. Now… I'll just go and say goodbye to Martin and Polly…'

Most of the guests had departed now, not wanting to linger when they could see that their host, too, had been taken ill. Bella carried the remaining crockery into the kitchen and, without anyone inviting her to do so, picked up a pot towel and started to dry the dishes, along with the chapel ladies who had been in charge of the catering. They smiled vaguely in her direction but, by and large, they worked in silence. Bella was only killing time whilst awaiting the arrival of the doctor. She intended to offer to help in looking after William, as she had done with his wife.

No…not in exactly the same way, of course. The wickedness of what she had so very nearly done came to the forefront of her mind again – although it was never far away at any time – and she almost dropped a cup. There had to be some way in which she could make amends, not only for the sake of her own guilty conscience, but to William as well for the loss of his wife. If she was given the chance she would look after him diligently and lovingly. Her love for him must not be allowed to show, though, until such time as William recognised himself that the two of them belonged together.

But supposing…supposing William were to die, as his wife had done? Then that would be God's judgement upon her, she reflected, for her wickedness. But could God really be so cruel as to punish her in such a way; a way which would cause others to suffer; Isaac, Patrick and Maddy as well as William? No, of course not. She was allowing her

imagination to run riot. Hurriedly she hung up her pot towel
and left the kitchen.

The other women glanced at one another and smiled
secretly as she went. One of them put a finger to her nose in
an eloquent gesture. 'Hoity-toity madam!' she said.

'Aye; far too big for her boots is that 'un,' said another.

'We don't want her looking after our dad,' said Maddy to
Patrick, when Bella had left them. 'You don't think Grandad
would be silly enough to let her nurse him, like she was
supposed to be doing with Mam, do you?'

'No, I shouldn't think so,' said Patrick. But he guessed that
Bella Randall would never let anything happen to his father. If
– and it was a very big 'if' – Maddy had been right in what
she had seen; if Bella really had been trying to do some harm
to their mam, then Patrick knew what the woman's motives
must have been. She must have wanted his father for herself...

The enormity of what that meant struck him forcibly now.
Bella...and his father! He remembered, now, little instances
that had not meant very much at the time. How he had seen
Bella smile at his father in a secretive sort of way, and how she
looked at him, sometimes, when he was not aware of it.
Patrick recalled, too, some of his grandfather's remarks; hints
of something that had gone on in the past between the two of
them; and he knew, of course, that Grandad had never liked
her.

Bella...and his father... As he thought of the two of them
now he almost cried out in horror. No! No...that was
something that must never be allowed to happen. Maddy
might not have realised the significance of what she had
seen; if, indeed, she had seen anything at all. And he,
Patrick, was not going to put any further doubts into her

mind by telling her that Bella might well have designs on their father. No...Maddy was too young to know about such things.

She was looking at him questioningly. 'No,' he said again. 'Don't be silly, Maddy. It wouldn't be right for Bella to nurse Dad, would it? She's not a relation or anything. Grandad'll probably get a nurse in while he's poorly.'

And that was exactly what happened. Bella lingered, trying to occupy herself until the doctor had been and gone. She went back into the kitchen, which the catering ladies had already left in apple-pie order, and started to re-tidy it, straightening the pots in the cupboards and making sure that the remnants of food in the pantry were covered up. She wanted to keep out of the sight of Patrick and Maddy; she imagined that the girl was still eyeing her malevolently. All the mourners had gone now apart from Louisa, who seemed to regard herself as one of the family; and Jack, a friend of William's from the chapel who had helped to get him into bed.

Normally she, Bella, would have departed by now. There would have been no reason to hang around; and she knew that by doing so she was really drawing attention to herself. But she had as much right as anyone, hadn't she? – certainly as much as Louisa Montague – to wait and hear the doctor's verdict. After all, she was now officially the shop manageress, a post which she had been doing for years anyway, and William's condition was as much her business as anyone's. Isaac might want her to help out again in other ways; she thought he had been rather more polite to her of late than he had used to be.

She ventured into the living room when she heard the doctor's voice. He had examined William and was talking to the family members – and Louisa – who were all hanging on his words. But they did not appear to be too anxious, which was a good sign.

'It's influenza, as I thought,' said Dr Metcalfe, steepling his fingers and tapping them together. He shook his head bemusedly. 'It's certainly got the upper hand in the town right now; one wonders how long it's going to continue… But I'm pleased to say that Mr Moon does not appear to have been affected too badly. He feels pretty groggy at the moment, of course. He is running a temperature and aching all over and his throat is sore. However, I've given him a dose of the new drug they're calling aspirin, and the rest of it is there, to be taken regularly. I realise it didn't help Mrs Moon very much in the end, but I have every confidence that William has a much better chance of recovery.

'I'm sorry…' He glanced round at them all with a sad sort of smile. 'Your family has already had a lot to bear, and we must make sure that no one else succumbs to this wretched illness.' He turned to Isaac. 'What I'm going to suggest, Mr Moon, is that you should have a full-time nurse to come and live in, then your son can be cared for night and day. Just to be on the safe side, you understand. I can make all the arrangements if you wish. In fact, I know just the lady.'

'Thank you, doctor,' said Isaac gruffly, tears of gratitude welling up in his eyes. He blinked rapidly. 'Aye, that seems like a champion idea. And never mind t' cost. Whatever it is it dun't matter. We've got to get the lad right again.'

Bella had the good sense to keep quiet. She knew that to say anything at all would make her look foolish. And when she thought about it logically she knew that she would never have been allowed to look after William. An unmarried woman who was not even a nurse? It would be considered most improper. But why, she wondered now, had they not thought of employing a nurse to look after Clara? If they had done so, she might still be alive today... If only...if only...

The thoughts in Bella's muddled mind were running away in all directions. She was losing control of herself again. No one was paying any heed to her, standing there in the doorway. The best thing she could do was to steal away quietly. Only Maddy glanced at her, then just as quickly looked away again, as she crept into the hallway and reached for her coat and hat.

Back in her own room she put a match to the fire she had lit earlier that day, then sat down, still in her outdoor clothes, to wait for the room to warm up. Of course she could not have nursed William; that had been a stupid idea. But she could, perhaps, do other things... When he started to feel a little better she could make appetising broths and tempting little delicacies, to coax his appetite back to normal. Then she frowned with irritation as she remembered how William had said that they were going to employ a housekeeper who would clean and cook for them as well. She must think of something, though – anything – to bring her closer to William again.

The nurse turned out to be a middle-aged woman, red-faced, bustling and rather bossy. A real old harridan, thought Bella, like a character out of a Dickens novel. But her no-nonsense approach did the trick. William was confined to bed for several days as the influenza took its course, but once on his feet again he made a good recovery.

During his absence Isaac had been obliged to engage another assistant. Joe Black was a young man who had come on loan from another firm, but had then decided to stay with the Moons. As this was agreeable to his previous employers it was settled amicably. But what was really needed was a woman to assist with the home visits, to take over the duties at which Clara had excelled.

William returned to work early in March and he soon realised that Clara had been – almost – indispensable to them. He qualified his thoughts with the word 'almost', because he knew that no one could be entirely indispensable. Didn't death prove that time and time again? 'Aye, the graveyard's full of indispensable folk,' his father was fond of saying. William missed Clara more than he could ever reveal to anyone. But life had to go on. That was a cruel cliché but such a true one. And so did the whole business of death in which they were involved.

He advertised in the local paper and in the window of their own shop for a suitable woman to assist with some aspects of the undertaking business. Bella, on reading the advert, remembered something that Polly had said to her a little while ago. Would she be helping Mr Moon with the 'laying out' jobs, she had wanted to know, like Mrs Moon had done? And Bella had scoffed at the idea. 'Of course not! Don't be silly…' And then she had thought about it afterwards…

She thought about it now. Why not? she thought. She had become, once again, nothing but an employee of the Moon family; in charge of the shop, to be sure, but what did that really mean? Not a great deal; certainly not the involvement with the family – with William – that she had wished for. Well, she could but ask. She could offer her services and try to convince him that it would be a very good move.

And, indeed, William seemed to think so too. He agreed, surprisingly quickly, to give it a try.

Bella has changed, thought William. He could see no reason now to fear her presence in his life. What had been between them was in the past, the dim and distant past. He hardly ever thought about it now, and neither, he was sure, did Bella. He had never failed to be surprised at the way in which his beloved Clara had coped with the sometimes unpleasant aspects of their business. If she had been repulsed then she had not allowed it to show. But then Clara had been able to tackle all things in her own loving and sympathetic way. Bella was a very different kettle of fish. He gave a wry smile at the aptness of the idiom. But if his lovely gentle Clara could adapt to it then Bella would most certainly be able to do so.

A picture flashed into his mind. He could see Bella as he had seen her that very first time, expertly gutting the herrings, the sharp blade cutting through the flesh and the bloody mess of the entrails being flung into the waste bucket. Yes, Bella would be ideal for the job.

Chapter Twenty

'Oh, it's fun to be here at the seaside,
It's good to be down by the sea...'

M addy was a little surprised to find herself joining in so readily with the Pierrots' opening song, along with Jessie at her side.

She had not felt like singing at all, for ages after her mother had died. But then gradually, as the winter turned to spring and then to summer her sadness had started to ease a little. She began to look forward to events that she had imagined she would never he able to enjoy without Mam there to share them with. And it was true that a few nice things had happened.

Her eleventh birthday in June had been a happy occasion. She had had a tea party and invited four girls from her class at school, two of them being also in her Sunday school class. Aunty Louisa had made the sandwiches and cakes and trifles, and iced a special birthday cake, just as her mother had used to do. The girls considered themselves too grown up now to play the usual party games of 'hunt the thimble' or 'blind man's buff' and so, instead, they had sung songs round the piano.

This was a recent acquisition to the Moon household. Maddy guessed it had been purchased at her grandfather's insistence. She had overheard a few conversations between her father and grandfather. She had sat on the stairs one night when they imagined her to be tucked up in bed, listening to what they were saying...

'That little lass needs bringing out of herself, Will lad.' That had been Grandad's voice. 'You remember how she allus used to be singing, all over t' house? Well, I've nivver heard her sing at all not since...well, not since...you know when.'

'I don't suppose she feels she has much to sing about, Father? Do any of us?'

'No, happen not... But I tell you what, Will, speaking for meself, it does me a power of good to sing me heart out on a Sunday morning along wi' t' rest o' t' congregation.' He had started to sing then, his voice a little croaky, but perfectly in tune...

'My chains fell off, my heart was free;
I rose, went forth and followed Thee...

'Aye – "And Can it Be"; a grand old hymn, that 'un; one of Charles Wesley's best. It fair lifts yer spirits.'

'Yes, I've missed our little Maddy singing meself, I must admit,' she heard her father answer. 'She's a lot quieter too. You know what a little chatter-box she used to be. But I dare say she opens up a bit when she's with her school friends.'

'She needs summat else though; summat to take her mind off things, like... D'you know, I've often thought we should get a piano. I wonder why you didn't get one for your Clara? She liked a nice tune, didn't she?'

'So she did, but she couldn't play the piano, and neither could I. I never learnt, and Clara never had the chance, did she, as a girl? Her parents were very poor. Aye, mebbe it's something we could have done, but we didn't, and it's too late now.'

'Oh, I don't know about that,' said her grandfather. 'It's never too late… I used to be able to pick out a tune meself, when I were a lad…'

Maddy had not heard any more just then, but she was not surprised when, a few weeks later, towards the end of April, a piano had been delivered to their home. Not a new one of course. She learnt that it had been bought from one of the old ladies at the chapel. Her two sons brought it round on a large trap pulled by a pony, and then the two men, with her father and Patrick helping, had pushed it through the back door and into its special place in the living room where it could get the light from the window. It was made of golden-brown walnut with a fancy pattern in the grain, and a cut-away design on the front showing panels of dark red velvet.

When Grandad had picked out a tune with one hand it had sounded rather tinny, but he decided that a good tuning would soon put that right, and so it did.

'Aye, that's champion now,' he had said, sitting down on the round red velvet stool which the old lady had included with the deal. He played with one hand, singing along at the same time,

'Amazing grace, how sweet the sound
That saved a wretch like me…'

'That's clever, Grandad,' said Maddy. 'D'you think I could have a go? I'd like to be able to play tunes.'

'Well now, I'll tell you summat,' he replied. 'That's the reason we've got this 'ere piano, so as you can learn to play. To play properly, I mean. Would you like to have piano lessons, Maddy?'

She had already guessed that that might be the reason for the purchase. She nodded enthusiastically. She had not felt so pleased about anything not since...not since her mam had died. 'Yes, please,' she said. 'I really would.'

'Well, that's champion then,' said Grandfather.

He was never one to let the grass grow beneath his feet. Before the week was out he had found a teacher – another of the chapel ladies – who gave piano lessons in between looking after her husband and her elderly mother. She was called Mrs Rafferty and Maddy knew her by sight. She was a plumpish comfortable-looking lady who sang in the choir on a Sunday morning and always wore a maroon felt hat trimmed with black petersham ribbon, a 'no-nonsense' sort of hat. All the choir ladies kept their hats on, and the men – there were six man and six women – wore their ordinary suits. They did not have a special uniform like they did in some churches.

Anyway, Mrs Rafferty turned out to be an excellent teacher and Maddy an eager and responsive pupil. Before a few weeks had passed she was able to play simple tunes, using both her hands, and Mrs Rafferty said she showed a very good grasp of what she called 'the rudiments of music'. She was learning about sharps and flats and key signatures, and how many beats there were in a bar, and what all those grand-sounding Italian words meant; crescendo and diminuendo, largo, adagio and allegretto. Her teacher had found a book that had a lot of simple tunes in it; a selection of hymn tunes, light classical pieces, traditional songs and folk songs from all parts of the British Isles.

Maddy's friends had looked on in admiration as she had played 'Drink to me Only', 'Golden Slumbers' and 'Dashing Away with the Smoothing Iron'. They had learnt those and

lots of others from their school National Song books and were
able to sing along with her. Then Grandfather Isaac had his
turn as well; he spent almost as much time at the piano as
Maddy did. And so to please him they sang, 'Jesus shall reign
where e'er the sun', and 'Eternal Father strong to save', hymns
that Isaac recalled singing as a lad and which were still sung
in day schools as well as in churches and chapels.

'Aye, music can be a great comfort, Maddy love, a real
solace,' Grandfather had quite often said to her since they
acquired the piano. She thought she understood what he
meant.

For a little while, as she watched the Pierrots performing on
the stage she almost forgot about her sadness. Not that she
would ever be able to forget her mam and never would she
want to, but she had grown used to the sadness being a part
of her. But what people had told her, that it would get easier
in time, was beginning to be true. She actually found herself
laughing out loud a couple of times at Uncle Percy and the
man called Pete – the one who was the 'bottler' – as they went
through the antics of their comic song, 'There's a Hole in my
Bucket'. Of course she had heard it before, but it seemed
funnier than ever with Pete scratching his head in a gormless
way and Percy getting cross with him.

Jessie turned and grinned at her at the end of the first half,
'That was great, wasn't it? Just as good as they were last year,
aren't they?'

'Mmm...yes, I think so,' replied Maddy. 'They've got a new
act though, haven't they? Those singers...'

'Didn't you like them?'

'Well... I dunno really,' said Maddy. 'I don't think they're
quite what my mam would have called "our cup of tea".' She

lowered her voice, adding in a whisper, 'I think she fancies herself a bit, don't you, that Queenie? And her voice wobbles when she sings the high notes, did you notice?'

Jessie nodded. 'And it's not all that wobbles, is it? You could see...well, you know...her chest wobbling.' She pointed vaguely at the area above her own waist and they both started to giggle. 'We shouldn't be unkind, though,' Jessie went on. She was really a very kind-hearted girl.

'No, we shouldn't,' agreed Maddy. 'She's probably very nice. And her husband seems all right. Not as – er – loud as she was. D'you think he is her husband?'

'Oh, I should think so,' said Jessie. She read out from the programme, a new innovation introduced that year. 'Carlo and Queenie entertain you with songs old and new... Yes, I should think they're married. They might appeal more to the older folk though, like my mother and your...father and grandfather.'

'Yes, Grandad came to watch the show – he's only been once though – and he said he liked them.'

'And did your father go as well?'

'No,' said Maddy briefly. 'I don't think he really wants to go anywhere yet without...well, you know... Come on, let's go and get an ice-cream, shall we? I don't think anybody will pinch our seats.'

It was a Wednesday morning during the first week in August. The Barraclough family had arrived on Saturday; that was to say Faith and the four children. There had been no mention of Mr Barraclough when Faith had called to see the Moon family on Sunday afternoon, accompanied by Jessie, Tommy and Tilly. Samuel had taken the opportunity to go fishing, rather to Maddy's disappointment. In fact, she had not seen him yet.

Her father had given her permission to meet Jessie today, and she knew there would be various other times when some of them, or all of them, might meet together. But although she would not have been able to put it into words or explain it to herself she knew there might be some sort of problem now, because her father no longer had a wife, and Mrs Barraclough...well, she did not seem to have a husband, at least not one who was living in the family home. She had asked Jessie if her father would be visiting them in Scarborough, but she had answered evasively, 'We hardly ever see him these days. I think he's living in another house in York, but Mother doesn't tell me very much.' And Jessie sounded as though she wasn't really all that bothered about him either.

Maddy tried to help out more in the house now, although her father did not expect too much of her. She kept her own room tidy, helped with the washing-up, made the breakfasts, and gave Mrs Brewster a hand with the meals when it was needed. Mrs Brewster was another of the chapel ladies who had been coming in to see to things for them ever since Dad had been taken ill at the funeral.

Maddy had insisted that she was quite capable and old enough herself to see to the family breakfast each morning; cereal and toast on weekdays and possibly bacon, eggs and fried bread on a Sunday. She felt proud that she was able to do this; she had watched and helped her mother often enough and knew to be careful with the gas and naked flames. Mrs Brewster came later in the morning when she had seen to her own family's breakfast. She washed up and tidied around, thoroughly 'bottoming' each room in its turn, as she called it. Washing was not a problem as the Moon family had always sent most of their household linens to the laundry, with Clara being a working housewife. Mrs Brewster also prepared a snack lunch each day, usually sandwiches and soup, which Maddy could warm up when she came home from school; and she returned later in the afternoon to prepare their evening meal. This was often a casserole dish or a hotpot, ready for Maddy to pop into the oven, with a rice pudding, fruit tart or a crumble for 'afters'.

She soon proved to be worth her weight in gold, as the saying went. She had insisted right from the start, however, reasonably enough, that Saturday and Sunday were her days off. And so fish and chips, or steak pudding and chips with mushy peas, from the shop round the corner in Castle Road, soon became the order of the day for Saturday, for a lunchtime meal.

And Louisa, of her own accord, had decided that she would take care of the Sunday dinner, always eaten in the middle of the day, promptly at one o'clock. Sunday had always been a lonely sort of day for Louisa. She had sometimes been invited along to the Moons' for dinner or tea, but she had never wanted to overdo her visits and be regarded as a nuisance. But now she felt that she really could help them and it was the least she could do for the family of her dear Clara. She shopped on Saturday afternoon for a nice joint of meat – pork, lamb or beef, whichever took her fancy – and vegetables from the Market Hall. She then took her purchases round to the Moons' place and she and Maddy prepared the meal in readiness for the following day; topping and tailing the carrots and sprouts, peeling the potatoes, and putting the joint in the coolest place in the larder, covered with a square of muslin.

Maddy put the meat into the oven at ten-thirty before they departed for church, and when they returned at midday – with Louisa, who had also been to worship – they were greeted by the aroma of gently roasting meat. Louisa insisted that she should see to the basting of the joint, the gravy and all the trimmings. Also the pudding, which was usually one of her home-made deep custards or curd tarts. All in all Sunday had become a satisfying day for all of them.

None of them ever mentioned how this had come about, why Louisa should be there cooking their Sunday dinner. But each of them knew in their hearts the reason for it; because the focal point of their family had been taken away from them. Clara had been the one who had held them together and there were times when each of them felt they might flounder without her loving presence in the midst of them. Louisa felt it as much as anyone.

But the saddest of all clichés, that life must go on, gradually began to prevail. They settled into a routine. Clara was still very much in their thoughts, but she came to be spoken of with a smile and a happy memory rather than with sadness and gloom.

And where did Bella Randall fit into this routine? Maddy had held her breath at first, quaking with apprehension lest her father should invite her to help out again with the domestic arrangements. But to her relief he had turned to Mrs Brewster. She was a jolly, friendly sort of lady and Maddy got along very well with her. She was more the age of a grandmother than a mother, so it did not seem as though another woman was taking over Mam's rightful place.

Bella had gone back to working in the shop. She was now known as the manageress, and they had another assistant. She was called Miss Muriel Phipps and she looked very prim and proper, with her hair swept up into a bun on the top of her head and rimless spectacles perched on the end of her longish nose.

And to Maddy's surprise Bella had started to accompany her father, or Patrick sometimes, when they went out on jobs; although it was Maddy's guess that Bella didn't seem to be any too happy about it. Maddy had feared that she might be trying to wheedle her way back into the family circle, but Bella, these days, seemed dispirited and low, as though much of the life had gone out of her. She and Maddy spoke politely to one another when they needed to do so. Much of the hostility, though, that Maddy had felt towards her had dwindled away; she was trying to forget all about the scene she had witnessed in the bedroom. The truth was that Bella did not matter to her anymore. She was no longer important.

The second half of the Pierrot show, to Maddy's mind, was more enjoyable than the first. Barney and Benjy had some new tunes and new dance steps; Nancy's dogs had some new tricks; and there were a lot of songs that the audience could join in with.

'I'll be your sweetheart, if you will be mine...'

Maddy sang along merrily as the Pierrots all came on the stage for their closing medley.

'Bluebells I've gathered; keep them and be true;
When I'm a man my plan will be to marry you.'

* * *

'Who are you thinking about?' asked Jessie with a roguish grin, nudging her friend.

'Oh...nobody really...' But Maddy had a twinkle in her eye.

'That's a man's song anyway,' said Jessie.

'I know, but it doesn't matter, does it?' They both giggled, then Maddy said, 'Shhh...Uncle Percy's saying something. Let's listen.'

Percy Morgan had come to the front of the little stage and held up his hand. 'Thank you, thank you, ladies and gentlemen for being such a wonderful audience, as usual. And the children, of course. Now, I have one or two things to bring to your notice before you go. Picture postcards of all the Pierrots are on sale, and my good friend Pete will be pleased to take your money.' There were cheers and applause from some members of the audience as he gestured towards his mate. 'Well worth a penny of anybody's money, ladies and gentlemen. Not only do you get a photo of your favourite performer, but in some cases the words of a song as well. And there are song books on sale, too, if you would like to sing 'em all again when you get home.

'We are here every day – three times a day – at half past ten, half past two and half past six, weather and tides permitting, of course. If the tide's in then we'll be up on t' prom. And two weeks today – that's the twenty-first of August – at two-thirty, we are planning a special event; a talent contest for our younger members of the audience. So if you're thirteen years old or younger come along and show us what you can do. Happen you can sing or dance, or tell jokes, or do some magic tricks, or play a mouth organ or a concertina. And if you need a pianist then my better half, Letty, will be pleased to accompany you.' There was an excited murmur in the audience, but also one or two long faces.

'Aye, I know some of you will have gone back home by then,' said Percy. 'That's a pity, but never mind. We've got a sandcastle competition tomorrow and we hope you'll all be there. And next week we're planning some races and games… Anyroad, I think I've talked for long enough. Cheerio for now. See you again soon. Ta-ra, folks…'

'Ta-ra, Uncle Percy,' called several of the children before going off with their parents to spend a little more time on the sands, or to make their way back to their digs for the midday meal.

'Let's have a look at those pictures, shall we?' said Jessie. 'I think I might like to buy one.'

'All right then.'

They walked over to where Pete was standing by a rack of brown-coloured photographs; Grandad had told Maddy that the correct word was 'sepia'. There were pictures, it seemed, of each one of the Pierrots, some on their own and some in groups. Jessie looked at first one and then another; looking just with her eyes, though, not picking them up and putting them back again like some of the children – and grown-ups, too – were doing. Mother had always told her that you look with your eyes and not your hands.

'Oh dear; the trouble is I don't know which one to choose,' she said, as though it was a matter of the greatest importance. 'Which one would you have, Maddy? Aren't you going to buy one?'

'No, I don't think so; not today,' replied Maddy. 'I might, when we come again. They're all good, aren't they? Why don't you get the one with the group of Pierrots, and then you've got them all?'

'And then you'll have a picture of me, won't you, luv?' laughed Pete. 'And look – there I am again with Percy. We look a real couple of idiots, don't we?'

Jessie and Maddy smiled at the picture of Percy and Pete doing their 'Hole in my Bucket' routine, with silly grins on their faces. Then there was Nancy with her performing dogs; Barney and Benjy in a tap-dancing pose, their white teeth flashing at the camera; the new lady, Queenie, dressed as the Fairy Queen – of all things! – with her husband, Carlo, by her side dressed as the sentry from the Gilbert and Sullivan opera *Iolanthe*; Susannah looking sweet and pretty, surrounded by baskets of flowers... Jessie could have spent a lot more time in deliberation, but most of the other customers had gone and Maddy was getting a little impatient.

'Hurry up and decide,' she said. 'I've got to get back to see to our lunch. I try to help a bit more when it's school holidays.'

'Oh...yes, sorry; I forgot,' said Jessie. She had finally decided, and she handed the 'Hole in my Bucket' postcard to Pete along with her penny. 'I'll have this one,' she said, 'because I think you and Uncle Percy are very funny and you make me laugh.'

'Well now, that's made my day,' said Pete, smiling at her as he popped the card into a little paper bag. 'See you again soon, I hope.'

'Yes, you will,' both girls replied as they walked away.

'What shall we do about the sandcastle competition?' asked Jessie. 'D'you want to go in for it? With our Tommy and Tilly, I mean? I don't think Samuel and Patrick would be interested, do you? Not now they're both fifteen. They'd be too old anyway.'

Maddy was thinking about it, and about the last time they had taken part. 'I don't really think I want to do it,' she said. 'Not this year. It all seems...different somehow.' She was remembering the fun they had had last year, the tea party back at their house and how happy they had all been together. And Mam had been there, so full of life. How could any of them have imagined that in only a few months' time she would be...gone. She was starting to feel sad again. These moments of sorrow crept up on her from time to time. But Jessie seemed to understand.

'It's all right,' she said. 'I don't mind either way. If you don't feel like it I might just go along and help the twins myself. It was a good show, wasn't it? And the Pierrots had some new costumes, hadn't they? I thought they looked very smart.'

'Yes; Louisa made them,' said Maddy. 'I call her Aunty Louisa 'cause she was a friend of...of my mother's. I told you about her, didn't I? She's a dressmaker and she has a shop.'

'Oh yes, so you did. And you said you would like to be a dressmaker when you left school, didn't you?'

'I said I might...' replied Maddy, 'but I don't know...' Jessie cast an anxious glance at her friend, then linked her arm as they walked up the cliff path. She could tell that Maddy was feeling sad. How awful it must have been for her when her mother died so suddenly.

'Maddy,' she said. 'What d'you think about this talent contest? I know you're still feeling a bit sad sometimes – I can tell – but I really think you should go in for it. You're a lovely singer and...well...I'm sure you'd win.'

To Jessie's surprise Maddy nodded. 'Yes... I might – go in for it, I mean. I didn't mean that I'd win. I've started to play the piano now. I told you, didn't I? And I've found that music

– singing and playing – it helps me to feel a bit better about – you know – about my mam and everything, not quite so sad. Grandad says music's a solace. He means it's a comfort... Yes, I think I will 'cause I do like singing. Not that I'd win though. There'll be all sorts entering, won't there? Conjurers and tap dancers and goodness knows what else. And a lot of 'em'll be older than me.'

'So what? There won't be anybody that can sing better.'

'And what about you then? If I go in for it, what about you doing something, Jessie, to keep me company?'

'Me? Oh no, I couldn't!' Jessie stood still in her tracks as though paralysed with fear, and her face turned pink beneath the mass of freckles. 'I can't sing. I can't do anything like that. Anyway, I'd die if I had to stand on that stage in front of everybody.' She stopped suddenly, aware of what she had said. 'I mean...no, I don't think so. In fact – no – definitely not.'

'All right then,' said Maddy with a little smile. 'I can see that you don't want to. I just thought you might like to recite a poem or something. You told me you have to learn all sorts of stuff at that posh school of yours.'

'Yes, so we do; pages and pages of it. And I like some of it too. "The Forsaken Merman" – I love that. It's about a merman who marries a mortal.'

'A what?'

'A mortal; an ordinary person like you and me.'

'No, the other thing you said...'

'Oh, a merman. Well, you've heard of a mermaid, haven't you, so this is a merman. And his wife leaves him and goes back to the land, and he's pining for her, and his children are too... "Come, dear children, let us away, down and away below..."' she recited in a melancholy voice. 'It's really sad.'

'Mmm; it certainly doesn't sound very cheerful,' agreed Maddy. 'But it would be very clever if you could recite it all. D'you remember Charlie, the old man they used to have in the show? He used to do long recitations, didn't he? And the audience seemed to like them.'

'Well, I couldn't do it; not in front of all those people.'

'Never mind then. So long as you're there to give me a bit of support... I'll have to ask Dad though, and Grandad. They might not want me to do it.' She wasn't sure why they might object, but she knew that when people were 'in mourning', as her family was, then they had to consider what would be considered right and proper.

Maddy found the song she thought she might like to sing, that evening, amongst the folk songs in her book of simple tunes. She tried out the melody with one hand, then softly sang the words along with it.

'Are you going to Scarborough Fair?
Parsley, sage, rosemary and thyme...'

'Aye, that's a grand old song,' said her grandfather. He came over to the piano and stood at the side of her, singing the first line again in his slightly husky tones. 'I've not heard that for ages. It takes me back years and years it does. I remember singing it when I was a lad at school.'

'I don't think we've learnt it,' said Maddy, 'but I think it's a nice tune... Grandad, can I ask you something?' she said in a quiet voice. Her father, with the evening paper stuck up in front of his face, did not seem to be taking much notice of them.

'Aye, of course you can, luv. You can ask me anything,' said Isaac. 'You know that.'

And so she told him about the talent contest that the Pierrots were holding in two weeks' time, and how she would like to sing, but she was wondering whether it would be the right thing to do.

'Whyever not?' asked her grandfather.

'Well, you know. Because of Mam...dying. I thought some people might think it was not...quite right.'

'Disrespectful, like?' said Isaac, understanding that she was not quite able to put her thoughts into words. 'No...' He shook his head. 'Not a bit of it, at least I don't consider it is. Especially if you're going to sing a tender little song like this. It's a sad sort o' song really, "Scarborough Fair". About somebody pining for their lost love.'

'It's really a man's song though, isn't it?' said Maddy.

'No, I don't think so. You just need to say "he" instead of "she", that's all. Come on then; let's have a go at it, shall we? Just listen to t' tune first, and then try singing the first verse.'

So while her grandad played the melody with one hand she sang the plaintive song...

'Are you going to Scarborough Fair?
Parsley, sage, rosemary and thyme;
Remember me to one who lived there
For once he was a true love of mine...'

'Champion!' said Isaac. 'You've got just the right sort of voice for it.'

'And the lady who plays the piano – Letty, she's called; Uncle Percy's wife – she's going to play for anybody who needs an...accompanist.' She stumbled a little at the unfamiliar word.

'Oh, you won't need one o' them,' said her grandad. 'Folk songs are meant to be sung unaccompanied. You just have to make sure you start on t' right note. Ask her to give you a middle C on t' piano and you'll be fine.'

'So you think it's all right then for me to sing?'

''Course I do. I've just said so, haven't I?'

'And what about Dad?' asked Maddy, glancing towards her father who seemed, now, to be just staring into space.

'Oh, don't you worry about yer father; you leave him to me,' said Isaac. 'He'll be real proud of you, you mark my words. And you can be sure we'll all be there to listen to you. And if you're still a bit worried,' he added quietly, 'then think how proud yer mam would have been an' all. Tell yerself that you're doing it for her.'

'All right Grandad.' She gave him a secret sort of smile. 'I'll try.'

William stood up at that point, shoving his newspaper untidily down the side of the chair. 'I'm off for a bit of fresh air,' he said. 'Blow the cobwebs away.' He nodded at Isaac and Maddy and strode out of the room. His father was used to him doing this a few evenings a week. And what did it matter if his breath of fresh air blew him into one of the nearby public houses. He never came back the worse for drink and the lad had to have some sort of an outlet for his sadness.

'What is Scarborough Fair, anyway?' asked Maddy. 'Do they still have it?' A travelling fair with sideshows and roundabouts visited the area occasionally, but never stayed for very long. She didn't think it was that sort of a fair.

'No, Scarborough Fair's long gone,' said Isaac. 'Faded away in the mists of time, but it's still remembered because of that song. It had gone long before I was born, but we learnt about it at school. It was started way back in t' thirteenth century by King Henry the Third. He granted the burgesses – those were the bigwigs, like, in the town – the right to have a fish fair on t' sands. And it went on for forty-five days, from t' middle of August to t' end of September, St Michael's Day.'

There wasn't much that her grandad did not know about Scarborough in the olden days, thought Maddy as she listened to his story of the fair. The colourful event had taken place every year from the thirteenth until nearly the end of the eighteenth century. That was…five hundred years! It must have changed a lot in that time. They hadn't sold just fish, of course. There had been a cattle market, a pig market and an apple market, and merchants – men selling their goods – from Belgium and Germany, as well as the local tradesmen. And there were minstrels, jugglers, ballad singers, fortune tellers, and men pretending to cure all sorts of ailments, called 'quack' doctors.

It was rather sad in some ways, Grandad Isaac said, that the good old days had come to an end. The street selling that had gone on for hundreds of years had been brought to an end when the Market Hall opened fifty years ago. He remembered that of course. But the old tradition of the ballad singers and minstrels was still being carried on by the Pierrots with their daily shows on the beach.

'Aye, "Scarborough Fair",' said Isaac. 'You couldn't have chosen a better song. And the audience'll love it, you'll see.'

Chapter Twenty-One

It seemed to Bella that whenever she set foot in the Moon's family living room Maddy was playing the piano, and sometimes singing along to the melody. This was usually in the late afternoon when she and William, or sometimes Patrick, had returned from one of their bereavement visits. If it had been a 'laying out' job Bella could not wait to get to her own rooms to wash away the odour of death from her hands and person. She felt that its miasma clung to her, although she realised that it could well be her imagination. Sometimes, though, if they had only been discussing funeral arrangements with the bereaved family, there were details to be finalised back at home. On those occasions Bella would be offered a cup of tea, although she had never, not even once since Clara died, been invited to stay and have a meal with them.

Maddy was still behaving coolly towards her, but Bella felt that the utter dislike and suspicion that had been so apparent at the time of Clara's death had now gone from the girl's eyes. There were times when they had no option but to speak to one another, and they did so politely but with little feeling.

Bella recognised the song, 'Scarborough Fair', that Maddy was playing and singing on that afternoon in August, oblivious to the rest of the people in the room. She had not looked round to greet her father and Bella when they came in and neither was she paying any heed to Patrick and Isaac, who were ensconced in easy chairs, having finished their work for the day.

'Hush a minute now, Maddy love,' said William gently, 'if you don't mind. It's coming on nicely, though, is your song. Happen you can give us a performance later, eh? But now... I wonder if you could make us all a cup of tea, please? We've got something important to discuss, y'see; business matters. And I'm expecting Miss Phipps to join us as well, any minute now.'

'All right,' agreed Maddy cheerfully, not showing any reluctance to do as her father requested.

Miss Muriel Phipps, the 'second-in-command' from the store, arrived almost at once, greeting everyone with a brief smile and a nod, in her usual diffident manner. It was a Wednesday afternoon, when the shop was closed for the half day. When Maddy returned some five minutes later she politely handed round the tea and biscuits and then sat herself down at the side of the room.

William had gathered them all together to discuss the future of Moon's Mourning Modes. He told them how he felt that they needed a more forward-looking image for the new century and the reign of a new monarch, King Edward the Seventh.

'We have provided a service in the town,' he said, 'but I feel now that perhaps we should not be concerned solely with death and bereavement, but with other aspects of life as well. I know that my dear wife – God bless her – was having thoughts in that direction, and it's partly for her sake that I would like to do this. She had been trying to introduce other colours – pale blues and mauves and lilac – instead of the deep funereal black. And I think we could go even further.'

'Other aspects of life?' said Miss Phipps. Bella was finding her to be a forceful character – in a quiet way – despite her prim and seemingly stand-offish appearance. 'You mean...birth, marriage...and death? That is what life is, is it not? In a nutshell, one might say.'

'Something like that,' agreed William. 'But nothing too drastic, not to begin with.'

'No, indeed,' said Bella. 'We wouldn't want a window full of bridal gowns, for instance. That would be too blatant. We must aim to be discreet.'

'We would do it all gradually, of course,' said William. 'We can't go making radical changes overnight.'

'I don't see why we have to change at all,' said Isaac. 'Folks know what we stand for in this town. They come to us for their mourning clothes when somebody dies: a new black frock or a coat or whatever. They've got used to us being here... But I'll not stand in yer way, of course, Will. You know that, don't you? The shop's allus been your baby, like, yours and Clara's, and I've left all t' decisions to you. So I reckon if it was our Clara's idea...well then, it must've been a good 'un. You'll still stock funeral stuff though, won't you? But happen not as much...'

'Yes, that's right, Father,' replied William. 'But I want us to think of a new name, instead of Moon's Mourning Modes. Has anybody got any ideas?'

They were all thoughtful for a few moments. Then Bella said, 'How about...Moon's Modes for all Occasions? Or...Moon's Modes for all Seasons. Yes, I think that sounds better.'

'Mmm...' William put his head to one side, frowning just a little. 'Moon's Modes for all Seasons,' he repeated. 'Yes, I like that. It has a good ring to it... Well done, Bella.'

'Aye; I must admit I quite like the sound o' that,' said Isaac, to Bella's surprise.

She was delighted to know that they all agreed to the new name, and William decided that the first thing to be done was to have the shop sign altered. Then they would put an advertisement in the local paper to tell clients about the future developments in their business and the new variety of their merchandise.

They would soon need to be thinking about clothes for autumn – almost at once, in fact – and then for the Christmas season. It was necessary to be always one season ahead of themselves. They discussed the warehouses they used in York and Leeds. And William reminded them that they must not forget Louisa Montague, who had always supplied a goodly number of their smaller garments.

Isaac and Patrick wandered away when the talk no longer concerned them, and Maddy, also, got up and took the tea things into the kitchen. William followed her. He re-entered the room a few moments later to tell Bella and Muriel Phipps that they were invited to stay and share the family's evening meal, if they wished to do so. He had ascertained from his daughter that it was something that would 'stretch': a shepherd's pie which Mrs Brewster had prepared earlier. She always made far more than enough and Maddy had said she could eke it out with extra carrots and swede.

Bella was astonished at the invitation, but she did not let her surprise show as she answered, politely, that she would be pleased to stay; and Muriel answered in the same vein. It was a step in the right direction, thought Bella, one for which she had been waiting a long time; her pleasure was somewhat

marred, though, by the fact that Miss Phipps had also been
invited. But her thoughts soon took her in another direction
as she started to imagine visits to warehouses, just herself and
William, with Muriel left in charge of the shop...

At the present moment, however, she knew that she should
offer to help Maddy who had been landed with the task of
organising the meal for six of them, no mean feat for an
eleven-year-old girl. She decided to act as though there was
nothing strange at all about her offering to help. She and
Maddy had worked together preparing the meals during the
time that Clara was ill in bed. But she hastily pushed those
memories away as she went into the kitchen.

'May I help?' she asked cheerily. 'You've got some
unexpected guests, haven't you? So the least I can do is to
come and give you a hand.' Maddy turned away from the
stove, where she was putting the plates to warm on the rack,
and looked at her; not speaking at first, just...looking.

'What shall I do then?' Bella went on. 'Set the table? Or do
you need some more vegetables doing?' She feared, for a
moment, that the girl was going to refuse her offer and say
politely – or otherwise – that she didn't need any help.

But after a few seconds she said, though not with a great
deal of enthusiasm, 'Yes, thank you. You could set the
table...Aunty Bella. There are six of us. You know where
the knives and forks are, don't you? And we'll need spoons
as well. There's some apple crumble that Mrs Brewster
made; I've put it in the oven to warm up... Oh dear!' She
put her hand to her mouth. 'We'll need some custard, won't
we?'

She looked so worried at that moment, a little girl with a
flowered apron that was far too big for her tied around her

middle, that Bella felt sorry for her, and a stab of something that might almost be affection.

'You've got a tin of custard powder, haven't you?' she asked. 'Bird's custard?'

'Yes, there's one in the cupboard.'

'Then I'll see to it,' said Bella. 'It's quick and easy to make. I'll have it done before you can say "Jack Robinson". I'll set the table first, then I'll see to the custard. You've got enough milk in the pantry, have you?'

'Yes, plenty,' replied Maddy. 'Er...thank you,' she said again. 'I'm usually all right. I can manage the meals perfectly well on me own,' she went on decisively. 'Well, after Mrs Brewster's done the donkey work, I mean.' She gave a half-smile. 'That's what Mam used to call it, donkey work. But it's with having extra people, y'see.'

'Of course; I understand,' said Bella smiling at her. 'I think you're doing splendidly, really I do. And we'll manage this lot between us, no trouble at all.'

Maddy nodded. 'I think I'll open a tin of peas an' all,' she said. 'Marrowfat peas. Our Patrick likes them and so does Grandad, and it'll make the rest of the veg go further...'

It was almost as though there had never been any constraint between them, thought Bella; but she knew she must go steadily with Maddy to win back the girl's confidence.

'That was a nice song you were singing,' she said cautiously as they worked along, together yet silently, after that initial burst of conversation.

'"Scarborough Fair"? Mmm...yes,' agreed Maddy.

'Are you practising for something special?'

'Yes,' replied Maddy, a trifle abruptly, and Bella wondered if that was all she was going to say. Then, after a few seconds' pause she continued, though not exactly in a friendly manner, 'I'm going in for a talent contest, at the Pierrot Show. It's next Wednesday afternoon.'

'Oh…that's nice,' said Bella, being careful not to enthuse too much. 'Can anybody come to listen?'

'S'pose so,' said Maddy, with a show of indifference.

'It's lucky then that it's my half day off. D'you think I could come and see the show?' asked Bella.

Maddy shrugged. 'If you like,' she said.

The menfolk and Miss Phipps were profuse in their praise of the shepherd's pie and apple crumble that was set before them. During the course of the meal Isaac told everyone about the song that Maddy had been singing and how she was entering for the talent contest. 'An' I'm just wondering if she'd like to give us a performance when we've finished eating?' he said, smiling coaxingly at his granddaughter. 'It'd be good practice, like, for you, Maddy love, singing for an audience. Only a little 'un though, not as many as there'll be next week.'

But Maddy could not be persuaded. In fact she was adamant in her refusal. 'You can come next Wednesday if you like,' she told them, 'but you'll have to wait till then.' For some reason, that she could not even explain to herself, she had suddenly gone all shy at the thought of singing in front of the members of her own family, plus the other two, of course. But, funnily enough, the idea of singing in the open air on the beach, with a much bigger audience, held no fears for her at all; at least, not at the moment.

'Leave her alone,' said William sympathetically. 'They'll have to wait, won't they, Maddy love? Anyroad, you can all come if you've a mind next Wednesday. And we've nowt much on at the moment, have we, Father? So with a bit of luck we'll all be there.'

'And Jessie and all her family as well,' added Maddy.

'Oh yes, that's right,' said William. 'Our friends, the Barracloughs, who are over from York.' He looked towards Bella. 'You remember Faith, don't you, Bella? You met her last summer, and she was at...at the funeral.'

'Yes, I remember...' said Bella in a voice that was devoid of expression.

After she had helped Maddy to clear the table and to wash up, with the willing assistance of Muriel Phipps as well, Bella was glad to return to the privacy of her own rooms. She had a lot to think about.

The proposed expansion of the store had come as good news to Bella. Perhaps now she would be able to broach with William the subject of her role in the business. She knew that she had jumped in with both feet on realising that William would need a female assistant for the undertaking work, without giving due thought to what might be involved. Whatever it was, she had convinced herself that she would be able to cope with it. But she had been unprepared for the abhorrence she was to feel at her first sight of a dead body and her experience of the work involved in the laying-out process. She told herself that she would get used to it; that it was early days and she had to give herself a chance to grow accustomed to the unpleasant, and what she considered to be gruesome, tasks. But, alas, she had never got used to it.

She had never been a squeamish person. In her days as a herring girl she had never flinched at the job of gutting the fish and had become used to the sight of blood and slime and mess. Her upbringing, too, in the small cottage in Morpeth, where she had lived cheek by jowl with her parents and her younger siblings, had been far from salubrious. From an early age she had been acquainted with the process of childbirth, and the sight of a red and wriggling newborn baby, just out of the womb, had never filled her with revulsion. Indeed, she had once witnessed, when the next but youngest child had been born, the whole process, from her hiding place behind the bedroom door, unbeknown to her father who had been skulking downstairs. At the time she had had no doubt, either, as to how the child came to be in the womb in the first place. She had oftentimes listened to the sounds coming from her parents' bedroom and had put two and two together. She had seen animals coupling on the nearby farms and guessed that the process with humans was similar.

She had had little experience of death, though, but had blithely imagined that she would be able to cope with that as easily as she did with most other things. She remembered telling William, on first learning that he was an undertaker, that she had seen a few dead bodies in her time and that she was not squeamish. But it was not strictly true.

She had seen her mother's body, but by the time she had come back from her work at the big house her mother had been prepared for burial and laid out in her coffin. And on another earlier occasion she had been taken by her mother to view the body of an old lady, a good neighbour, who had passed away. The viewing of the body was a custom to which even children were accustomed, but it had all been very clean and respectable. Bella had remembered, though, the sickly-sweet smell that had pervaded the atmosphere, not entirely due to the profusion of flowers in the room.

It had been a rude awakening, therefore, when she had accompanied William earlier that year to assist with the laying out of a middle-aged woman. She had felt shamefully embarrassed as she had watched William ease away the nightclothes in which the woman had died to reveal the naked limbs and torso. But he had done it all so reverently and gently, and then had persuaded Bella to wash down the body in the warm water from the bowl provided by the woman's daughter. She had tried not to show her revulsion at the task. After all, it was more fitting that she, another woman, should do this rather than William; although the poor woman was now what was known as a corpse, rather than a living and breathing female person.

Bella had not known, either, about the expulsion of bodily fluids, which was one of the first things to occur following death. The first time she had experienced this she had been unable to disguise her distaste, but William had dealt with it swiftly and competently and assured her it was something she would get used to. But she never had.

She well remembered an instance when she had been with Patrick, not his father. The body was that of an old lady and Bella had turned away for a moment to fill the bowl on the washstand from the kettle of warm water. Suddenly there was a groan from the body, 'Aaargh...' which made her shout out in fright and almost drop the kettle.

'She's still alive!' she gasped. 'Patrick, do something... Go and tell them...'

To her amazement Patrick was laughing, not uproariously, but chuckling quietly to himself. 'No, she's not,' he said. 'She's dead all right...poor old soul,' he added. 'Is it the first time you've seen that happen?'

'Yes, it must be,' whispered Bella, white-faced and shaken.

'It's the last breath of air being expelled from the lungs,' said Patrick. 'Aye, it gave me a shock an' all the first time I heard it. You'll get used to it, don't worry.'

But she never had. She knew now, in fact she had very soon realised, that this side of the business was not her cup of tea at all. She had tried, but with all the will in the world she could not get used to it. Now, with the expansion of the retail trade, she knew it was time to point out to William that she would be much better employed concentrating on her position as manageress of Moon's Modes for all Seasons. She had gained her experience in the gown trade years ago when she had worked with Madame Grenville, alias Maud Green. Who better, then, than she, Bella, to locate and check out new warehouses for the purchase of their more varied stock? It would mean, of course, that she would not longer be able to accompany William on his home visits, but she was sure he would understand. And if he could be persuaded to take more part in the transactions at the warehouses...

Bella was unable to sleep that night. She found that the words and the melody of the song that Maddy had been singing were going round and round in her head. She had not heard all of it, but it was a song that she had known since girlhood, and one phrase in particular had struck a chord with her.

'...Remember me to one who lives there,
For once he was a true love of mine.'

Yes, there had once been a time when she and William Moon had been lovers. Had she really believed for a while that he was her true love, or was the passage of the years lending enchantment to the scene? They had been happy and carefree together during those summer months when she had been working at the harbour. Yes, she had loved him. She had never met anyone quite like him before; so gentlemanly in his behaviour towards her, and yet there had been another side to him, a passionate nature which she had so easily awakened and brought to fruition. But he had let her down. He had been unable to face up to the result of their intimacy, and so they had parted.

She had often thought of him, though, during the years she had spent back in the north country; William Moon, the canny lad from Scarborough whom she had loved...and lost.

'...Remember me to one who lives there,
For once he was a true love of mine.'

Her disappointment had been great on her return, when she had discovered he was married and with a child on the way. But now...now the pathway was clear again. She was finding it easier as the months went by to set aside her ambivalent thoughts with regard to Clara. And she had made headway tonight with Maddy. If she proceeded with caution she was sure she could win the girl's acceptance, if not her affection. The love that there had once been between herself and William could be rekindled. It was unfortunate, of course, that she found herself unable to work along with him in some aspects of his profession – she knew she must tell him this very soon – but there would be other ways of winning his admiration and, eventually, his love.

The beautiful face of Faith Barraclough suddenly loomed, unbidden, into her thoughts. She banished it quickly to the outer reaches of her mind. That woman would be here for the next couple of weeks, that was all, then she would have gone. Whereas she, Bella, would always be here...

Chapter Twenty-Two

Percy Morgan noticed the two little girls – Jessie, the ginger-haired lass from York, and Maddy with the pale golden hair – on the front row, where they usually sat at each performance they attended. He noticed, too, that Maddy, the granddaughter of Isaac Moon, the undertaker, was dressed in mourning clothes. Not the deepest black, to be sure, but a sombre shade of purple and with a black ribbon tied around her curls. It was obvious that someone close to her must have died recently, and he guessed that it might be old Isaac. Not that he was so very old – roughly the same age as Henry, his own father, whom was still hale and hearty – but the cold Yorkshire winters were treacherous, particularly the bitter east winds on the coast, blowing across from Scandinavia.

When he made enquiries, however, he discovered to his surprise and sorrow that it was Clara Moon who had died, young William's wife, carried off suddenly in an attack of pneumonia. Percy wondered if he should go round and offer his condolences, but already six months had passed since Clara's death and he did not wish to reawaken their feelings of sadness; especially with regard to young Maddy who might be starting to recover from the worst of her sorrow. He noticed that she sang along cheerfully enough when the audience was invited to join in with the choruses, although he had seen a pensive expression on her face, too, at times.

And then he noticed Maddy's name on the list of entrants

for the talent show; Madeleine Moon, age eleven, singer; that was all it said. Percy was pleased. He guessed she would make a good impression on the audience. From what he had heard of her singing, her voice was clear and tuneful and she didn't seem to be afraid of making herself heard. It was different, of course, when you had to stand up on a stage facing an audience. It was good, though, that the girl was doing this and he felt sure it would be with the encouragement of her family. Life had to go on... A worn-out old platitude but one that, nevertheless, was very true. He would probably see Isaac and William Moon on the afternoon of the contest and would be able to have a word of commiseration with them then.

The discussion of the forthcoming talent show was just one of the items on the agenda when Uncle Percy's Pierrots met together on a Saturday afternoon in mid-August. Their meeting place, once again, was at the comfortable home of Mrs Ada Armstrong on Castle Road, where Percy and Letty and Henry Morgan, and other members of the troupe, had stayed for several seasons. Their first of what might be called business meetings had been in May, near the beginning of their Scarborough season; and this later one was to evaluate the new ideas they had introduced that year, and to discuss plans for the following six weeks or so, after which the season would end. And to hear about the bookings which Percy and Henry had already procured for the autumn and winter season, an item of particular importance to the younger members of the troupe, Barney and Benjy, the tap dancing duo, and Susannah, the soubrette, who were not as well off as some of the older members.

The customary fish and chip lunch they had enjoyed, followed by the strong cup of tea, had kindled a feeling of contentment and self-satisfaction throughout the troupe.

'I think we have good reason to be pleased with ourselves so far this year,' said Percy. 'Our takings are up on this time last year, our new innovations seem to have gone down well, and as far as I'm concerned I'm right proud of us all.'

'That goes for me an' all,' said his father, Henry. He did not perform any longer but took an active part on the managerial side. 'Aye, I'm as happy as Larry, you might say, whoever he is; I'm blessed if I know. We can all give ourselves a good pat on the back.'

They talked about the programmes which the audience were now given at each performance; so that they could follow the acts and get to know the names of the artistes, and also pass the programme on, maybe, to somebody else in their holiday digs to encourage them to come along to the show as well. This list of acts was changed each week and banged out by Letty on her old typewriting machine. She also made posters in – hopefully – indelible inks advertising forthcoming attractions such as the sandcastle competition, children's races, the talent contest, and the gala performance which would take place at the end of the season.

They were all vociferous in praise of the new picture postcards which were sold at the end of each performance. Percy's Pierrots had enjoyed a day out earlier that year. They had travelled by train to the little Yorkshire town of Holmfirth near Huddersfield to have their photographs taken by a man called James Bamforth, who was becoming very well known in his own field of work. He was an artist who had started a family firm, painting backgrounds for thousands of Life Model Lantern slides which he had been producing for a good number of years. His other interest was photography, and more recently he had started using his slides to illustrate postcards which incorporated the words of hymns and songs of the day. These were often sold in sets of three or four, so if the buyer wanted all the verses of the song, then all the postcards had to be bought. Postcard collecting was becoming very popular at the beginning of the new century, also the idea of sending a picture postcard home when on holiday.

And so Percy had contacted the firm of Bamforth's who had been pleased to fit in with his ideas. The result was a collection of photographs of the Pierrots, two dozen pictures in all. They were photographed singly, in pairs, or in groups posing against painted backgrounds of trees and hills, flower gardens and fountains, rustic cottages, or a vista of cliffs and sea and sand. And each picture contained a verse of a song or a telling phrase from the artiste's repertoire.

'Which of the cards has sold the best?' asked Susannah. Percy knew she was longing to be told that it was the one of her in the flower garden, but he was determined not to give her the satisfaction, or, on the other hand, to disillusion her.

'There's little to choose between them,' he said. 'The group photos all sell very well.' Actually, although he did not say so, it was the one of himself and Pete in the 'Hole in my Bucket' song which had proved the most popular, with the one of Nancy and her dogs, Daisy and Dolly, as a close second. They had had a devil of a job, he recalled, keeping the dogs – a couple of adorable little West Highland terriers – still, and Nancy had been photographed with an arm held tightly round each of them, seated on high stools similar to the ones they used in their performance.

'Some folks buy one every time they come,' said Pete. 'That little red-haired lass – the real ginger-nut, I mean, not her friend – she bought one, then she was back for another couple the next day. I asked her if she was sending them to friends back at home, but she said no, they were souvenirs, like, of her holiday. It's nice to feel that folks want to remember us, isn't it, when they've gone back home?'

'Indeed it is,' said Percy, 'and the song sheets help as well. They can sing their favourite songs over and over again. A pity about the music though. That's summat we've not got round to yet. But happen by the end o' t' season we'll have enough pennies saved up to have some music sheets printed an' all. So they can have jolly old sing-songs round the pianner. Like Pete was saying, it's good to remember happy times, especially when the weather's turned cold and dreary.

'Now, the talent contest next Wednesday is the next thing on the agenda. It's the first time we've tried one for the younger members of our audience, so we want it to be a success. I think we've got the age limit right, haven't we? Aged thirteen and under?'

'Aye, I reckon that's right, boss,' said Frank Morrison, the 'Jack of all trades' of the group. He was proficient at the harmonica, banjo and concertina, could sing reasonably well and also act as a 'funny man'. 'Most youngsters leave school at thirteen or so, so I think we should limit it to those of school age. Anyroad, the lads' voices start to break at round about that age and they find their singing's gone all over t' show.'

'How many entries have we got?' asked Susannah. There had been a notice pinned up on the events board for the last week on which entrants could place their names, age and the type of act.

'Oh, about a dozen so far,' said Percy. 'But there'll be several more I'm sure. The list so far only includes those who

are staying for a fortnight or longer. I know there were quite
a few kiddies disappointed because they were going back
home today. But that's the way it goes; we can't have one
every week. Those who are just starting their holidays won't
know about it yet. And there are the local children of course.
One or two that I know are residents in Scarborough. Little
Maddy Moon, for instance; she's down to sing a song.'

'Yes, poor little lass,' said his wife. 'You know the girl we
mean, don't you?' The rest of the troupe nodded their
agreement. 'We found out she lost her mother not long ago,
so it's very brave of her to enter.'

'Happen her father thought it might help her to take her
mind off things,' said Henry Morgan. 'Aye, she's sure to get a
good ovation.'

'We mustn't let it influence us, though,' Percy pointed out.
'I know we feel sorry for her and I dare say she'll do quite well
– she's got a nice little voice – but we must make sure we are
absolutely unbiased, in fairness to the other entrants.'

'Of course,' said Benjy.

'Here, here…' said Barney.

'Who is going to judge the contest?' asked Nancy. 'What
have you in mind, Percy? Just two or three of us, maybe?'

'No…' replied Percy cautiously. 'I think it would only be
fair for us all to have a hand in it. We all have our preferences,
haven't we, for different kinds of acts? We've got singers
amongst us, and musicians and dancers and funny men
and…recitationists. Is that the right word? And performing
dogs, of course, although there aren't any of those so far.'

'What sort of acts are there?' asked Frank.

'Oh, a pretty mixed bag,' said Percy. 'A few singers; another
girl as well as Maddy, and two boys. Three doing recitations,

a lad doing conjuring tricks, a juggler, two who call
themselves comedians, and a dancer. I'm not sure what sort
though, tap or ballet or whatever; it's a little girl aged eight.
And Letty will be pleased to play for them if they bring their
music along.'

'Do you think it will work, though, if we all have a finger
in the pie?' asked Pete. 'I'm sure we could all trust the
judgement of just two or three of our members, couldn't we?'

There were nods of assent from most of them; only the
dancing duo and Susannah seemed unsure.

'No, that's the way I want it,' said Percy decidedly. 'What I
have in mind is summat like this. We all of us give marks out
of five – or happen ten – when each boy or girl has performed,
then at the end we can add the marks together and see who
has the most. It seems to me to be the fairest way of doing
things.'

'Yes, that sounds like a good idea,' said Nancy. 'There are
eleven of us altogether, so I would suggest marks out of five,
not ten.' She laughed. 'Maths was never my strong point, I
don't know about the rest of you.'

'Very well then; marks out of five,' agreed Percy.

'Supposing there's a tie for the first place?' queried
Susannah.

'Well, in that case I suppose we would all have to get
together and cast votes,' said Percy. 'But let's not make
difficulties. It's meant to be fun, not deadly serious.'

'And what are we giving for prizes?' asked Carlo, whose
real name was Charles Colman. He and his wife, Queenie,
were the newest members of the troupe.

'I've got a trophy for the winner,' said Percy. 'Just a small
one, a little silver cup on a black stand, and I thought we

could have it engraved – when we know who's won it, of course. There's a chap in the market who does it the same day, and he's very reasonable. And perhaps a monetary reward as well for the first three. What do you think? Seven and sixpence, five bob and half a crown? Or is that too much?'

It was agreed that that was just about right, and it was decided that each child taking part should be given a set of the Pierrot postcards. That would be of more lasting value than a stick of rock or a lollipop.

'Now… I have some news regarding our future bookings,' Percy went on when they had exhausted the subject of the talent contest. They had decided on the name of 'Morgan's Melody Makers' before they had started their new venture the previous autumn. It was short and snappy and to the point and the show had proved to be a success in the Yorkshire towns such as Leeds, Bradford, Halifax, Sheffield and Huddersfield where they had performed in small theatres, assembly rooms or community halls.

'Yes, we've been booked again at most of the places we visited last winter. Morgan's Melody Makers have made their mark, I'm pleased to say. And this year, of course, we have our new members, Carlo and Queenie, who I am sure will be very popular with our audiences.'

Queenie turned and looked at her husband, beaming all over her plumpish face, and Carlo nodded and smiled too. She was a regal-looking woman as befitted her name; not exactly fat but certainly well upholstered and with a magnificent bosom. She loved to wear rich purple or emerald green satin with strings of pearls on stage, when she was not in her Pierrot costume. Her husband, tall and slim, dressed accordingly in full evening attire. Their Gilbert and Sullivan songs had gone down particularly well and Percy could see already that they were an asset to the troupe. Queenie's grandiose manner was largely put on for show. When off her guard her accent, acquired in the suburbs of Wakefield, was as pronounced as that of any of them.

'I have a list here which I'll pass round,' Percy continued, 'then you can see the locations and the dates of the bookings. You will see that we will be venturing "over the border", as you might say, this time. Not very far though; Rochdale and Oldham and a variety theatre in Manchester. And I'm sure you will be pleased to see that we are invited back to Scarborough in December, to the Spa Pavilion, no less! A week in the city of York; that's in January. And Blackpool! Now that's a feather in our cap if ever there was one. We'll be going there in February. So all in all I think we have every reason to be pleased with ourselves.'

Percy allowed a few moments for the members of the troupe to chatter amongst themselves. They all seemed satisfied with the good work that he and his father had done for them.

'Well done, Percy lad,' said Pete. 'And you too, Henry. You've done us proud.'

'Aye; the bookings are well up on last year, aren't they?' said Frank. 'That means more time away from home. Oh dear! My missus isn't going to be very happy about that.'

'You should do what I do, and Pete and Carlo,' said Percy. 'Bring your wife along with you. I'm sure we could fit her into the programme somewhere. I dare say she can sing as well as you can, can't she?' Percy was smiling though. He knew that Hilda Morrison ran her own second-hand clothes business in York and was quite self-sufficient. He guessed, too, at Frank's reaction.

'Not on your life!' replied Frank. 'She's all right where she is. Anyroad, what is it they say? Absence makes the heart grow fonder?'

Percy grinned. He knew that in Frank's case it was more likely to be 'out of sight, out of mind'. 'I will leave you to make your own arrangements regarding digs,' he said. 'There should be plenty of adverts in the stage magazines for all the towns we're booked in. They're well used to variety performers. My father and I will see to the travel arrangements. Sunday trains, of course, but they're all pretty much on the main line so there shouldn't be any problems. We managed to get through last winter without too many hitches.'

'Apart from Susannah and her hat-box,' laughed Frank. Susannah always seemed to have more items of luggage to carry than anyone else, and when alighting at Bradford one Sunday in January she had left behind possibly her most vital item. The collection of large-brimmed, flower-trimmed hats for which she was renowned had continued on the journey to Leeds where, fortunately, the troupe was booked for the following week. Susannah had been forced to pay a visit to Bradford market early on Monday morning to buy a replacement from the hat stall; and, to her annoyance, she had to wear the same headgear for every appearance.

'You've no room to talk, Frank Morrison,' she retorted now. 'Who was it who missed the train to Sheffield? I've never seen Henry in such a panic, pacing up and down the platform. He thought you'd gone and left us in the lurch.'

'As if I would!' said Frank. 'You should know me better than that, sweetheart. Anyway, I didn't exactly miss it. I was what you might call otherwise engaged.' With his current woman of the week, in the town of Wakefield, Percy guessed, seeing the twinkle in Frank's eye. 'I caught the next one a couple of hours later, so no harm done.'

'And may I ask who is going to have top billing?' asked Barney. 'I think I should point out that Benjy and I have been with the troupe a long time.'

'Not as long as some of us,' Pete reminded him. 'Anyway, we've never bothered about things like that, have we? We're a team and we all work together. As far as I'm concerned we're all of equal importance, and I'm sure that Percy and Henry are of the same opinion.'

'Quite so,' agreed Percy. 'We've never had arguments about who is top of the bill, and we're not going to start now. We can take it in turns if you like as to whose name appears at the top. But the heading will be "Morgan's Melody Makers". So long as nobody objects to the use of our family name?' He looked around at them all in turn; but no one objected.

'Well then, that seems to be all the important matters dealt with. Has anyone anything further to say?'

They all shook their heads. Percy had the knack of smoothing away difficulties in the nicest possible way. All the same, they were all well aware of who was the one in charge.

The following Wednesday started off as a miserable grey sort of morning with even a drizzle of rain. Maddy, peering through her bedroom curtains at the dismal scene, felt quite let down. She had felt so sure that the day of the talent contest would be bright and sunny. She looked up anxiously into the sky but there was no break to be seen in the clouds. She knew, though, that the sun must be shining somewhere up there to give the light to the day.

But there was nothing she could do about it except, perhaps, say a little prayer and ask God to send some sunshine. She was never sure, though, whether or not you should worry God with such trivial little requests. Could He really be bothered when He had all the other people in the world to look after?

By lunchtime, however, it seemed as though He might have been listening because, sure enough, there was a patch of blue to be seen in the sky. 'Big enough to make a sailor a pair of trousers,' her mother used to say. And that meant that the rest of the day would be fine.

She had practised her song for the very last time, giving herself the note on the piano and then singing it without any accompaniment, which was how Grandad said the song should be preformed. They were all coming to listen to her; Dad and Grandad and Patrick, because they had no important work to attend to that afternoon. Bella and Miss Phipps from the shop were coming as well, and Aunty Louisa; and, of course, her best friend Jessie and her family; Mrs Barraclough – Aunty Faith as she now called her – and Tommy and Tilly and Samuel... At least she hoped Samuel might be there, if he considered the talent contest to be more important than his fishing or his fossils.

'Come on now, you must eat summat, Maddy love, to keep yer strength up,' her grandad told her at lunchtime. She managed to eat half a bowl of soup and a ham sandwich, but then her tummy felt so full of butterflies dancing around that she couldn't eat any more.

'Ne'er mind; you've put a lining on yer stomach,' said Grandfather, 'and it'll help to settle you down. Now then, you've nowt to worry about. You sing like you sang an hour ago and you'll do champion. An' we'll all be there cheering you on.'

'I know that, Grandad,' said Maddy. And she knew, too, that her mother would be there with her in spirit. She was not sure if Mam would be watching her, but she would certainly be there in Maddy's mind. She would be singing the song, partly, in memory of her mother. Her father had persuaded her to wear the black dress she had worn at the funeral, which Aunty Louisa had afterwards made less sombre by adding a large white lace collar and cuffs, and she was wearing a white satin ribbon in her hair. She wished everyone would leave her alone now, to be quiet and to collect her thoughts. She hadn't expected to be nervous, but people telling her not to worry only made her feel worse.

She felt much better, however, when they arrived at the beach and Jessie immediately ran over to greet her. Jessie, to everyone's surprise and despite her earlier protestations, had decided to enter the contest as well. She was going to recite a part of her favourite poem, 'The Forsaken Merman'. Maddy guessed that, at the last minute, she had felt rather left out of things, and no one was more pleased than Maddy that Jessie was taking part.

'Let's go and look at the list of acts and see when we're on,' said Jessie. They discovered that Jessie would be the third one to perform and Maddy was number seven, right in the middle of the programme.

'Oh, thank goodness for that,' said Jessie. 'I won't have very long to wait. I'm feeling really nervous, aren't you?'

'I was earlier but I'm not so bad now,' replied Maddy. 'My family kept pestering me, but I feel better now I'm with you. Are your family all here?' She glanced around looking for the familiar faces.

She saw the twins sitting on the front bench and they waved excitedly to her. And Aunty Faith waved, too, from her deck chair a little further back. She noticed that her dad had sat down next to her with Grandad and Patrick further along the row. There was no sign of Samuel but she didn't want to mention his absence to Jessie. But Jessie told her that Samuel would be coming later after he had been to the library in town.

'He'd better hurry up then,' said Maddy. 'They'll be starting in a few minutes. I hope he gets here in time to hear your poem.'

'Oh, he says he's not bothered about that,' said Jessie. 'He's heard it dozens of times. He says he's tired of listening to it. I keep reciting it for Mother, you see, to make sure I know it; although I learnt it ages ago. I'm frightened though, that it'll all suddenly go out of my head.'

'Don't worry, you'll be fine,' said Maddy. 'Look, all the Pierrots are sitting in the audience. Don't they look funny – well, different, sort of – in their ordinary clothes?' They were all there, even Nancy's dogs on leads, sitting obediently. The Pierrots had papers and pencils on their laps and Maddy guessed that they were all going to act as judges. All except Letty who was seated in her usual place at the piano at the side of the stage.

Percy stood up, then took his place on the stage. He was nattily dressed in a light-coloured jacket and trousers with a striped tie, and a straw boater on his head. 'Now, ladies and gentlemen, boys and girls,' he said, 'I think it's time we made a start. And thank you for bringing the sunshine with you. It will make all the difference. Would all the competitors please come and sit on the seats at the front that we have reserved for them? And if you have brought any music give it to Letty at the piano. Now, when we are all ready...' The children who were taking part sat down and the folk in the audience fidgeted a little and then settled themselves. '...we will have the first competitor. And he is Timothy Laycock from Leeds, and he is going to sing for us. Give him a big hand, everyone – Timothy Laycock.'

Maddy felt sorry for the poor lad having to start the performance. She guessed he was about her age, possibly a bit younger. He sang 'Early One Morning' – a song she knew from school – in a piping little voice, but growing in confidence with each verse. He received a good round of applause, then he blushed furiously and ran off the stage.

The next act was a lanky lad of thirteen or so who told jokes, waiting eagerly at the end of each one for the laughter. The audience did laugh, although they had heard most of the jokes before at the Pierrot shows.

Then it was Jessie's turn and Maddy felt her own heart give an extra beat in sympathy with her as she stood there on the stage. She was an appealing little figure in her apple-green taffeta dress with matching ribbons tied on the bunches of her bright ginger hair. Maddy glanced round anxiously and she saw, to her relief, that Samuel had arrived and was standing at the back of the audience. He did not notice her, Maddy, but there was a pleased smile on his face as he looked at his sister. She guessed he was proud of her no matter how much he pretended not to be. She knew what brothers could be like.

Jessie began to speak, quietly at first, but then, like the boy singer, she gained in confidence as she went on. Maddy thought, as she listened to her, that her friend's education in the swanky school in York must be rather different from that of her own.

She could not imagine any of the girls – or boys – that she knew being able to recite great long poems like Jessie was doing. And in such a posh voice too. When she had first met Jessie, Maddy had been conscious of the other girl's lack of any Yorkshire accent, such as was common to her and her school mates. She did not notice it so much now, but it was clear from the way she was reciting the poem that Jessie and her fellow pupils were encouraged to speak 'properly'. Not that Maddy had any reason to criticise her own education at the 'Friarage' school she attended. They were taught to read and write very well, to do all sorts of sums and problems and they knew all their times tables. And they learnt poems by heart – much shorter ones, though – and songs, and verses from the Bible in Scripture lessons.

The members of the audience were attentive as they listened to Jessie reciting the long poem, without faltering once.

'We will gaze, from the sand-hills,
At the white sleeping town;
At the church on the hill-side –
And then come back down;
Singing, There dwells a loved one,
But cruel is she;
She left lonely for ever
The kings of the sea.'

When she had finished there were murmurs of 'Ahhh…how lovely!' and 'Well done!' from the audience, then they all clapped loudly. Jessie gave a wide grin, obviously glad it was over, bobbed a curtsey and quickly left the stage.

'Jolly good,' Maddy whispered. 'See, you didn't forget it, did you? It was great. I hope I do as well as that.'

There followed a boy who tap-danced, quite accurately, but with not very much enthusiasm or confidence; another boy comedian, a slight improvement on the first one they had heard; and a boy from Bury who recited 'You are old, Father William' in a broad Lancashire accent.

Then it was Maddy's turn. Jessie squeezed her hand and smiled at her, whispering 'Good luck' as she went to take her place on the stage.

'Ladies and gentlemen, boys and girls,' said Percy. 'Here is our next contestant, Miss Madeleine Moon from Scarborough. And she is going to sing for us.'

Maddy smiled round at the audience, hearing the ripple of applause. She was pleased that Uncle Percy had announced her as Madeleine. It sounded much more grown up than Maddy. She caught sight of her family and grinned at them, noticing that Samuel had sat down now, next to her brother, Patrick. She still felt a little bit churned-up inside, but she was looking forward to giving a good performance, as she knew she could do if she tried.

'I would like to sing for you an old folk song called "Scarborough Fair",' she said, speaking to the audience; and then to Letty at the piano, 'Could you just give me a Middle C, please?'

And as she began to sing all traces of her nervousness vanished.

Chapter Twenty-Three

'Are you going to Scarborough Fair?
Parsley, sage, rosemary and thyme;
Remember me to one who lives there –
For once he was a true love of mine...'

All eyes were drawn towards the girl on the stage, a poignant little figure in her black dress with the large white collar, and her golden-blonde hair tied round with a white ribbon. She was a pretty child. 'The image of her mother,' some whispered to one another, those who knew she was little Maddy Moon who had lost her mother only quite recently. That was why she was in mourning, poor lass... Others who did not know her were struck by her charm and modesty, and yet there was a quiet self-confidence there, too, when she started to sing.

She sang the whole song unaccompanied. Her voice was clear and vibrant and melodious, never once straying away from the accuracy of the simple tune. The audience fell silent, drinking in every tender phrase, every joyous note of the old melody, and thinking that never before had they heard it sung so movingly.

That was what Percy Morgan thought as he listened in amazement. He had expected that she would do quite well, but he had been determined not to let sentiment get in the way of his judgement. But there was no doubt about it; the girl was excellent. And glancing at his fellow artistes he could see that they were all as enraptured as he was.

'When you've done and finished your work,
Parsley, sage rosemary and thyme;
Then come to me for your cambric shirt,
And you shall be a true love of mine.'

When the song came to an end Maddy stood perfectly still, her hands folded in front of her, smiling gently at the audience. There was complete silence for several seconds; Percy knew that this happened on occasions when the listeners were completely overcome by what they had heard. Then there was an outburst of applause, loud and long, such as had not been heard before that afternoon, although all the contestants had been well received. Maddy looked startled for a moment, then she smiled more broadly, bobbed a curtsey, and went to sit down next to her friend.

'There goes our winner,' murmured Pete, who was sitting next to Percy.

'Hush!' said Percy. 'We mustn't influence one another, remember? All the others have to have an equal chance... Superb, though, wasn't she?' he added in a whisper as he went forward to announce the next act.

There followed a juggler of balls and hoops who got through his performance with not too many mishaps; two more singers; two reciters of poems, shorter ones than Jessie's; a boy conjurer who did card tricks and produced miles of silken scarves from a tiny box, finishing off with a white rabbit in a hat; and a little girl, the youngest competitor, who was a ballet dancer and performed very daintily to the music from *Swan Lake*.

Percy then announced that it was the end of the contest and that everyone had done very well. 'Give them all a big hand, ladies and gentlemen; they deserve it... Now, if you will give us a few moments, my friends and I will add up the marks and then I will announce the winners. Exciting, isn't it, folks? But not too long to wait now...'

All the children who had been taking part ran to talk to their families and friends and to receive congratulations on their performances, but they all returned to their former seats in time to hear Percy announce the results.

The Pierrots had found that their system of awarding marks to each contestant had worked well. They had decided, however, to adopt the first suggestion of marks out of ten rather than five, as it was felt that that would give a wider range to the results. They found that there was a clear winner, several marks ahead of any of the others, and a runner-up who was judged to be a performer who showed great promise. The rest of the marks were somewhat lower, although none of the judges had awarded very poor marks, remembering their own first appearances on a stage and how nerve-wracking it could be. There was only one mark separating the third and fourth places, so it was decided unanimously to award a 'highly commended' prize of two shillings to the child who had come fourth.

There was a buzz of excitement as Percy took his place on the stage again. 'And now, ladies and gentlemen, boys and girls,' he began, 'the moment you have all been waiting for. My fellow Pierrots all agree that it has been a very successful afternoon and I feel sure everyone has enjoyed it. And what a display of talent! I can see we'll have to watch out because these young folk may well be starting their own Pierrot show!'

After the laughter had died down he continued, 'You have all done very well indeed, and there's a little gift for all the contestants as a memento of the competition. Pete has some packets of postcards that you can collect from him afterwards. But there can only be three – no, sorry – four prizes, although you are all winners in a way because you have been plucky enough to take part. So – are you all listening? Yes, I can see you are – so, here we go then...

'We have decided to award a fourth prize – a "highly commended" – to a girl with an outstanding memory and a lovely speaking voice. Jessica Barraclough from York, for her recitation, "The Forsaken Merman". Come along, Jessie...'

The little ginger-haired girl blushed bright pink and the delight and surprise showed on her face as she went up to collect her prize money in an envelope, and a certificate from Uncle Percy. Her friend, Maddy, looked pleased, too, and was clapping like mad.

'And in third place, Dora Featherstone from Beverley, our delightful little ballet dancer.' Dora, at eight years of age, was the youngest competitor and received a big round of applause as she ran on to the stage, her ballet dress covered now with a bright red jumper.

The second prize went to Frederick Nicholls from Halifax, a very competent conjurer whom Percy believed could have a future on the stage if he persevered. He was confident and self-assured – perhaps he had hoped he might win? – but he seemed well pleased with his runners-up prize.

'And now...' Percy paused dramatically, '...our first prize winner, a little girl – or maybe I shouldn't say little – a charming girl who has thrilled us all this afternoon with her wonderful singing. Ladies and gentlemen – Madeleine Moon, from right here in Scarborough. Come along, Maddy love, and receive your award. Very well done!'

Percy saw the two little friends hug one another joyfully before Maddy came up on to the stage. She looked pleased, but bewildered too. Surely she must have had some idea that she had done very well? She received her envelope and certificate and the little silver cup in open-mouthed surprise, and Percy could see a tear glistening in the corner of one eye. What a dear little lass, he thought. She was just the sort of child that he and Letty would have loved to have as a daughter, but it was not to be. He felt sure that the tear was for her mother, but he knew that her family and her little friend would soon cheer her up again. And Isaac and William would be so proud of her.

She walked off the stage to loud applause and resounding cheers from the more exuberant members of the audience. Her family and friends all crowded round her, congratulating her, as did some other people who were complete strangers.

'I knew you'd win,' Jessie told her.

'Well done, little sis,' said Patrick.

And Samuel smiled at her and said she had a very pleasing voice.

'You must be very proud of your daughter,' Maddy heard a lady who had been sitting nearby remark to Faith.

And she heard Aunty Faith reply with a smile, 'She's not my daughter, just a very dear friend. But you are right; we are all proud of her.' Then she turned to Jessie, stroking her fiery hair. 'This is my daughter, Jessica, and we are proud of her as well. What a wonderful afternoon it has been.'

'Oh, you are the clever girl who recited the long poem,' said the lady. 'Very well done! What a marvellous memory you must have, my dear.'

Maddy and Jessie were quite dazed with all the excitement. Jessie was still bright pink with pleasure, but Maddy felt that she would like to get away from it all soon and have a few minutes' quietness.

They were all going back to the house where the Barraclough family were staying whilst they were in Scarborough. It was on Blenheim Terrace, the road that led up to the castle, overlooking the sea. Well, not exactly all of them... Just the family: herself, Patrick, and her father and grandfather. The other people who had come to watch the show – Aunty Louisa, Bella and Miss Phipps – hadn't been invited because Faith didn't know them quite so well.

When all the talking had finished – Maddy had seen Uncle Percy chatting away to her father, and then he had come over to her and Jessie, telling them how well they had done – and all the goodbyes had been said, Maddy and Jessie set off across the beach ahead of the others, then up the steps and the cliff path which led to the holiday home. They did not say very much because they needed all their breath for the stiff climb.

Maddy was thinking about Bella who had been acting rather strangely. She and Miss Phipps and Aunty Louisa had all come to look at her little silver cup and certificate and to tell her how nicely she had sung. She had not expected Bella to be too enthusiastic in her praise – she had heard her remark several times in the past that she didn't like children who were 'too big for their boots' – but to her surprise she had noticed that Bella's black eyes were shining with unshed tears and there had been a little catch in her voice when she said, 'Very well done, Madeleine.' It was hard to understand, but as she had often heard Grandfather say, 'There was nowt so queer as folk…'

She quickly put Bella out of her mind, though, when they reached Jessie's home and waited for her mother to arrive and open the door. It was a jolly tea party which Faith had prepared beforehand, and Maddy was glad when the conversation drifted on to other topics instead of the successes of herself and Jessie.

'Percy Morgan was telling me that the Pierrots are coming back to perform at the Spa in December,' said William, 'for two weeks. Well, not exactly the Pierrot show; the same artistes, but they have a travelling company called Morgan's Melody Makers during the winter season. I was wondering if we might go and see them? It would be a nice treat, just before Christmas. What do you think about that, Maddy?'

'Ooh, yes please!' said Maddy. 'All of us, do you mean?'

'Well, yes…of course. But I can't speak for your Aunty Faith and her family.'

'Ooh… Could we, Mother, please?' asked Jessie. 'On a Saturday, when there's no school?'

Faith looked thoughtful. 'Maybe…' she said. 'We might be able to manage a weekend. Some of the hotels on South Bay open during the winter. We wouldn't be able to stay at this house, not just for two days. I'm not promising…but we'll see.'

Maddy and Jessie exchanged excited glances as Faith went on to say, 'Percy Morgan told me they have a week booked in York as well, in January. He thought we might be interested with us living there. So…that might be another possibility.'

Maddy was not sure if anyone else noticed the look that

passed between her father and Faith. Each of them had a sort of half-smile on their face, and she thought she saw her father raise his eyebrows a little as though he was asking a question, and Faith gave the merest nod of her head in reply. She didn't know whether she should mention it to Jessie, but in the end she decided not to. She knew that sometimes fathers – and mothers – got married again when their partners had died. A girl in her class at school had a new stepfather, and a boy she knew had a stepmother. The both seemed quite happy about it.

Her mind started to leap ahead to what might happen. Supposing…just supposing that her father and Jessie's mother were to get married? Not yet, of course. She knew that her father was still very, very sad sometimes when he thought about her mother. She could always tell when he was unhappy, but at other times he was able to laugh and joke, like he had been doing today. Of course Jessie's mother – Aunty Faith – still had a husband. They didn't live in the same house any more, but he wasn't dead. She wasn't sure what they might be able to do about that…

It was odd to think about it, but the idea of being Jessie's stepsister – is that what she would be? – didn't displease her. But the thought that Samuel might become her stepbrother, and Patrick might become Jessie's stepbrother…and then there were Tommy and Tilly as well. Oh dear! It was all too confusing to even think about…

William was thoughtful, too, as he buried himself behind his newspaper at home, later that evening. Faith had confided in him that she and her husband were now living apart, but he was continuing to support her and the children very generously. She had even told him, in hushed tones, that there was another woman involved and that the question of divorce had been raised. At least, that was what her husband wanted, but divorce, to Faith, was such a shameful and scandalous matter that she could not, at the moment, consider it. For the sake of the children, she had added.

William had loved Clara deeply and faithfully. But there could be no harm, he told himself, in continuing his friendship with Faith. After all, she had been Clara's friend as well. Perhaps he could suggest a meeting during the winter, just for the two of them, himself and Faith. Or perhaps it might be more suitable to have a family get-together? Maddy and Jessie would enjoy that; the little Barraclough girl had become a close friend to his daughter. So far he and Faith had exchanged a few meaningful glances, born out of friendship, nothing more; and in a fortnight's time she would be returning to York. He knew he must leave the question of his feelings for her in abeyance for the moment. But he was beginning to look forward, not backwards all the time and regretting what might have been. The future no longer looked quite so black.

And this was partly because of his dear little Maddy. Who would have believed that she would turn out to be such a resounding success on the stage? He had been moved almost to tears by the purity and clarity, the sheer beauty of her voice, and he could tell that his father had felt the same way too. She was modest, though, and had seemed truly surprised that she had won, although he knew that her self-confidence would be an asset to her. Percy Morgan had been quite overwhelmed too at hearing Maddy's singing. He had described her to William as a 'rising star' and said she had a rich talent that should be encouraged. He had even requested that she might be allowed to perform occasionally with the Pierrots.

'Mind you, I don't believe in exploiting children,' he had added. 'I reckon nowt to taking 'em away from their education; that's what's important. But it is the school holidays at the moment and there's no doubt about it that she would be a crowd puller.'

William had been taken aback and said that he would think about it. For next year, though, he had insisted; it was far too soon at the moment for Maddy to be singing what you might call 'professionally'. Probably Maddy herself would be thrilled at the idea, but he decided not to tell her about Percy's suggestion; not just yet.

Bella was in a despondent mood that evening after Miss Phipps had gone home. She had felt that she had no choice but to invite the other woman to go back with her for a meal. She had watched the Moon family and the Barracloughs all disappear en masse and had felt a deep hurt right at the heart of her. Louisa Montague had not been invited either, to the family gathering, which did console Bella to a certain extent, but it didn't seem to bother Louisa. She said a cheerful goodbye and scurried off back to her little shop. Bella was relieved; she would certainly not have wanted to invite her along as well.

Is this really all that I deserve? she wondered as she listened to Muriel's desultory conversation about her boring family or customers from the shop: the company of a fifty-odd-year-old spinster with nothing in her life but her far-distant family, her job and her chapel, because, like the Moons, Miss Phipps was a staunch Methodist.

Bella breathed a sigh of relief when the woman had gone, but her thoughts were not happy or uplifting ones. She had felt strangely moved by Maddy's singing and she had known it would be ungracious not to go and tell the child how much she had enjoyed it. Although enjoyment was not the correct word for what she had felt. There had been the poignancy of the song, so applicable to her own situation, a girl – or woman – longing for her lost love; the undoubted beauty of the girl's voice and the delicate loveliness of her face and form. Bella, watching and listening to Madeleine, had been reminded forcibly of Clara. Her daughter was growing up to be the image of her. Seeing her up there on the stage – the golden hair, the facial features, and the selfsame mannerisms – had evoked memories which Bella would have preferred not to bring to mind.

Chapter Twenty-Four

Flags were flying from flagpoles and red, white and blue bunting was fluttering in the breeze along the promenade at Scarborough. And not only at Scarborough. All over England loyal subjects were preparing for a coronation. King Edward the Seventh who had succeeded to the throne in the January of the previous year was to be crowned in Westminster Abbey on the 26th of June, 1902.

The shop windows along the main street of the town, from Eastborough, near the harbour, right up to the top of Westborough, were declaring their allegiance to the new monarch with displays of merchandise in patriotic colours, and many windows held large portraits of the king and his queen, the lovely Queen Alexandra, who was much admired by the womenfolk.

The ladies' gown shops, in particular, were paying tribute to her by displaying high-necked lace blouses, elegant dresses with tightly fitting bodices, and silken toques trimmed with ostrich feathers, such as the queen might wear. Some of the more daring stores showed, in a separate window, bathing dresses, navy blue cotton edged with red, or royal blue with white ribbon trimming to the short skirt and knee-length drawers.

At the Moon emporium, now known as Moon's Modes for all Seasons, it was felt, by those in charge of it, that the window dressing, as always, must be quite discreet. Many folk, in particular the older ladies, had looked askance at the changes that had come to pass. Moon's establishment had always been associated with mourning, and some people did not take kindly to the multicoloured array of garments which, little by little, had been introduced to the once sombre windows.

The new innovations in the store had begun the previous autumn, starting with the changing of the sign over the door. One window had still remained more or less faithful to the convention of darker-coloured clothing, but as to the other window, that had undergone quite a transformation. A cherry-red costume trimmed with ermine and with a matching muff had held pride of place during the Christmas period, followed by springtime shades of daffodil yellow and leaf green at the changing of the season.

Now, in keeping with the national trend, patriotic colours were on display. Nothing too garish, however; afternoon dresses in two shades of blue, white lace blouses, and a splash of red from a feathered hat and a parasol. Bella Randall and William Moon had decided, in deference to some of their clients, not to trim the windows with flags and bunting. Instead there was a portrait of their Majesties placed to one side, and a discreet sign which read 'Loyal Greetings to King Edward and Queen Alexandra'.

Bella, by this time, was in almost full control of the store, although she was always careful to consult William before any important decisions were made. He had understood perfectly when she had told him, in the summer of the previous year, that she felt she was no longer able to accompany him on his funeral visits. She had explained that her time would be taken up now with the reorganisation of the store, but she soon realised he was well aware of the real reason.

'I understand, Bella,' he had said, with just the slightest spark of amusement in his eyes. 'I know it has not been what you might call...your cup of tea. Actually, I was waiting for you to tell me; I didn't want to be the one to suggest you might give up. You mustn't feel bad about it. I must say you have coped with it very bravely considering how repugnant you found it all... Yes, I could tell. Don't worry; I know a woman at chapel who I think might be willing to help us out. We've got Joe Black, of course, and he's a great asset to the firm, but we do need a woman as well for some of the jobs...Clara was a real treasure, though; there's no doubt about that,' he had added reminiscently...and to Bella's annoyance.

She had hoped, even though she would no longer be working in such close proximity to him – for all the good it had done her! – that William might have accompanied her on trips to the various warehouses, to choose the new range of clothing. It was a feather in her cap, she supposed, that he had given her free rein on these excursions, telling her that he trusted her completely to make the right choices without referring to him. He had suggested, too, that she should take young Polly along with her sometimes so that she could learn the procedures, leaving Miss Phipps in charge of the store.

Which was all very well for Bella career-wise. She had been given quite a substantial rise in pay, she had the comfortable flat above the shop; but she and William were as far apart, emotionally, as they had ever been. More so, in fact. She realised that he had come to regard her as a business colleague, albeit a tried and trusted one, but nothing more.

Moreover she knew that he had seen Faith Barraclough, the woman she regarded as her rival, on at least two occasions.

Last December, just before Christmas, the whole Barraclough tribe – Faith, Jessica, Samuel and the twins, but minus the father – had come to Scarborough. They had stayed at the Crown Hotel, so Maddy had informed her, and there had been a jolly outing to the show at the Spa Pavilion for both the Barraclough and Moon families. Bella supposed it was unreasonable of her to hope that she might be invited along as well. After all, not even Louisa Montague had been included in their party. Bella had gone with Muriel Phipps on a different occasion to see the show. It was very entertaining, there was no doubt about that; light-hearted and colourful and amusing. But the heaviness in her heart had not been alleviated at all by the lively performance of the Pierrots, alias Morgan's Melody Makers.

It had been Maddy who had also informed her, in great delight, that she and her father – just the two of them – were going to York at the end of January to see 'Uncle Percy and all the others in a show there'.

'Oh…that's very nice, Maddy,' Bella had said, trying to sound interested and not at all patronising. She still found it hard to speak normally to the girl, although Maddy did talk to her now without any of her former animosity or reluctance. 'You will be pleased to see your friend, Jessie, again, won't you?' Bella didn't want to appear too inquisitive, but she did venture a question to which she badly wanted to know the answer. 'Will you be staying at Mrs Barraclough's house, dear? Or…somewhere else?'

'Oh no, we're not staying with Aunty Faith,' Maddy told her. 'Dad's booked us in at a hotel near to the railway station. But I 'spect I shall see Jessie quite a lot. She's going to show me all round the city; all the old streets and the castle and the big church called the Minster. I've never been to York before so I'm getting real excited.'

'I'm sure you must be,' Bella had replied, wondering if William was looking forward to seeing Jessie's mother with the same eagerness. It wasn't often that Maddy spoke to her with such enthusiasm, and Bella felt that maybe she was getting somewhere at last in gaining the child's confidence. But with regard to her father she seemed to be making very little headway.

Maddy had not said a great deal about the York visit on her return, except to reply politely that yes, thank you, she had enjoyed it. Bella had resisted the temptation to question her further. She did not know whether William and Faith had met at all during the intervening months, but one thing was certain. All the Barraclough clan would be there again in Scarborough for the month of August.

In the meantime, though, there was the coronation which would be celebrated in the town, as in towns and cities throughout the land, with various events; parties and concerts and special church services.

It was during the late afternoon of 24th June that the townsfolk started to realise that something was amiss. People were talking together in little groups in hushed voices, and the red, white and blue bunting which decorated the streets was being removed.

'Have you heard about the poor old king?' A woman who was quite a regular customer had brought the news to the Moon emporium, but this time she had not come in to shop but to spread the unhappy tidings. 'He's been taken ill, summat called appendicitis and he's got to have an operation. And the coronation's had to be cancelled.'

'Are you sure? How do you know?' asked Bella.

'Oh, word's come through from London. I heard it from somebody on t' town council, no less. It's true enough, more's the pity.'

Bella decided to shut the shop straight away out of respect for the king. It was nearly closing time anyway and it was doubtful if there would be any more customers that day.

'Oh deary me!' sighed Miss Phipps. 'The poor king. Just imagine; we've only just got used to being called Edwardians instead of Victorians, and now it's doubtful that we will be for much longer. I do hope he recovers.'

'Of course he'll recover,' said Bella. 'We'll have to try and look on the bright side. He's got the best doctors in the land looking after him, hasn't he, so he should be all right.'

'Yes, I expect so...' replied Muriel a little doubtfully. 'We'll all have to say a special prayer for him.'

And that, indeed, was what happened that evening in churches and chapels throughout the country. Prayers were said for the recovery of King Edward the Seventh. Miss Phipps remarked to Bella the following morning that she had been along to a prayer meeting at her chapel.

'I must admit though, Bella, my dear,' she added, in a confidential manner, 'that I think his conduct is somewhat...scandalous at times. But he is our king when all is said and done and we've got to try and look up to him.'

'Quite so,' replied Bella, smiling to herself. She knew that King Teddy was not the sort of man that Muriel would approve of wholeheartedly, but she, Bella, thought he was a real good sort, though admittedly a bounder. 'He certainly enjoys himself with his big cigars and his race horses...and his lady friends,' she said. 'Let's hope he gets better again to enjoy them.'

'Yes…lady friends.' Muriel sniffed. 'He does have a wife. A lovely wife and he should be more considerate of her.'

'Oh well, I dare say there's one rule for royalty and another for the rest of us,' said Bella with a shrug, and with her tongue in her cheek. She guessed that Muriel knew nothing of her 'affair' with Ralph Cunningham. It was all ancient history anyway.

'Perhaps he will alter his lifestyle after he's had a close encounter with death,' Muriel went on. 'It's sure to make him think about what he's doing. Kings and queens are only human like the rest of us underneath all the pomp and glory.'

'Yes, it's possibly he might change, but I doubt it,' said Bella. 'Some folk thought he might change his ways when he became king, but there hasn't been much sign of it.' She gave a quiet laugh. The king's weaknesses and misdemeanours only made him the more likeable as far as she was concerned.

Long before the closing years of his mother's long reign and the start of the new century Prince Albert Edward – Bertie – had been a well-known national character. Everyone had seen, in newspaper photographs or in advertisements for various products and shop window displays, his large and splendid uniformed figure performing his ceremonial duties as the representative of the queen. But the public also knew about his large appetites, for food and drink, for shooting, horse-racing and gambling, and for beautiful women.

'Queen Alexandra must be a very understanding wife, that's all I can say,' said Miss Phipps. She pursed her small mouth before going on to say. 'I have heard that she is very fond of small animals. She collects lapdogs while her husband collects ladies.'

'Yes, it's amazing what some women have to put up with,'

said Bella a trifle wearily. She was beginning to get bored with this conversation. Muriel Phipps, like many woman of her age, loved to tittle-tattle when the opportunity arose.

The doorbell rang as a customer entered; a well-dressed woman who would usually, with gentle persuasion, purchase several garments.

'Good morning, Mrs Hetherington,' said Bella, with just the slightest touch of subservience in her tone; a manner that befitted a shop assistant, even one in a managerial position, but one that was completely assumed. Bella Randall considered she was as good as anybody. She stepped forward to greet the lady. 'A lovely day, isn't it? Apart from the news about our dear king, of course.'

'Yes, indeed,' said Mrs Hetherington.

'Miss Phipps and I were only just this minute saying that we hope the prayers of the nation will be answered... I will attend to Mrs Hetherington, Miss Phipps. Would you go over and see if Polly needs any help with her customer, please? She seems to have taken out every pair of gloves in the store...'

Seemingly, the prayers of King Edward's loyal subjects were answered because, in a few days' time the news from London was favourable. He was making a good recovery, far more quickly than had been expected. And before long a new date had been fixed for the coronation. It was to be on 9th August, which fell on a Saturday. An odd choice of day, many people thought, assuming that it would have been in the middle of the week.

'Hmm...not a good day for a special performance,' said Percy Morgan to his troupe. They had already planned one for the earlier date, 26th June, which had been a Thursday, but that, of course, had had to be cancelled. 'Saturday's change-over day for one thing. One lot of visitors leaving and another one coming in. Folks haven't got themselves settled enough to come and watch a show.'

'It doesn't have to be on exactly the same day,' Pete pointed out. 'So long as it's after coronation day and not before it. There's many a slip...as they say.'

They decided to have the Coronation Special, as they called it, on the Tuesday following the big day. Percy pleaded with Louisa Montague to do a 'rush job' on their costumes, with which she was pleased to comply. She added red, white and blue ribbon trimming to the ruffles on their tunics and red and blue pom-poms to their hats, working until almost midnight on the Monday evening. They would wear them for the rest of the season, of course, and be proud to do so in honour of the king. And Louisa, along with the Moon and Barraclough families, had a special invitation to the show, an afternoon performance so that young and old alike could enjoy it.

Maddy was as excited as anyone about the forthcoming show, especially as she had been invited to sing a solo. She had been astonished, but delighted as well, when her father had told her, earlier that summer, about Percy's suggestion that she might take part in some of the shows.

'Percy mentioned it to me last year, to be honest,' he told her, 'just after you won that talent thing, but I thought you were a bit too young then. Besides, it was not long after – you know – your mother... But you're twelve now, and next year when you're thirteen I dare say you'll be leaving school. You're growing up fast. So...what d'you think of the idea, eh?'

'You mean...to be a Pierrot?' said Maddy. 'With a costume and hat and everything?'

'Well, not an official one,' her father smiled. 'Just a guest artiste, like, now and again. And not until August, mind, when the school holidays start.'

Maddy could hardly speak for excitement. 'It'll be wonderful!' she gasped. 'Ooh, thank you, Dad, for saying I can do it. And Jessie'll be here an' all, won't she? I must write and tell her straight away...'

The coronation concert would be the second time she had performed. The first time had been the previous week when she had sung last year's song, 'Scarborough Fair'. But she had a new song for the show on Tuesday and it had been decided that she would, again, sing unaccompanied by the piano. Uncle Percy and Letty had told her that she had a lovely lilting voice that was just right for singing folk songs.

'What are you going to sing?' asked Jessie, the day before the concert.

'Wait and see!' said Maddy mysteriously. 'It's another folk song, sort of, but it's an Irish one. And I'm wearing a white dress; Aunty Louisa made it.'

'When you wrote and told me you were going to be in the shows I thought you might be wearing a costume like the others,' said Jessie.

'No... I'm not really a proper Pierrot,' said Maddy. 'Not yet anyway...' she added thoughtfully. 'Don't tell anybody, will you, Jessie, but that's what I'd like to do when I leave school. I'd like to join the Pierrot troupe, for all the time, I mean. But I don't know whether Uncle Percy would want me all the time; and probably Dad wouldn't let me anyway...'

'I thought you wanted to be a dressmaker,' said Jessie, 'and work in a shop like Miss Montague's.'

'Oh, that was before,' replied Maddy, going all starry-eyed

again at the thought of becoming a fully fledged Pierrot. 'But I suppose I'll just have to wait and see,' she added with a shrug of resignation. 'I've got the rest of this summer, anyway, haven't I? I'll probably do a few more shows.'

It was a memorable performance, which was talked about long afterwards by the folk who watched it. There was a patriotic feeling to it throughout. Susannah, dressed in a royal blue satin dress with a red feather boa, sang saucy musical hall songs, such as might be enjoyed by His Majesty; Carlo sang the Major General's Song from *The Pirates of Penzance*, then he was joined by all the Pierrots in the chorus of 'When the Foeman Bears his Steel'; and Queenie, not to be outdone, sang 'Poor Wandering One' with scarcely a wobble on the high notes.

There was the usual mixture of wisecracks and dances and sketches, and a rousing medley of national songs to end the performance, finishing off with 'Here's a Health unto His Majesty' and three deafening cheers.

One of the highlights of the show was Maddy's solo spot. She was introduced again as Miss Madeleine Moon. She stood all alone in the centre of the stage, a diminutive figure in a simple white dress with a white satin ribbon in her hair.

'I know where I'm going,' she sang,
And I know who's going with me;
I know who I love,
But the dear knows who I'll marry...'

Those who had not heard before remarked on her simplicity, her totally unaffected manner and the lyrical silver-toned sweetness of her voice. And those who knew her felt justly proud of their own little local lass.

Her own family members did not over-praise her. William did not want her to become swollen-headed, not that he thought she ever would, but he wanted her to retain her modesty and innocence as long as she could.

His tender feelings for Faith were growing stronger. She and her husband were living apart permanently. Faith had told him the previous year that Edward wished to marry his lady friend eventually, which, William supposed, was to the fellow's credit when he could have continued to keep her as his mistress, as many men did. But they seemed to be no nearer in reaching a divorce settlement, and divorce was still, to Faith, a disgraceful matter, even though she was the completely innocent party. There was one rule for men and an entirely different one for women, regarding divorce. A man could divorce his wife for adultery, but she could not divorce him, however unfaithful he might be, unless he committed another matrimonial offence, such as cruelty. And Edward, whatever his other faults, had never been cruel to her.

It was towards the end of August when William confessed his feelings to Faith, although he knew she must have been aware of how he felt about her; just as he had guessed how she felt about him. They had managed to spend a little time together away from their families, but they both knew they must behave with the utmost prudence. However, William had decided, for once, to throw caution to the winds, and he invited Faith to accompany him one evening to a concert of classical music at the Spa Pavilion.

He put his arm around her instead of holding her elbow as they walked back over the Spa Bridge and through the town, then up to her holiday home near the castle. All the children, who had been left in the care of Samuel, had gone to bed, including her elder son.

As soon as they stepped over the threshold William gently put his arms around her and she rested her head on his shoulder. When she turned to look up and smile at him he lowered his lips to hers, kissing her, for the very first time, tenderly and reverently.

'Faith, my dear, I think you know how much I care for you, don't you?' he asked. She nodded.

'Yes, William; I think I do...'

'Faith... I love you,' he whispered.

'And I love you too,' she replied.

They sat and held hands, contented to be in one another's company with their feelings out in the open at last. But they both knew that they must be circumspect in their behaviour. It could be quite a long while before they were able to be together as they wished, openly and for the rest of their lives.

Chapter Twenty-Five

Bella caught sight of William and Faith one evening during the first week in September. She was at the Theatre Royal in St Thomas Street enjoying a performance of *The Importance of Being Earnest* by Mr Oscar Wilde. She had seen the play before and she found the character of Lady Bracknell particularly amusing. She had decided to visit the theatre on her own as she found the company of Muriel Phipps to be somewhat irksome at times. Sometimes Bella preferred her own company to that of anyone else, seeing that she could not have the company she would have liked.

At least she had been enjoying the play, until the interval, when she caught sight of two familiar heads a few rows in front of her in the stalls. One dark head and the other with hair of a bright chestnut colour. She was not absolutely sure until she saw William turn to smile at his companion. Quickly Bella looked down, studying her programme until the lights dimmed again. She did not want them to see her.

Her appreciation of the rest of the play was quite spoilt, and when the performance ended she loitered, making doubly sure she had her programme and her bag and hat, and stooping down to retrieve a dropped glove until the couple had passed along the aisle.

Their way home – for she felt certain that William would be going back to Faith's place – led along the same route for part of the way. She followed them, keeping a good distance behind them as they walked along St Thomas Street. She knew she was only rubbing salt into a very tender wound, but she could not stop herself from watching them. The street was fairly busy, not as much as it would have been during the daytime, but there was a fair number of theatre-goers making their way home, some of them hailing passing hansom cabs. William and Faith, however, seemed oblivious to the people passing or following them. She saw William put his arm around Faith's shoulders; she saw Faith turn to smile up at him, and then he lowered his head to place a kiss on her forehead.

At the junction with Castle Road the couple turned right, with Bella continuing on until St Thomas Street merged with North Marine Road. She let herself into the door at the side of the shop and went up the stairs to her flat above the store. Bitterness and anger and frustration were building up inside her, more than ever before. She pulled off her hat and jacket and flung them on to a chair.

It wasn't fair! It just wasn't right... She had been William's willing slave in all sorts of ways for the last – how long? – it must be seven years or more since she had first come to work at Moon's Modes. She would have loved William faithfully, if only she had been allowed to do so. She did love him, and when Clara had...gone, she had felt that there might really be a chance for her.

Then...along had come that vision of loveliness. How could any man resist beauty such as that, for Bella had to admit that Faith was a beautiful woman. William was infatuated. That, maybe, was all it was. He had allowed his head to be turned by a pretty face. But it could not come to anything, could it? The woman was married and it was more than likely that her husband would not want a divorce. And she could not imagine William Moon – the steadfast and highly principled William Moon – 'living in sin'. As she, Bella, had done with Ralph Cunningham, a little voice in her head reminded her.

Deep down, though, she knew that she was trying to delude herself. William was not merely infatuated; he was in love with the woman. She had seen tender glances pass between the two of them before and had guessed which way the wind was blowing. She felt tears of anger and unhappiness welling up inside her and she was powerless to stop them. She raged and sobbed for a while, beating at the sides of the armchair with her fists until her fury was spent. Then she went to the sideboard cupboard and took out a bottle of whisky. She poured a good measure into a glass and gulped it down. She felt the fire in her belly at once and already a slight lessening of her mental anguish. She would take the next measure to bed with her, diluted with hot water. It was one of the few comforts she enjoyed at the moment. At least it guaranteed her a good night's sleep and, hopefully, respite from her despair and the demons that possessed her...until the next day.

Maddy and Jessie, too, could not fail to notice the growing friendship of their respective parents.

'D'you think they've fallen in love?' Maddy said to Jessie as they sat together on Jessie's bed, one early evening during the first week of September. Maddy had returned to school that week and had been invited to tea at 'Jessie's place'. Her friend would be going back home to York the following weekend.

The idea of her father and Faith did not trouble Maddy too much. Her father often talked to her about her mother and when he said that he would never forget her...well, she believed him. They were able to talk about her mother now and smile together as they remembered the happy times they had enjoyed together as a family. But Aunty Faith was a very pretty lady, and she was nice and friendly as well as being beautiful. Maddy could not blame her dad for liking her a lot, as she knew he did. There was a girl in her class whose mother had died, a few months after Maddy's mother. And her father had got married again just before the summer holidays. Agnes – that was the girl's name – didn't seem to mind about it.

'I think they might have done,' said Jessie, in answer to her question. 'Fallen in love, I mean. I wonder if they'll get married…'

'They can't, can they? Your mother's got a husband, hasn't she?'

'We hardly ever see my father now,' said Jessie. 'But it doesn't really make any difference. We didn't see him all that much before he…before he went to live somewhere else. I mean…he didn't take much notice of us, not like your father does with you and Patrick. And he wasn't all kind and friendly, either, like your father… I like him very much… Your dad, I mean,' she added pensively.

'It's funny to think of it, though, isn't it?' said Maddy. 'If they got married – your mum and my dad – you wouldn't be able to marry Patrick, would you? Because he'd be your brother, sort of…'

Jessie blushed bright pink. 'Who says I want to? Anyway, he's got a girlfriend now, hasn't he? I saw him talking to a girl at that Pierrot show, the one when you sang.'

'Oh yes, that's Katy. She goes to our chapel; she's in the choir. Our Patrick has started going there on a Sunday evening and he never used to do. He might be seeing her, but he never lets on.'

'I'm not bothered anyway,' said Jessie with a shake of her ginger plaits. 'And if – you know – that happened, then Samuel would be your brother as well, wouldn't he?'

'Yes...' said Maddy thoughtfully. 'Oh, let's not think about it, eh? It's far too complicated... I'm real sorry you're going back this weekend, Jess. But we might see one another during the winter, like we did last year, if there's another show on in York...or here.'

'I hope so,' said Jessie. 'We have such a good time in Scarborough that it always seems so dull again when we get back home.'

Bella's distress and anguish did not abate even when Faith Barraclough and her family had gone back to York. Indeed, they seemed to intensify.

The days were not too bad. She could busy herself with her work in the shop and keep her tormented mind more or less in check. She went on excursions with Polly to warehouses in Leeds and York, to choose a range of garments for the autumn and winter seasons. Polly's excited chatter, for the girl had come out of her shell a lot recently, amused her momentarily, and she had always taken pleasure in the latest fashionable clothes. But there was nothing in her life anymore that she could say she thoroughly enjoyed or looked forward to. Her life, or so it seemed to her, had become meaningless. The evenings were the worst, especially now that the nights were drawing in.

She had never cared for the autumn, which she thought of as the dying of the year; the shortening of the days and the early darkness and, particularly on the coast, the fog that rolled in from the sea. She stood at her window one evening towards the end of September, looking out at the swirling mist. She knew that she was not well, either physically or mentally, but she was determined not to see a doctor. There was no doctor, anyway, who would be able to cure her malaise.

No one seemed to notice, however, that she was suffering. During the day she was able to put on a brave face, being her usual forceful self; her bossy self, as she knew only too well. She had lost weight because she was not bothering to eat as she should, but no one had commented on this, and the headaches she suffered from, which were occurring quite frequently, she kept in check with soothing powders.

Alone in her flat in the evenings with no company other that the whisky bottle – and she knew she was imbibing too much – she frequently gave way to despair. The alcohol, which had been a nightly solace, was no longer having the desired effect. But the worse she felt, the more she went on drinking.

She knew now that William would never be hers. She had been nurturing a hopeless love for the last...goodness knows how many years. And although at one time the bold and confident Bella Randall would have been able to pick herself up and start again, she knew she could not longer do so. It was not only the fading away of her futile dream that was tormenting her, but the memory of her wicked actions, her murderous intent; there were times when she really believed that she and she alone had been responsible for Clara's death. If she had not succumbed to that moment of positive hatred – she recalled how she had looked down at Clara's uncovered body and the enmity she had felt for the woman – then Clara would be alive today. William would not have fallen in love with Faith Barraclough. What had happened had all been her,

Bella's, fault. And it served her right that she had lost him now.

There was nothing left for her, nothing at all, and there was not one person in the world who cared whether she lived or died...

It was half past eleven at night and Constable Harry Perkins, peering through the mist up Valley Bridge Road, could see a figure loitering there, near to the railings of the Valley Bridge. He stood and watched as, some twenty yards away, the figure – a woman in dark clothing – after hesitating for several moments, put her hands on the railings and began to haul herself up.

Harry shone his torch in her direction and shouted, 'Hey! Miss...you can't do that. You mustn't... Wait; I'm coming...' He knew it was a favourite spot for suicides. There had been umpteen over the years since the bridge had been opened in 1865; folk who were tired of life flinging themselves down onto the road far below. But he had never, until this moment, encountered one himself.

He ran as fast as his corpulent figure would let him, praying he would get there before she jumped. But he could see that she was having difficulties; her long skirt was caught on the railings and she was trying to lift one leg up behind the other.

'Miss! Don't, please don't...' he cried, grabbing hold of her skirt and pulling at it.

'Let go of me!' she shouted back. 'I've made up my mind. I can't go on... I can't...'

'Now steady on, luv,' he said, holding fast to her skirt. 'There's nowt so bad that you need to try and kill yerself. Come on now, luv. Come down...and happen you can tell me all about it…if you want to. I'm a good listener.'

The woman cast an anguished look in his direction. 'Go away,' she said. 'I've told you I can't…' Suddenly her voice broke in a sob, and he could see her frightened black eyes, like two gleaming lamps in a stark white face. He felt that he had won the battle as she began to sob, and then she climbed slowly down.

He looked more closely at her face. She was a good-looking woman, fortyish, he guessed, with a mass of black hair uncovered by any hat. He thought she looked familiar but he couldn't quite place her. She was staring at him in a bewildered manner and as she began to speak he could smell the alcohol on her breath.

'I was going to do it,' she said. 'I'd made up my mind, and if you hadn't come along… Why did you?'

'Just doing my duty, luv,' he replied. 'And it's my duty now to see you safely home. You've got a home to go to, have you? Or is that what's troubling you?'

'No; I've got a home,' she replied, 'such as it is. But I don't want to go back, not yet. Leave me alone, please; I'll be all right.'

'I most certainly will not leave you,' said Constable Perkins. 'Now, come along, there's a good lass. Nothing is quite so bad as it seems.' He took hold of her arm and, to his surprise, she started to walk along with him. 'Now, you show me the way,' he said, ''cause I don't know where we're heading for. You've decided to go back home, have you?'

She nodded numbly. 'But I don't know why. There's nothing here. There's nobody who cares…'

All the same she steered him away from the bridge, across Newborough, and then along Castle Road. It was as they

neared the site of the undertaker's premises, Isaac Moon and
Son, that Harry realised who she was. She was that Miss
Randall from the shop. Bella, they called her. He had been a
constable in Scarborough for a good many years and he
remembered that there had been some sort of a scandal about
her a while back; living with a married man or summat o' t'
sort. He didn't let on that he knew her, though, and by the
time they reached her door she seemed more composed. She
hadn't wanted to talk so he hadn't pressed her.

'So this is where you live, is it?' he said. 'Now, think on
what I've said. Go and have a good night's sleep and you'll
feel better in t' morning. It's not a bad old life, y'know, all
things considered. And I'm sure there's somebody, somewhere
who cares about you.'

'Thank you,' she said. 'It doesn't seem like it at the
moment… I'll be all right though. Don't worry. Thank you for
seeing me home.' Fortunately, and surprisingly enough, she
had her key in her coat pocket and she quickly opened the
door and disappeared inside.

Harry Perkins was worried though. He decided he must
keep a watchful eye on her.

Bella flung herself on the bed fully clothed and, still
befuddled by the whisky she had drunk before her aborted
suicide attempt, she slept for several hours. When she awoke
it was still dark and her alarm clock told her it was five-thirty
in the morning. She could not tell whether she was glad to be
back home, glad to be still alive…or what. She remembered,
though, the kindness of that corpulent policeman with the
ruddy cheeks, and it occurred to her that maybe she was being
given another chance. She had done wrong; the Bible would
say she had sinned, but maybe God had forgiven her.

'There's somebody, somewhere who cares for you...' the policeman had said. But she did not know about that. If she had died, would there have been anyone to grieve for her? There might have been, though, if her life had taken a different direction.

Her thoughts, more lucid now, took her back to the child she had borne and then given up for adoption. Henrietta...no longer a child of course; she would now be a young woman, twenty-one years of age. She had been a tiny girl when Bella, secretly, had last set eyes on her, living in the town of Ashington with her adoptive parents. Was she still there? Or had she moved on, got married, maybe? Well, there was only one way to find out.

She pulled a large suitcase and a canvas holdall from the top of the wardrobe and, working swiftly, filled them with as many of her possessions as they would hold. She stopped for a wash, realising suddenly how grubby she felt, and breakfasted speedily on a cup of tea and a slice of bread and butter.

It was half past six and still dark when she stole down the stairs and out of the door. She locked the door behind her and posted the key through the letter box. She had not left a note to say where or why she was going. It was nobody's business but her own. She dragged her heavy luggage to the corner of the street and hailed a passing hansom cab.

'Scarborough railway station,' she told the driver. 'As fast as you can.'

Constable Perkins opened the door of Moon's Modes for all Seasons at eleven o'clock the following morning and entered the shop. It was the first time he had been inside the premises, although his wife had bought garments there occasionally, and he was struck now by the feeling of warmth and opulence, especially for a store that had once dealt solely in mourning wear. A middle-aged woman stepped forward to greet him.

'Good morning, sir.' She addressed him as sir although he was wearing his uniform. 'How can I help you?'

'I am looking for Miss Randall,' he said, looking around. 'Isn't she here?'

'Oh deary me!' The woman seemed covered with confusion. 'No, I'm afraid she isn't. We don't know where Miss Randall is.' She looked at him in consternation. 'Why? You don't want to see her about...something, do you? It's not...a police matter?'

'No, madam,' he replied. 'At least... I hope not.' He was beginning to feel worried. Surely she hadn't gone and made another attempt? 'You say you have no idea where Miss Randall is?'

'No; she didn't turn up to open the shop this morning. So Mr Moon went to look for her and all her things have gone from the flat... You'd better go and talk to Mr Moon,' she said. 'It's really nothing to do with me.' The poor woman was looking frightened to death by now.

'Thank you, madam; so I will,' he said. 'Round at the back, is he?'

'Yes, I think so. That's where he usually is.'

William Moon, also, was very worried at the disappearance of Bella Randall, and even more so when he saw the policeman. He guessed why he might be there before the constable said, 'I've come to see you about Miss Randall.'

William stepped out of the workshop and into the yard so that they might speak privately. 'She isn't in any trouble, is she?' he asked. 'She's disappeared. Done a moonlight flit by the look of things. Do you know where she is... Constable Perkins, isn't it?' He had met this policeman before.

'Yes, that's right,' he nodded. 'But, no; I'm afraid I don't know where the lady is. But there is summat I think you should know. I came across her on t' Valley Bridge last night, trying to throw herself over. That's why I came, to see if she was all right.'

'Oh...no!' said William, aghast at the news. 'Bella...trying to commit suicide? But...why?'

'Well, she'd been drinking for one thing,' said Harry Perkins. 'That might've had a lot to do with it. And she'd got herself into a right maudlin state of mind, thinking that nobody cared about her.'

'But that's not true,' said William. 'She's very well thought of here. Everyone thinks highly of her...' A niggling thought intruded, though, at the edge of his mind. Thinking highly of someone was not the same as caring. 'You don't think...? Might she try to do the same thing again?'

'I doubt it,' replied Harry Perkins. 'I was worried myself at first, when I found out she'd gone. But your shop assistant said she'd taken all her belongings. Now, you don't do that if you're intending to do away with yerself, do you?'

'No... I suppose not,' said William. 'No; of course not. I can't help feeling worried though.'

'She was calmer by the time I left her. She kept mithering on about there being nothing left for her, nobody to care. But I told her there must be somebody, somewhere who cares for her. That was the last thing I said to her. Happen she's thought of somebody and gone to find 'em, eh?'

'Maybe...perhaps so,' said William. 'Anyway, thank you,

Constable Perkins, for looking after her last night and for showing concern. I'll let you know if we hear anything.'

'Very good, sir. I was only doing my duty, but sometimes you're called upon to do a bit more than duty, aren't you? An' I was concerned, like. But from what I know of Miss Randall – I've heard tell of her before, y'see – I would say she was a survivor. She'll pick herself up and carry on.'

'Yes, I hope so,' said William. 'I would have thought so at one time, certainly. But she's kept herself to herself pretty much lately...'

He pondered on that after the policeman had gone. Had Bella been obliged to keep herself to herself, he wondered, because of the behaviour of the Moon family and, particularly, himself? Had she felt ostracised, not wanted...? He remembered how, when she had first come to work for them, he had been wary of her because of their past association; and he and Clara had agreed to be friendly with her, but not too much so. He thought the policy had worked and he no longer saw her as a threat. He believed that any residual feeling that she might have had for him had long gone, and that she now regarded him only as her employer and as a friend. Since she had been in full charge of the store, especially since the new innovations and the buying of stock which she had undertaken, he had assumed she had been contented; quite satisfied with her position of authority and with her life generally.

'So she's done a bunk, has she?' said Patrick, when he found out that Bella had gone. 'Where's she gone to, d'you think?'

'I don't know,' said William, although he had an idea that she had probably gone back up north.

'Ah well, I reckon we'll be able to get along wi'out her,' said

Isaac. 'Although I must admit she's been better lately. Me and her, we've never really hit it off, but we've managed to put our bad feelings to one side, at least I thought we had. Why d'you suppose she's gone?'

'I've no idea,' said William. 'I would've thought she had a pretty good life. A steady job, a comfortable place to live and...friends. And since her...companion died she hasn't seemed to seek the company of men...' He was aware that Patrick was looking at him strangely. 'What's up?' he asked. 'What have I said?'

'Father, have you never realised?' said Patrick. 'Bella Randall was in love with you.'

'What? What nonsense!' exclaimed William, without stopping to think what he was saying. 'However did you get that idea?'

'Nah then, lad,' said Isaac to his son. 'The boy's got eyes and ears. An' he's old enough now to know what's what. Happen it's time you spilt the beans, eh? You've nowt to reproach yerself with. It isn't as if you were ever unfaithful to Clara.'

'What?' asked Patrick. 'What on earth are you talking about?'

William looked his son straight in the eyes. 'I used to know Bella...' he began, 'when we were both a lot younger. Eighteen I was, and she was about the same. She was working down at the harbour... I never mentioned it because, as your grandfather says, I didn't have any reason to reproach myself.' He knew that he did, of course; there was the matter of a child born out of wedlock, but his father and Patrick did not have to know about that.

'It was long before I knew your mother. And so when she

came back to Scarborough – Bella, I mean – I met up with her again. And then, a good while afterwards, she came to work here; that was your mother's doing. But your grandad knew. He had always known that I had met Bella before… It's all ancient history, believe me, Patrick. I have had no feelings for Bella, other than friendship. Your mother was the only woman for me. And I shall never forget her. My feelings for Faith make no difference to the love I have for Clara… And as for Bella…' He shook his head in a bewildered manner.

'I believe you, Father; of course I do,' said Patrick. 'Actually, I'd guessed there might've been something, once, between you and Bella. But Bella…well, obviously she didn't see it all the same way, did she? She must have kept on loving you. And since you became friendly with Faith… I suppose that must've been the last straw.'

'Do you really think so?' asked William. He was stunned to think that Bella had been moved to take such drastic action because of her feelings for him. Patrick did not know about the suicide bid, although William had told his father about it. 'I had no idea…'

'There's none so blind as those who won't see,' commented Isaac. 'Aye, that's my opinion an' all. It was all too much for her…poor lass,' he added. 'I was never all that fond of her, but I hope she makes out all right.'

'I'm glad really,' Maddy said when she, too, heard that Bella had gone. 'I didn't like her all that much. I think she caused a lot of trouble,' she added.

She saw Patrick frown at her across the table, shaking his head slightly. She got the message. He didn't want her to mention about what she had seen that time. As if she would be so stupid! But now Bella had gone and she wouldn't need to think about her anymore. 'I mean...she was bossy, wasn't she?' she added. 'Perhaps we won't ever see her again...'

Probably not, thought William. Just as suddenly as she had reappeared in Scarborough some sixteen years ago, so had Bella Randall disappeared again.

Chapter Twenty-Six

I t was on a Saturday afternoon in late September, 1905, when a young dark-haired woman alighted from the train at Scarborough Station and hailed a hansom cab to take her to North Marine Road. It was her first visit to the resort, but she knew where she was going; to the undertaking premises of Isaac Moon and Son. It had been described to her as a substantial-looking house, with the workshop and stabling and small office at the back, and, next door, a high-class store, Moon's Modes for all Seasons.

She stood on the pavement, her small holdall at her side, and surveyed the property in front of her. Her eyes were drawn to the store; to the window with sombre, but stylish mourning wear, and to the second window in which were displayed garments of rather brighter hues; autumn shades of russet, deep gold and olive green. Well worthy of a browse around, she decided, in a little while maybe. But first things first...

It was obvious that there had been some changes over the past few years. The house that had been described to her now had a large plate-glass window at the front with purple drapes on either side. There were a few vases and urns on show, suitable for placing on graves, and in the centre an eye-catching display of mauve and white chrysanthemums. Through the window she could see that the downstairs premises must have been converted to an office, and seated behind a long mahogany counter was a man with dark hair, busily writing in a ledger. From his age she guessed that this must be William Moon.

The young woman picked up her bag, took a deep breath and opened the door. The bell gave a quiet jingle and the man looked up from his work.

William Moon gasped at the sight of the young woman who had just entered. His pen dropped from his hand, causing a splodge of ink to fall on the white page, and he felt himself blanch. He half rose from his chair. 'Bel...' he began. Then as he came to his senses, 'I'm sorry,' he said. 'Of course it isn't. Please forgive me, miss...madam. For a moment I thought you were someone else.'

'I'm not surprised,' said the young woman, smiling at him in a most friendly way. 'I am very much like her. You mistook me for Bella Randall, didn't you?'

'Well...yes. Just for a moment. But I can see now, of course, that you are much younger...' His voice petered out as he started to realise who, in fact, this person might be.

He was not surprised therefore to hear her say, 'I am Bella's daughter. And you, I presume, are Mr William Moon?'

'Yes, indeed I am,' he replied in a quiet voice.

'Then...please forgive me if I am wrong, but I have to find out.' She was looking at him half-pleadingly, half-apologetically. 'According to what Bella told me, you are...my father.'

William gave a deep sigh as he gazed at her. She was Bella to the very life. The same dark curling hair, half hidden beneath a small-brimmed hat of natural straw, and the same dark flashing eyes. But he could tell at once that this young lady had a far different disposition from that of Bella. He was

sure that she was kind and considerate and fair-minded and
that he would have nothing to fear from her. So he had no
qualms at all in answering her.

'Yes, my dear; that is so. What Bella – your mother – told
you is quite right. I am your father. And you...you must be
Henrietta?'

'Yes, Hetty; that's what I'm usually called.' She smiled and
held out her hand. 'I'm very pleased to meet you...at last.'

He took hold of her hand, holding on to it for a few
moments. Then, 'Come on through to the back,' he said.
'We'll have a chat over a cup of tea. I'm here on my own. We
usually close on a Saturday afternoon, but I had some work
to finish so I left the door open. Very lucky that I did...' He
felt that he was babbling incoherently, but the young lady –
Hetty – was nodding agreeably.

The kitchen at the rear was pretty much the same as it had
always been. He invited Hetty to sit down, and she took off
her hat and lightweight jacket whilst he made a pot of tea.

'You have made some changes then?' she asked, when they
were both seated. 'Bella told me that you lived here, on the
premises.'

'So we did,' said William, 'but I got married again two years
ago and we needed more room. We bought a house over the
other side of town, on South Bay, and this property has been
given over, more or less, to the business. My son, Patrick, still
lives here in the upstairs part. He is nineteen now and he likes
his independence, and it means that there is someone here all
the time to keep an eye on things. We still have our own two
horses, but the way things are going they might soon be put
out to grass.' He smiled. 'My father always said it would be
over his dead body if we ever went on to those "new-fangled

horseless carriages"; but we all have to move with the times.'

'Your father? Is he still with you?'

'If you mean is he still alive, then yes, he is, very much so. He's almost retired though now. He lives with us, with me and my wife, Faith, and my daughter...' He hesitated, looking at her a little ruefully. 'You will know, I expect, that I have a younger daughter, Madeleine; Maddy, we call her. She lives with us most of the time. She is here at the moment, but she will soon be off travelling with the "Melody Makers"; that's a group of entertainers she belongs to. She's a singer; a very good one actually.'

'And she is...how old?'

'Maddy is fifteen. I thought she was too young at first to be away from home, on the road, as they say. But she has persuaded me to let her go this time. I wouldn't do so if I didn't trust the man in charge of the troupe. Percy Morgan; I know he'll let no harm come to her.

'And then there's Jessie; she's my wife's daughter. She's still at school, a private school in Scarborough; she's the same age as Maddy. And the twins, the terrible twosome, I call them,' he laughed. 'Tommy and Tilly; they're eight now.'

'A big family then,' Hetty observed. 'And...do you all get on well together?'

'Very well, surprisingly,' said William. 'I must tell you though... I loved my first wife, Clara, so very much. We had a very happy marriage and I will never forget her, neither will my children. But then... I met Faith. We found each other, you might say. She was in the throes of an unhappy marriage, so we had to wait. But it was all sorted out eventually. Faith's elder son, Samuel, is away at university, so we see him only occasionally. He is the only one who might, possibly, be somewhat difficult... But that's enough about me for the moment. Tell me about yourself, Hetty. Why did you decide to come to Scarborough? Now, I mean, rather than earlier? And...what about Bella? I guessed when she left here so suddenly that she might have gone to look for you.'

'Yes, you're right,' said Hetty. 'But I'm sorry to tell you that Bella died six months ago.'

'Oh! Oh dear; I'm sorry to hear that,' said William. He truly was sorry, but the thought came to him that she had not died alone. She had met someone who cared for her; he felt sure that she and Hetty must have established some sort of bond or she would not be here.

'Yes, she died of pneumonia, following influenza,' said Hetty. 'But to begin at the beginning...'

She told William how Bella had travelled to Northumberland, starting and ending her search for her daughter in the town of Ashington. It was the place where she had last seen her, living with her adoptive parents and, fortunately for Bella, the place where Hetty was still residing.

'My parents had both died a few months before,' Hetty told him. She looked at William a trifle apologetically but her tone was positive. 'They were really and truly my parents; Hilda and Simon Collier. I couldn't have wished for a better mother and father, although they told me, when I was old enough to understand, that I had been adopted. It was pretty obvious anyway; I was so dark and they were both so fair.'

'What happened to them?' asked William. He was warming to this young woman more and more.

'My da had a weak chest. That was why he worked in the office at the coal mine instead of going down the pit. He died of bronchitis in March, and then Mam was knocked down by a horse and cart a few weeks later. I'm afraid it was largely her own fault. She wasn't looking where she was going; she was so distressed at losing my father.'

'How very sad... So you were left on your own?'

'Yes; I suppose you could say I've been lucky, in one way. My parents owned their house; only a little cottage but at least it was their own. And so it was left to me and I stayed there.'

'You have a job, I suppose, Hetty?'

'Yes...' William noticed she said 'yes' and not the more usual 'aye' which was a word more often used in the Northumberland area. She had an accent that betrayed that she was a Geordie, along with her way of speaking of her father as 'my da'; but William guessed that her parents had done their very best for her and that she had been brought up to speak correctly.

'I have a good little job,' she continued, 'in the office at the coal mine, the same one where my da worked. I stayed at school till I was fifteen and then I had shorthand and typing lessons.'

'So you have a job to go back to when—' William stopped, not wanting her to think that he was anxious to see the back of her. 'They know you've come down here, do they?'

'Yes; I asked for a week's leave of absence. Don't worry,' she grinned, 'I won't be moving in with you.'

William smiled at her. 'You are most welcome to come and stay with us while you are here.' He was realising that the time had come for him to be completely honest, with himself and with others, about his past. This had been forced upon him, sure enough, but he knew it was time to speak out. He knew that he must tell his son and daughter that they had an older sister, who was the daughter of Bella Randall. He had told

Faith, however, before they were married, about his one-time friendship with Bella and about the child he had never seen. She had been surprised but very sympathetic.

'That explains a lot,' Faith had told him. 'I realised she had tender feelings for you, although I would never have guessed at the extent of them. Poor Bella! It's not so surprising then, is it, that she disappeared when you and I became...friendly.'

'Tell me...' William said now, putting his empty cup on the table and leaning forward to look keenly at Hetty. 'What did Bella tell you about me? Don't be afraid to say. I have lived with it all these years, thinking about what happened when you were...conceived. I know I behaved badly.' He shook his head. 'I was young; I couldn't cope with the enormity of it all, although I know that is no excuse.'

Hetty was looking at him understandingly. 'Bella – I always called her Bella, y'see; that was what she wanted; it wouldn't have seemed right to call her Mam – Bella told me all about it, quite bluntly. She was that sort of person, wasn't she? I knew at once who she was when she came knocking at my door that September day, three years ago. It was a shock for me though, as you can imagine.'

'Just as it is for me now,' said William. 'A nice shock though,' he added.

'Anyway...she stayed; that's the top and bottom of it. She had nowhere else to go and we found that we rubbed along together quite well. And bit by bit she told me her story...'

He knew it all, of course; how Bella had returned to Scarborough several years later and found out that the man she had once loved, and believed that she still loved, was married. She had told Hetty, quite openly it seemed, about her anger and bitterness at the time, and then how she had found happiness for a while with Ralph Cunningham.

William nodded. 'And then she came to work for us at the shop. She had become quite friendly with Clara, my wife. One thing that I regret was that I was never completely honest with Clara about knowing Bella. In fact I wasn't honest at all. I was very wary of Bella at first, I must admit, but it all seemed to work out quite well. She had a good job and a comfortable home. I believed she was quite content.'

'But she was nursing a hopeless love for you...William,' said Hetty. It was the first time she had addressed him by name. It seemed natural to him that she should call him William; he knew he could never be 'Father' and certainly not 'Da'... 'She admitted it, how she kept on hoping you might see her in a different light, and then Faith came along.'

'Yes...Faith,' said William quietly. 'I told Faith about Bella before we were married, and about the child...you, my dear.' He smiled at her. 'I felt so guilty, you see, about never having told Clara, and I knew I had to start off with a clean slate, so to speak.'

'Bella told me about her friendship with your wife,' said Hetty. 'How she was very fond of Clara in spite of everything. But there was something troubling her, and I never found out what it was. She mentioned Clara quite a lot, and then she would go on to say how badly she had behaved towards her... That would usually be when she had had a few drinks. I'm afraid I was never able to make her give up the whisky. There was something on her mind though...'

'Maybe it was just that she was jealous,' said William. 'Clara and I were very close, it was a good marriage. Feelings of envy can take a hold of you and make you harbour bad thoughts, I suppose. I didn't notice anything out of the ordinary, though. Bella always behaved correctly. She was a good help at the end when Clara was ill... And very distressed when she died. I really thought that any fondness she might have had for me had long gone. Poor Bella... And you say she died six months ago, of pneumonia?'

'Yes, it was a bad winter, but then it usually is up in the north. She caught influenza, then it turned to pneumonia and she went very quickly after that, as though she had no resistance left. "It serves me right," she kept saying. Almost the last thing she said was, "I've been a wicked woman, what I did to Clara..."'

'Poor Bella,' said William again. 'She didn't do anything except, perhaps, to feel envious. It's only human nature to envy what another person has. But she had found you, Hetty, in the end. I'm glad about that.'

'Yes...' There was a tear in the corner of the young woman's eye. 'I was glad too,' she said, 'that I'd got to know her. "Thank you, Hetty," she said to me, just before she died. "You've been a good daughter." And that was the only time I called her Mam. I said, "That's all right, Mam." Then she smiled at me and closed her eyes.'

William's eyes were moist, too, as he said, 'Thank you for telling me, Hetty. It's a chapter closed, but I hope it might be the start of another one.'

They took a cab later that afternoon across to the South Bay. Hetty, as was to be expected, was a little ill at ease, but no more so that William felt. 'It will be all right,' he assured her, with more confidence than he was feeling. 'I have a lot of explaining to do, but it is time all secrets were out in the open.'

'You mean...no one knows about me?' asked Hetty.

'My wife does,' he replied, 'as I told you. And my father

knew about my former friendship with Bella, and my son guessed. But not about...'

'Not about me? Oh dear! Perhaps it might be better if you were on your own, William. I would hate to cause trouble.'

'No...' He patted her hand. 'It will be all right. I promise.'

There was only Isaac at home, reading the newspaper in the sitting room. He looked up, and on seeing the young woman with his son he gave a startled exclamation.

'Good God, it can't be!' He rose to his feet, scattering the pages of the newspaper far and wide and his glasses dropped to the end of his nose. 'Bella... No, no, of course it isn't. Oh dear, I'm sorry luv. My eyesight isn't as good as it was.'

'No, Father,' said William, taking her arm and leading her right into the room. 'You were almost right. This is Henrietta Collier. She is Bella's daughter. And...she is my daughter, too,' he added decidedly. 'Hetty, this is my father.'

Isaac was rendered speechless, but only for a few seconds. He soon got over his shock and he didn't, then, seem terribly surprised by the revelation. 'Aye, I suppose I might've guessed,' he said with a chuckle 'And where have you sprung from, luv?'

Hetty laughed, not at all put out by his outspoken comment. And as for Isaac, he seemed charmed by his latest granddaughter. William began to feel easier. Faith and the two girls came in later, after a shopping expedition in the town, followed by Tilly and Tommy. Their reactions at seeing the newcomer and hearing her introduced as Bella's daughter were mixed. The twins, as usual, took it all in their stride, and Jessie looked puzzled. But Maddy was the one that William was watching more closely. She stared at the newcomer, not rudely, but not all that welcomingly either. Faith, though, making up for all the others, smiled charmingly and held out her hand.

'How do you do, Henrietta. You are very welcome.'

'There is something else you should know,' said William when they were all sitting down. 'Henrietta – Hetty – is not only Bella's daughter... She is my daughter as well, and I have met her for the first time today.'

Jessie gave a gasp of surprise; but once again William was watching for Maddy's reaction. She looked shocked, horrified almost, as she cast a searching, unsmiling glance, first at Hetty and then at her father. There was a silence which seemed interminable before Faith spoke.

'Well then, you are doubly welcome, my dear,' she said. 'Maddy love, would you pop into the kitchen, please and tell Mrs Baker that there will be... How many will there be for dinner tonight? There are usually seven of us, so with Patrick – he's coming tonight – and Hetty, that makes nine. Goodness me, what a large family we are! And how nice it will be to have a celebration.'

Maddy nodded. 'Come on, Jess,' she said 'Let's go and see Mrs Baker.' She was the cook and live-in housekeeper.

'Whatever do you think of that?' said Jessie when they were out of earshot. 'What a surprise! You could have knocked me down with a feather.' She looked closely at her friend who had suddenly gone very quiet. 'What's the matter, Maddy?' she asked anxiously. Maddy had turned quite pale and Jessie could see the glimmer of a tear in the corner of one eye. 'Oh... I'm sorry,' she continued quickly. 'How stupid of me to ask what's the matter. It's your father, isn't it, and...Bella. Oh dear, what an idiot I am! It must be much more of a shock to you than it is to me.'

Maddy nodded. 'Yes…it's a shock, sure enough. I can't quite take it in yet.' She lowered her head and closed her eyes tightly, trying to prevent her tears from falling. Jessie put an arm round her and Maddy leant against her, glad to have the support of a good friend. 'Jessie…' she said. 'You go and tell Mrs Baker, will you, about the arrangements for dinner? I would like to be on my own for a little while.'

'Of course,' said Jessie. 'You go and think things out. I can understand how you feel; at least, I think I can. I remember my father, you see, and…and the other woman he went to live with.' She paused before going on to say, 'That Hetty, though… I thought she looked rather nice, really.' She lowered her voice. 'Nicer than Bella; I never liked her very much.'

Maddy managed a weak smile. 'Yes, I thought so too. She looks friendly, but she seemed a bit embarrassed, didn't she? It must have been an ordeal for her as well, meeting us. She's so much like Bella – to look at, I mean. That's what gave me such a shock.' She opened the door of the dining room. 'I'll just sit in here for a few minutes. Don't worry; I'll be all right.'

They would be dining in there later, nine of them, round the long mahogany table which would be set with the best linen, silverware and china. Maddy sat down now on a low velvet armchair at the side of the fireplace. The grate was laid with sticks and paper and small pieces of coal, ready for lighting in a little while. It was turning chilly in the evenings now and there was usually the need for a fire.

Maddy took several deep breaths, something she had learnt to do whenever her nerves started to get the better of her. She soon began to feel calmer and the threatening tears did not overflow. She was determined not to give way to a bout of weeping. After all, what was there to cry about? Her father was happy. He had been so ever since he married Faith; and she, Maddy, and Patrick had come to love their stepmother too. They both thought of their own mother, very often, as they knew their father did; but their thoughts of her now brought back memories of happy times and they were able to smile instead of feeling sad.

Seeing that young woman, though, who was the very image of Bella, had evoked unpleasant memories, things she had tried so hard to forget. And then to discover that she was her sister! Her...stepsister? No, Jessie and Tilly were her stepsisters. This Hetty was her half-sister because they both had the same father. Hadn't she always suspected, though, that there was something between her father and Bella? Maddy had come to realise that Bella had loved him and had been jealous of her mother. But she pushed away, as she always did, the dreadful memories of the time when her mother died and the shocking scene she had witnessed.

How old was this Hetty? Twenty-five or thereabouts, she guessed. Certainly much older than herself and Patrick. So what had happened between her father and Bella must have been long before he met their mother. She gave a deep sigh and rose to her feet. It was time she went back into the sitting room or else her father and Faith would start to get anxious. And she knew what she had to do.

Faith smiled at her encouragingly as soon as she entered the room. 'I am sorry,' said Maddy, looking straight at the young woman, Hetty, who was half smiling at her, a little unsurely. 'I'm sorry if I seemed rude and unwelcoming. I didn't mean to be. It was quite a shock, seeing you. You are so much like Bella, and of course I had no idea...'

'I understand perfectly,' said Hetty. 'I said to William – your father – that it might be better if he broke the news to you first. But he insisted that I should come and meet you all.'

Maddy nodded. 'It was very brave of you.' She held out her hand. 'How do you do, Hetty? It is good to meet you.'

'So it is,' agreed Hetty with a warm smile as she took hold of Maddy's hand. 'There is something you should know, though, Maddy... My mother – Bella – she died, six months ago. That is why I decided to come, now, and find... William. She had told me about him, you see.'

'Oh dear!' said Maddy. 'I am sorry to hear that.' It was, of course, not strictly true. She could not be sorry for her own sake that Bella was dead. She regarded it, in fact, as an unhappy and worrying chapter that had now closed. But it was sad for this young woman to have lost her mother at an early age as she, Maddy, had done. 'I know what it's like to lose a mother,' she said. 'You must miss her.'

'So I do,' replied Hetty, 'but I hadn't known her for very long really.' Maddy realised there was a lot she didn't know about her new half-sister. But she was beginning to learn that everyone went through periods of sadness as well as joy in their passage though life. 'I am just glad that I knew her for a year or two before she died.' Hetty smiled a little sadly, and the two young women looked at one another in perfect understanding. Suddenly her face brightened 'But now,' she said, 'I have a new half-sister. I do hope we can be friends, Maddy?'

'So do I,' replied Maddy. And she knew that she really meant it.

Author's Note

You may have found yourself humming along to some of the songs I have mentioned in the book. These have been quoted from a number of popular songs from the era, listed below:

The Band Played On – JF Palmer and Charles B Ward
Here We Are Again, Happy As Can Be – old music hall song
The Boy I Love is Up in the Gallery – mid-nineteenth-
    century music hall song made famous by Marie Lloyd)
Soldier of the Queen – Leslie Stuart
Goodbye-ee – RP Weston and Bert Lee
How Sweet the Name of Jesus Sounds – hymn by
    John Newton
And Can It Be That I Should Gain? – hymn by
    Charles Wesley
Amazing Grace – hymn by John Newton
I'll Be Your Sweetheart – Harry Dacre
The Forsaken Merman – Matthew Arnold
Scarborough Fair – traditional song dating from the
    seventeenth century
I Know Where I'm Going – traditional Irish song